EXTRAORDINARY PRAISE FOR
SARA BLAEDEL
AND THE LOUISE RICK SERIES

"Blaedel is one of the best I've come across."

—Michael Connelly

"Crime-writer superstar Sara Blaedel's great skill is in weaving a heartbreaking social history into an edge-of-your-chair thriller while at the same time creating a detective who's as emotionally rich and real as a close friend."

—Oprah.com

"She's a remarkable crime writer who time and again delivers a solid, engaging story that any reader in the world can enjoy."

—Karin Slaughter

"One can count on emotional engagement, spine-tingling suspense, and taut storytelling from Sara Blaedel. Her smart and sensitive character, investigator Louise Rick, will leave readers enthralled and entertained."

—Sandra Brown

"I loved spending time with the tough, smart, and all-too-human heroine Louise Rick—and I can't wait to see her again."

—Lisa Unger

"If you like crime fiction that is genuinely scary, then Sara Blaedel should be the next writer you read."

—Mark Billingham

"Sara Blaedel is at the top of her game. Louise Rick is a character who will have readers coming back for more."

—Camilla Läckberg

THE LOST WOMAN

"Leads to...that gray territory where compassion can become a crime and kindness can lead to coldblooded murder."

—*New York Times Book Review*

"Blaedel solidifies once more why her novels are as much finely drawn character studies as tightly plotted procedurals, always landing with a punch to the gut and the heart."

—*Library Journal* (starred review)

"Long-held secrets and surprising connections rock Inspector Louise Rick's world in Blaedel's latest crime thriller. Confused and hurt, Louise persists in investigating a complex murder despite the mounting personal ramifications. The limits of loyalty and trust, and the complexities of grief, are central to this taut thriller's resolution. A rich cast of supporting characters balances the bleakness of the crimes."

—*RT Book Reviews* (4 stars)

"Sara Blaedel is a literary force of nature...Blaedel strikes a fine and delicate balance between the personal and the professional in *The Lost Woman*, as she has done with the other books in this wonderful series...Those who can't get enough of finely tuned mysteries...will find this book and this author particularly riveting."

—BookReporter.com

"Blaedel, Denmark's most popular author, is known for her dark mysteries, and she examines the controversial social issue at the heart of this novel, but ends on a surprisingly light note. Another winner from Blaedel."

—*Booklist*

"Engrossing."

—Toronto Star

THE KILLING FOREST

"Another suspenseful, skillfully wrought entry from Denmark's Queen of Crime."

—Booklist

"Engrossing...Blaedel nicely balances the twisted relationships of the cult members with the true friendships of Louise, Camilla, and their circle."

—Publishers Weekly

"Blaedel delivers another thrilling novel...Twists and turns will have readers on the edge of their seats waiting to see what happens next."

—RT Book Reviews

"Will push you to the edge of your seat [then] knock you right off...A smashing success."

—BookReporter.com

"Blaedel excels at portraying the darkest side of Denmark."

—Library Journal

THE FORGOTTEN GIRLS

WINNER OF THE 2015 RT REVIEWER'S CHOICE AWARD

"Crackling with suspense, atmosphere, and drama, The Forgotten Girls is simply stellar crime fiction."

—Lisa Unger

"Chilling...[a] swiftly moving plot and engaging core characters."

—*Publishers Weekly*

"This is a standout book that will only solidify the author's well-respected standing in crime fiction. Blaedel drops clues that will leave readers guessing right up to the reveal. Each new lead opens an array of possibilities, and putting the book down became a feat this reviewer was unable to achieve. Based on the history of treating the disabled, the story is both horrifying and all-too-real. Even the villains have nuanced and sympathetic motives."

—*RT Times* Top Pick, Reviewer's Choice Award Winner

"Already an international bestseller, this outing by Denmark's Queen of Crime offers trademark Scandinavian crime fiction with a tough detective and a very grim mystery. Blaedel is incredibly talented at keeping one reading...Recommend to fans of Camilla Läckberg and Liza Marklund."

—*Library Journal*

"*The Forgotten Girls* has it all. At its heart, it is a puzzling, intricate mystery whose solution packs a horrific double-punch...Once you start, you will have no choice but to finish it."

—BookReporter.com

"Tautly suspenseful and sociologically fascinating, *The Forgotten Girls* demonstrates yet again that the finest contemporary suspense fiction emanates from Europe's snowbound North."

—*BookPage*

"Sara Blaedel's *The Forgotten Girls* is an emotionally complex police-procedural thriller set in Denmark. With a gripping premise, fast-paced narrative and well-developed characters, *The Forgotten Girls* is an incredible read."

—FreshFiction.com

"Tightly knit."

"*The Forgotten Girls* is without a doubt the best the author has delivered so far…strikingly well done…The chances are good that *The Forgotten Girls* will become your favorite crime novel for a long time to come."

"[*The Forgotten Girls*] is gripping when it depicts some horrific crimes…[An] uncompromising realism…distinguishes this novel at its best."

BOOKS BY SARA BLAEDEL

THE LOUISE RICK SERIES

The Missing Persons Trilogy

The Forgotten Girls

The Killing Forest

The Lost Woman

The Camilla Trilogy

The Night Women

The Running Girl

The Stolen Angel

The Homicide Trilogy

The Midnight Witness

The Silent Women

The Drowned Girl

THE FAMILY SECRETS SERIES

The Daughter

THE DROWNED GIRL

SARA BLAEDEL

Previously published as *Only One Life*
Translated by Erik J. Macki and Tara F. Chace

GRAND CENTRAL
PUBLISHING

New York   Boston

Copyright © 2007 by Sara Blaedel
Cover design by Eliazbeth Connor
Cover photo of woman on dock © Maxim Chuvashov / Getty Images
Cover photo of stormy sky © Nicolas Kipourax Paquet / Getty Images
Translated by Erik J. Macki and Tara F. Chace; translation © 2011 by Sara Blaedel
Excerpt from *The Daughter* copyright © 2018 by Sara Blaedel
Cover copyright © 2018 by Hachette Book Group, Inc.

Grand Central Publishing
Hachette Book Group
1290 Avenue of the Americas
New York, NY 10104
Hachettebookgroup.com

First published in the United States as *Only One Life* by Pegasus Books in 2012
First Grand Central Publishing edition: December 2018

Grand Central Publishing is a division of Hachette Book Group, Inc.
The Grand Central Publishing name and logo is a trademark of Hachette Book Group, Inc.

The Hachette Speakers Bureau provides a wide range of authors for speaking events. To find out more, go to www.hachettespeakersbureau.com or call (866) 376-6591.

The publisher is not responsible for websites (or their content) that are not owned by the publisher.

Library of Congress Cataloging-in-Publication Data

Names: Blaedel, Sara, author. | Macki, Erik J.—translator. | Chace, Tara, translator.
Title: The drowned girl / Sara Blaedel ; translated by Erik J. Macki and Tara F. Chace.
Other titles: *Kun ét liv*. English
Description: First Grand Central Publishing edition. | New York : Grand Central Publishing, 2018. | Series: Louise Rick series | "First published in the United States as *Only One Life* by Pegasus Books in 2012."
Identifiers: LCCN 2018022060 | ISBN 9781538759851 (trade pbk.) | ISBN 9781549141959 (audio download) | ISBN 9781538759844 (ebook)
Subjects: LCSH: Women detectives—Denmark—Fiction. | Honor killings—Fiction. | Murder—Investigation—Denmark—Fiction. | Copenhagen (Denmark)—Fiction. | Mystery fiction.
Classification: LCC PT8177.12.L34 K8613 2018 | DDC 839.81/38—dc23
LC record available at https://lccn.loc.gov/2018022060

Printed in the United States of America

LSC-C
10 9 8 7 6 5 4 3 2

For Leif and Annegrethe

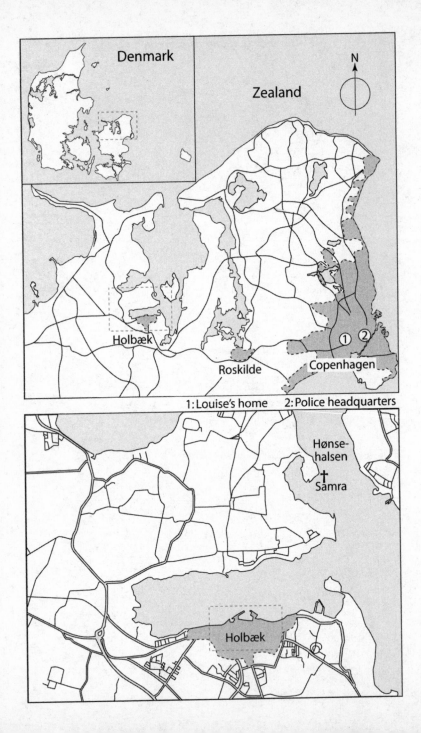

Denmark

Zealand

N

Holbæk

Roskilde

Copenhagen

1: Louise's home 2: Police headquarters

Hønse-
halsen
† Samra

Holbæk

When women are seen as the carriers of a family's honor they become vulnerable to attacks involving physical violence, mutilation and even murder, usually at the hand of an "offended" male kin and often with the tacit or explicit assent of female relatives.

—Navi Pillay, United Nations High Commissioner for Human Rights, "Opinion Piece for International Women's Day: Honor Killing and Domestic Violence," March 2010

An honor killing is the murder of a family member due to the belief that the victim has brought dishonor upon the family.

The United Nations Population Fund estimates that perhaps as many as five thousand women and girls a year are killed by members of their own families. Many women's groups in the Middle East and Southwest Asia suspect the number of victims is about four times greater.

The perceived dishonor can be the result of dressing in a manner unacceptable to the family or community, wanting to end or prevent an arranged marriage, engaging in heterosexual acts outside marriage, or engaging in homosexual acts, among other things.

The most famous honor killing case in Denmark was that of Ghazala Khan, a nineteen-year-old woman who was shot and killed outside a train station in Slagelse, west of Copenhagen, in 2005 because her family disapproved of her choice of a husband. Nine people, including her father, brother, three uncles, an aunt, and two family friends, were convicted of murder or accessory to murder in this case.

THE DROWNED GIRL

1

She could just make out the blue flashes of light between the dense tree trunks, but she couldn't see how many police vehicles were at the scene. The forest road was bumpy, with stacks of lumber on either side blocking out the bright morning light.

Søren Velin sped up, shooting small rocks against the undercarriage of the car, which skidded a little whenever the road turned. They waved him through the police blockade, and he parked next to one of the squad cars.

Louise Rick got out. The road ended at a small cliff where a narrow path led down to the bay, which extended smooth and calm across the sound to the tree-lined shore of Orø island in the distance. From here, Louise didn't recognize any of the men huddled at the edge of the bluff, so she grabbed her jacket from the backseat and waited for Søren to lead the way.

A dark-haired, powerfully built man came up to greet them. "A fisherman found her," he explained, walking past Søren to offer his hand to Louise.

"Storm," he said. "I'm grateful you were willing to help us out." Louise shook his hand and smiled. Storm was the captain of the Unit One Mobile Task Force with the Danish National Police, and he knew as well as she did that willingness had nothing to do with why she was out here, on the shore of the sound just north of Holbæk an hour west of Copenhagen. Higher-ups had made the decision before she was even asked, and they had just been lucky that she was in fact willing to help.

"We still don't know how long she's been in the water," Storm continued as the three of them headed back toward the bluff. "The fisherman notified Holbæk Police this morning at eight thirty-five, saying he had spotted a motionless figure in the water. The girl had a heavy concrete paving slab tied to her torso, which kept her submerged under about four and a half feet of water, stuck in an old fishing net. The fisherman gave up trying to get her loose with his oar and called the police, who showed up along with an ambulance. The Falck Rescue Squad just finished recovering the body."

Louise watched the search-and-rescue van's trailer for the rubber raft that they had used to recover the girl. One diver had gone into the water to cut her free, then passed her off to the other diver, who had hoisted her up into the raft. Now they were loading the rescue raft back onto the trailer. Louise walked all the way over to the edge of the bluff and saw the white sheet covering the dead girl's body and the crime scene technicians in their coveralls busy combing the shore for evidence.

"The local police have cordoned off the site, and as you can see the CSI techs are already at work," Storm continued. "But we're still waiting for a couple more cars."

When they reached the others, he introduced each of them in turn. "That's Bengtsen; he's been with Holbæk's major crime squad since before anyone can remember," he said with obvious respect. "He knows everything worth knowing about Holbæk and the people who live here."

Bengtsen nodded at her, but kept his hands in the pockets of his tweed trousers.

Storm stepped over to a man with an olive complexion. "Dean Vukić," he said. The man shook hands with Louise. There was something hypercorrect about his well-dressed style, the shirt and tie under his leather jacket making him look more like a banker than a detective.

Another man offered his hand to Louise. "Mik Rasmussen," he said. Like Vukić and Louise herself, Mik was in his mid- to late thirties.

"Louise Rick," she replied. Out of habit she almost added *Department A*, but caught herself. Instead she quickly took in the new faces. It was quite a small group, and she wondered how she would fare at finding her place in this pack.

After the briefing that morning back at Copenhagen Police Headquarters with Department A—her homicide investigation unit—Captain Hans Suhr had opened the door to the office that Louise shared with her partner, Lars Jørgensen. Louise had just set her tea mug on her desk and was asking her partner about his adopted twins, who were home sick with the flu, when Suhr interrupted to tell her that her former partner Søren Velin was on his way to pick her up.

"Starting today you've been temporarily reassigned to the Unit One Mobile Task Force with the National Police," he said, already on his way back out the door.

Louise quickly jumped to her feet and stopped him in the hall, wanting to know why she was being reassigned. Suhr's response was curt and clear: because she was deeply familiar with cases like this one. Then he hurried off.

Louise went back to her office and took a sip of her tea, shaking her head in response to her partner's raised eyebrows to indicate that Suhr hadn't given her anything to go on.

"Rape, I'm assuming," she said on her way out the door with her bag over her shoulder, telling Lars she hoped his twins felt better soon. It was only later, when she was sitting in the car next to Søren Velin and heading out toward Cape Tuse—more specifically, a nature preserve out there with the unusual name of Hønsehalsen, "the Chicken Neck"—that she realized she had misunderstood her boss.

"I have no idea whether rape was involved," her former partner told her. "But it looks like the girl is from an immigrant background, and my understanding is that *that's* why Storm really wanted you on this case."

Louise sighed. She had just wrapped up a case like this, and she was still having such a difficult time letting go of it that she was considering seeing one of the police psychologists at the Counseling Services Unit to avoid any permanent trauma. As a young officer she had always struggled whenever she was confronted with people's personal tragedies, and she had worked hard to learn how to handle this. Even so, she still sometimes found herself succumbing again. That's what had happened with her last case, an attempted "honor killing." It had ended with a charge of aggravated assault, but Louise and the rest of her investigative team had absolutely no doubt that certain members of that family had actually intended to kill the sixteen-year-old girl, but had botched the job. Now their eldest daughter was a vegetable in the neurology department of Rigshospitalet, the National Hospital in downtown Copenhagen.

"She was floating on her stomach," Storm explained, pointing to a spot on their right not far out into the sound. "We don't know who she is, but we think she's between fourteen and sixteen years old, give or take. She didn't have a purse or any type of ID on her."

"The canine unit is on its way. We'll see whether they can find anything that could identify her," Bengtsen reported, coming over to stand next to the Mobile Task Force captain. "We can probably assume she was thrown into the water from a boat," he continued, both hands still in his pockets, his eyes scanning the water. "It's too deep here for anyone to have carried her out. A slab of concrete like that weighs a lot."

Louise heard car doors slam shut and saw a blue van now parked next to the other vehicles and two men putting on their work clothes. She recognized one of them as Frandsen, head of Copenhagen's Forensics Division, which had just been renamed the Forensics Center. She walked over to say hi. Frandsen had recently turned sixty, and the Forensics Center had thrown a big reception for him at their offices on Slotsherrensvej, in Copenhagen's Vanløse district. Louise had given him a little pipe holder carved out of mahogany for the pipe he always carried with him even though she had never seen him light it in all the years she'd known him. Whenever Frandsen pulled the pipe out of his pocket and stuck it in his mouth, she knew it meant he was concentrating.

"I guess we're back in business," Frandsen said, pulling a large wooden box out of the back of the vehicle. "And here I was just getting a taste for the golden years."

Instead of throwing a big birthday party for the family, Frandsen and his wife had chosen to spend two weeks in Thailand on vacation. They must have just gotten back, Louise thought. She smiled because he hadn't spent even a second wondering what she was doing at a crime scene so far from Copenhagen, a sure sign that he was wholly focused on the task at hand.

After he got all his equipment together, he followed his team out to the bluff, and Louise walked over to the people standing with Dean and Mik. They had just gotten back from talking to a woman who'd been out walking her dog.

"Nothin'," Dean said. "She lives on a farm right around here and takes her dog on walks through these woods twice a day."

A big, black Citroën rolled up. "It's Skipper," Søren said, waving at the car.

Louise had heard of him over the years. He was a fixture at the Mobile Task Force and National Police, and he had a reputation for unparalleled skill with crime scene investigation and details. She could hear the muffled sound of music booming behind the closed windows of his car. *Looks like Søren was right*, Louise thought. On their way out here, he had told her about Skipper's enormous passion for jazz fusion, which stood in stark contrast with his understated sweater, proper Windsor knot, and otherwise distinguished and reserved appearance—including his neatly groomed gray hair, which was combed back in a soft wave.

After Louise introduced herself to Skipper, Søren added that she had been his partner before he joined the Mobile Task Force.

"Well then, I'm sure we can't get anyone better," Skipper said with a warm smile. "Glad to have you with us."

"Thank you," she said, wondering what Søren had told him. She watched Søren as he spoke to two of the local uniforms. He had been with Department A homicide at the Copenhagen PD for a while when Louise was offered her job there, and they had enjoyed a really good working relationship for a couple of years before he moved to his current job.

The CSI techs were working on the bluff and at the edge of the water. Since she had been in the water, there would be hardly any traces of DNA left on the girl, but they were taking thorough photographs of the body and scene and bagging items from along the shore. Two men were focusing exclusively on finding footprints and tire prints. The coroner from Copenhagen had also arrived, Louise discovered—Flemming Larsen's six-foot-six frame was impossible to miss. He was standing with his back to her as he balanced his bag on his knee to fish something out of it. When he turned around and caught sight of Louise, he set the bag down and walked toward her, his smile beaming.

"Does your being here mean this girl's from Copenhagen?" he asked, surprised, giving her a hug that lasted a bit longer than Louise would have liked. She had worked with Flemming on many of her cases, and lately they had also been seeing each other a little outside of working hours, but no one else needed to know that.

"They sent me out here to assist the Mobile Task Force," she replied.

"Well, I'll be damned," he said, still smiling. "I didn't think Suhr and the rest of Department A could spare you. Is it permanent?"

"It's just for this case— I'll think they'll manage," she answered, thinking that the only person at Copenhagen PD who seemed to have a problem with her working with the Mobile Task Force was Michael Stig. But that was probably just because he thought they should have picked him.

"Good luck, and give me a call some night when you've got time to go out and have a glass of wine." He walked over to pick up his bag as Frandsen returned from the shore, announcing that the coroner could proceed with his in-situ examination of the body.

Louise followed him to the bluff and watched as Flemming removed the sheet and squatted next to the girl. She was lying on her back on the black, wet shore of the sound, her eyes closed, and the slab of concrete still tied to her stomach.

Her long-sleeved T-shirt and lightweight beige jacket had slipped off, revealing how the rope had dug into her skin. Her long dark hair was plastered to her face like yarn; the coroner carefully pushed it to the side. Then he started his examination of the body.

Louise listened in as he reported to Skipper, who had appeared at his side with a notebook to record keywords.

"Unidentified woman found a short time ago," Flemming started, focusing initially on the face. "No petechiae in the conjunctiva or surrounding the eyes. Around the abdominal region a"—he studied the rope—"blue nylon rope is visible, approximately three to four yards in length tied with a square knot with one end wrapped around the subject's waist and the other around a concrete paving stone measuring sixteen by sixteen inches. Livor mortis visible on the abdomen, which does not disappear when pressure is applied, meaning the victim has been dead for at least four to five hours. Rectal body temperature is eighty-one degrees, and the water temperature is sixty-two," he said.

"What do you think about the cause of death—did she drown? And how long has she been here?" Skipper asked, stepping closer.

Flemming stood up and crossed his arms as he contemplated the girl on the ground. Then he shook his head.

"I can't tell how she died. There are no signs of force, but I don't think she was breathing when she was put in the water. Otherwise she'd have foam both in her mouth and around it. Still, that may have washed off. The petechiae are sparse and reddish; she has goose bumps over her entire body, which we often see in individuals who have been in water. And there is pronounced wrinkling on the fingers, palms, toes, and soles—but that shows up only after a few hours."

He concluded by saying that, judging from the rigor mortis, petechiae, and body temperature, he would tentatively estimate the girl had been dead somewhere between nine and fifteen hours.

"When can we get her autopsied?" Skipper asked, waving Storm over.

Flemming looked at his watch and then at the two men. "We can get started at one o'clock, provided you can get Falck Rescue to dispatch their bone bus out here that fast," he said darkly.

The bone bus. Louise shook her head. The nickname for the ambulance with covered windows had stuck. In some cases, it made literal sense, but in others—like this one—it was jarring.

They put the girl into a white plastic body bag, and she was ready for transport to the forensics lab. It felt impersonal and cold for someone whose identity they didn't even know. For a moment Louise had an urge to ride along with the girl so she wouldn't have to make the trip alone, but the bone bus wasn't like an ordinary ambulance with a seat for a family member. It was stripped bare so there was room only for two stretchers and a large exhaust fan in the ceiling.

After the coroner left, Storm headed for the vehicles to drive back to Holbæk PD Headquarters. "That means she might have been in the water since midnight," he said, opening the door of his car. "Let's get going."

Louise took one last look at the scene before climbing in next to Søren, and they drove back along the forest road.

2

Holbæk Police Department was headquartered in an elegant, old-fashioned building of red brick with white window trim, making it look both impressive and well maintained. Louise followed Storm as he led them up one hallway and down another before reaching the Criminal Investigation Division. The offices were arranged in a row—some detectives shared, while others, like Bengtsen, had their own. His was a corner office with windows facing both the front of the police station and the large green lawn and pond at the end of the building. By contrast, Mik Rasmussen and Dean Vukić shared a smaller, darker office where there wasn't room for much other than desks and bookshelves.

Louise had a hard time imagining how they were going to find any room for the extra help they had called in. Earlier Søren had told her about a case in which they had squeezed in an extra detective at a little elementary-school-style desk out in the hallway, and another case in which they kept moving a detective around. But just as she began to worry, her old partner emerged from an empty office. He ran his hand through his longish blond hair as he looked at the weekend bag and two computer bags he had set down on the floor in front of him.

"Are you moving in?" she asked, walking over to him.

"It'd probably be smarter to wait until we know who we'll be working with, but it'd be nice to have a proper place to sit," he said. At that moment Storm stuck his head out a door at the end of the corridor.

"Everybody's meeting in here," he called, waving for them to join him.

They entered what must have been the division's conference room. Louise guessed this was likely where the Criminal Investigation Division normally held their morning briefings. The walls were painted a warm yellow reminiscent of a child's drawing, with the sun a little too heavy and saturated with color—over the top for a small room, but the light from the tall windows compensated for the cramped feel. In front of one window they had a large whiteboard set up similar to the one in the briefing room at the Copenhagen PD, with bits of blue and green lines that the eraser had missed. On another wall there was a large dry-erase calendar next to an enlarged map of the area around Holbæk. Someone had decorated the opposite wall by tacking up a Matisse print, and an overhead projector was tucked away in the corner behind the door. Louise sat next to Søren, grabbing one of the lined legal pads stacked on the table with a few pens, which must have been left over from a previous meeting.

"I think he's going to split Mik and Dean up, and you'll get partnered with one of them," Søren whispered to her.

Louise looked at both of them. One would be just as good as the other. It was standard procedure to form teams by mixing local and backup officers. She had also quickly determined that she was the only woman in the group, so it might well be that the local boys were sitting here wondering about their prospects of being partnered with her. She had heard stories about local police officers calling in sick because they felt invaded when officers suddenly showed up from the Mobile Task Force and started screwing with their routines.

Her thoughts were interrupted when Storm started speaking.

"Nobody has reported the girl missing, so we've put out notices to all police districts about the discovery, and we'll be going to the press with a missing person report," he said, opening the meeting. "Without a photo, initially," he added. "We'll stick to describing just the clothes she was wearing when she was found. If that doesn't turn anything up, we'll have to release one of the forensic pictures. We just don't want to risk her parents' finding out that way." Several people in the room shook their heads. "We'll set up three teams…"

At that moment the door opened, and a woman with elegant orange hair and red lips came in with a bag over her shoulder and a laptop under her arm.

"Hi," she said, smiling.

"Ruth Lange," said Storm, gesturing toward her. "Ruth is our administrative assistant."

Warm hellos filled the room.

"Ruth and I will hold down the command center, which will be here in this conference room," Storm said.

"The teams are as follows," he continued, once Ruth had set her things on the table and taken a seat. He looked around the room. The local officers were sitting next to each other. Louise was sitting next to Søren, who stood out in his cargo pants and black turtleneck. Skipper was to her left.

"Skipper and Dean," said Storm, "you two are responsible for the site where the body was found. In other words, all of the technical evidence."

The two men smiled and nodded to each other.

"Louise Rick and"—he looked down at his papers—"Mik Rasmussen. We're putting you two together to identify her family and social circle. We've got to find out what the motive might be. Rick has some experience working with ethnic minorities," he continued. Louise furrowed her brow. She wouldn't have gone that far, but she wasn't going to correct Storm right now.

"Bengtsen, you and Søren will handle telecommunications and question potential witnesses in the area."

Bengtsen set his pad on the table and nodded in satisfaction. Louise guessed it was probably more the telecommunications and any subsequent wiretapping that he was happy about and not working with Søren, because she had noticed Bengtsen sizing up her former partner. They would make an odd couple, Bengtsen with his tweed and corduroy and Søren with his casual style.

People started talking a little across the table, especially Skipper and Dean who seemed quite happy to be working together. Louise smiled at her newly assigned partner, who quickly looked down after having given her a brief nod.

Storm told everyone to quiet down and took control of the meeting again.

"We don't know anything about the victim. Flemming thinks she was dead before she was placed in the water, but he can't say with any certainty, so we'll need to wait for the autopsy."

Storm got up and pointed at Louise and Mik.

"You two will attend the autopsy. I just got off the phone with Frandsen—the head of the Forensics Center in Copenhagen," he said. "He'll make sure one of his people is ready around one o'clock so the autopsy can get started on time."

Bengtsen nodded his head.

Louise stood up as Storm gestured at the door.

"I've put in a request for an official car for you," he told Louise.

"You can pick it up when you're done with the autopsy. And Ruth will make sure to get you set up with your own laptops."

She gave him a questioning look at his use of the plural.

"One laptop for our secure internal network and intranet, and one for external access," he explained.

Of course they work on two computers, she quickly thought. The Mobile Task Force operated on a heavily firewalled secure police network, but they naturally also had access to the Internet and an open email system. The laptops would be some of the new gear suddenly available to her.

"You'll also get one of our cell phones, but keep your own with you so ours isn't busy when we need to reach you."

As though that's going to be a problem, she thought, but she just nodded.

"We'll be staying at the Station Hotel, which is just a little way up the street across from the train station," he said, pointing out the window. "I hope you'll be able to make it back from Copenhagen by dinnertime. Afterward we'll touch base here again and keep working."

"Sounds good," Louise said, following him to the office they had cleared out for Mik and her to share. They stopped outside the empty room where Søren was standing with his things. He had been given a spot in Bengtsen's corner office, and as he walked past her in the corridor she could tell from the look in his eyes he was quite satisfied with this.

The room she was going to be working in was small and spartan. The walls were a dull eggshell color. The desks and two office chairs reminded her of old school furniture, with names and symbols scratched into the desktops. Mik Rasmussen had already begun to move his things in, but Louise's area was completely empty. She settled into her chair and watched Mik stock his desk with paper and set out pencils in a mug from a local soccer club.

"Do you play?" she asked.

He looked over at her with a confused expression and then followed her eyes to the mug.

"I used to," he replied curtly. When she kept looking at him, he explained that he had played soccer for several years with the Holbæk Ball & Sports Association.

"But we never got further than the Zealand playoffs."

"But you don't play anymore?" she prodded, keeping the grilling going.

He shook his head. "Now I paddle sea kayaks and teach kayaking down at the Rowing Club."

Louise smiled at him. At no time during their brief acquaintance had she suspected him of being particularly athletic. He was just too lanky and reserved for her to connect him with any form of outdoor recreation.

"Do you know when they're going to notify the media?" she asked. Bengtsen was taking care of that.

"I doubt it'll go out right away, but once it does I'm sure it will get a lot of airtime," he replied, pulling on his windbreaker.

His accent had a distinctly Zealand ring to it, which hers did as well—she'd grown up in central Zealand. She had worked hard to rid herself of the accent, but sometimes it still came through.

She looked at the clock. It was nearly noon. She stood and pulled her bag up over her shoulder; they had to get going.

"Time to go?" he asked, and she let him lead the way out, through the back entrance to the lot where the squad cars were parked.

They drove in silence. It suited her just fine that neither of them felt the need to entertain the other. Gradually, though, the silence got to be too much for her, so she broke it as they drove through Roskilde.

"Have you worked with the MTF before?" The Mobile Task

Force was an elite National Police unit dispatched throughout Denmark, Greenland, and the Faroe Islands to assist local police departments investigating serious crimes.

When he nodded, Louise explained that she wasn't permanently assigned and that this was her first case with them.

The September sun was blinding them, so he pulled the visor down and positioned it carefully before he finally started talking.

"We had a murder up here a few years ago when they called in the MTF after a few weeks. That was under our old boss, and for that case in particular it probably would have been smart to have called for assistance earlier, because the perp was never found. But that's not how things run anymore. Now they call in assistance the moment a murder is discovered."

There wasn't a trace of sarcasm in his voice.

"How long have you been a detective?" she asked with interest.

He did the tally in his head before answering. "Eight years, but I've been here eleven. I became a uniform right out of the police academy."

That confirmed for Louise that he was in his mid-thirties. Actually, thirty-six, a year younger than she was.

"I assume you live in Holbæk?" she said, thinking she sounded like a reporter doing a lengthy interview, although it didn't seem like it was bothering him.

"On a farm just outside town. Do you know Holbæk?"

She nodded and told him that her parents lived not far from there and that when she was a teenager she used to spend all her free time at The Alley, one of Holbæk's nightclubs.

He turned his head and studied her, and she knew he was wondering whether he had seen her before.

"Maybe we've danced together," she joked, glad that the conversation was starting to loosen up and become less formal.

But his eyes were already back on the road, concentrating on a couple of bicyclists. He politely mumbled that if that were the case he probably would have remembered it.

She was about to try again, but just then he turned off onto Frederik V Avenue and parked up alongside Fælled Park across from the morgue. Flemming Larsen was waiting for them when they entered.

"Åse is already here, so let's just head up and join her," he said, starting toward the elevator.

Louise smiled. Åse was one of her favorites among the forensic pathology staff. The tiny woman—whom Louise initially took as fresh out of college and green—was in fact extraordinarily competent and thorough. Åse had her own quiet style whenever she set to work photographing a corpse, moving through the lesions on the body and internal organs, and it was clear that she considered every detail important. Now she was already ready to go, waiting for them in the little corridor that led into the autopsy section, wearing scrubs and blue medical booties carefully secured over her shoes.

"Well, we meet again," Louise said.

Mik went straight into the rear autopsy room, commonly called the murder room. It was twice as large as the other rooms where autopsies were performed so any law enforcement officials who needed to observe would be able to. Louise and Åse stayed outside talking while they waited for the fingerprint expert to finish taking the girl's prints, in the faint hope of identifying her that way. When Flemming asked them to come in, they walked past the line of smaller autopsy stalls where other forensic pathologists were working. They continued to the autopsy room, joining the forensic team in charge of preparing the body and Mik Rasmussen, who was sitting on a stool in one corner with a pad of paper on his knee, ready to take notes.

Louise grabbed another stool and sat next to him. Åse pulled her camera out of her bag and started taking pictures of the fully clothed corpse from various angles while speaking quietly to Flemming. When she finished the photos, the other forensic techs stepped forward and removed the girl's clothes. Åse took pictures of each garment separately, and then at last they were ready to start on the external examination.

During a brief break, Louise stood up and stepped forward to take a close look at the naked girl. She looked so very young. Her long dark hair lay out over the table; around her neck she was wearing a thin gold chain with a tiny heart. She had no makeup on. It could have been washed off by the water, Louise thought, but there was no dark residue around her eyes.

She stepped back again when Flemming and Åse were ready to continue. The coroner reiterated his comments from the examination at the crime scene: "No clear signs of violence, no signs of pathology or specific identifying marks."

Mik scooted his stool over to the windowsill on the back wall so he could use it to hold up his notepad. He wrote extensively as everyone continued speaking behind him. Flemming Larsen also repeated that there were petechiae in and around the victim's eyes, and then the forensic techs went over every inch of the girl's body, using an arsenal of cotton swabs to dab for evidence before turning the body over.

Åse photographed every detail. When Flemming finished examining the back of the body, he straightened up.

"The top left side of the neck shows two yellow, slightly rounded abrasions," he announced. Åse stepped closer, and together, they bent down.

"These are quite unusual and were sustained after death. I can't exclude the possibility that they occurred during transport here," he said before asking the men standing in the corner by the door to open the girl up.

Louise stepped out with the others while the forensic techs did their work, drinking tea as she waited. She finished half a cup in Flemming's office before they called her back in.

The body had been opened with a long, straight cut, and the internal organs had been lifted out in one block and rinsed. Now the last stage of the autopsy could get under way. The light from Flemming's work lamp, which hung from the ceiling, was intense, reflecting a glare out into the room wherever it struck the white tiles of the end wall and the shiny surfaces of the stainless steel tables. A long hose hung over the deep sink where the block of organs lay, and Louise could hear the echoing sound of regularly spaced drips whenever a drop of water hit the basin.

"She is a healthy young woman," said Flemming, mostly directing his comments at Mik for his notes. Flemming announced that her last meal had been rice and beans.

He worked a little more in silence before saying: "There is no water in the lungs or sphenoidal sinus, so there is no indication that she drowned, but she was underwater for a few hours. She has acute hyperinflation. The lungs are large and pale, which may be because she had difficulty breathing, but I can't give you a cause of death," he said, completing the autopsy.

Everyone said thank you, stepped out, and pulled off their masks and white coveralls. Louise hung back a moment to talk with Flemming before following Mik over to the elevators to head down to the car. They agreed that he would drop her off at the Polititorvet, the large, red-brick neoclassical building that housed the Danish National Police Headquarters, where she could pick up the car she had been assigned. Then she planned on stopping by her apartment in Copenhagen's Frederiksberg neighborhood to pack a bag.

3

After Louise packed a few things, she did a quick walk-through of her apartment with her weekend bag in hand. She had packed both warm- and cold-weather clothes. Even though they were halfway through September, they were still having days so hot that even shorts and T-shirts seemed like overkill.

Her answering machine was blinking. She pressed PLAY and walked over to the windowsill to grab the vase of flowers she had bought the day before. It would be easy enough to bring the flowers wrapped in a bit of newspaper to her room at the Station Hotel in Holbæk.

"…you can call anytime today. We're supposed to be getting together tomorrow, and it would be nice to know if we're all set or if I should just wait on standby until it suits you to call me back!"

Camilla Lind's voice was cut off by the answering machine's shrill beep.

"Yeah, yeah, yeah," Louise said to the machine, reaching for the phone.

"Hi—and I'm sorry," she began, heading off Camilla's initial reproach for her laxness in returning calls. "I've got to cancel for tomorrow."

"Well then, let's set up a different time to get together," Camilla said.

Louise's best friend worked the crime desk at *Morgenavisen*, and she was used to Louise's canceling when she was working on a case. In turn that usually also meant that Camilla could expect to get some kind of story lead out of her. Their jobs were connected in a way, even though they approached homicide cases from different angles.

Even so, it surprised Louise a little that Camilla didn't protest more vigorously, which left Louise feeling guilty. She knew that her friend could really use her support right now, and she wanted to be there for her. It just wasn't possible today.

"I'll give you a call in a couple of days," she promised, explaining that she was on her way out the door.

Then she hung up and changed her voice-mail greeting: "This is Louise. I'm not checking my messages, so call me on my cell. Bye."

Camilla Lind stepped up her pace so she'd be able to make it to Markus's private school on time and then take the subway with him all the way back to the Frederiksberg Community Center so he wouldn't be late to his break-dancing rehearsal at Hot Stepper again. She had planned to buy a bottle of water and some fruit for him on the way, but she dropped the idea when she checked her watch at Nørreport Station, instead bounding down the stairs and darting onto the subway in a quick leap.

She was sorry that her date with Louise had fallen through. Camilla had been looking forward to slumping down onto Louise's couch and venting. But after talking with her, Camilla had called the Copenhagen PD to find out what was up, since Department A was apparently involved. Camilla had sensed that they were giving her the runaround when the duty officer insisted he was unaware of any new case. Annoyed, she'd quickly packed up her things and shut down her computer to head out the door. On the way she'd run into her editor, Terkel Høyer, who was coming to see her with a missing person report from Holbæk involving the body of a teenage immigrant girl.

Camilla quickly realized that her workday wasn't over yet after all. Both of her colleagues were out: Kvist was taking some well-earned extra vacation days, and their intern, Jacob, was in New Zealand with his girlfriend for the entire month of September, so everything fell to Camilla. Her editor just nodded when she announced on her way out that she would be right back after she dropped her son off at home. Her cell phone was already in her hand so she could get hold of her irreplaceable babysitter, Christina, and have her watch Markus after his break-dancing session.

"Be back as fast as you can," Terkel called after her.

Walking quickly out the door, she raised one arm in the air in acknowledgment. She knew where he stood: The paper should be in on the story from the get-go. She agreed. The stories of eighteen-year-old Ghazala Khan, who had been shot by her brother on the square in front of Slagelse Station in September last year, and the even younger Sonay Mohammad, who had been slain by her father in February 2002 and thrown into Præstø Harbor, had filled many front pages and garnered a great deal of media attention during their investigations and subsequent trials. There was no reason why this story would be any different.

Markus was waiting for her on the sidewalk in front of his school, wearing his backpack, looking for her. She started running toward him and waving as soon as he spotted her. Hurrying hand in hand, they raced off and made it just before rehearsal began. Markus quickly changed shoes and put on his hoodie and baseball cap while Camilla went to the food court to buy a bottle of water and a banana, handing them off to him. The door closed, separating her from the loud pounding music and the fifteen tough eight-year-old kids—fourteen boys and one girl—who would spend the next hour practicing the Baby Freeze and various other moves. She sat down on a bench in the lobby for a moment.

Christina had promised to be at the community center in forty-five minutes so she could take over by the time rehearsal was done. Then she and Markus would go home and have some dinner together. Camilla had already braced herself for a fairly late night.

She had just stood up when she saw him—and sat back down again, heavily, as though two powerful hands had given her a rough shove. She knew instantly that he had been watching her, and her stomach turned as he approached. She couldn't stand; she just sat and stared up at him as he spoke.

"For the love of God, you've got to stop calling me and sending me emails," he said. "You have got to respect my boundaries and stop contacting me."

Then he was gone. Out the door and down the sidewalk. Camilla felt as though the whole interaction had played out in slow motion, and yet she had not had time to react or say anything.

She sat frozen. Anger and pain filled her, both fighting to take over. She wanted to run after him and make him understand. Tell him that she needed to stay in touch. That she needed him, and that they had been good together. But she couldn't stand up; her muscles felt weak and useless. He ignored her phone calls and didn't respond to her emails. He didn't want her. It was over, and that was unbearable.

She tried to collect herself, taking deep breaths and trying to ignore the pangs in her diaphragm. Finally, she stood up and started walking back to the subway.

4

The body of an unidentified teenage girl was found this morning in Udby Bay on Cape Tuse, north of Holbæk. The girl is approximately fourteen to sixteen years old and appears to be of Arab origin. She has long black hair and was wearing a beige summer jacket over a dark-blue T-shirt with long sleeves, faded Miss Sixty jeans, and white Kawasaki shoes. If you have any information about this girl, please contact Holbæk Police."

Louise heard the missing person report break on the news on the local P3 radio station during the drive back to Holbæk. It was almost five o'clock when she parked behind the police station. Upstairs in the corridor she nodded at Mik Rasmussen, who was talking with a colleague.

Inside the sun-yellow command center, someone had set up a fourteen-inch TV that was playing in the background at low volume, and there was coffee in a carafe. Ruth, the administrative assistant, and Storm were talking to Bengtsen about coordinating first interviews with witnesses who might have known the girl. A communications guy was walking around, almost finished running a few extra outside phone lines, and Ruth was just getting a large database system up and running.

"Have you taken a look around the Station Hotel?" Ruth asked.

Louise shook her head and said she would drop her things off when they headed back there for a bite to eat. "Have we gotten any leads from the missing person report?" she asked with interest.

"A few tips have come in, but not really anything we can use," Ruth replied.

"But we have ten men circulating a description of the girl in town, so I don't think it'll take long for something to turn up," Storm added as he stood up. "Let's head over to the hotel and grab some food."

Ruth flipped the lid of her laptop shut and pushed aside the stacks of binders, pens, and pads that she had been quick to requisition before the investigation really got going. No one was going to have time to keep filing requisitions for everything they would need once the case was really under way. The mobile command center was almost ready.

At that moment one of four telephones in the office rang. "DNP Unit One Mobile Task Force, Ruth Lange speaking," she said, pulling back her voluminous hair. "Okay, send her in. We'll come meet her."

She hung up and looked at Louise. "There's a young woman here who thinks the victim we found may be a friend of hers. Can you talk to her? I just told your partner he could go home for a few minutes before dinner."

Louise nodded and poured a cup of coffee from the thermal carafe in the middle of the table before grabbing a pad of paper and a ballpoint pen in case her computer hadn't been set up yet. The coffee sloshed over the rim and down the side of the cup, burning her fingers as she walked down the corridor. Swearing, she set the plastic cup down on the desk a little too hard, causing it to slosh more. She quickly wiped her hand on her pants and went out to meet the witness.

A tall, attractive, very young blond teenager was walking in slowly, uncertainty filling her eyes.

Louise approached her with an outstretched hand and a welcoming smile.

"Hi, I'm Louise. Let's go in here." She pointed toward her office, which still seemed cluttered, although her partner had already put his things away.

"Would you like a glass of water?" she asked as they stepped in. The girl shook her head and sat down on the edge of the hard wooden chair that Louise had pushed toward the end of her desk.

The bags containing her laptops were still the way she had left them. She hoped that a little informal chat would get the girl to relax.

"What's your name?" Louise began, leaning back slightly in the office chair.

"Benedicta, Dicta for short..." The girl cleared her throat and repeated her name a little louder. "Dicta Møller. I'm in ninth grade at Højmark School."

"And you're worried that the girl we found out at Hønsehalsen may be someone you know?"

It wasn't that uncommon for girls to worry about their female friends and contact the police if a girl was reported missing in the media.

"There's a girl in my class who wasn't in school today," Dicta began.

Louise didn't rush her.

"She and I were going to get together this afternoon, and I haven't been able to get hold of her. She's not answering her cell, and no one answers when I call her at home." Louise nodded and waited for her to continue. "I've been calling all afternoon."

"Do you think she might have taken off somewhere with her

parents and forgotten about your plans this afternoon? Something unexpected may have come up."

Dicta thought for a moment, considering the possibility, but then shook her head.

"She wouldn't have forgotten this. We were going to go through the photos," she said, now with more strength in her voice. "She was over at my house yesterday after school, and we talked about it then. One of the photos is going to be published this weekend in the paper."

Louise asked her to explain what kind of photos she was talking about and what paper she was referring to.

"I'm a model," the girl explained. "I model for a few stores, including Boutique Aube, and the paper is supposed to run their big ad on Saturday. The photos were ready, and Samra was supposed to come to the photographer's and take a look at them. So she wouldn't have just taken off."

Tears started streaming down Dicta's cheeks, but she continued: "She w-would never do that. She keeps…"

Dicta broke into tears, her words turning into an incomprehensible mess. Louise held out her hand to stop her.

"What does your friend look like?" she asked when the girl had calmed down a little.

Dicta straightened up and carefully dabbed away her tears so they wouldn't ruin her makeup.

"She has long dark hair."

Louise sat up and grabbed her notepad.

"And is your friend ethnically Danish?" she asked, waiting for the next crucial answer.

"No," the girl replied hesitantly, as though she was afraid that was the wrong answer. "She's from Jordan."

"Does she have any distinguishing marks that you can think of? Or things she usually wears?"

Dicta fell silent, picturing her friend in front of her.

"She usually wears a watch. It's a Dolce and Gabbana knockoff. I bought it for her in Thailand—and she's also got a ton of bracelets. You know, bangles, where each individual one is thin, but you can wear a lot of them at the same time."

She used her index finger and thumb to indicate a width that Louise estimated at about four inches. "Anything else?"

"Nothing that she wears regularly, but she does have jewelry."

"What about her clothes?" Louise asked instead.

"Just the usual. Jeans and T-shirts…a lot of times she'll wear a top with a little blouse over it, and she has a beige jacket like they mentioned on the news on the radio."

Louise glanced down at the girl's feet and saw a pair of black Kawasakis. She pointed at them.

"Does she have a pair like those, too?" she asked, knowing most of the girl's friends likely had them. She couldn't understand how the floppy little sneakers managed to stay in style. They'd been popular when she was in school, as well.

Dicta nodded. "We bought them together; hers are white."

The girl stopped, unable to think of anything else. Louise didn't pressure her, instead saying, "Okay, I've got all this information written down. The last thing I'll need is just your friend's full name and address, and also how to get hold of you in case we want to talk with you again."

"She usually always responds to text messages. I've been texting her, but she doesn't reply," Dicta said instead.

"What's her name again?" Louise asked, trying to direct Dicta back to her question.

"Samra al-Abd. She lives out at Dysseparken, apartment 16B," the girl said. She seemed to consider her words before continuing. "She comes over to my house a lot when her parents let her, but her father can be pretty strict; sometimes she's afraid of him. And now she's suddenly missing…"

Louise tried to reassure her by repeating that there could be any number of good reasons why her friend had missed school or blown off their plans.

"There's no need to assume the worst," she said. Louise knew that lots of people saw ghosts in broad daylight when it came to persecuted immigrant girls and their fathers. Still, she had to admit that many of the things Dicta had told her might well indicate this was the right girl.

"Could I get your friend's phone number?" Louise asked, watching Dicta take her cell phone back out and browse through her contacts. Louise took down the number and also asked for her friend's home number at Dysseparken.

Once she had written down both numbers as well as Dicta's, Louise nodded toward the cell phone and asked if Dicta happened to have a picture of her friend on it.

A moment later Dicta passed her phone across the table and told Louise she'd taken the picture outside of school the week before.

Louise quickly leaned forward and took the phone, but the picture was taken from so far away you could see only the long black hair and a blurry face. There was a certain similarity between Dicta's friend and the dead girl, but it was impossible to tell for sure if it was her.

"Unfortunately, this was taken from too far away for me to make her out properly," Louise said, handing back the phone. "Do you think you have a better one?"

The girl shook her head and explained that she'd had more pictures on her old phone, but she had lost it.

"I might be able to find one at home," she offered, saying she would be happy to stop by with it the next day.

"It's a deal. Then hopefully we can rule out your friend as the girl we found," Louise told Dicta, thanking her for coming before walking her back out to the reception area. Then Louise quickly returned to the command center, but it was empty, and the lights were off. She surveyed the offices, but Bengtsen was the only person still at his desk.

"Did everyone else go over to the hotel?" she asked. Bengtsen nodded without looking up from his copy of *Venstrebladet*, Holbæk's left-leaning daily newspaper.

Louise went into her office and found Storm's cell phone number, so she could call and update him on her conversation with the girl. "Hurry over here and get some food, we'll go over it after we've eaten," he said curtly.

"If it really is the friend, shouldn't we get in touch with the parents right away?" Louise objected.

"Of course, but we also need to eat; it's going to be a long night," he said. "Afterward we'll check out what other tips have come in on the missing person report, so we know where we stand before we start talking to people."

Louise knew protesting would be pointless; Storm called all the shots. Instead, she went back in to see if Bengtsen wanted to join her.

He shook his head, but this time his eyes at least left the paper to look at her.

"Aren't you going to eat?" she asked before leaving his office.

"Yes, but I prefer to eat at home," he said, briefly explaining that she should just head left when exiting the police station, and then take a right. Then she'd come to the Central Station Square where the train station and the Station Hotel were located.

"See you later," Louise said, heading back to retrieve her bags from the car before she set out on foot toward the hotel.

5

Last night he cut deep gashes into his own face. He can't take it anymore; I have to keep an eye on him.

Camilla teared up as she read the old email in her inbox. She was still upset that Henning had shown up at the community center just to tell her to her face that she should stay away. When she got back to her office at *Morgenavisen*, she immediately checked her email to see if he had sent an explanation, but there wasn't any word from him. Now she sat there depressed, skimming through his old email instead.

They used to talk to each other, she and Henning. They had both thought their relationship was strong enough to handle what happened in Roskilde. Camilla couldn't recall ever being so determined to fight for a relationship. Not even when she and Tobias had started drifting apart when Markus was about one year old.

A few weeks after Henning's brother was arrested, they had lunch at one of the colorful eighteenth-century restaurants on Franciscan Square, right off the pedestrian shopping district downtown. After coffee, they sat holding hands across the table, promising each other their relationship would survive, despite the trauma they had shared when his brother was arrested in a headline-grabbing online-dating case involving several brutal rapes.

"It's settled. It will always be the two of us," he said, and at the time that had filled her with relief. But then everything suddenly went to hell—ending with that email he'd sent saying he had to focus on taking care of his brother.

As she sat staring at her screen, she would have given anything in the world to just let go of him and move on, but she couldn't. He was all she could think about, and she was close to exploding from the pain of longing to have him back in her life. He was the man who had finally shown her what it felt like to come home. He was the one: She had known it after their first week together.

Her hands were still trembling a bit when she opened the door to her editor's office to announce that she was back.

Terkel Høyer was sitting behind his desk and didn't look like he was going to be heading home anytime soon, either.

"No word from Holbæk since they issued the missing person report," he said.

Camilla had been on the crime beat at *Morgenavisen* for several years and had gotten good at reading her boss. She could sense that he was all fired up about running something in the paper the next day.

"We've got to include every angle on the story. You're going to have to get someone local to talk, otherwise we'll just be rehashing what we did out in Slagelse the first few days after Ghazala Khan was killed. There wasn't any depth to our coverage, and people lost interest in the story."

Camilla watched him for a moment. She didn't actually think there was anything strange about readers avoiding the tragedy of an entire family joining forces to kill a young woman—someone's daughter, sister, and niece—because she had sullied their familial honor by marrying someone they didn't want her to.

Camilla really couldn't blame readers for turning their backs on that one in disgust. At the same time, she understood what Terkel was saying. Over time, all the reporting on cases like these started to sound the same, so their coverage of this case would pack more of a punch if she could land an interview with members of the family. That probably wouldn't be easy, but she welcomed the challenge.

"And then of course you'll byline a report from Holbæk with local reactions and whatever else you can dig up."

She nodded and got to work packing up her laptop and throwing a few things into a small bag so she could spend the following day in Holbæk.

"But we still don't know if the girl is actually from there," she pointed out.

He conceded her point but thought it wouldn't hurt to stick to the plan all the same.

"I talked to Storm," he explained. "The MTF already has a team in town. It's probably not a bad idea to stick close to them. He agreed to give us a call to update us on the case once they've gotten a little more information to put out. You stay here and write the story tonight so we can run it in the next edition, and then drive out there tomorrow morning."

Camilla nodded and thought about Storm, with whom she had a great working relationship. He didn't have the same aloofness from the press that several of the other lead detectives had, which undeniably made it a little easier to enjoy friendly rather than irritated interactions with the police.

She went back to her office to pull out her calendar. Sometimes she was organized enough to jot down her family's and friends' plans. This was usually limited to her mother in Skanderborg, Markus's dad, and Louise. She started by calling Tobias to find out if he could take their son a day earlier than planned.

This week he was supposed to pick Markus up from school on Friday and keep him until Monday morning, but if he didn't have other plans he was usually more than happy to take Markus for an extra day.

She sent a text message and quickly got a reply that the change of plan was okay; Tobias would pick Markus up Thursday afternoon. So that was covered. Camilla pondered briefly calling Storm and asking if he had any more information besides what she already knew, but she decided to give him a couple more hours. She still had plenty of time until her deadline. Instead, she printed out the missing person report to have it ready, and then she went down to grab some dinner.

Louise carried her weekend bag to the reception desk, and the woman at the counter handed her the room key along with a message that the others were already at the restaurant. She rushed up to her room with her bag, quickly scanning the large, airy space. It had yellow walls and gaudy curtains on the large windows. The decor included light-colored birch furniture, a large framed America's Cup poster from 1987, and a painting of the crowns of some trees densely packed together under a blue sky. Next to the bathroom there was a small vanity.

She went into the bathroom and washed her hands, splashing cold water onto her face. Then she removed her hairband and shook out her long dark curls before gathering them back into a

ponytail again. That would have to suffice. Before heading to the
restaurant, she sat down on the bed and dialed the two numbers
that Dicta Møller had given her, but no one answered at either.
Dicta's friend's cell phone went to voice mail, and her parents'
landline rang and rang until Louise hung up.

"Hi," everyone said as she came in.

"I ordered something for you," Søren said, "but you should tell
them what you want to drink."

There was no one in the restaurant besides them, and the waiter
was busy talking through the swinging door that led off to the
bar. She walked over to him and ordered a Coke before taking the
empty seat her former partner had saved her.

"So, you think it may be the girl's classmate?" Storm asked as
she sat down.

"Can't rule it out. There are several similarities," Louise replied,
looking at him. He was speaking from across the table four seats
away from her, so she had to raise her voice.

"She said her friend is from Jordan, she has a beige jacket, and
she wears white Kawasaki shoes. I think we have to take her information seriously and follow up on it."

Storm nodded.

"How long has it been since she was heard from?" he asked.

"She wasn't at school, and she missed a date with her friend this
afternoon, so it's only really been today," Louise replied.

"None of those things are uncommon," said Mik, who was
sitting across from Storm. "What was her name—the girl you
talked to?"

Louise hesitated until she realized he was asking because he
thought he might know her. That's how it was with small-town
life, she reminded herself. People knew each other.

"Dicta Møller," she answered, adding that the girl and her missing friend were in ninth grade at Højmark School.

Mik shook his head; apparently the name didn't ring a bell. Apparently Holbæk wasn't quite small enough.

"Shouldn't we focus on our food now? That way we can throw ourselves back into work afterward," Storm suggested, apparently forgetting entirely that he had started the conversation.

The waitstaff started bringing in huge plates of Wiener schnitzel, with slices of veal as thick as phone books. The meat was served with pan-fried potatoes, peas, anchovies with lemon, and horseradish on the side. Gravy was set out in a little boat next to each place setting. Normally Louise would have lost her appetite when confronted with such enormous portions, but the last thing she had eaten was some oatmeal she'd dished up at seven that morning. So she tried to ignore the size of the portions, remembering her grandmother's words: *No shame in not cleaning your plate.* Nowadays, if anything, there was more shame associated with overeating. After dinner, several of the others ordered apple cake with whipped cream, while she made do with tea.

She could already tell what direction things would go if she was to be living and eating with a pack of hungry men like this for any period of time. She was going to have to keep an eye out, or she'd just end up having to run off the weight during her morning jogs.

"Let's meet again in the command center for our briefing," Storm said once everyone was almost done with their dessert. They split up and left the restaurant in small groups, chatting away.

Bengtsen was waiting for them when they got back. He had made a fresh pot of coffee and had a baking sheet of chocolate cake on the table in front of him.

"It's from Else," he said, passing it around.

Louise tried to call the two numbers, the girl's and her parents', again, but since there was still no answer, she sat next to Bengtsen and was happy to take a piece of cake. She had regretted not ordering the apple cake almost immediately, even though she'd felt as if she were bursting at the seams.

"Is Else your wife?" she asked, slicing a corner off the cake and tipping it onto a piece of paper towel. She had decided to ignore the rigidly square grid Bengtsen had begun when he took the first piece.

He nodded, drawing the ends of his narrow lips up only just enough that Louise dared interpret it as a smile. But whether the smile was an expression of a lifelong devotion to his wife or whether it was because he was a little shy about having food made for him, she couldn't say. She was quick to praise the cake as soon as she had gotten a bite into her mouth.

"How did it go out at the crime scene today?" she asked Dean, who was sitting on her other side, loosening his tie a bit. "Did anything turn up?"

"The Frogman Corps has been doing dives up and down the cove, but they haven't found anything," he replied, referring to the elite special forces unit of the Royal Danish Navy. He poured her a cup of coffee before saying that forensics had kept the girl's beige jacket out at the scene so the dogs would have something to go by.

"Various things have been collected from the scene," he continued, till Storm interrupted asking him to speak up so everyone could hear.

Dean Vukić looked around and reiterated that the divers hadn't found anything they could link to the girl or her murder and that the canine units weren't finished yet.

"There are some tire prints we'll research. We have several footprints that we need to take casts of. And the CSI team has secured some evidence from the soil in the form of cigarette butts, chewing gum, mucus from globs of saliva that will be checked for DNA, and then we'll see what we have," he said.

Yes, we'll see, Louise thought. But first they had to find out who the girl was.

"We haven't located a purse, bag, or cell phone," Dean finished after a pause.

Now it was Mik's and her turn. Mik updated everyone on the autopsy.

"We're obviously ruling out an accident, given the concrete paving slab," Storm stated when they finished.

"What about suicide?" Søren asked.

"In that case she would have had to jump into the water from a boat," Skipper said, but he added that they had not come across any unmoored boats in their survey of the area.

"If she had been attacked at that location, there would have been prints in the dirt or on the bluffs near the water," said Dean, who had spent the whole day working with the CSI team. "There were no signs of any struggle. And, again, there would have had to have been some kind of boat to get her so far out into the water."

"There are some boats moored out at Hønsehalsen that the fishermen use," Bengtsen, who evidently had in-depth knowledge of the area, interjected.

"All those boats are accounted for," Skipper said. "They're all moored, so she couldn't have used them herself, in any case. But we should take a closer look at them."

"Most likely she was killed somewhere else and brought out to Hønsehalsen," Dean added. "Otherwise, the dogs would have responded at the scene. We ran the dogs through the little marina with all the dinghies, too, and they didn't find anything."

Everyone nodded and seemed to agree.

Storm sat sorting some scraps of paper as though they were playing cards.

"These are the tips that have come in response to the missing person report so far," he said, dropping them nonchalantly on the table. "Probably nothing of much interest. All of the girls are native Danes, but let me flip through them quickly." He fished out his glasses. "There's a Lisette Andersen, age seventeen, from Kalund-borg. Her mother called in. Her daughter has short blond hair."

"Didn't it say that our girl has long dark hair and might be Arab?" Søren asked pessimistically, disqualifying Andersen. "A Tove Mikkelsen called in about her daughter, age twenty, from Roskilde, but she pointed out that her daughter looks very young and could well pass for sixteen."

"We get a couple hundred missing person reports about teenage girls every year," Ruth interrupted, looking at the men around the table. "Some of them make their way to Christiania," Ruth continued, reminding them of the appeal of Copenhagen's downtown hippie commune, "or they get settled into a co-op building or communal house somewhere and come home again once the exoticism of their adventure has faded and they miss hot baths and decent food. But there isn't anything you can say when a mother is worried something has happened to her daughter."

"True enough, but there's no reason to spend more time on that now," Storm replied. He asked Louise to tell Bengtsen about her conversation with the teenage girl, as Bengtsen had not been at dinner at the hotel restaurant.

She quickly updated him on her conversation with Dicta Møller and on the similarities that were of interest.

Bengtsen nodded several times as Louise spoke. "Given that so many things match, we definitely need to reach Miss Møller's friend or her parents so we can figure out what's going on," he said. "We can't proceed with the investigation until the body has been identified."

"I've called her and her parents a few times, but there isn't any answer at either number," said Louise.

Storm looked from Louise to Mik Rasmussen.

"You two drive out there right away. We've got to determine whether we've found the right girl. And then we'll go from there."

6

"There is a lot of ethnic diversity in this neighborhood," Mik Rasmussen explained as they parked next to some town houses at the end of a large block of apartments. The town houses were dingy yellow stone, and there were two apartments in each.

Samra and her family lived in an upstairs unit. From down in the parking lot Louise could make out a light in the room facing the front of the building. Judging from its faintness, it was probably from just a single lamp in the room, she guessed, walking closer. The downstairs neighbors were clearly at home. That unit had lights on everywhere, and she could see a person through the window.

They walked up the stairs together and rang the bell. As they waited, Louise jotted down the name on the door: Ibrahim al-Abd. There was no woman's name. After a few minutes and several rings they gave up and went down again.

"Let's just go and talk to the downstairs neighbor," Louise suggested, walking over and ringing the bell before her partner could object.

The door opened almost before her finger had released the button. They were observed with curiosity by a woman with a crutch under one arm.

Louise introduced herself and asked whether the woman knew if the upstairs neighbor had been home over the course of the evening.

The woman at the door took a small step back when she learned they were with the police, but a spark of curiosity gleamed in her eyes.

"Is anything wrong?" she asked.

Louise shook her head and said she assumed not, but they had a question for the family upstairs.

"Have you seen their daughter at all today?" Mik asked over Louise's shoulder.

The neighbor thought about it and shook her head. "I don't think I've seen any of them today at all. But you can just check if their car is parked in the lot. Maybe they all took the car somewhere together."

Louise stepped aside so Mik could move in closer. "What kind of car is it?" he asked.

"It's a run-down red one."

"What make?"

Louise was already sure this woman was clueless about makes and models, so they would have to take whatever she said with a grain of salt.

"A Honda," the neighbor said, after a long pause.

Louise took a notepad from her pocket and wrote, *Red car, older-model Japanese. Check vehicle registration.*

"How many kids do they have upstairs?" she asked before they left.

"Four. Two older ones, and two little ones," the woman said, explaining that the children were Aida, a four-year-old girl, and Jamal, a boy of about two. Louise and Mik thanked her and apologized for disturbing her. The neighbor stayed in the doorway watching them until they got back to their car.

Right as they were about to exit the lot, Louise yelled, "Stop!" There was a red car parked there matching the description. She jumped out and went over to an older-model red Peugeot 306. She wrote down the vehicle registration number and walked back over to her partner.

"Should we just try to go upstairs again and see if they'll open the door?" she suggested, but she could tell that he really wanted to get going and thought they had already done enough. "You can wait," she added. "But it does look like their car is here."

Mik stayed in the car with the engine running while Louise quickly ran back upstairs and pressed the bell. She stepped away and looked in through the window next to the front door. She could see the kitchen, and it was completely dark. There was a bedroom on the other side. Louise leaned over the railing and peered in. That was the window with the light on, but the room was empty and the door to the hallway closed. It was a girl's room, she noted.

After pressing the doorbell a second time, she went back down again and went over to the other side of the building, but everything upstairs was off and dark. So she returned to the car.

The drive back to the police station took ten minutes. They agreed that Mik would check the car's registration when they arrived to find out whether the Peugeot was registered at that address. Again, Louise had a feeling he was eager to get the job done so he could go home.

"Not much new information. No one was home," she reported to the others sitting in the command center. "But what we do know about this girl fits the description we have. Samra al-Abd is from Jordan. She has long hair, and her clothes also match the description pretty well."

"We need to find someone who can come to the morgue to identify her," Skipper said, filling his mug with coffee.

"With her parents' permission we could take Dicta in to do that," Søren suggested. "We have to be sure it's someone who knows the deceased well."

"She's too young," Bengtsen interrupted. "We should use Dicta only as our very last option. It's too hard for such a young girl to be confronted with a corpse, especially if it turns out not to be her friend."

It surprised Louise to hear him make that objection.

"What about her homeroom teacher?" she suggested. "She would know her student well enough."

Storm nodded and asked her to get in touch with the teacher so they could get the identification done that night.

"The press has started pushing for more details. But I'll take care of them," he continued.

That sounded good to everyone because it wouldn't be much help if all of them were so busy taking calls that they didn't have a chance to coordinate the information before it leaked out.

Louise got up and left the meeting to call Dicta and get the name and number for their ninth-grade homeroom teacher. Mik stayed in the office to check the red car in the motor-vehicle registry and had an answer ready when she came back.

"It's good enough: It belongs to Ibrahim al-Abd," he said, pronouncing the name slowly and trying to put the stress on the right syllables. "The address also matches," he added. "And there was a cell phone number registered for the same name, but the phone seems to be off."

"We should be prepared for things to go late tonight," Louise said. She told him about the impending identification before dialing Dicta's number and waiting for the girl to answer. Mik and Louise had family living in the area around Holbæk, so the task had fallen to them. To her surprise he nodded absentmindedly and stood up, pulling on his jacket.

"Well then, I've got to run a quick errand." He left the office without another word.

"Jette Petersen," Dicta said when Louise had gotten her on the line and asked for her teacher's name. In the same breath Dicta asked if it was Samra who had been killed.

Louise could hear how anxious she was.

"We don't know yet. But we are certainly taking your concern seriously," she said to dampen the girl's fears. Then she asked if there were any friends Samra might be staying with. "Does she have a boyfriend?" she asked more specifically.

"No," Dicta said quickly. "She's not allowed to have a boyfriend or anything like that, and she doesn't usually get permission to go out that much. Sometimes she bends the rules, but that's mostly when she's supposed to be coming over to my house and her father won't let her."

Louise wrote this down. If it proved relevant, Louise wanted to hear more about how Samra managed to sneak out and be with her friends, but she would not probe into that right now. Dicta found their homeroom teacher's phone number, and she gave Louise both her home number and her cell.

"Thank you so much, and I apologize again for bothering you," Louise said before hanging up. Louise could hear Dicta's voice choking up as they said good-bye and knew perfectly well that calling her had only added to the girl's worries.

She dialed Jette Petersen's home number, glancing at her watch. It was nearly half past nine, a bit late to be calling people, but the way things were, they couldn't wait until the next day.

"This is Helge," a man's voice said.

Louise introduced herself and asked to speak to his wife. She didn't think it was necessary to fill him in on the reason for her call.

There was a moment's silence, then the homeroom teacher got on the line. "Yes?" she said.

Louise introduced herself again and apologized for the late call. "I'm calling because I'd like to talk to you about one of your students."

"Has something happened?" Jette asked anxiously.

Louise heard a chair being dragged over the floor. Based on her voice, Louise guessed the woman was middle-aged, but it was hard to say.

"That's what we're trying to find out," Louise answered. "And I need your help."

"Who are you talking about?" the teacher asked quickly, and Louise could tell she was holding her breath, waiting for the answer. Likely not because hearing one name would be any better than hearing another, but because the teacher was nervous about what was coming.

"This is about Samra al-Abd," Louise said.

"What's happened?" Her voice was shrill with anxiety.

Louise told her that the police had received a visit from Dicta Møller, who linked Samra with the girl who had been found dead early that morning.

"Oh, I heard about that. But it didn't occur to me it might be one of my kids!"

"It's certainly far from sure," Louise hastened to say. "But there are some similarities, which means we have to look into whether it could be Samra or not. How long have you had Samra in your class?"

"Ever since she moved to Denmark four years ago. She started fifth grade just after the summer break."

"We haven't been able to get hold of Samra or her family, and despite the late hour I need to ask if you could accompany me to the morgue in Copenhagen tonight and tell us if the deceased girl is your student."

"Of course." Her voice grew slightly hoarse. "I can be ready in ten minutes."

"That's great. We'll come pick you up," Louise said, silently cursing that her partner had just taken off. They could have the girl identified before midnight if they got going now.

She went out and found Storm, telling him she was ready to drive to Copenhagen with Samra's teacher.

"If you leave now, I'll get Bengtsen and Velin to see if they can track down any family members who might know where the parents are."

Skipper and Dean were sitting with Ruth, reviewing the technical evidence that had come in during the day so it could be entered into the database. They had turned up some tire tracks, which might be of interest, and the technical investigation would continue the next day.

"Well, I'll be on my way," Louise said, but at that moment she saw her partner walking toward her again, ready to go. She couldn't help thinking it was some kind of retribution that he'd ended up having to make this late trip into Copenhagen even though he was obviously itching to get home.

7

Dicta and Samra's homeroom teacher lived in a yellow house on the outskirts of Holbæk. Forty-five years old, Louise guessed, plus or minus. She was an attractive woman with short dark hair tucked behind her ears, her glasses pushed up on top of her head, and her lipstick a subdued hue. Her voice made it clear that she was not quite as composed as she seemed, and she was clenching her hands tightly together in her lap.

They didn't say much in the car. Mik assumed the role of chauffeur and hadn't uttered a word since they left the police station. He drove with a local's familiarity through the residential neighborhoods, all of them named after various flowers, and he nodded subtly when Louise volunteered to walk up to the teacher's door by herself.

Now Louise sat leaning her head against the window on their way to Copenhagen for the second time that day. Jette Petersen obviously had her mind on her student, the possible victim in this case.

Before they left Holbæk Police Headquarters, Louise phoned the on-call pathology lab technician in Copenhagen, asking to have the body brought out so it would be ready for viewing when they arrived.

"Is it normal for Samra to miss a day of school?" Louise said, breaking the silence as she turned around in her seat to look at Jette.

She quickly repeated that they still weren't at all sure that the victim was her student, but this was the only relevant tip they had gotten on the missing person report. The fact that they weren't able to get in touch with the girl or her family was a contributing factor in their suspicion.

"Yes, she misses a day every now and then. Most of the students in this class do. But she hasn't had any major absences. In fact, it's fairly uncommon for her not to show up," the teacher said after thinking a bit.

"What's her family like?"

"I don't know much about them," Jette replied, saying that Samra had an elder brother, Hamid, but she knew him only by sight. He was a few years older than she was and had attended the school for only a year before moving on to the business school. "She's a very pretty girl, and I've gotten the impression several times that the parents had the son keep an eye on her. He was often standing around waiting for her when school got out, and then would accompany her home. Occasionally she would run into trouble if she stayed late after school or if we had a special-topic week and were working on class projects into the early evening. The last time we did that, Samra asked me to call her parents at home to confirm it was true she would be staying at school that late. So I guess you could say they keep a pretty close eye on her, but she never complains about it. I probably couldn't put up with it myself, though," Jette said quietly.

"What's your impression of her parents?"

"I've met them only a few times. Her father showed up just once for a parent-teacher conference; otherwise I haven't seen him. But last winter we did 'Food Week.' We have several immigrant kids in class, so we spent a week focusing on food from different cultures, and we invited all the students' parents for an evening in the home-ec classroom and had the parents prepare a special dish together with their children. It was really great—homey and pleasant and fun—and we ended up with a huge buffet of Danish and international dishes from all over the world. Samra's mother, Sada, is a lovely, sweet woman. We laughed a lot and ate a lot, and I don't think I might otherwise have had the opportunity to talk as openly and freely with the mothers as I did that night. Everyone's dishes came with lots of funny stories. Sada had her two littlest ones with her as well, Aida and Jamal, and Samra's sister was a big hit strolling around the room in her little white apron, holding her mother's fancy serving dish in those little hands of hers and asking, 'Would you like any more, ma'am? Sir?'" Jette smiled at the memory.

"Does Samra have relatives in the area?" Louise asked. "Or farther away, for that matter, that her family might be off visiting?"

"They do have some family here in town. I'm not sure whether they're on her mother's or father's side, but Samra does have a cousin. She's in the other ninth-grade homeroom, and I have her for math," Jette said. "Also, I think there's an uncle who lives somewhere around Ringsted, or somewhere between Holbæk and Copenhagen, I'm not exactly sure. But during vacation last summer I ran into Samra at a flea market in Ringsted, and I think she said she was visiting family. My sister lives just outside Ringsted," Jette said by way of explanation.

"Do you know what her uncle's name is?"

The teacher shook her head.

Louise knew that Bengtsen and Søren were already looking into locating other people with Samra's last name, and she thought there was a decent chance the families had the same last name. Louise wondered if she should ask any more about the girl but decided to wait until she knew whether it was actually Samra al-Abd whose body was lying out waiting to be ID'd.

A man was waiting to let them into the Teilum Building, which was otherwise dark at this late hour, and he led them through the waiting room to the left of the main entrance and then around a corner where he opened the door to a smaller waiting room. He asked them to take a seat on the blue sofas for a moment. There was a box of Kleenex on the table, and the blinds were rolled down over the window into the viewing room.

The technician opened the door to the room and asked Jette to come in. Louise stood up and walked over to the door. He had pulled the white cloth down to reveal the girl's face, and her hair was neatly arranged over her narrow shoulders. She had no wounds or bruises. She looked the way you often hear corpses described: like she was asleep.

It was over after the first glance. Jette nodded and confirmed that the dead girl was fifteen-year-old Samra al-Abd, who was a student in her ninth-grade class. Louise nodded at Mik, who stepped out to make the phone call so they could start focusing the investigation.

The teacher placed her hand on her student's cheek and let it rest there for a moment as she looked at Samra's face with her eyes shut. Jette's eyes were filled when she turned, and Louise left her in peace as her tears started to fall.

When Mik came back in, to Louise's great surprise he stepped over to put his arm around Jette's shoulders and stood there for a moment comforting her. Louise couldn't hear what he said, but she noted that the teacher stopped crying, and shortly after she heard him ask if Jette was ready to go back to Holbæk. She saw the small nod, and they slowly began to walk toward the exit. Louise stayed back a bit as Mik helped the teacher into the car.

They drove back in silence. There were suddenly a number of important questions to ask, but Louise didn't feel it was the right time to ask them. It was late, and Jette was sitting with her eyes closed, taking deep breaths as though she was struggling to regain control over her emotions. Her willingness to come had been an enormous help to them. Louise received a text message from Søren, who wrote that the family in Ringsted had been located, but they were going to postpone getting in touch with them until morning, hoping this would allow them to inform the parents first.

Before dropping Jette off, Louise asked her not to mention anything at school. They wanted to make sure that the family had been told before there were any rumors in town. They agreed to meet the next morning when the teacher had a free period in her schedule so they could talk about Samra.

"Good night, and thank you so much for being willing to do this so late in the evening and on such short notice," Louise said.

Mik got out of the car and shook the teacher's hand good-bye.

"Do you know her?" Louise asked as he pulled away from the curb.

"I know who she is, and she knows who I am, but I don't know her any more closely than that. But it's never nice to take a blow like that while other people are looking on, let alone people who know you."

Louise just sat and watched him, surprised by the thoughtfulness that had shone through Mik's reserve and awkwardness.

"I'm heading home if that's okay with you," he said when they arrived back at the police station. After they dropped Jette off, they had stopped at Dysseparken 16B to inform the girl's parents, but there was still no answer at the door.

Louise nodded at her new partner and said good night before heading up to see whether the others were still at their desks. The lights were off in most of the offices, but Ruth Lange was sitting at her desk working. Ruth told her that everyone had just taken off, and they would regroup again at eight.

Louise sat down in her office and found to her satisfaction that the IT guy had managed to set up her two laptops. She took out her personal cell phone and saw a long list of messages from Camilla, who asked her to call. But now it was too late.

She turned it off and flipped it shut, and then started walking over to the hotel with an extra key that had been dropped off for her that opened the hotel's main door when the front desk was closed. She suspected there wouldn't be anyone at the front desk this late, but she still went over to see if she could get anything to drink and take up to her room.

Søren Velin was sitting in one of the roomy armchairs in the lobby waiting for her. With two beers.

"Hey," he said, asking if she wanted one.

She nodded and sat down. There was a pack of cigarettes on the table, but she quickly looked away. She had relapsed and started smoking again over the summer but had decided to quit again.

"How's it going?" he asked, holding out a beer to her.

"All right," she replied. "We got the girl ID'd."

He nodded and said he actually meant how Louise herself was doing.

Louise smiled and said that she was all right, too.

"What about your partner? Is he okay?" he asked.

Louise took care not to say too much because she knew she couldn't afford to complain. "I haven't really figured him out yet," she said. "It's like we're not communicating on the same frequency."

"Well, everything is pretty new. Are you still happy about being in Department A back in Copenhagen?" he asked, shifting the subject away from the local situation.

She nodded and asked if he had plans to come back.

"Yes, but I don't know when," he replied. "Right now, things are going well here."

"What about at home? Are you guys able to stay connected with you gone so much?"

"Actually, it's working pretty well," he said. "As long as Lisbeth is enjoying working from home, I think we can make it work."

Søren and Louise had been partners back when Søren's wife was deciding to quit her job and start up her own web-design business, so Louise had been privy to all the considerations that had entailed.

"Working from home, she takes care of Soffie alone, and things have been working really well for them when I'm away."

Louise estimated that his daughter must be about two and a half now. She thought the girl's name was a little pretentious. She knew Søren had preferred the spelling *Sophie*, but he hadn't won that battle.

"Are things going well with her job?"

Louise knew only that his wife designed websites; she had no idea whether it was a proper business or more a hobby.

He nodded. "At least right now. If things change we'll obviously have to sell Strand Boulevard," he said, referring to their place in an affluent neighborhood north of downtown Copenhagen.

Yes, and either buy somewhere out in Hvidovre or smack-dab on City Hall Square, depending on which direction things went, Louise thought, picturing one of the beautiful old brick buildings with ornate, wrought-iron balconies near the fancy hotels across from City Hall. But he was right. You had to adapt.

"How about you?" he asked, lighting a cigarette. "Did you keep the apartment after Peter moved out?"

She nodded. "That was my place when I was single, too, before he moved in," she reminded him.

He smiled. "Ah, right. And do you think there will be two names on the door again at some point?"

She shook her head and loosened up a bit. There weren't many colleagues she felt like inviting into her private life, but back when Louise and Søren used to be partners, he had managed to break down her barriers, and she felt a little of their old familiarity starting to rekindle.

"At first Peter wanted to move back in. Or, I don't fucking know exactly what he wanted, but in any case, he had second thoughts about the breakup at one point."

When Peter had dumped her for someone else after eight years together, Louise had told her partner, Søren, everything. It was some other girl Peter worked with. Then shortly after he had moved in with that girl, Louise found him standing in the stairwell outside her place again, asking if they couldn't work things out after all.

"I just couldn't," Louise said. "And when I thought the whole thing through carefully, I came to see that the right thing had happened—it probably should've even happened a little sooner."

Søren nodded in understanding and asked if she was only saying that with the benefit of hindsight.

She shrugged.

"I spent a whole month with Camilla and her son in the South of France. We rented a little house and sat gazing out over the water drinking Kir and discussing everything that had happened to us at the start of that summer. I don't think I'm seeing it this way only because he's gone. We were too different, and we wanted different things from life."

He nodded. "Yes, but it can be hard to get perspective on stuff like this while you're in the middle of it, especially if two people's everyday routines seem to work without major conflicts."

She conceded his point, but reminded him that there had been a few clear signs along the way.

"For example, I never thought about joining him when he would fly to Aberdeen for work."

"Well, you're not exactly the archetype of the follow-him-loyally-at-his-heels housewife," Søren replied drily.

"No, but I probably would have gone with him if he'd been the most important thing in my world," she said, taking a sip of her beer.

"Do you miss him?"

She nodded. "I miss him as a person, but I don't miss our life together."

"Incidentally, what happened with Camilla after that arrest down in Roskilde? Is she still together with that guy's brother?"

Louise shook her head and suddenly felt overwhelmingly exhausted. "They broke up before we took that trip to France. The whole thing knocked all the wind out of her, and I don't really know what I should do to help her. The only sensible thing for her to do is forget him and move on."

Søren stood up and grabbed another beer, and she nodded when he asked if she wanted to share it.

"I feel like giving her a firm shaking. The relationship between those two was completely lopsided, but instead of getting angry and flicking him off, which is much more her style, she's doing just the opposite."

"That doesn't sound like the Camilla Lind I know," Søren conceded, lighting another cigarette.

"Uh-uh, not the one I know, either."

"The best thing would be if she met someone else who completely swept her off her feet," he said after a moment's thought.

"You're right. But that kind of thing just doesn't happen that often, and certainly not when you need it to."

Louise glanced at her watch and downed the rest of her beer. "I think I'm going to call it a night," she said, standing. "It's been great seeing you again—thanks for the beer. Next time they're on me."

"Same here," Søren said. "I'm looking forward to working with you again."

They went up together and parted ways at the top of the stairwell.

It was nearly nine thirty when Ibrahim al-Abd arrived at Holbæk Police Headquarters. Louise had just returned to the office and grabbed a cup of tea, and her hand was on her phone. Earlier that morning, Mik Rasmussen and she had stopped by the family's apartment again. Since there was still no answer, Ruth Lange helped them look up where the father worked, which was a lumberyard by the harbor. When they arrived there, the manager said the father had just left.

He was a small man, with thick black hair and a solid, well-groomed mustache. Louise had been about to leave for the Højmark School and her appointment with Jette Petersen, but had canceled when Storm asked her to come with him to notify Samra's father.

"Let's go in here," Louise said, leading Ibrahim into the office. She asked him to take a seat on the chair next to her desk and nodded at Mik, who had already grabbed an MP3 recorder that he was setting up. She offered the father coffee and water while she prepared for the conversation. Right as she was about to shut the door, Storm waved her out into the corridor.

"Try to get him to tell you a little bit about his daughter before you tell him that she's the person we identified."

Louise raised an eyebrow but nodded and turned to walk back into her office.

"You wanted to talk to us about your daughter?" she began.

He nodded and said he had left work when he heard the news at nine that morning, which had included a report about the dead girl the police had found.

"What is your daughter's name?" Louise asked.

"Samra al-Abd," the girl's father said, pronouncing her name clearly. He added that his daughter was fifteen years old and was in the ninth grade.

"How long has she been gone?"

He shrugged his shoulders all the way up to his ears and, holding out his palms in despair, said it was hard to know.

"We haven't seen her since she said good night and went to bed Tuesday night."

The night before she was found out by Hønsehalsen, Louise thought, feeling sorry for the man, who in a moment was going to find out his daughter was dead. Still, she wanted to get as many facts as possible about Samra al-Abd as long as the father was talking.

"What about the next morning when she was supposed to go to school?" Mik asked. "Didn't you notice if she left for school?"

He was obviously also determined to get the father to explain himself, and he watched the man intently as he answered.

"No, my wife doesn't get up when our older kids leave for school."

He briefly said that he had to be at the lumberyard down by the harbor at six thirty himself, and his eldest son had a job at the same location three mornings a week before his business school classes started.

"He and I are already gone when Samra gets up."

"Has your daughter disappeared from home and stayed away for a whole night before?" Mik asked.

At first Ibrahim shook his head, but after thinking for a while he said, "Sometimes the other young people she hangs out with infect her, like a rotten apple in a basket," he said, looking accusingly at Louise for a moment as if she bore part of the blame. "So it can be hard to figure out exactly what she's up to."

"What other kinds of things does your daughter do?" Louise asked, seizing the opening.

She could see how torn he felt as he considered the question.

"She doesn't always listen to what we tell her," he said finally. "Then she comes home when it suits her."

"Does she often come home late?" Mik wanted to know.

"A few times it's been several hours past what we agreed on," said Ibrahim.

"But right now, we're talking about almost thirty-six hours—has she ever been gone so long before?" Louise asked.

"No, which is why I think something must have happened. She wouldn't dare," the girl's father replied, and Louise noted that Samra apparently had reason to fear her father's reaction.

"Does your daughter have a boyfriend she might be staying with?" Louise asked, following every movement in his face.

His expression suddenly seemed less open and he shook his head.

"She's too young for that sort of thing. She's fifteen," he said, looking Louise straight in the eye when he replied. Louise felt as though she were gazing directly into the abyss of a father's deep worry.

If he thought a fifteen-year-old girl was too young to have a boyfriend, then he also probably thought the girl was too young to marry off, thought Louise, making it fairly unlikely that it was an "honor" killing triggered by a conflict over marriage.

Louise excused herself for a moment and went to ask one of her colleagues to check on whether there were any past reports of violence in the family. But when she entered the command center, Ruth Lange had anticipated Louise's request and had a printout of the information ready for her.

"We've got one report against the father for domestic violence. His wife filed it six months ago. Apparently he beat both her and her daughter, and subsequently the wife stayed at a women's shelter in Nykøbing Sjælland. Other than that, we don't have anything on him or the elder brother. The father came to Denmark in 1998, but the rest of the family did not arrive until 2002. At that point, the youngest hadn't been born yet, and the little sister was still an infant. They come from a town fifty miles south of Amman, Jordan, called Rabba. Since early 2001 he has been working at Stark, a lumberyard down by the harbor," said Ruth.

Louise hurried back to her office and sat down quietly so she wouldn't interrupt the interview.

"Do you have a picture of her?" Mik asked.

Samra's father gently pulled a photo out of his jacket pocket. He set it on the table. It must have been taken on Midsummer's Eve; Samra was wearing a light-colored summer dress, and you could see the bonfire in the background. Her long dark hair fell onto her shoulders, and she was holding her little sister's hand. Both of them were smiling widely for the photographer. It struck Louise that she actually hadn't known whether Samra wore a head scarf, but apparently she hadn't.

"Is she the one you found?"

Louise glanced quickly at Mik, who nodded to her, and she turned to the father and said she was deeply sorry to have to tell him that it was his daughter whom a fisherman had found in the water out by Hønsehalsen in Udby Bay.

All the color drained out of his face. His shoulders slumped, and a moment later he burst into tears and began to wail. With a sudden jerk, he rose and started to pace back and forth in shock, moaning that it couldn't be true. He kept breaking into streams of Arabic they couldn't understand, but there was no mistaking the despair in them.

Louise approached cautiously, pulled him back toward the chair, and tried to get him to calm down.

"My little girl," he repeated between deep sobs, sitting with his face hidden in his hands.

The air in the office was heavy with misery and grief. Finally Ibrahim calmed down a little.

Mik turned the MP3 recorder back on and attempted to resume the interview. "We need to talk more with you about your daughter's disappearance."

The father looked at them with a distant gaze and tear-laden eyes. "How did it happen?" he asked.

"We don't know quite yet," Mik said, making no mention of the rope and concrete.

"Could you please repeat for us when you and your wife last saw Samra?" Louise asked, turning the conversation in another direction.

"Tuesday night, when my wife said good night to her at eight thirty."

"Yesterday one of your daughter's friends from school came forward when she heard we had found a dead teenage girl. Didn't you see or hear the news yesterday?"

Ibrahim al-Abd was frozen, sitting as if encased in ice for a moment. Finally, he shook his head. "Was it on TV? So then everyone knows what happened...?"

Mik interrupted him. "We put out a description. No picture was shown."

Louise couldn't tell from Ibrahim's face whether he thought it was good or bad that the missing person report had gone out.

"Last night we went out to talk with you and your wife after the

tip from Samra's friend, but no one answered. Where were you?"
she asked.

It took a moment before Samra's father replied.

"At my brother's house in Benløse, outside of Ringsted," he explained.

Louise just nodded. "How did you travel down there?" she
asked.

"By car."

Tears were making his eyes shiny again.

"We drove," he continued, diverting attention from his fresh
bout of weeping.

"When did you come home?"

"Midnight, maybe one a.m., I think."

"But you didn't answer this morning, either, when we stopped
by again," Mik interjected.

The man looked over at him and explained that he and his son
had gone to work.

"My wife is very worried and didn't sleep at all. After my son
and I left, she took the little ones to her sister's house."

"When we went out to talk with you last night, your car was
parked in the parking lot, and it was at just past ten. Does your
wife have a car?" Louise asked.

He shook his head, but she knew the answer already. No other
cars were registered to their address.

"If you didn't drive your car, then what car did you drive?" He
didn't seem to understand what she meant.

"You drove down to your brother's house, you say. But your car
was in the parking lot last night," Mik clarified.

"No, no," he said, jumping up from his chair and pacing back
and forth again. "We didn't drive. My son drove."

"There is no vehicle registered in his name," Louise interrupted.

"He's buying one. It's not all worked out yet, but he'll get it settled," the father assured them.

Louise asked for the car's make and registration number, but the father could only say it was an older-model BMW.

"Could I just get your brother's name and phone number?" she asked, to be on the safe side, so they could compare that with the information Søren had dug up.

He sat down and gave her both.

"What happened? What happened to her?" he mumbled again, rubbing his forehead as his face once more took on an absent look.

Mik took over and pointedly asked Samra's father to describe in detail the period of time when he was last with his daughter.

Ibrahim calmed down a little. Louise could see that he was pulling himself together, preparing to go through the last time he was with his daughter. They waited for his breathing to become regular again.

"Tuesday," he said, savoring the memory of the weekday. "I was down at the boat," he continued, explaining that he had a small sailboat moored in Holbæk's marina.

Louise asked him to clarify where it was and wrote a note that she should have someone look into how long it took to sail from Holbæk over to Udby Bay, where the Hønsehalsen peninsula jutted out.

"When did you get home?" Mik asked after they had noted all the details about the boat so they could locate it later.

"Around seven o'clock."

"Was Samra home when you came back?"

He thought carefully before nodding.

"Did anything peculiar happen that night?" Louise asked.

He shrugged slightly and said they'd had a visit from family.

"Who from?"

Louise was starting to get annoyed that they were having to

drag everything out of him. She had hoped that they would be able to get him talking without having to squeeze each word out so they would have his own description and sequence of events to go by.

"My brother," he replied.

"The one from Benløse?"

He nodded.

"You see each other a lot," she noted.

"That's normal in my family."

"Was Samra with you?" Mik asked.

The father shook his head and said that she had spent the whole evening in her room. "She was doing her homework," he added.

"But you said good night to her?"

Again there was a pause before he explained that usually his wife was the one who took care of that sort of thing. "I was in the living room."

"We know that you were reported for domestic violence previously against your wife and daughter. Will you tell us what happened?" Louise asked.

The father winced and looked down at the table.

"Have there been problems between you and your daughter since then?" she continued.

He still didn't respond, and they let him sit in silence. "It was a misunderstanding," he finally said. "Nothing bad. I lost my temper."

"What set you off?" Louise asked quietly.

"It was my son, and Samra stuck her nose into it."

"How?"

"It's not her place to make a fuss about the way I raise my son," he said simply.

"What did your son do?" Mik wanted to know.

"I thought he had lied to me. But I had misunderstood and

made a mistake. I apologized, and my wife came home again. You can see that everything got sorted out."

Mik coughed briefly before meeting the father's eyes and asking: "Did you kill your daughter?"

Ibrahim al-Abd's face shut down completely and he started crying as he vigorously shook his head and looked back into Mik's eyes without shame.

Louise and Mik glanced at each other and agreed that would have to be enough for now. They asked for his son's cell phone number so they could get in touch with him.

"Can we see her?" the father asked, turning around in the doorway on his way out, tears still streaming down his cheeks.

They both nodded and said they would call him about a time when he and his wife could drive over to the morgue in Copenhagen and see their daughter one last time.

He nodded his thanks and zipped his jacket all the way up to his throat before turning around and heading down the corridor past the offices where everyone was hard at work on the investigation into his daughter's murder.

Louise stood watching until he disappeared out the door.

8

Louise and Mik sat in their office together with Storm and told him how it had gone, and Louise called Samra's teacher and principal and asked them to notify the students before the news got out.

"We need to find out how that family works," the lead investigator said. "If her father or another member of the family did it, we need to close in on them before they start covering their tracks with uncles and alibis."

Storm stood up and strolled down the corridor, summoning everyone to the command center.

Louise felt strangely relieved that Storm had just said straight out what everyone undoubtedly suspected. Yet another "honor killing," or liquidation of women, as some had begun calling it, because they could not accept that there was anything honorable about such an act.

Louise had brought the picture of Samra with her. She tossed it out onto the conference table so it could make the rounds.

"This is how she looked in June, so about three months ago."

At that moment the door opened, and a young man came in with two white boxes he was balancing in one hand. Storm had ordered fancy open-faced sandwiches from the local butcher's shop.

"Here are your sandwiches," the man said. A girl with plates, silverware, and napkins followed him in.

Bengtsen got up and returned a moment later with a blue lunch box that he set in front of himself.

"Aren't you having any?" Skipper asked, nodding at Bengtsen.

"No, I prefer to eat what I bring from home."

"We're definitely going to have to meet this Else soon," Skipper said.

Bengtsen ignored him and started opening his lunch box, while Louise hurried to reach for a Veterinarian's Midnight Snack—an open-faced sandwich of buttered rye bread topped with liverwurst, corned beef, aspic, and red onion—before anyone had a chance to call dibs.

"Did the father say anything?" Søren asked, getting everyone's attention again now that they had food on their plates.

"He said he got home around seven Tuesday night," Mik said, wiping his mouth, "and his daughter was home then. They had a visit from the uncle from Benløse, but Samra was in her room, and he has not seen her since."

"Ibrahim al-Abd also has a sailboat moored down at the marina," Louise added, looking at Storm.

He set his knife and fork down, and a deep wrinkle appeared over his brow as he let that information sink in.

"So far we've got only the one crime scene. We should look into getting the girl's room and the rest of the apartment searched in a hurry, and we can do it under the pretext that there may be important information about her disappearance. Then we should bring the mother and brother in immediately, and of course we've also got to get the sailboat searched, as well as the dinghies anchored out in the cove." He paused briefly. "We also need to ID her closest friends, so we'll be able to get their take on the relationships in the family."

The boss looked around and asked who else they should get hold of.

"The father's brother in Benløse," Mik quickly said.

Storm nodded and repeated that everyone related to the al-Abd family needed to be brought in as soon as possible.

"And you two need to help with all the interviews," he told Bengtsen and Velin, adding that they were also responsible for obtaining a printout of the girl's cell phone records.

Søren said that Samra's cell phone had not yet been found; he had already requested a court order for the phone company to turn over all of the information pertaining to her phone number, so they could get a list of all calls, times, and cell towers.

Storm nodded in satisfaction.

"Shouldn't we call in an interpreter?" Louise asked. "Based on Mr. al-Abd's statement, his family speaks and understands Danish, but aren't we obliged to make sure that everything is being understood correctly?"

"We'd better," Storm conceded and then looked at Bengtsen. "Who do you usually use for cases like this?"

Bengtsen said that there was a woman they had been extremely satisfied with in the past who worked as an interpreter at Holbæk Hospital.

"Couldn't it present a problem if we use someone local?" Louise interjected. "Interpreters can be more loyal to the person being interrogated than to the police. If we want to be sure that the interpreting is correct, we should use double interpretation and bring in one of the department's own translators."

She spoke from experience. The first crucial interrogations in the Nørrebro case had gone horribly wrong because the interpreter turned out to be from the same area in Pakistan as the suspect. That meant he did not dare convey the uncomfortable questions the police were actually asking, and instead made things up.

"Rick is right," Søren said. "We don't have any way to control for that, and Holbæk is a small town."

"We've got a good guy, Fahid—let's see if he's free so he can assist her," Storm said and asked Søren to get hold of him. Then he turned to Skipper and Dean, who were following up on the technical investigation. "We've been looking into the family's cars."

Louise briefly updated the others on the old BMW that Samra's brother was apparently in the process of buying, and on the father's red Peugeot.

"I understand you've already got something around the crime scene that might be of interest?" Storm continued, asking them to report.

Dean explained that they had secured several tire prints, but one in particular was interesting. Close to the bluff, the forensic techs had found a tire print manufactured by Bridgestone with the brand name Europa II 195/50 R15 82V.

"So, it's a fifteen-inch tire, and it's a little unusual," Skipper added. "Most of us drive on sixteen-inch tires. Bridgestone explained to us that this tire is unique in its design and size, and it was for sale in Denmark for only a short period of time. A car dealer here in Holbæk, Hans Just, sells Bridgestones, and he said that on March tenth, 2006, he sold a red Peugeot 306 to an Ibrahim al-Abd who lives at Dysseparken and that vehicle just had four completely new tires put on, brand Europa II 195/50 R15 82V."

"That car needs to go to forensics," Storm said. "They'll secure the tires and put on some equivalent ones before he gets the car back, and then of course we can go over the interior in detail. We also want them to investigate the BMW, and I want that to happen today."

Dean and Skipper nodded in agreement and got ready to return to work.

Louise got up as well, and on her way out of the command center she tossed her paper plate and plastic silverware into the trash. She liked this phase of an investigation, when the tasks were assigned and everyone was scrambling to get going on them.

9

When Louise got back to the office, she first called Samra's teacher to get the names of the school friends Samra had been closest to. She also called Dicta Møller and left a message on her cell phone.

It only took a minute for Dicta to call back. Louise could hardly hear what she was saying and asked her to speak louder.

"Are you in the middle of class?" she asked.

Dicta explained that she had stayed home from school. She was sick.

"I'd like to talk to you about Samra if you think you are ready for that," Louise said, sensing that the girl was about to cry.

The girl inhaled deeply. "I just heard," Dicta sobbed, unable to keep her emotions at bay. "The school called, and of course I knew right away."

Louise offered to drive to her house so Dicta didn't have to come down to the police station. It would be helpful to get Dicta's views as quickly as possible on how Samra's family worked.

She told Mik across the desk that she wanted to drive out and have a quick talk with Samra's friend, and they agreed that Mik would continue questioning the family members. Then Louise could join back in once she returned.

She hurried down to the parking lot to the car, tucking the slip of paper with Dicta's address in her mouth as she pulled on her jacket and opened the car door. She felt privileged to have been assigned her own vehicle. Back at the Copenhagen PD, a number of cars were allocated to each investigative team, but that didn't mean there was always one free when she needed one.

She had no idea where Holbæk's Østby neighborhood was in relation to the police station, but thankfully the car had a GPS; she keyed in the address. Normally she considered it a point of honor to have some feel for a place, but the only thing she knew in Holbæk was the downtown area. She didn't have a very good handle on anything outside that. When she saw the route, however, it dawned on her that instead of a car she should have asked them to issue her a bike. Even though the address was on the edge of town, it wasn't very far, and it would have done her good to bike out there.

She started driving and soon found herself in a showy neighborhood of newly constructed family homes not far from Beach Mill Meadow Park and the sound. The houses were close together, and Louise drove down the street slowly, studying the houses. All were built in individual styles with impressive driveways, and several had sunporches facing the street or were in a functionalist style with sleek surfaces and lines, while others were done in an older style with arches and balconies. Although the residents had clearly gone to some trouble to turn their homes into something unique and special, there were three things they pretty much all had: Poul Henningsen designer lighting, either outdoor sconces on exterior walls or conspicuous table lamps in windows facing the street; Swedish-style white wooden benches; and large lion statues carved from white stone gracing the driveways.

Louise noted all of the details. There were kids' bikes in most of the driveways, and she didn't doubt that this was a neighborhood for privileged children. Yet you couldn't feel much life on a Thursday morning like this, probably reflecting the fact that both parents had to work to afford to live here.

If she hadn't already known that Dicta attended one of the city's public schools, she would have guessed that the parents who lived here would rather send their children to the one-hundred-year-old Stenhus School in Holbæk, one of Denmark's largest university preps, or to any of the city's other private schools. But apparently the Møller family had not made that sort of thing a priority.

The Møllers' house had a white plaster exterior with a large balcony that went all the way around the top floor. Louise guessed that the view was impressive: the sound, the marina, the open fields, the forest, and the city. Parked in the driveway was a large, new SUV. Louise was a little puzzled. As far as she had managed to figure out, both parents worked in Holbæk; the father had a chiropractic clinic on the main street, and the mother worked part-time as a medical secretary. Yet they had opted to equip themselves with a Jeep Grand Cherokee with yellow license plates, normally reserved for business cars that were eligible for lower fees. It irked Louise when people, who didn't have a really good reason to, chose to drive big, heavy cars like that.

As she approached the front door she heard fierce barking. There was a wall to the right of the house with a white gate in the middle. She had the feeling there was a nice pack of medium-size dogs just on the other side, and she got a glimpse of the shadow of a German shepherd and an Old English sheepdog before quickly taking the three steps up to the front door and ringing the bell.

Ding-dong. The sound echoed and further agitated the dogs; now there was barking from inside the house, too. Louise began to regret not asking Dicta to come down to the police station after all. Not that Louise had anything against dogs, but all the noise and frenzy was annoying as she tried to gather her thoughts and prepare her questions.

Dicta was wearing a gray tracksuit, she had no makeup on, and her long blond hair was gathered into a loose ponytail. The ditziness and flightiness of the other day were now entirely gone. Louise was standing opposite a young girl who was either trying to be a grown-up or striving to give an impression of maturity. Pale and deeply upset, Dicta invited Louise inside, into something Louise would have described as a laundry room—or scullery, as people still called them out where she was from. A woman was busy grooming a large black poodle there.

The woman wiped the dog hair on her hands onto an apron that was mostly covered by a picture of a dog jumping through a car tire. Underneath were the words STOCKHOLM 2006.

"Hi, I'm Anne Møller," she said, offering her hand to Louise. "Dicta's mother."

Louise could see the similarities immediately. The two of them resembled each other uncannily. Anne was looking at her daughter with great concern. "I came home as soon as Dicta got the call from school," she explained. "She called me at the medical practice where I work." She let the dog go and pulled her shoulder-length blond hair behind her ears as she explained that she did competition-level agility trial training for other people's dogs. Those were the dogs running around out in the yard right now.

That explained all the barking, and probably the SUV, Louise thought.

The poodle began to sniff her.

"Charlie, down," Dicta's mother commanded. The dog hesitated only for a moment before going under the dining table and lying down.

Anne Møller asked Louise to follow her into the kitchen, where she pointed at the large, oval Piet Hein table that filled the room. "Do you drink coffee? I just put a pot on. My husband is on his way home. He just has to pass off his patients to the two chiropractors who work for him at the clinic."

Anne's speech seemed a bit frantic, and her cheeks were flushed. During pauses, her eyes would dart over to see how her daughter was doing.

Louise had taken a seat opposite Dicta. The girl seemed to be tuning out her mother's stream of words, sitting with her eyes trained on the table. Dicta was obviously somewhere else entirely.

"Do you take milk? I'll just warm some up!"

Louise looked up at Anne and said cold milk was fine, but Dicta's mother ignored her and placed a carafe of milk in the microwave.

After clicking the door shut and punching in the heating time, she appeared to calm down. She came over and stood behind Dicta, laying her hands on her shoulders. She had taken off her apron and was dressed classically in a lightweight cardigan over a white blouse and beige linen trousers. Her face looked fresh and youthful with nice, smooth skin.

"It doesn't make any sense at all. Samra was just here a couple of days ago," Anne said.

She started stroking her daughter's arms and then walked over to the cupboard, took out a plate, and piled it with chocolate cookies. She did the whole thing reflexively; there was something safe and reassuring about setting out cups and cookies on the table.

Louise looked intently at Dicta, saying she wanted to chat with her a little about Samra's friends and her relationship with her family.

Dicta slowly raised her eyes toward Louise, as if she were coming back to reality. Louise let her take her time. Mechanically, the girl took a cookie from the bowl. Crumbs fell on the table as she broke it into small pieces, rattling off the names of three other girls from school she knew Samra spent a fair amount of time with.

"I only know one of them really well," Dicta said. "She's my friend, too; the other two I don't know that well."

Louise wrote down the names and signaled that the mother was welcome to come over and sit with them. She'd been hovering in the background since they started talking. Now she brought her cup over and sat down.

"I think they mostly hung out together at school," Dicta continued, regaining her composure. She explained that it was rare for Samra to get permission to take part in anything that happened after school. "Her parents were really strict. She was supposed to go straight home and do her homework, and she often had to help watch her little sister and brother, too."

Louise detected a sweet sort of pride when Dicta explained that her friend Samra had been one of the smartest students in their class—but then you'd damn well expect that, Louise thought, if you were forced to pore over your schoolbooks for so many hours every day. "You're some good kids," her mother interjected, stroking her daughter's cheek.

Dicta looked at her as though she didn't understand where that comment had come from.

"She was a good kid," Dicta stressed, turning her eyes back to Louise.

"You work hard, too," the mother insisted.

Dicta ignored her, and Louise hurriedly stepped in.

"But her parents did give her permission to come over here?" Louise asked.

"Yes, but definitely not as often as Samra would have liked, as far as I understood."

Anne was the one who had latched on to that question, and Louise listened in interest as Anne explained that she had met Samra's mother several times.

"At the medical practice where I work," she said. "She stops by there relatively often, either by herself or with the two children, and then we always chat about the girls and their school. She knows that Dicta is a stable, sensible girl, and that probably contributes to their feeling comfortable having their daughter at our house. But I never got the impression Samra was allowed to spend much time with anyone else after school, either."

"She also had permission to sleep over here," Dicta said, adding that she hadn't gotten permission to sleep over at Liv's, another of the girls in their clique.

They heard a car engine stop and a door slam shut. Anne got up and hurried out—to prepare her husband for the fact that there was a police officer visiting, Louise guessed.

He was a tall, handsome man, blond with bright-blue eyes. It wasn't hard to see where Dicta had gotten her looks from, with parents like these, Louise thought, standing to shake his hand.

"I'm Henrik," he said once Louise had introduced herself and explained why she was there.

He gave his daughter a kiss on the cheek before going to get a cup from the cabinet and joining them.

"It's so terrible you can hardly bear to think of it," he said.

"I can't think of anything else," Dicta said.

He looked with worry at his daughter. "Of course you're thinking of her," he said, turning to Louise. "It's just so incomprehensible when it's a girl you know. It's been all the talk at the clinic the whole morning. People are afraid this will lead to something more."

"It might, too, if there's a killer on the loose in town," said Anne.

Henrik looked at his wife, and Louise could tell that he was about to say something reassuring when Dicta suddenly stood up and left the kitchen.

They watched her go.

"The police still don't know much?" Henrik asked, looking at Louise.

She shook her head. "We've started interviewing the family and are looking for witnesses who might have seen Samra during the period of time we think she went missing. But it's a gap that extends over twelve hours—from when she said good night to her mother in her room at eight thirty Tuesday night to when she was found the next morning."

Neither of the parents asked Louise whether the police thought the family was behind it, and she was happy about that. She looked over toward Dicta's room to assess whether enough time had passed for her to go in to talk to her more.

"She was a good kid," Dicta's father said, using the same wording that his wife had used earlier. "Even if her family had a different set of rules for her than the ones her friends lived by, it seemed like she accepted them. There was no anger in her voice and she talked openly about the things that were off-limits to her. I actually had quite a lot of respect for that. We also hear about girls at school who are very disruptive to class unity because they let all their pent-up frustrations spill over onto their classmates."

Charlie had come in and was now resting his soft, furry head in Louise's lap. She scratched behind his ear.

"Many of these young immigrants are also put into an unreasonable situation—especially those who come here after spending their childhoods in another country," Anne added, backing up her husband. "They get pressured to step into a life they are never given full access to. That has got to be frustrating. Especially for young people who aren't that aware yet about the differences between Muslim and Danish ways of life."

Louise listened without interrupting. She liked Dicta's parents, and it wasn't hard to see why Dicta's friends liked to spend time at her house. They were very down-to-earth and forthcoming.

"Nor is it easy to come to this country," the father continued. "It's not like we're trying to meet them halfway. That much is clear here, even though Holbæk is a relatively small town. Lots of immigrants have moved here, and it's obvious when you visit our schools or walk around in town."

"But he doesn't mean that in a bad way," Dicta's mother hastened to interject.

"No, of course not," her husband said quickly, "but the tension has been growing more visible in recent years."

He stood up and walked out to find his jacket and pull a pack of cigarettes from the pocket.

"Do you mind?" he asked before he tapped one out.

Louise shook her head, hoping in a moment of weakness that he would offer her one, but he didn't.

"The children of immigrants are placed in public schools, which causes many Danish families to choose private schools for their children—which is pretty much a ridiculous system," he said, "particularly at the secondary level, from seventh grade up. They may be good at reading and writing, but they have no idea who the prime minister is because they never watch Danish TV or read Danish papers, and it doesn't help that there aren't any Danish students in class to pick these things up from. It leaves our public-school classrooms full of only disadvantaged students with limited resources. And that's not good for anyone."

"I assume that's why you're sending Dicta to Højmark School, which is public, right?" Louise asked.

They both nodded.

"Some Danish kids have to stay in the public-school system if we don't want the country to crack down the middle." Anne's voice sounded tired, as though she'd had to explain her position one too many times. Louise thought of Camilla, who was of the opposite opinion when it came to her son, Markus. He was attending a private school because Camilla felt he had only a limited number of years to attend school and so his experience had to be as close to perfect as possible—and she definitely didn't want him held back by students without family resources who slowed the pace down for everyone. Torn between the two points of view, Louise was momentarily happy she didn't have kids herself.

She stood up and said she wanted to go see if Dicta was ready to continue. The poodle's eyes followed her, as though he was trying to figure out whether she was going to come back or whether he might as well go take a nap.

She knocked quietly on the door and waited till Dicta invited her in. The room was large and bright and had its own French doors opening out onto the yard. Several posters hung on the walls, but, considering the girl's aspirations of becoming a model, Louise was surprised there were no pictures of herself. When Louise asked about that, Dicta pulled a photo album off a shelf and flipped through the last few pages in it. Then she went to the closet and got out a box that was crammed so full its lid would no longer stay in place without a rubber band.

"My parents don't know much about this," she explained as she opened the box and carefully spread the pictures out on the bed.

"Surely they can't help but notice when the pictures are printed in the paper," Louise said.

Dicta laid out the last picture. "They do know a little bit about it. Just not that I'm working on becoming a professional model, and that we've taken so many pictures."

Louise looked at Dicta and thought she had a curiously grown-up way of relating to a modeling career that she hadn't even really embarked on yet. She must have been mimicking the photographer's words.

"Who took the pictures?" Louise asked, contemplating one where Dicta was sitting on the deck of a sailboat with her long blond hair fluttering in the breeze and her feet hanging over the edge. She turned the photo over to see if there was a copyright stamp on the back, but there was nothing.

"His name's Michael Mogensen, and he's the best in town," Dicta said, sitting up straight. "We've spent a lot of time taking the pictures that are going into my portfolio. Now I'm just waiting for him to finish them. There's something about the background he needs to correct in Photoshop, but once that's all set, the portfolio will be ready to be submitted to the major modeling agencies."

Louise smiled at her. Dicta had a youthful joy and exuberance when she talked about her dreams. It was sweet—but it didn't take a professional's eyes to see that there was something naive and rigid in Dicta's poses, which a more talented photographer probably would have done something about.

"It sounds exciting," Louise said.

She fished out a picture in which Dicta was standing between Samra and a man who was in his mid-twenties.

"That's Michael," explained Dicta. "He is a staff photographer at *Venstrebladet*." She seemed impressed by him, pleased that he had taken on the responsibility for shepherding her to the top.

Louise looked at the picture for a long time. Samra's smile beamed and her hair hung down loose. It had been taken on a summer day down by the water. Louise recognized the bridge out to Holbæk's public beach, and she thought she could just make out the red-painted main building and little changing cabins in the background.

"He looks nice," Louise said, examining the very average-looking guy with blond hair and thick eyebrows. "Did Samra have her photos taken, too?" she asked out of curiosity.

Dicta shook her head. "She just came with me a couple of times. Her father would totally flip out if he knew."

Dicta stacked up the pictures and put them back into the box before carefully hiding it away again and making sure it was hidden by other boxes and a bag in the bottom of her closet.

"Was she seeing any boys?" Louise asked once Dicta emerged again.

It took a while before she answered. "What do you mean by seeing?"

Louise explained that she was trying to find out whether Samra had a boyfriend, or whether there was a boy she'd had an especially big crush on.

"She wasn't allowed to do that stuff."

"Not being allowed to do something is not necessarily the same as not doing it." Louise was trying to phrase it in a way that would not force Dicta to snitch on her friend for breaking her family's rules. Dicta herself obviously felt other people didn't necessarily need to know everything about Samra's life.

Louise asked how Dicta perceived Samra's relationship with her family.

Dicta shrugged, and when the silence stretched, Louise stepped over and opened the door to leave.

"Over time she preferred spending time here more than being at home," Dicta said finally as Louise stood in the hallway, "but that may also have been because there was always so much noise and so many people at her place," she continued, following Louise.

Louise went back out to the kitchen and said good-bye to Dicta's parents, who were still sitting at the table talking softly. They got up and went outside with her.

"Did Samra mention anything about her family recently? Did she give the impression that anything wasn't as it should be?"

Louise glanced at the parents to see if they understood where she was headed with the question.

Dicta's shoulders sank a little, and, without warning, all the tears she had been holding back suddenly flooded out. Her slender body began to shake. Charlie got up uneasily from his place under the table and watched Dicta. When she began to sob, Dicta's father took his daughter in his arms and rocked her gently back and forth.

"Had you noticed anything about Samra that might indicate she was afraid of something the last few times you saw her?" Louise persisted.

But Dicta didn't answer, and her father closed his arms tighter around her. Louise nodded at him and said good-bye to Dicta as she let Anne accompany her the rest of the way out.

They stood for a moment on the front steps. Anne said she thought she had noticed a change in Samra recently. She said Samra had seemed sullen and sad.

"She used to enjoy helping me out a little with the dogs, when I was training them in our dog run out in the backyard. But lately she's been staying up in the bedroom with Dicta. Maybe they just had a lot of homework to do, or a lot of things to talk about."

Louise nodded. It was impossible to know if Dicta knew something, but didn't want to say what was going on. Louise thanked Anne for the coffee and asked her to tell her daughter that she could call or stop by the police station at any time if anything else came up.

She was just stepping off the end of the driveway onto the

sidewalk when a blue station wagon parked at the curb. She immediately recognized the photographer as he got out of the car and started walking up toward the front door.

"Hello," she said, offering a hand. "Detective Louise Rick, I'm with the Holbæk Police Department."

The man shook her hand and introduced himself. "Michael Mogensen," he said, seeming a bit hesitant.

"I know," Louise said, smiling. "I was just looking at the pictures you've been taking of Dicta. Those are some big plans the two of you have been cooking up."

He nodded a little self-consciously. "I'd really like to help her."

"I noticed that you also knew Samra."

"Yes, a little," he said. "I promised Dicta I'd drive her out to Hønsehalsen so she can lay a bouquet of flowers and light a candle."

The door behind Louise opened.

"I'll be right there," Dicta yelled, disappearing back into the house. A moment later she returned with a jacket on, ready to go.

Louise went to her car and smiled at them as the photographer gallantly opened the car door for the young woman.

10

When Louise got back to the police station, she met Samra's father and a woman in the hallway. She guessed it must be the mother, Sada, because she was wearing a head scarf and keeping her eyes glued to the floor. They were following Søren Velin to the corner office where Bengtsen and both interpreters were waiting. Louise nodded to them and hurried to her own office. She knocked cautiously before entering and found her partner in the middle of questioning Samra's older brother. Without interrupting, she took a seat.

"Where'd you get the car?" Mik asked.

"From a friend, like I said!" There was no trace of anger in the young man's tone, just a stubbornness that told them they shouldn't count on finding out more than he'd already told them.

"But it isn't your car?" Mik continued.

Samra's brother shook his head.

"Does that mean other people might have used it in the last week?"

There was no response.

Mik Rasmussen leaned forward and asked, "Did you use the car Tuesday night?"

Hamid nodded. "Yes, but I wasn't anywhere near Hønsehalsen."

His Danish was very good considering he'd only been living in the country for four years, Louise noted, although he did have a tough time pronouncing *Hønsehalsen*.

"I'm not saying you were," Mik interrupted. "I really just want to know if anyone else might have driven that car out there."

Samra's brother shook his head.

"Did your sister have a boyfriend?"

Mik had changed topics so quickly that it seemed as if Hamid needed a moment to reboot before he could answer. He shook his head.

"Who do you hang out with?"

"People from school."

They had determined that he went to trade school, and in addition to a morning job where his father worked, he also had an after-school job at the local Kvickly supermarket. Ruth was already working on getting a list of his classmates in case they needed to talk to them.

Louise leaned back to listen in on the session. She was surprised that her partner was being so aggressive with his questioning. Louise was more a fan of the cognitive interview method, in which you guided the subject through an explanation in his own words at his own pace. She had always found that more productive. But every now and then it just failed to get anything out of a subject and then of course you had to be more aggressive.

"Does it bother you when girls have male friends?" Mik asked, changing topics again.

"Why the hell would I care about that? Girls can have male friends. What kind of stupid prejudices do you have?"

"So you feel that way even when your sister is involved?" The question's tone was filled with confrontational sarcasm.

There was a bang as Hamid angrily slapped his hand against the desk instead of responding, and in a way Louise couldn't blame him for losing his temper, especially if the interview had been going like this from the beginning.

"Was your sister dating anyone?" Mik asked again, in a more subdued tone.

The brother shook his head and hid his face in his hands as he shrugged.

Mik set down the pen he had been holding in his hand. "That's enough for now," he said and asked Hamid to wait until the interview had been typed out so he could read through it and sign it. Once that was done, Mik said, "We may need to talk to you again." He followed Samra's brother to the hallway and held out his hand, but the young man ignored it and just scurried off.

"I guarantee you that got to him," Louise exclaimed as Mik stepped back in and closed the door.

"He spent the first half hour evading every question, so I did that to get a reaction," Mik responded, and Louise got the sense that he had taken her comment as criticism. Instead of getting into it, she started focusing on her computer to avoid spoiling the mood just because they approached things differently.

"All right. I admit that he got to me, too," Mik said after they had each sat staring at their screens for a few minutes. "But I'm having a hard time accepting his attitude toward immigrant girls and their male acquaintances. There must be a fundamental acceptance of what's permitted for girls. And yet here it seems like everything is divided into two categories. There's plenty of tolerance toward immigrant girls in general, but that tolerance is severely curtailed when it has to do with the female members of your own family."

Louise thought about that for a moment and then nodded. "She was kind of viewed as the family's property and then suddenly that turns into something else," she said, remembering what a sociologist from the University of Southern Denmark had explained to her when she was on the Nørrebro case.

"That's really the crux of it when you're talking about honor and shame," Louise continued after a moment. "In families where those concepts are significant, people don't care that much about honor or shame when it doesn't have to do with their immediate family members. And in those cases when something does happen to offend the family's honor, it doesn't become dangerous until someone from the neighborhood starts talking about it. As long as the problem is only known within the family's four walls, no one has to react to it. It's so strange that there's such a huge difference between the world in general and the inner circle."

She could tell by the way Mik was looking at her that he wasn't putting much stock in her explanation. But that was one of the important things she had learned during the case she had just wrapped up. It wasn't until it became publicly known that the family couldn't control their own daughter that the girl had to die. In the case in Nørrebro, the death sentence had been pronounced by an uncle and his three sons. They wanted the girl killed before any of the other girls in the family became infected by her loose behavior.

"The world is a strange place. I don't understand that way of thinking," Mik admitted, shrugging.

Louise smiled at him and said that there weren't many Danes who did.

"Jette Petersen is here," Ruth announced from the doorway. She asked if they were ready for her and when they wanted the classmates to come in.

"Maybe we ought to see about borrowing a room at the school so we can do it while school's in session tomorrow?" Mik suggested. He received a nod of confirmation from the adminis-trative assistant.

"That'll save us a ton of coordination. Good idea," Louise said, standing up to go receive Samra's homeroom teacher.

"I'll write up the parents' and brother's interviews and update what we have in the case file on the family from before," Ruth said, before heading back to the command room.

Storm came in to ask them if they could also talk to the women's shelter the mother had stayed at to find out what information they had on the family. Louise took a seat on the edge of her desk as he spoke.

"We just need to find out if the parents were having problems with the girl before we latch on to our suspicions," Storm said.

"I'll call the shelter right away," Mik offered, pulling out his papers and flipping through them. He left the office to find some-where quiet to call from so Louise could start her conversation with Samra's teacher. Louise followed Mik into the hallway and asked Jette Petersen to come in.

"Would you like some coffee?" she asked.

The teacher looked as if she'd been crying. Her eyes were red and there were streaks of mascara under her bottom lashes. "We told the students right after their lunch break," she said, "and then we gathered Samra's classmates in the gym afterward and told them what had happened. It was the single worst experience of my twenty years of teaching." Louise let her sit for a moment.

"I'd actually thought the girls would take it the hardest. But several of the boys reacted quite strongly. It's unfortunate."

"In what way?" Louise asked.

"Obviously they were all really shocked, but I don't think they'd ever thought much about the fact that Samra and two of the other students in the class who aren't ethnically Danish came from dif-ferent cultures. But now they all think that Samra's family hurt her, and they're cursing all immigrants and wanting them to go home. Of course, they're mostly reacting to the feelings of helplessness and grief," she said after pausing to think for a moment.

Louise nodded.

"There've already been journalists outside the school asking the students about Samra's family. About whether they'd tried to force the girl into an arranged marriage, whether maybe that was what triggered the killing. And that kind of thing is enough to stir up trouble with the kids."

"But there wasn't anything like that as far as we know," Louise said.

Jette Petersen shook her head. "Now we just need to help them stick together and talk about what happened so we don't end up with a worse schism in the class or the school, for that matter. No one has been charged yet and we don't know what happened, but they've already made up their minds." She added that it was both good and bad that the newspapers had been featuring stories about honor killings so prominently—because of course that affected the kids' opinions about what must have happened when a girl like Samra was murdered.

Louise agreed with her, but had a hard time seeing how it could be any other way. At the moment she couldn't think of a single murder case where a young immigrant girl had been killed and it wasn't the family that was behind it. But of course, you had to be careful about leaping to conclusions, even though that was also where the police had been focusing.

They both sat lost in their own thoughts for moment before Louise asked Jette to describe Samra—both how she fit into the class socially and as a student, anything that might help the police put together a more nuanced picture of the girl that could lead them to a motive.

11

It's clear she was very well liked and got along fine in class," Louise said, addressing the others in the command room later. "Her parents didn't forbid her from attending class events and school activities, but even so, there were problems at times. Sometimes her father wanted proof that she was really at school if there were late classes or something."

"And Jette Petersen didn't have the impression that Samra had much to do with her classmates outside of school hours," added Mik, who had been present for the last part of their conversation.

"As we already know, Samra occasionally saw a couple of the girls," Louise continued. "For the first few years after she started school here four years ago, she played handball with a bunch of kids from school, but that only lasted a couple of years. Then she quit."

"Something happens around the time girls start puberty," Dean explained. " They no longer have the same freedom they had when they were children. Up until that point, their fathers are in charge of their upbringing and they are welcome to play and spend time with other kids their age. But once the girls menstruate for the first time, all that's over. Then the upbringing becomes the mother's responsibility and their freedom is noticeably curtailed. And if things go wrong for a girl, it's the mother's fault. So they're kept at home and not allowed to hang out with boys the way they could before."

"Are you Muslim?" Louise blurted out. She knew he was from the former Yugoslavia and was now married to a Dane, but she wasn't sure it was polite to ask.

He shook his head. "Catholic," he replied. "But where I come from there were a lot of Muslims."

"Well then, your familiarity with the cultural concepts will give us a head start," Skipper said.

Louise noted that their little group was quite diverse: a woman, a couple of older men with years of experience and strange habits, and a couple of young bucks who really wanted to make their mark. She smiled at Dean when he joked, "Now I'm afraid of disappointing you."

"We'll assume that Samra al-Abd didn't have that big a circle of friends. She occasionally spent time with some of her girlfriends after school and on the weekends, but she was kept under relatively tight rein at home," Storm concluded, looking at Louise and the others to see if there were any objections.

"I agree that she was under very tight control from her parents," Søren Velin said, and gave a recap of his and Bengtsen's questioning session with the parents. They had both denied knowing anything about their daughter's disappearance.

"They say that their daughter didn't have many friends and preferred to spend time with her family," Bengtsen began before pouring some coffee into a plastic mug. "Yet her father maintains that he didn't really get worried about her being gone until she still wasn't home when they got back from visiting his brother in Benløse. And that sense of worry was only reinforced when he heard the news on the radio the next morning at nine."

Now it was Mik's turn to report. "I spoke to the women's shelter," he began. "She was there six months ago, and the woman I talked to remembered the family quite well. She said that Samra was rather beaten up when they arrived. She wouldn't talk about what had happened, so they got the story from her mother. The family voluntarily returned home after about five days and there haven't been any more reports of violence since then."

Everyone in the room digested that for a moment before Storm spoke again.

"The preliminary results are back from the forensic examination of the father's boat," he said. "They didn't find any traces to suggest that he was carrying a concrete slab in the boat. It's likely it would have left scratches or cement particles. There was also nothing to suggest that the boat was the scene of the crime. They're still studying the pictures."

Storm looked over at Skipper. "You head out to the house and examine her bedroom."

Skipper nodded so his hair billowed gently.

"How's it going with the cell phone records?" Storm asked Bengtsen and Velin.

Bengtsen pointed to the table in front of him where there were two sheets of paper.

"They're here," he replied. "She mostly sent text messages, and we've located the numbers. Her family and some of the girls from school. No unknown numbers, no surprises," he said, sounding disappointed that he didn't have anything more helpful to report.

Skipper and Dean stood up to go help the crime scene technicians examine the girl's room.

"Remember to check if she had access to a computer," Storm called after them. "And if she did, obviously bring it back." He turned his attention to Bengtsen and Velin.

"We need to set up audio surveillance in the home," he said. "Maybe next time the family comes in for questioning."

This was Søren Velin's specialty and he nodded right away, so Louise guessed that he'd already done the prep work.

"Maybe you should head out there while the others are working on the bedroom just so you can get an overview of the apartment. We have a warrant, so there's no problem with your having permission to be there," Storm said.

Velin nodded again. Louise suspected he must have already been by the place and presumably had a very good idea of what he would need to set up the audio surveillance.

"The phone is easy, and you'll know best how to capture the conversations that take place in the various rooms." Storm avoided going into detail. The custom was that only the officers who set up the equipment would know where the devices were located. "Check the place out and get everything ready so we can start the surveillance tomorrow."

"We should have it up and running today," Bengtsen cut in. "It would be crazy to wait until tomorrow."

There was a second of silence. He was right.

"Well, then we need to get the family out of the house again," Storm said, without showing any sign of irritation at having been rebuked by the local officer.

"We're not ready for our next questioning session yet. We need a little more time to prepare," said Ruth, who was responsible for gathering all the details about the family's background and past.

"Then we'll do something else," Bengtsen suggested. "We'll invite them to come in for an update on where things stand in the case. Then we can also set up a time for them to view the body. It'll be totally informational, no questioning, just an update of what our plans are, what the school has told the other students, and the fact that they're having a moment of silence for Samra tomorrow at noon. We also owe it to them to prepare them a little for what's going to come now that the press is starting to get interested in the case and in them."

The others nodded. They hadn't had a chance to discuss this yet. Of course, the family should be provided the same courtesies others would be in that situation, even if suspicions were starting to point in their direction.

"We mustn't treat them as if they've been charged," Mik Rasmussen added. "They're only just suspects."

Louise could tell that Søren was starting to get irritated. No one had been treating Samra's family as if they'd been charged. Still, even though he and Bengtsen were looking as hard as they could for witnesses who might have seen Samra and they were receiving assistance in those endless interview sessions from local officers from the Holbæk Police, it hadn't led to anything. That meant that for the time being the suspicion was still focused on the family. She guessed that he thought treating them with kid gloves was overkill.

Louise looked out the window as she listened, remembering how Søren's impatience used to drive her crazy. He wanted action and progress constantly. It would do him good to get out and mess around with his eavesdropping equipment, she thought.

"Right. We'll just invite them in for some coffee and pastries and I'll have a chat with them," Storm said as he sent everyone out the door.

It was after five and there was no guarantee the family would even be home, but everyone agreed that this was the right approach.

Mik and Louise started to follow Søren down the hall, but Storm waved for them to remain behind.

"We also need to pay the uncle a visit and find out what happened when he saw the family Tuesday night," he said. "And find out why Samra's parents visited him in Benløse the following day, when they'd just seen him."

"I'll get hold of him. Louise and I can drive down there this evening," Mik said, pulling his car keys out of his jacket pocket. "The uncle has a shop, so he won't be home until after he closes at seven."

They took the back stairs down to Mik's car to drive out and invite the al-Abd family in for a chat. In the yard Bengtsen and Velin were checking to see if they had all the necessary equipment for the audio surveillance. Louise would send them a text message once the family was safely out of the house.

Half an hour later, Louise and Mik were back with Samra's parents. Storm ushered them into a meeting room next to the chief's office.

Back in their own office, Mik familiarized himself with Ruth's printout about the uncle and his family. There wasn't much, just a little about the business he owned, his wife and kids' Social Security numbers, information about their immigration and residency permits. Louise offered to bring her partner a soda if he needed a pick-me-up. "Good thinking," he said, tearing himself away from the papers for a second to let her know that she would find whatever she wanted in the cafeteria.

Her tour of the Holbæk Police Station had not included the cafeteria, so she stood in the doorway a little unsure.

"Fourth floor," Mik said.

She walked out to the secretary's office and took the stairs up. The passport and DMV offices were on the first floor, and administration, the police's legal department, and the cafeteria were on the fourth.

There was a small group of officers around one of the tables when she walked in. She said hello and felt their eyes following her as she walked over to the vending machine. Something told her it wasn't because she was a woman but because she was an outsider. Even from a distance she could tell there were only Pepsi and Faxe Kondi. Irritated, she wondered why she couldn't just get a Coke, but with the men's eyes on her back she couldn't just spin around and walk back out empty-handed. She decided to just get something for Mik.

On the way back, she met Ruth, who was headed for the hotel with her bag over her shoulder to take a nap before dinner. She smiled at the Pepsi in Louise's hand and said there was a bunch of soda and bottled water down in the command room.

"The investigation would grind to a halt if the boys were forced to drink that stuff," she said, and apologized for not having mentioned this to Louise sooner. "There's also a cupboard full of crackers and things for the days when we're forced to skip breakfast or when work drags out late into the evening."

Louise thanked her for the information and returned to the office to give her partner the Pepsi. They agreed that they wouldn't let the uncle know they were planning to visit him that evening. He shouldn't have time to prepare.

When Mik stood up and said that he had to go home before they set out again, Louise wasn't surprised. She decided to follow Ruth's example so she would be fresh for their visit to Benløse. She grabbed her bag and headed for the hotel, wondering why her partner always had to check in at home.

12

Louise glanced at her watch as she entered the hotel. She could squeeze in half an hour of relaxation before they were supposed to meet for dinner. On her way to her room she stopped by the restaurant to pick up a cup of tea. She had her back to the tables, waiting for the waiter to return from the kitchen, when she heard a familiar voice say, "There's tea in the pot over here…and warm milk, if that's any enticement." She spun around in astonishment.

Camilla was sitting at a table way over in the corner. Louise had walked right by without noticing her.

"What the hell!" Louise exclaimed. "When did you get here?" She gave her good friend a hug.

"I got here this morning, and I'm only staying until tomorrow for right now."

"You're writing about the case?" *I don't even know why I'm both-*

ering to ask, Louise thought as soon as the question was out of her mouth. Of course, word had already gotten out. Obviously *Morgenavisen* was going to run the story.

Camilla poured tea into a second cup and set it on the table. Then she proceeded to scold Louise.

"Now, obviously it's not like I'm entitled to know everything, but you damn well could have told me that you'd been assigned to the Mobile Task Force. That's big news!"

Louise took a seat and filled the rest of her cup with warm milk. "It's going to be a challenge," she admitted, instead of starting in on the excuses. "Do you know Storm?"

Camilla nodded and said they'd known each other since he'd been put in charge in 2002, when the Mobile Task Force was resurrected after having been dismantled a couple years earlier and merged with the Forensics Department.

"Storm's a great guy," Camilla said. "And, after all, Holbæk is practically like coming home again."

"Well, it's a ways from Roskilde to Holbæk," Louise pointed out. She and Camilla had known each other ever since they went to Roskilde Amtsgymnasium together right after high school.

"We used to get drunk and make out with boys here in town," Camilla responded with a grin. "But enough reminiscing." She drew Louise's attention to the notepad lying on the table in front of her. "I have to get to work now," she said, explaining that she had a meeting with Storm later that evening, and that until then she was planning to poke around a little.

Louise realized what that meant right away. Camilla was going to do her best to find someone who had known Samra.

"The girl's mother ran off to a women's shelter several times. A woman doesn't just go do something like that unless she has a real reason," Camilla said with certainty.

"She went to the shelter once," Louise corrected, then stopped, realizing too late that she had just confirmed what Camilla was probably only guessing at.

"Was Samra rebellious?" Camilla asked.

Louise shook her head. "You're not getting anything else out of me."

"Either she didn't want to get married, or she had a Danish boyfriend, or…" Camilla plowed on, undaunted.

Louise shook her head again and got up to leave. "The others will be down here in a bit. We're meeting for dinner in fifteen minutes. I'm just going to pop up to my room beforehand." She excused herself and thanked Camilla for the tea.

Camilla walked Louise out to the lobby, where she wrapped a crocheted shawl around her shoulders and pulled her shoulder strap over her head so her bag rested securely on her back.

Louise gave her a hug as they parted and hurried up to her room to wash her hands and splash a little water on her face before joining the others for dinner. Running into Camilla had reinvigorated her; she no longer felt the least bit tired.

Louise stood up from the table after dinner, wishing she'd passed on dessert. She had just started a brisk stroll back to the police station when she spotted Mik pulled over to the curb, waiting for her. She started to head toward him, but noticed a figure leaning against a streetlight behind the car. When she got closer, she recognized Dicta Møller, even though the girl was wrapped in a large scarf that was covering the lower part of her face and wore a cap pulled down to her eyes. Louise motioned to Mik that she was just going to run over and talk to the girl.

"Hi," she called out before she got too close so as not to frighten Dicta. "Are you doing better?"

The young girl shook her head and asked Louise if she had time to talk. She had been to the station to ask for Louise and had been told she would be back around seven.

Louise thought it over quickly. Then she strode over to the car and explained that Dicta was there to talk to her.

"I'll just head down there," Mik said without hesitation and agreed that it was important Louise find out what the girl had to say. He pulled away from the curb, and Louise turned back to Dicta.

"Do you want to come inside, or would you rather go to a café?" Louise asked, hoping Dicta might tell her more now than she had with her parents present.

The young girl thought about it for a moment, as if she were contemplating where it would be least embarrassing to be seen—at the police station or at a café, where people could see that she was talking to a cop. Finally, she chose a café that was at the end of Ahlgade. Once they got there, Louise realized there wasn't much risk of running into anyone else Dicta's age. Yellowed lace curtains were drawn over the large windows, so the late-evening sun had no effect on the dark atmosphere in the café, and the wall sconces cast a greenish sheen over the room, leaving the customers in a shadowy darkness. They ordered soft drinks and chose a table in the back.

"How did your trip out to Hønsehalsen go?" Louise asked. "I assume they didn't let you go all the way out."

Dicta shook her head and said that Michael had gotten one of the policemen out there to lay her bouquet down by the cliff. "When you're a photographer, you know most of the people in town," Dicta said with a small smile.

"How did it go with the pictures? Did they turn out well?" Louise asked, pouring soda into a glass.

Dicta shrugged. "I haven't seen them. I didn't want to. He just drove me home again afterward."

Dicta's answer hadn't left Louise with any easy way to keep the conversation going, so she waited for the girl to start telling her why she had been standing outside the police station waiting for her.

"I came to tell you that I'm not sure something I said was true," Dicta finally began. "I don't know if it's true that Samra was afraid of her father, and I'm afraid I might have told you something incorrect."

Dicta said it tersely; the self-confident poise she'd had during her visit to the police station had disappeared. Louise found herself sitting across from a hesitant little girl, who seemed to have been anxiously scrutinizing every single word she'd said.

"She liked her parents," Dicta continued. "But she just wasn't ever allowed to do anything, and it's been like that since her mother found a picture of one of the boys from our class. It was in Samra's wallet, hidden in a bunch of other stuff."

There was a long pause as Dicta gathered herself. Then she started to explain how Samra had falsified her school schedule after summer vacation when they started this school year.

"She always had to be home right after her last class. But on Monday and Tuesday, when we got out earlier, she wrote extra classes on her schedule to give herself some time to hang out with the rest of us. We promised not to say anything because she said something terrible would happen if her father found out about it."

"So, what did you guys usually do?" Louise asked.

"We either hung out at school or went to my place. Every once in a while she'd come down to Michael's photography studio or to a café where she knew she wouldn't run into anyone. There was this one time when we ran into her dad down on Ahlgade at a time when he thought she was still in school. He was furious even though she told him one of the teachers had been sick and we'd had a free period. He wouldn't even listen to her and he ordered her to go straight home.

"Her brother was allowed to hang out with his friends in town.

I didn't get why her parents treated the two of them so differently," Dicta said, sounding offended on her friend's behalf.

"He's older, and he's a boy," Louise said, knowing that a Danish teenage girl was not going to find that answer sufficient.

"Yeah, but he got into fights and all that kind of stuff," Dicta replied indignantly. "I just didn't think it was fair." She took off her scarf and hat, letting her blond hair loose. It hung down almost to the edge of the table.

Louise just nodded.

"Samra didn't think so, either," Dicta continued. "That's why every once in a while she would run away."

Louise couldn't blame her. But she did think there was something wrong with parents moving an eleven-year-old to a country with such a dramatically different culture and putting her in school there without making it possible for her to fit in with the other kids. It was only natural for a girl like that to try to fit into her new life. Danish kids who moved from one part of the country to another would try to do exactly the same, but they would have a much easier time adjusting. In this case, there was an ominous demand that girls had to adapt, but only to a certain extent; otherwise all hell would break loose.

"Did it seem like her parents were pressuring her to maintain their traditional culture?" Louise asked, curious.

It took a little while for Dicta to respond, but eventually she shook her head. "Not pressuring, no. She felt like her parents' attitude toward tradition was normal, you know? But sometimes it irritated her."

"Had you noticed anything about Samra? Had anything happened lately that had affected her?" Louise asked.

"Just that she had been a little quiet lately, but she didn't say anything, so I don't know if there was anything wrong."

"Which boy from class did she have a picture of?" Louise

wanted to know, flagging down the waitress at the same time so she could pay.

Dicta hesitated a little before responding.

"His name is Mads, but that's over. He's dating Emilie now."

"Has she dated anyone else?" Louise asked as they were on their way out.

An older man with a pint of porter and an aquavit in front of him watched their motions with interest.

"No, they weren't dating," Dicta replied loudly to emphasize that Louise had misunderstood. "She just liked him. I don't even think he knew about it."

"Okay," Louise said, holding the door. "Was there anyone else she had a crush on or was maybe interested in? I mean, I suppose it's practically unavoidable at your age."

When that went unanswered, Louise asked instead if Dicta had a boyfriend.

The girl quickly shook her head. "I'm making my modeling work a priority," she said, explaining that she and Michael Mogensen had devoted a lot of time to taking those pictures, and that they were going to help her reach the next level in her career.

Louise was again surprised by Dicta's maturity and her attitude toward modeling. Not that it was unheard of for a girl that age to go after her dreams in such a purposeful way. And Dicta was a pretty girl.

It was almost nine o'clock when Louise returned to the police station. Mik wasn't back yet. She considered waiting for him, but she was tired, and since his cell went straight to voice mail she figured he'd turned it off, either because he was still with Samra's uncle or because he was already back home. She powered down her computer and started walking back to the hotel.

most prudent man, who rose from private life to achieve great renown. If this man had defeated Pisa, no one would deny that the Florentines would have had to remain under his command, for, if he had become a soldier for their enemy, there would have been no solution for them; and if they had held on to him, they would have been forced to obey him. If we examine the course followed by the Venetians, we see that they managed to operate safely and gloriously as long as they themselves conducted their war (this was before they turned to fighting on land); with their noblemen and common people armed they fought with great courage; but as soon as they began to fight on land, they abandoned this strategy and followed the customary means of waging war in Italy. When they first began to increase their holdings on the mainland, since they did not have much territory there and since they did enjoy a considerable reputation, they had nothing to fear from their captains; but, as they increased in power, which was the case under the command of Carmagnola,[8] they got a taste of this error; for, having seen him in all his fearlessness they fought the duke of Milan when under his command, and knowing, on the other hand, that he had cooled down in his fighting, they decided that under him they could no longer conquer, for he had no desire to; nor could they discharge him, through fear of losing what they had acquired; so to safeguard themselves, they found they had to kill him. Then they had as captains Bartolomeo da Bergamo,[9] Roberto da San Severino,[10] the count of Pitigliano,[11] and the like; under such leaders they had to fear their losses, not their gains; as it happened later on at Vailà, where, in one day, they lost what had taken them eight hundred years of considerable struggle to acquire. For from such troops as these come only the slow, tedious and weak conquests and the sudden and astounding losses. And

Avete dunque a intendere come, tosto che in questi ultimi tempi lo imperio cominciò a essere ributtato di Italia, e che il papa nel temporale vi prese più reputazione, si divise la Italia in più stati; perchè molte delle città grosse presero le armi contro a' loro nobili, e quali, prima, favoriti dallo imperadore, le tenevono oppresse; e la Chiesa le favoriva per darsi reputazione nel temporale; di molte altre e loro cittadini ne diventorno principi. Onde che, essendo venuta l'Italia quasi che nelle mani della Chiesa e di qualche republica, ed essendo quelli preti e quelli altri cittadini usi a non conoscere arme, cominciorono a soldare forestieri. El primo che dette reputazione a questa milizia fu Alberigo da Conio, romagnolo. Dalla disciplina di costui discese, intra li altri, Braccio e Sforza, che ne' loro tempi furono arbitri di Italia. Dopo questi, vennono tutti gli altri che fino a' nostri tempi hanno governato queste armi. E il fine della loro virtù è stato, che Italia è stata corsa da Carlo, predata da Luigi, sforzata da Ferrando e vituperata da' Svizzeri. L'ordine che elli hanno tenuto è stato, prima, per dare reputazione a loro proprii, avere tolto reputazione alle fanterie. Feciono questo, perchè, sendo sanza stato e in su la industria, e pochi fanti non davono loro reputazione, e li assai non potevono nutrire; e però si ridussono a' cavalli, dove con numero sopportabile erano nutriti e onorati. Ed erano ridotte le cose in termine, che in uno esercito di ventimila soldati non si trovava dumila fanti. Avevano, oltre a questo, usato ogni industria per levare a sè e a' soldati la fatica e la paura, non si ammazzando nelle zuffe, ma pigliandosi prigioni e sanza taglia; non

13

When Camilla stepped across the threshold of the al-Abd family's apartment a little after 8:30 a.m., she noticed how densely packed the place was with furniture. Dressers, shoe racks, a display case, a row of hooks above so that a thick blanketlike layer of clothes hung over the rest. She smiled and introduced herself to a short, thin woman who only came up to Camilla's shoulders and wore an attractive black scarf over her head.

"I'm Camilla Lind. I'm with *Morgenavisen*," she said and then hurriedly continued, "My deepest condolences."

Even though it was cliché to say, Camilla meant it sincerely. After she had arrived in town the day before, she had taken a spin through downtown Holbæk to track down some teenagers who had known Samra and were willing to talk about her. The picture of the young immigrant girl that had emerged was heartrending and made her murder even more incomprehensible.

Extremely sweet, helpful, fun, smart…it had been a long list of superlatives. But what had struck Camilla most was how raw the teenagers' grief was. They had been genuinely floored by a level of pain and turmoil they didn't comprehend. They understood that the worst had happened, but they had in no way been prepared to have the foundations of their lives yanked out from underneath them that way. The safe and innocent world they'd known had suddenly disappeared, pushing them several steps closer to the seriousness and sorrows of life.

"I'd really like to talk to you for a minute," Camilla continued. Sada al-Abd started retreating back into her apartment, eyes downcast. Camilla knew she was thirty-seven years old and that she understood and spoke some Danish. She heard a young girl's voice from the living room, and a second later a cute little girl with dark curls dancing around her head came to the doorway, looking shyly at the female stranger. In the background Camilla spotted a boy, who was sitting on the floor playing with some blocks.

The mother said something to her daughter in a language Camilla didn't understand, and the girl smiled, her mouth full of chalk-white teeth that would have made a great ad for Arla, the dairy company, and disappeared back into the living room to join her little brother.

"I didn't want to bother you," Camilla quickly told the mother. "But I was talking to some of Samra's friends in town yesterday and they told me such nice things about your daughter. I thought you might like to hear what they said."

She waited to see how much of her Danish the mother seemed to understand. The woman's eyes were still trained on the floor, but she had nodded weakly at Camilla's words. As soon as Camilla finished talking, however, the woman shook her head and softly said, "You have to go."

Camilla stood there for a moment, looking at the Jordanian woman. She couldn't tell if there was fear mixed with her profound grief.

"We could meet somewhere else to talk," Camilla suggested, making another attempt. "I'm going to have to write about this story, with or without your help. But it would be better if you would talk to me."

Again, the woman shook her head.

"I can't talk to you." She had a thick accent in Danish, but she was understandable.

Camilla sensed motion behind her before she heard a voice say, "What are you doing here? Leave us alone."

She hadn't heard the man enter. When she turned around he was standing right behind her.

"How dare you come here and bother us..."

The man's voice grew louder and Camilla tried to explain that she was not trying to bother anyone, that she just wanted to talk to them about what had happened. But everything she said was drowned out by his shouting.

Then he turned his rage on Sada. "What did you tell her?" he yelled.

She shook her head. "Nothing."

"I'm calling the police," he screamed at Camilla. "You need to get out of here *now*!"

She watched how he punched the buttons on his phone. The woman stood still, her eyes on her own feet.

Camilla moved a step closer to her and said, "I know you reported him for abuse and spent some time at a shelter, but then you came back to him. How could you do that to your daughter?"

The mother jumped as the words hit her. She looked up and stared Camilla right in the eyes, but didn't say anything.

The man's infuriated voice was echoing in the background. He had finally gotten through to someone.

"I'm staying at the Station Hotel and I hope you'll decide to talk to me. But I'm going to be writing my articles whether you do or not." Camilla nodded a quick farewell before the husband returned.

As she walked down the stairs, she wondered if she ought to call the Holbæk Police herself and let them know she was the one who had stopped by to see the family and triggered this outburst of anger. But that might be blowing things out of proportion, she thought.

The sun was shining, painting the parking lot between the buildings in a soft, golden glow, and there was some warmth in its rays despite the season. Camilla buttoned her cardigan and climbed into the driver's seat of her car. *Well, that didn't go well*, she thought. It would be hard to recover from that introduction. She supposed the ball was in Samra's mother's court now since she just hadn't had a chance to say she would come back. The father would skin the woman alive if he found Camilla interviewing her in the apartment. Plus, there were the two little kids. It would end in chaos.

Camilla had been sitting patiently in her car since eight o'clock in the morning, waiting for the husband to leave. She'd known he had called in sick to work, and she'd been determined to keep an eye on the place until she was sure he'd gone out. She'd realized that if he was home, the door would be slammed in her face. At least now she'd had a chance to introduce herself and ask for an interview, but she didn't think the odds were very good that it would pan out.

"I'm going to kill that bitch."

"You mustn't say kill. Or die. What are you doing to us? Can't you understand that they're going to come and take my children away from me if you say things like that? Stop it!"

Despite the heated voices from the surveillance, the interpreter's unaffected monotone translation remained calm.

"You're ruining it for us, and we'll all end up in there…"

"In jail," the interpreter explained, glancing up at Louise, who was standing with the rest of the team, listening.

"For God's sake, don't ruin anything else," the interpreter continued.

Again, a man's voice on the tape: "I didn't say kill. I said I'll hit her!"

"Why are you saying these things?"

"I'm going crazy. I'm going to kill myself, too."

"You mustn't say that word at all. They're going to take my babies away from me."

The woman started crying loudly.

"Get out, get out! I don't want to hear any more…"

A door slammed and Storm impatiently asked for the tape to be stopped so they could discuss what they'd heard.

During the morning briefing, Storm had informed them that they were going to have to do without him for the rest of the day. With a little embarrassment he had explained that he knew it was impractical and that it was coming at an unfortunate time, but the appointment had been made a long time ago. He was going to teach a continuing education course at the police academy in Avnø and he had to be there until ten o'clock that night because they were having a big farewell dinner.

Louise got the sense that he was anxious to get out of there, but he obviously also felt like he had to be present while they prepped for the next round of questioning with Samra's family.

The task force was brought into the interrogation room at ten o'clock. The National Police's staff interpreter, Fahid, had arrived early that morning so he could listen in as the family woke up. Normally, they would have had the audio material transcribed and waited until they had the translated transcript in their hands, but Storm had decided that there was not a moment to lose in this case, so they had skipped that step. Instead, they had the interpreter doing a simultaneous interpretation directly from the tape, which would allow them to pick up the last few important details before the couple arrived.

"He calls his daughter a bitch," Søren Velin said, offended.

Fahid shook his head and explained that it wasn't Samra but the female interpreter who was being called a bitch. "He's accusing her of stabbing him in the back during the questioning. He was very upset during this conversation," Fahid said. "They were apparently just visited by a reporter, who was standing in the doorway talking to his wife when he came home; he feels like everyone is against him."

"What was that stuff about the kids?" Louise asked.

"That has to do with the problems stemming from Sada's stay in the shelter. A note was placed in the file that the state was considering removing the two youngest children from the home if the internal family problems continued."

"She's accusing him indirectly of having killed their daughter," Skipper concluded, referring to the statement that the father mustn't ruin anything else.

"I don't get it," Louise said heatedly. "He was completely crushed when he found out the murder victim was his daughter. What the hell kind of charade is this?"

Mik nodded in agreement. He was apparently also having trouble reconciling how this could be the same man who'd been so upset to learn of his daughter's death.

They stood around quietly, digesting what they'd heard, before moving into the command room and taking their seats around the table. Storm pulled on his jacket, grabbed his computer bag and the large, square, black briefcase that contained all his teaching materials, and then he was out the door with a brief nod.

Ruth had a stack of plastic folders ready that she handed out. "Here are all the facts on the al-Abd family," she said. "About their stay at the shelter, too."

"The father can be a real prick," Bengtsen began, explaining that he had some peripheral awareness of Ibrahim al-Abd, both from the local street scene and from Stark, where Bengtsen's brother-in-law worked along with Samra's father and brother. "But he's also very well-liked by his co-workers. As long as things run smoothly he's cheerful and amenable, but he's got a short fuse."

"I can believe that," Mik said, rubbing his nose and seeming lost in thought for a moment.

"Well, despite everything, Samra's mother must have some backbone," Louise said, thinking it would take guts to report your husband for domestic abuse and then end up going back home again. "She's not a coward."

Skipper got up, took a couple of sodas out of the fridge, and put them on the table, passing the bottle opener around.

"Nah, but if it was the father who was responsible for Samra's murder, then it didn't really pay off for the mother to have reported him for his violence, did it?" Velin contributed.

"The father's brother in Benløse says that he visited Ibrahim and the family on Tuesday evening the way he does every week," Mik said, glancing down at his notepad. "He describes Samra as a sweet girl, but at the same time he said that there had been a few problems lately, trouble getting her to stay away from the boys. The Danish boys."

"That sounds a little exaggerated," Louise exclaimed in surprise.

"Did he want to go into any more detail on that?" Dean asked.

Before Mik had a chance to respond, Louise started to tell

everyone about the picture Samra's mother had found in her daughter's wallet.

When Louise finished, Mik shook his head and said the father's brother wouldn't say anything concrete. "He does not generally consider Ibrahim to be particularly violent, but he did say that if that kind of thing happens, of course you have to strike back and get the girl in line before things get totally out of hand."

"But we're not talking about a dog that needs a little behavioral correction," Skipper commented.

"It doesn't make any sense that a fifteen-year-old girl would do anything that went so much against her parents' wishes that they'd rather kill her," Ruth Lange said, plopping down onto the edge of the table.

"This kind of thing isn't logical," Skipper countered. "We'll never accept that things like this happen. And I don't give a damn if this is part of their religion," he continued.

"Cultural tradition," Louise interjected, but she really didn't want to get into that with a group of co-workers she'd just met. It was easier to have this conversation with people who knew each other, because every time someone made it clear where they stood on this issue, you found yourself in deep water.

"It doesn't have anything to do with religion or Islam. Honor and shame are part of their cultural heritage. Men fight for their honor and fear that women are bringing shame to them. Therefore, all women must be controlled so they don't mess things up for everyone," Dean explained.

"There's also that thing about some families regarding women as property, thus making it totally okay to beat them and treat them as objects," Velin said, both indignant and baffled that people could think that way.

Dean nodded at him, agreeing that unfortunately that was not uncommon.

"Did the father's brother say anything else?" Bengtsen asked, putting an end to their assessments of global cultural differences. "Did he say why Samra's parents went out to see him in Benløse again so soon, when they'd just seen each other?"

Mik sat studying the folder Ruth had given him, and then shook his head. "Just that it was because they were worried about Samra."

Before they wrapped up the meeting to get ready for the next round of questioning with Samra's parents and her older brother, Louise reported on her conversation with Dicta Møller the previous evening.

"It turns out that Samra tinkered with her school schedule to give herself a couple of free periods each week when she could escape her parents' control for a little while, so she did occasionally do something they didn't know about," Louise concluded just as the phone rang to let them know the al-Abd family had arrived.

❧

She and Mik walked to their office together.

"I'll be back from the school as soon as I've spoken to Samra's four friends," Louise said. "And we'll see if I can get anything out of them."

They had agreed to split up. Mik went to participate in questioning the family while Louise went to talk to Samra's school friends, and they had both turned down the offer of help from a couple of local detectives. Louise realized she had misjudged her new partner when she had assumed he was lazy. He actually took more work on himself than he assigned her.

"Good luck," he called after her as she walked away.

"Same to you. You'll need it more."

Mik smiled at her and tipped his chair back a little, running his hand through his hair and making a face. "I suppose I'll have to try to go a little easier on Hamid if I want to keep him from shutting down right away." Louise got the sense that her new partner was finally starting to feel less uptight with her.

"I'll see you," she said, stuffing her car keys into her pocket on her way out the door.

14

Louise looked around the empty faculty lounge. There was a long table and several small clusters of sofas, stacks of books and newspapers, and a couple of empty coffee cups that had been left behind. It was bright and airy with a couple of colored prints hanging on the walls, and though it was an old school, it had obviously been renovated within the last few years. She had an appointment when classes got out to meet the four girls who'd been closest to Samra. School was canceled for the rest of the day but Jette Petersen had asked permission for their class to meet for a memorial service in the gym before Louise took over.

"I'll just get them all out the door," Jette had said when they had spoken that morning.

Maybe I should have waited until Monday, Louise thought, walking over to the window, but then a whole weekend would have passed before she got a sense of the girl's circle of friends. She watched a rented bus park along the sidewalk, emptying its load of small children, all with wet hair and carrying swimming gear. She followed them with her eyes as the herd disappeared across the playground.

The door opened. Louise turned around and said hello to a man, who gave her a funny look, wondering who she was.

She introduced herself and explained that she was waiting for Samra's teacher. Jette Petersen's co-worker just nodded at her and walked over to the table that served as a kitchenette to pour water into the coffeemaker.

"It's a sad story," he grunted when he was done. The machine started gurgling a second later.

Louise quietly agreed with him.

"But who says the family's behind it?" he asked, nodding at the morning papers that were sitting on the long table. Both front pages prominently featured the words HONOR KILLING. "She may just as easily have been the victim of a crime the family wasn't behind. Isn't that kind of jumping to conclusions?" he asked in a tone that made Louise feel as if he was holding her accountable for the coverage.

She hurried to say that of course someone else could easily have been behind it. "But there's not really any motive to suggest that," Louise continued, trying not to sound defensive.

Silence hung in the air between them and she took a seat. The coffeemaker finished gurgling and the man pulled a couple of clean mugs out of the dishwasher. He asked her if she wanted anything in hers. She said, "Milk please," and asked if he might know anything the police hadn't heard yet, since he had brought all this up.

He shook his head and said that it just seemed to him as if they were taking the path of least resistance. "You're going after the easiest target," he said, taking a seat. "If it had been a Danish family, you'd be searching for the perpetrator everywhere but inside the family."

Really? You think so? Louise thought. "The second we have any other leads to follow, I promise you we will."

"Even though Holbæk isn't that big, there are crazy people here, too. We've had a number of rapes," the man began.

"Well, Samra wasn't raped," Louise interrupted sharply. "She was murdered, callously and coldheartedly. She was asphyxiated, tied to a concrete slab, and dumped in the water."

"Yeah, well, you don't know it was the family," he said once more.

Louise sighed and conceded that he was right. No, they didn't know. "But I can tell you that two of my colleagues have been looking for witnesses since she was found and no one saw her leave her parents' home," she said, thinking about all the interviews Bengtsen and Velin had done in Dysseparken and the large residential area where the family's apartment was located.

"But that also means no one saw her father drive off with her," he pointed out, and again Louise had to concede. Samra could easily have left home without having been noticed.

"You're just starting out with the assumption that the family is guilty…"

The door opened, and he stopped talking.

Louise was starting to get irritated. She got up and walked over to put her mug in the sink. "We're not assuming anyone is guilty," she said, standing right across from him. "We're following the leads we have as we investigate the case."

She turned around to greet the girls Jette Petersen was just leading into the teachers' lounge.

"We can go down to the classroom at the end of the hall," Jette said after they'd greeted each other. There were three girls in addition to Dicta Møller.

"Great," Louise said, leading the way out the door without saying good-bye to Jette's colleague.

Two of the girls, Fatima and Asma, were from immigrant back-grounds. Liv was Danish. Louise pulled a couple of tables together so they could sit across from each other. Jette Petersen sat down a little way in the background as an observer.

"I'd really like to get a better sense of who Samra was," Louise began, looking at the girls. She had thought about whether or not she ought to meet with the girls individually, but had decided that having them all here together might help them loosen up. "As I understand, you were the ones who were closest to her."

She could tell they'd been crying. The memorial service in the gym must have been tough on them.

"She's my cousin," said Asma, the thinnest of the girls, whose pretty, slender face was framed by a head scarf that was so tight fitting Louise couldn't see a single strand of hair.

Louise sat for a moment, watching her. It would have been hard to find someone sending more mixed signals than this girl. Of the four, Asma was the most provocatively dressed, so the demure head covering seemed completely out of place in combination with the plunging neckline and tight skirt. Louise's eyes moved on to Fatima, who was a little stockier and seemed more relaxed about her appearance. She was wearing a pair of baggy pants and a styl-ish pink T-shirt and had a lot of curly black hair surrounding her face in a rather unruly hairdo.

Louise got down to business and explained that she had already spoken with Dicta and that she wanted a better idea of who Samra had hung out with. Who had known her?

She looked first at Fatima, who had been in Samra's class. "Our families know each other. We moved to Holbæk because my fa-ther grew up with Samra's father back home in Rabba. So I played with her a lot during the years we've lived here."

Louise was particularly struck by the girl's use of the word *played*. That wasn't a word Dicta would have used about the time she spent with Samra.

"When was the last time you saw her?" Louise asked.

"We saw each other last weekend," Fatima said and nodded at Asma, adding that Asma's family had been there, too.

Asma explained that her mother was Sada's sister. Asma was in the same grade, but had a different homeroom.

"How do you guys think Samra was doing?"

"Well," Fatima began to answer, but then gave Asma a questioning look. Asma, however, was lost in her own thoughts and didn't respond to Fatima.

"Do you also think Samra seemed to be doing well when you were together last weekend?" Louise prompted.

Asma hurriedly nodded, and Louise felt herself starting to get a little exasperated. "You know, I'd heard that she seemed like she was under a little pressure lately, but you guys hadn't noticed that?" Louise prompted.

Fatima shook her head, but Asma looked Louise in the eye and said that there were times when Samra wasn't that happy.

"Had she been like that lately?" Louise asked.

Asma shrugged. There was something vulnerable about her. She didn't look at all cheap in her tight-fitting clothes; it was more like she radiated a strong sense of feminine elegance, one that she was just way too young to carry off and that wasn't fully realized because she was hiding one of the most feminine of bodily adornments: her hair.

"Did Samra say anything to you? She must have needed someone to talk to?" Instead of waiting for an answer, Louise asked the girls whom they talked to when they were sad. "Each other," all four of them replied.

Dicta added that she also talked to her parents, and there was nodding all around the table. The others obviously did too, when all was said and done.

The silence in the classroom was oppressive until Louise asked if anyone thought the family might have been planning a wedding for Samra and that maybe that was what had been making her feel pressured.

Suddenly everyone was talking over each other.

"They wouldn't do that," Fatima exclaimed loudly and was interrupted by Liv, who exclaimed, "Well, they could just forget about that!"

"My aunt and uncle aren't like that," Asma said, once everyone had calmed down. "They're not into that kind of thing."

"But that's what you Danes always think about us, isn't it?" Fatima mumbled angrily.

"Samra would never have put up with that. She was way too independent to accept a decision like that," Liv interjected, and the other girls agreed.

Louise studied Liv for a moment. She was hardly the first person Louise would have picked as one of Samra's closest friends. Her leather jacket was worn, and the red T-shirt with the black dots she wore underneath it was faded. Louise couldn't figure out whether the girl's hair was standing up in stiff tufts because it was beyond greasy or if she'd painstakingly achieved this look with multiple hair products. It was hard to tell what color the girl's eyes were behind all that thick, black eyeliner.

"Well, good, we'll forget about that then," Louise said. "Do you think Samra would have snuck out of the house at night without telling her parents?" she asked instead.

Both Dicta and Liv nodded, while Asma and Fatima took a little longer to acknowledge that she might well have done that. "Samra's parents usually went to bed around ten, because her father had to get up early," one of the girls added.

"Who would she have gone to visit if it wasn't one of you guys?" This time there was no rapid outburst of answers.

"She was very careful," Liv said, pulling her leather jacket tighter around her, as if she was a little uncomfortable talking under such scrutiny.

"If they found out, her father would have been furious and then she would have been grounded for several months."

Dicta agreed with Liv and said that Samra had been grounded a few times in the past.

"You can't just fucking do that! I'd dare my parents to even try it," Liv said, her tone indignant. Louise thought that they would have a hard time reining her in.

"Her parents hadn't seen her since her mother said good night to her Tuesday evening. They thought she'd gone to school the next morning. But by the time the alarm clock rang at eight Wednesday morning, Samra was already lying out in Udby Bay."

Louise knew it would be hard on them to hear her say it so matter-of-factly, but she felt she needed to shake them up a little. They weren't giving her anything and she had to get them talking if she was going to have any chance of making headway.

"Did she show up at any of your homes on Tuesday night?" Louise asked, and she was prepared when all four of them shook their heads. "Did any of you go out gallivanting with her and you're not mentioning it now because you're worried your parents will find out?"

Her voice had become sharp, and she noted the look the teacher shot at her, but she didn't stop. She carefully studied the young girls to try to determine what was going on behind their expressionless faces, but none of them seemed to be trying to cover up a lie.

"She must have disappeared in the evening or at night," Dicta said softly, when the silence became unbearable.

Louise had the sense that a distance was growing between the girlfriends and it wasn't hard for her to figure out what they were divided over. Accusers on one side and defenders on the other. Against the family and for the family. She was afraid to put any words in their mouths, but they were dealing with facts here, and she had to confront them with those. If anyone could come up with an alternative chain of events, they were more than welcome to do so.

"I already asked Dicta. But now I'm asking the rest of you if you know whether she had a boyfriend or a friend whom she saw in secret?"

Louise was ready for another round of loud protests from Fatima and Asma but they just shrugged and said there wasn't anyone they were aware of. Dicta repeated that there hadn't been anyone.

"You wouldn't know shit about it," Liv remarked caustically. "The only thing anyone can talk to you about is your hair and your advertising jobs."

"Modeling jobs," Dicta corrected her.

"I just mean it's not like Samra would have wanted to tell you anything—if there was anything to tell—since you're always off in your own egocentric universe."

Louise considered interrupting, but before she had a chance, Dicta managed to do so herself.

"Give it a fucking break already," Dicta swore. "I don't think I spend any more time on my hair than you do, so just drop it." Louise's eyebrows were halfway up her forehead. There was something out of place about words like that coming out of Dicta's pretty young mouth, but it was effective. Louise had obviously misjudged her. And it surprised her just as much that Liv took it without any kind of comeback.

"Do you know something?" Louise asked, directing her question at Liv.

"I don't know what it was, but I think there was something," Liv replied cryptically.

"Well, how about a few more details, please!" Louise's tone was harsher than she'd intended, and again she noticed a look from the girls' teacher, who wished to protect her students.

Liv's face was full of regret, as if she felt she had promised more than she could deliver. The young, black-haired rebel seemed to oscillate between reckless bluntness and strong discomfort at being noticed, which once again caused her to pull her leather jacket tighter around herself. But there was nothing flippant about her charm, Louise noted, studying Liv with interest as she began her response.

"I don't know anything about any boyfriend," Liv explained, "but it's very clear that there was something. Something had hurt her, she had been upset, something had been painful."

Dicta looked skeptical. "Well, I certainly didn't notice that," she said, looking over at Fatima and Asma. "Did you guys?"

"Maybe, but not the way you mean," Fatima told Liv. "I think she seemed happy, as if she had butterflies."

Louise looked at each of the girls in turn. This was almost worse than no information at all, she thought. Everyone was going off in separate directions.

"At some point did she maybe confide something in one of you?" Louise asked, hoping they would confide in her. But all four of them shook their heads.

Louise thanked them for their time and for the information they'd given her. She said good-bye to Jette Petersen and thanked her as well. Then she left Højmark School to drive back to the police station with the sense that she hadn't gotten very far.

15

"I know you used to call the school office and ask about your sister if she was even ten minutes late coming home from school. And now you're claiming you don't know shit about what she liked to do?"

Louise heard the voice through the door, just as she was about to enter her office. She stopped, quickly realizing that her partner's plan of maintaining a more convivial tone hadn't gone so well. Louise considered going to the command room to wait until Mik was done questioning Samra's brother, but ended up standing in the hallway while Hamid heatedly defended himself and claimed it was all a bunch of lies.

"You used to follow her on your moped when she walked home after visiting her friends. Am I making that up, too, or shall we accept that as credible since Dicta Møller's parents say they saw you several times?"

Louise continued down the hall before Hamid answered. She

knew Mik had the upper hand. Samra's classmates had already described several incidents that confirmed Hamid had indeed followed his sister.

Louise went in to see Ruth and sat down with a Coke in her hand. "How did it go when Mik questioned the parents?" she asked, hoping that he'd gotten a little more out of them than she had from her visit to the school.

Ruth leaned back in her chair and pressed her cherry-red lips together. A look of annoyance flashed across her face as she placed her hands behind her head and pushed her ample orange mop of hair upward to form a crown over her head.

"This has not been a good day, to put it mildly," Ruth said. "First, Storm decided to leave us." Then she explained that the mood had been rather tense after the day's questioning sessions.

"Ibrahim al-Abd has started waffling about when he came back from the marina Tuesday night and when his brother went home. If Storm had had time to attend to his responsibilities here, maybe he could have forced through a detention order for the father, but the deputy commissioner didn't think we had enough to hold him."

"Couldn't you just call Storm on his cell?" Louise asked.

Ruth irritably shook her head. "He's not picking up and hasn't responded to the messages I've left. Maybe giving his PowerPoint presentation down there will eventually earn him another star on his lapel, but he'd be doing a hell of a lot more good right now if he were here."

Louise pictured the look on Samra's father's face when they'd told him about his daughter. "If we forget about statistical probabilities and everything we have to go on so far, I'd say I'm reasonably sure the father didn't know it was his daughter's body that had been found," Louise said. "It would be almost impossible to fake that much despair."

The administrative assistant shrugged. "They haven't given us a thing—either the mother or the father—that would give us the slightest reason to cross them off as suspects. One minute the father is yelling and screaming and making a big scene because the police suspect him of having something to do with his daughter's death and the next he's refusing to say anything about the family's acquaintances and what Samra had been up to in recent weeks. He's completely shut down. The mother cried most of the time and didn't give us anything useful. We let them go and we'll have to see what Storm says whenever he finally gets back."

"Are you going to be in town this weekend?" Mik Rasmussen asked after he'd said good-bye to Hamid, who had given the detective an obstinate look and an almost invisible nod before quickly scurrying away.

Louise nodded. Before Storm left, he had made it clear that everyone was going to be staying in town over the weekend. Not that he was expecting all that much to happen, but he wanted to be able to call in his troops if there was a sudden breakthrough. It didn't bother Louise. She was in no hurry to go home to her empty apartment.

"I'm teaching a sea kayaking class for beginners tomorrow," Mik said. "If you want to give it a try, stop by."

Louise stared at him blankly. "Sea kayaking?" she repeated.

Mik nodded and smiled at the look on her face. "We go out on the sound," he explained. "It's amazing. I think you'd actually really like it."

Louise started laughing. "And just what makes you think that? It sounds strenuous, cold, and wet. Definitely not something for me."

"You wear a wet suit, so you won't get cold when you're in the water," he countered. "Besides, you don't need to paddle all the way out to the Sjællands Odde peninsula on your first trip."

"Isn't this a little late in the year to start kayaking?" she asked, trying to shoot down the idea, but her partner brushed that aside, explaining that as long as they were wearing wet suits, they could keep going until well into October.

She stood there for a moment, watching him as he gathered his papers into a neat pile. Then he shut down his computer and said he was heading home to do the next feeding.

"Feeding?" she asked. Now she was totally in the dark.

He explained that one of his hunting dogs, a black Lab, had had puppies who were three weeks old now and that the mother needed all the food she could eat so she could produce enough milk for them. Which is why he had to go home several times a day.

She had to smile. Suddenly everything made sense.

"The Rowing Club is behind Hotel Strandparken," Mik said on his way out the door.

She waved after him, but her cell phone rang just then. When she saw that it was Camilla, she pushed the office door shut a little with her foot before answering.

"I don't think we'll be working that late tonight," Louise answered after her friend asked if she had an estimate for when she'd be done.

"There's a restaurant down by the harbor that looks promising. Let's meet there at eight. I'll have my articles turned in by then," Camilla said. "Maybe some of the others would like to join us. You guys can't keep hanging out at the Station Hotel, and it's usually pretty easy to tempt Søren Velin into tagging along."

Louise had no doubt he could be tempted. When they worked together in Department A, Søren was known as a joiner. She headed down the hall to find him and hadn't even finished asking before he'd suggested they start with a beer at the brewpub before heading to dinner. Skipper stopped as he walked by and asked what time they were meeting.

"Who's going to convince Bengtsen?" Louise asked, heading down the hall to see if Dean had left yet.

"I will," said Ruth, who had appeared in the hallway.

Suddenly Louise had the impression that the prospect of a little socializing had improved everyone's mood. They'd all been buried in work since the group had been formed. Now people's voices sounded more upbeat.

They all had more than one beer at the little brewpub, which was walking distance from the hotel, and when they made it to the nice restaurant by the harbor they agreed it probably wasn't the best fit for them. They were no longer in the mood for quiet conversation, so they decided on a nearby Indian restaurant instead. The group was a little too big for the one table that was available, but no one seemed to mind squeezing in. Not even Bengtsen, who had ordered an orange soda at the brewpub, although that had only lasted until Camilla stuck a foamy draft beer into his hand.

Louise sat crushed between Skipper and Søren, well entertained because Skipper pulled his iPod out of his pocket and started showing off his knowledge of fusion jazz. She listened with concentration, trying to hear the tranquility in the notes, but kept getting thrown off because the music kept switching tempo and style. She noticed that he smiled whenever she periodically grimaced.

"Do you like it?" he asked.

She felt like she'd been caught and shrugged a little.

He said a lot of people felt that way about this kind of music:

They either loved it or hated it. The people who loved it took pleasure in the unpredictable notes, and the ones who weren't captivated described it as irritating noise. He explained that he'd been in a band when he was younger.

"Now we just mess around for fun, whenever I get together with a couple of the other old guys back home in Svendborg."

Louise had a hard time picturing him with a saxophone in his mouth. Skipper was in his mid-thirties and in great shape, muscular in an outdoorsy way. It was much easier to picture him with a golf club or a fishing pole.

Søren ordered another bottle of red wine while Ruth and Camilla made Dean retell a story that had made them erupt in raucous laughter, so that everyone else could hear it, too.

"Shortly after I arrived in Denmark, I was living in a refugee center in Lyngby," Dean began, getting everyone's attention. "And if I have anything funny to say about that period it was that we discovered that on the door to the boss's office it said PEDER PEDERSEN. Because where I come from, *peder* means 'gay.' So you can appreciate why all the kids laughed every time they saw him and the rest of us had a little trouble taking the head of the refugee center seriously. The guy resigned after just two weeks."

The laughter spread around the table and Søren generously refilled people's wineglasses.

When they were having coffee after dinner, Ruth got a call from Storm, who had just returned to the Station Hotel. For a second it sounded like he was considering joining the party, but when Ruth made it clear to him how irritated she was that he hadn't been there doing his job when they'd needed him, he reconsidered.

Louise smiled as she listened, thinking that it must have taken years of working together closely for Ruth to achieve such a sharp tone without him taking it the wrong way. She was yanked out of her musings when Skipper spoke to her.

"Are you happy with Department A and Suhr?"

As she nodded, she reminded him that he, too, had worked in Department A once upon a time. "But that was many years ago," he said. "A long time before Hans Suhr became chief of the homicide division. He and I worked together a long time ago, at Station Three—or Bellahøj, as they call it now."

Well, she supposed it wasn't surprising that Skipper and Captain Suhr knew each other. They were remarkably similar, even though it was hard to spot a gruff side to Skipper. But maybe that was because she didn't really know him yet.

"I've been there three and a half years and so far, so good," she replied, explaining that she was in Henny Heilmann's squad.

Skipper knew her, too, and told Louise a couple of anecdotes, ending with a story about Thomas Toft, who had seniority on the investigation team Louise was currently part of. She laughed out loud when Skipper called him a stubborn terrier who wouldn't let go once he'd bitten into something, because it was the perfect description.

After coffee they split the bill and got up to go check out Holbæk's nightlife. Dean and Søren led them back to the brewpub, where they had live music, and Louise gladly accepted the pints Skipper passed across the table to her each time he returned from a trip to the bar. As she let herself into her hotel room a couple of hours later, she realized she was a bit tipsier than she had realized. It didn't take long before sleep overcame her.

16

Camilla was lying in her hotel room reading through her article in *Morgenavisen*. They'd been out late the night before, and they'd had plenty of beer and wine with their food. That had been nice. Bengtsen had stubbornly denied that he'd let Else down on a Friday night because of Ruth's special persuasive abilities. He had insisted to Camilla that he was very social as long as the company was right, so she'd taken it as a compliment that he'd chosen her as a tablemate and had made sure he was aware that in the future she would include him on her list of police sources.

The paper was featuring her story prominently, with a set of statistics on recent honor killings. She'd hoped that Samra's mother would show up so she could interview her, but deep down she knew that it wouldn't happen. And certainly not now that her boss had thoughtlessly rewritten the headline of Camilla's article on the mother's visit to the women's shelter. Samra's mother failed her, it now said, and with those words her last chance of an interview was gone, Camilla thought angrily.

Camilla felt rotten about the headline. It made her feel sick to her stomach. Plus, there was no way she could back it up since the title promised quite a bit more than the article actually contained. She had carefully described the police report about the father and how Sada had sought help. That was all information she'd gotten from the police. It wasn't like she'd been poking around to find that out on her own, and nowhere in the article had she suggested that the mother had failed her daughter, costing the girl her life.

Camilla had spent most of her Friday afternoon trying to find someone who would talk to her about their impressions of Sada al-Abd, both as a mother and a wife. It was hard to get anyone to talk, but she had finally managed to find two other immigrant women who had agreed to speak to her. They had been very positive and had told her in their limited Danish how Sada devoted all her time to her children, especially the two little ones. On the other hand, when Camilla brought up the spousal abuse Samra's mother had been subjected to, the two women shut down. Either they didn't know anything about it or, more likely, they dared not get involved. That was something you kept in the family.

Camilla quickly skimmed through the rest of the paper, and was lazily lounging around in her hotel bed when the phone in the room rang. She tripped over her suitcase as she darted to answer it. She had packed her things before breakfast and was planning to head back to Copenhagen later that morning.

"There's a guest in the lobby who'd really like to speak with you," the person at the front desk said.

"Is it Louise Rick?" Camilla asked.

"It's a foreign woman."

Camilla grew tense; she knew instinctively that something unpleasant was coming.

"I'll be right down," she said and put on her shoes.

The woman was sitting in the large, dark-brown armchair to the left of the front desk. Camilla recognized the veil that was hiding her face. She took a deep breath and straightened herself up before walking over and saying hello.

The girl staffing the front desk, one Camilla hadn't seen before, watched them with curiosity.

"Come," Camilla told Samra's mother, nodding toward the restaurant. "Let's find a spot where we can talk privately."

She said it so loudly that the girl behind the desk quickly looked away.

Sada al-Abd still hadn't said a word, but she rose and followed Camilla. The restaurant was empty. All the same, Camilla asked the waiter cleaning up after breakfast if there was a place where she and Sada could speak undisturbed. He showed them what was likely the hotel's conference room, although it did not look as if it was used very often. There was a heavy, stuffy odor in the room and a layer of dust over the rectangular rosewood table that filled the room lengthwise.

When the waiter left, shutting the door behind him, Camilla turned to Sada, ready to take whatever the woman was going to dish out.

"You mustn't write things like that," Sada exclaimed in despair.

Camilla winced, pulling back reflexively from the distressed woman.

"How could you do that?" Sada stepped toward her and started crying loudly, her voice growing more shrill as she continued to yell.

Camilla stepped back farther, now waiting patiently for Sada to finish. When she collapsed into quiet, miserable sobs, Camilla put her arm around her shoulders and led her over to a seating area by the far wall.

Once Sada was sitting, Camilla stepped out into the restaurant and asked the waiter to bring them some tea. Then she sat down across from Samra's mother and let her cry.

Camilla felt the knot in her stomach again. Her article had been restrained, but she was fiercely angry at her boss and the sloppy way he came up with headlines. It never cost him anything, but that damn well wasn't the case for her. Here she was, sitting across from the woman they'd maligned, who very obviously couldn't take any more pain.

When the tea arrived, Camilla poured it into two large, floral teacups copied from the best of traditional English style and passed one to Sada in the hope that it would distract her.

Sada reluctantly accepted it, avoiding eye contact with Camilla as if she was ashamed of her angry outburst. After she took her first sip, she finally said something: "I have always taken good care of my children."

There was a long pause. Camilla was about to speak when Sada continued.

"Now they're going to take my children away. But what do you care? You don't understand," she said, wringing her hands together.

Not caring was not Camilla's problem at the moment. Her boss had sold her out and it was going to cost him. She did care about Sada, although she was irritated that the woman hadn't come to see her until now that the article was already printed instead of the day before so they could have talked to each other beforehand. At any rate, Camilla began by defending herself in a way that could easily be interpreted as an attack.

"No one needs to understand or accept anyone being abused to the point that they have to go to a women's shelter," Camilla said. She knew this might put an end to the woman's willingness to talk, but on the other hand she felt it was necessary to indicate where she stood.

But her statement didn't seem to bother Sada al-Abd. The woman just shook her head. There was obviously something else Camilla didn't understand.

"Try to explain to me what led up to your going to the shelter. What I especially want you to explain is why you went back to him," Camilla said.

"Why should I?" Sada asked. "You're just going to write whatever you want anyway."

Camilla had heard that one many times before.

"You wrote that I killed my own daughter." Sada spoke quietly, with a determination in her voice. The tears were gone and she seemed almost fearsome.

"I didn't write that you killed her," Camilla exclaimed indignantly, wishing that instead of accusing her, the mother would give her new information. "I wrote that you went to a shelter for help and that shortly after that you went back to your abuser."

Camilla took a sip of tea and again asked Samra's mother to talk about what had happened when she went into hiding with her children.

As Sada drank a little more of her tea, it looked as if she was fighting some kind of battle within herself. Camilla had the sense that the woman across from her really wanted to tell her story, but that she was afraid of the consequences.

"I won't write anything until you've given me permission," Camilla said. "And I'll let you read through it before it goes to print."

That was really all she had to offer, but it seemed to have an effect.

"My husband got mad at Hamid, our older son," Sada began. "Hamid didn't want to hand over some money he'd earned, and that made Ibrahim so mad, he struck out."

Camilla had brought her bag down with her; she pulled out a

notepad and started taking notes. Sada didn't seem to notice and kept talking.

"He was hitting Hamid hard, and I tried to stop him."

"You fled with your children because you tried to come between your husband and your son?" Camilla stated in surprise, a little shaken. She knew that Hamid had not gone to the shelter with the other children.

The woman nodded.

"If it was your son Ibrahim was mad at, why were you the one who had to flee?"

"Samra was also yelling at her father and defending her brother. My husband can get very angry. He lashed out with his hands many times and said he would kill the little ones if I got involved again."

"And did you?"

"No, but he hit Samra to show that he meant it."

"Didn't he threaten to kill Hamid?"

Sada looked directly at Camilla and maintained the eye contact for a long time.

"He would never kill his eldest son," she finally said.

Camilla had her notepad in her lap and sat for a bit, gathering her thoughts. She bent her head back to stop the shivers that were running up and down her spine.

"So, you reported him to the police and the four of you got out of there?"

Sada nodded.

"How could you go back to a man who had threatened to kill your children?" Now she set down the pad, sensing how the room seemed to close in as she asked her question. "Why?"

Tears began to flow down Sada's cheeks once more. "Lone-liness," she finally whispered so softly that Camilla had to lean forward to hear her. "If I had left him, we would have had no one.

I might have been okay, but it wouldn't have worked for the children. Our lives would have been shut out."

"What do you mean?" Camilla asked. "You would have been free."

The thin woman shook her head. "Freedom is not the same for me as for you."

Camilla sat motionless.

"I would rather be home with my husband than be free and lonely."

Camilla didn't understand.

"Why would you be lonelier away from a man who abuses you?" Camilla asked.

"If you don't belong anywhere anymore, then you have no one. No one will talk to you. You don't get invited anywhere. The children are not allowed to play with other children, and there's not even any guarantee you will get to keep your last name. You will be totally alone, an outcast."

Camilla was speechless at the way Sada rattled this all off, as if it had come straight from some kind of list of rules.

"Who says all that?" Camilla asked.

Sada gave her the smallest of smiles.

"It's not something anyone says. That's just how it is, and how it has always been for those who bring shame to their families."

"Yeah, but you damn well can't avoid things happening in a family that will make waves, and you don't necessarily have to become an outcast because of it," Camilla said heatedly. It wasn't that she hadn't heard of honor and shame before, but this was completely crazy.

Sada sat for a moment before responding, searching for the right words.

"It's only in the closest family that honor and shame really mean something. If it's someone you don't know, who cares? Then it doesn't mean anything."

Camilla had no idea what Sada was talking about.

"There can be conflict within a family without it necessarily resulting in any consequences. It's only once the extended family hears about it that things get tricky."

"You mean if other people start talking about it?"

Sada nodded. "You don't want that," she said. "You don't want anyone speaking ill of your family."

Camilla was with her so far. She urged Sada to explain what kinds of issues could be so important that they would result in abuse or expulsion.

"I can certainly appreciate that some people might feel it was impinging on the family's honor if one family member did something wrong, but I can't understand how this would result in such a physically violent outcome," Camilla said.

"Danish families also expel people," Sada said, after pausing a moment to think.

Camilla was about to protest.

"Pedophiles, for example," Sada continued.

Camilla's eyebrows shot up. "That's not a fair comparison."

Sada nodded and said that that was precisely the same way one might be excluded from a family unit in her culture. "People who do that are the worst kind of scum. No one wants to be with them and people won't protect them, either," the slender immigrant woman said.

Silence settled between them as Camilla considered Sada's words. She regretted promising she wouldn't write anything without obtaining permission first, because it was pretty easy to see that she wasn't going to get it in this case. She sensed a peace between them as well as a new intimacy, which was what made her decide not to even try to pressure the woman for permission to use anything from their conversation.

"Would your husband have been able to kill your daughter if

she had violated the family's honor?" Camilla took a deep breath once that question was out there. She had been wanting to ask since they'd sat down.

She noted that Sada's shoulders had risen a smidge at the question, but they slowly fell back into place again as she answered.

"He might. But our daughter didn't do anything to violate our family. To the contrary. She was our pride. He took care of her," she said, taking great pains to emphasize the words, making them unwavering.

"Are you afraid of him?" Camilla asked.

Sada looked at Camilla in surprise and then responded with a convincing "No." She continued, "On those occasions when something happened, he had a reason to react. He didn't have one in this case."

This statement made Camilla suspect that Ibrahim had hit Sada more than once, but just hadn't been reported to the police.

"I'm not afraid of my husband," Sada said, "even though he can lose his temper and do stupid things. But I am afraid that they will come and take the little ones away."

"Who will?" Camilla asked, her thoughts still on the rest of Sada's family.

"The government. I won't be allowed to keep my children after what you wrote."

And with that, they were back where they'd started, but the feeling in Camilla's stomach was totally different now than the one she'd had when Sada had started scolding her.

"They're not going to come take your children away. You're a good mother. They have no reason to."

"They don't know how it is. They only see what's in the paper."

"Well, I don't believe that," Camilla said, but she knew that the other woman wasn't entirely wrong. Camilla had stoked the fire and possibly set something in motion that she had not understood the repercussions of, but she hadn't been thinking about her article as something that could have such a direct consequence. Now she regretted that she hadn't just written a sentimental piece about a town where some teenagers were grieving the loss of a beloved classmate.

Repercussions, Camilla thought, afraid it was a word that was going to follow her for the entire story.

"I'd really like to write about what you told me today. It might help your case."

"No, no." Sada vigorously shook her little head. "You mustn't."

"I don't need to say the two of us talked. I can write something about honor and shame, about the loneliness and fear of becoming an outcast, and why it might be necessary to act as you did."

"No one will bother reading that to try to understand," Samra's mother said, suddenly sounding tired.

Camilla smiled at her.

"You leave that to me. I'll just throw something together." Before they stood up, Camilla pulled out her card with the paper's number and her own cell phone number on it. "Call me. Also, if you just want to talk," Camilla said. "I'll be back in Holbæk again next week."

Sada nodded and took the card.

"Take care of yourself," Camilla said as they parted. "And thank you for coming."

She stood there outside the hotel watching Sada walk across Banegård Square to catch a bus home.

17

Louise quietly coasted down the street and parked next to a red wooden building with a big sign reading HAMAM. She sat looking at it for a moment, wondering why it seemed familiar, until she remembered that she had once read an article about a Turkish bath opening in Holbæk. She and Camilla had even toyed with trying it out. *So this is where it is*, she thought, getting out of the car. The Rowing Club was on her right, and a little way out in the water, along a pier, were the Oceanside Baths—a small redwood building with a number of small, attractive cabins all painted white.

She wondered for a second if she should head back up the road and try going in through the clubhouse to find Mik, or go down to the water and see if she could get through that way.

"Hi!"

He had spotted her first. He was standing along the shore in a wet suit and a life jacket, which wasn't buckled shut yet, but what she noticed first were his bright-yellow plastic clogs.

They were not at all attractive and yet they were all the rage—
and they were one of the last things she would have expected to
see her not-all-that-hip partner wearing. He was standing with
a bunch of men and women in wet suits and fluorescent-yellow-
and-orange life jackets. There was a line of sea kayaks, ready to
put into the water, and she realized she had interrupted the class,
which was already under way. A little embarrassed, she walked
over and greeted the others.

"I got one out for you," Mik said, pointing to the red Dagger-
brand kayak, which was the one farthest away.

She walked over to stand next to it and listened as he explained
that the sea kayak had two sealed compartments, which meant it
couldn't sink, and which also served as storage space if you were
going on a trip.

He held up something that looked pretty much like a skirt and
explained that it was a spray skirt, which you attached around
your waist before you climbed into the kayak and then pulled taut
and secured over the opening.

"Start from the back," he said, demonstrating how to secure it.
"That way you won't get water in your kayak. It will come off easily if you capsize in the water, so don't be afraid of getting stuck if
that happens."

Louise looked around at the other students, listening attentively
to his explanation. Personally, she didn't have the slightest desire
to capsize, whether she had one of these skirts on or not. She was
having a hard time paying attention. It was totally discombobulat-
ing to see Mik Rasmussen in the role of kayaking instructor.

He showed them how far to pull their kayaks out into the water
before climbing into them and then he came over to Louise and said
that he'd laid out all her equipment for her up in the dressing room.

"But you didn't even know I was going to come," she protested
as they walked back up to the clubhouse.

"Of course you were going to come. No one ever turns down a free kayaking lesson," he said, holding the door open for her.

She refrained from saying that her presence today had less to do with wanting to go kayaking and more to do with the fact that she didn't have anything else to do; it had just been an alternative to an afternoon at the movies.

"Did you bring your swimsuit?" he asked.

She shook her head.

"Then you'll have to make do with underwear under your wet suit, but I hope you brought an extra set. Otherwise you'll be uncomfortable once you've been in the water."

"Yeah, but I'm not going in the water," she protested.

"Well, we'll see." He found her a life jacket and asked if she wanted to wear a parka underneath. "I don't think it's cold enough for you to need that," he added helpfully.

Louise just nodded, hoping he wasn't expecting her to start pulling on the wet suit while he stood there watching.

"Come down when you're ready," he said, turning his back to her. The suit was still a little wet, and she was already having regrets as she felt the clammy neoprene against her skin. She kept her sneakers on, annoyed that she hadn't given any thought to what she ought to bring, but then again she hadn't really been planning on coming. She didn't even have a towel.

The others were already sitting out on the water when Louise reached the shore. Mik was standing there waiting for her as he yelled his instructions to the class. He helped her with the kayak and held it while she climbed in. He carefully pushed her the last little bit out into the water.

"Find the balance point," he said, and she took the paddle he passed her.

"The curved side should go down next to the water," he reminded her.

She turned to give him an irritated look, but noticed how the kayak started tipping when she turned around. She quickly straightened back up and took a first cautious stroke in the water. She let the paddle rotate in the palm of her hand and switched to the other side. Then she started moving forward, stroke by stroke. She was surprised that she didn't feel more unsure of herself; it actually felt nice. She gradually, gently reached the other students, who already seemed to have such control over their paddles and kayaks that they could maneuver around without bumping into each other.

Mik had hopped into his own kayak and was already on his way out. "We're going to paddle down to the other side of Strand-parken," he yelled. "And when we return, I'll show you how to get back up again if you land in the water."

In the beginning her arms hurt, especially the left, but then she straightened her back and stretched it out at a right angle and could feel that things were going better. Once they'd rounded the hotel and were on their way back she realized she was actually enjoying this. She had never pegged herself as a water-sports enthusiast, but this was great. The autumn sun was shining low in the sky, and she was gliding through the water peacefully. She'd quickly figured out how to control her turns by back-paddling so the motion of the water acted as a brake, and the boat would slow down and start to change directions.

"If you fall in the water, you'll need to do an assisted recovery," Mik explained as the kayaks bobbed in a group in the water in front of the Rowing Club. He had everyone's attention.

"First you empty the water out of the kayak. Let's just try. Hop in," he said, and for a second Louise thought he was talking to her. She held her breath until she realized he was talking to a guy with long hair behind her. The man was down in the water quickly and Mik paddled over to him and positioned himself alongside.

"Start by flipping the kayak over and emptying out the water," he instructed, and, along with the long-haired man, he pulled the kayak up over his own so the front part was resting on his.

"The water empties out like this," he explained as he demonstrated. "Then you have to get back in." He turned the kayak over again and pushed it into the water so it was parallel to his. "You support it while your buddy climbs in."

Louise was glad it wasn't her. It didn't look easy. *Although I probably ought to learn what to do in a situation like that*, she thought. Just then, she felt a sharp jerk on her own kayak and before she had a chance to react, she was halfway over. She barely had time to wonder if her spray skirt would come loose so she wouldn't be trapped under the water. But it had already come free and she was out by the time her kayak was floating bottom-up beside her.

"Sorry!" exclaimed one of the older men, who had accidentally bumped into her.

"Well, I suppose you two might as well do the next assisted recovery," Mik said.

Louise got the kayak flipped over and drained the water out of it. She quite easily crawled up so she was lying on her stomach with her legs half down into the hole. With her kayak being held good and steady, she slowly turned around so she was lying with her head over the back end, and cautiously slid down into the kayak. She felt victorious having succeeded on her first try.

"Bravo!" Mik yelled, paddling over and giving her a high five.

She felt great when the class ended and they helped carry the kayaks back to where they were stored. She accepted Mik's offer of an extra towel and headed inside to get dressed. She wrung out her undergarments, and although she wasn't crazy about wearing her jeans and T-shirt with nothing underneath, she decided there was really no way around it.

"That went extremely well," her partner complimented her as they walked out of the clubhouse together.

She smiled and thanked him for having enticed her to try it. "It was a lot more fun than I thought it would be," she admitted before climbing into the car to drive by her hotel room and put on some dry underwear. Just after she'd arrived in Holbæk her mother had invited her to come over for dinner since she was so close, and tonight was the night. Her brother, Mikkel, and his girlfriend, Trine, would be there, too, along with their two little hellions, and as she drove back to the hotel she realized she was actually looking forward to spending a nice evening with her family.

18

It was almost eleven when Louise, full and in a good mood, pulled into the parking lot by the hotel. In the car on the way home from her parents' house, she had decided she would go for a run the next morning before work. She walked over to the train station on the other side of the street to look at the big map of Holbæk and the surrounding area that was posted by the entrance, trying to decide whether she should drive out a ways and go for a run in the woods or make do with a run along the shore, following the sound out of town.

She was preoccupied with planning her route when she registered the sound of someone vomiting behind her and turned around. At first, she didn't recognize the person, doubled over supporting herself with one arm on the train station's bike racks as she threw up. Then she realized who it was and hurried over in concern.

"Dicta! What's going on?"

It took a moment before the girl shakily stood up. She had on heavy makeup, which was now messy and smeared.

Louise walked over and put her arm around Dicta. She found a pack of Kleenex in her pocket and took one out to dab the remaining vomit away from the girl's mouth and chin.

Even from a distance, she'd sensed that Dicta was pretty drunk, and they wobbled as Louise started walking toward the hotel with her. She got her seated in the restaurant, which had been empty of guests for a while. Then Louise went into the kitchen for a glass of water and found a bag the girl could throw up into if necessary. She set the glass down in front of Dicta and took a seat next to her.

"What did you do?" Louise asked.

Dicta didn't respond, didn't even look at Louise. She seemed to be falling asleep. Louise took a firm hold of her shoulder and shook her. "Where have you been? Hello!"

The girl shook her head a little and tried to focus on Louise's face. She spasmed and Louise only just barely managed to get the bag in place before Dicta threw up yet again.

Goddamn it, Louise thought as some of it hit her hand. She went back to the kitchen, washed her hands, found a new bag, and went back in to ask the question again.

"In Copenhagen," Dicta finally answered. "All day," she said, looking up at Louise.

"And what were you doing in Copenhagen besides drinking yourself into a stupor?" Louise asked, trying not to sound like a mother.

For a second it looked like Dicta was going to throw up again, but she was just shaking. She rubbed her face and looked at her hands. "I was working," she said in a weak voice. She looked like she felt wretched, and Louise felt bad for her. She guessed it was the first time Dicta had gotten really drunk.

"A photography job?" she asked.

Dicta nodded, and now she was shaking so much that Louise was beginning to fear that it wasn't just alcohol she'd consumed.

"Did you take drugs? Pills? Or smoke something?"

Dicta vehemently shook her head. "I just drank champagne."

Louise forced her to drink some more water and relaxed a little to hear it had just been champagne. Although that could be bad enough when you were fifteen and almost certainly hadn't had much of it before. It struck Louise that she probably ought to call the girl's parents instead of sitting here herself with the sad dregs of their daughter.

"What about your parents?" she asked. "I have to call them."

Dicta shook her head again.

"Were you with your photographer?" Louise asked, already prepared for the scolding the *Venstrebladet* photographer was going to get after dropping his young model off outside the train station in this condition.

Dicta suddenly looked proud as she told Louise that she'd been photographed by one of the big-name photographers.

"He photographed Lykke May, too," she said, assuming that Louise would be familiar with the name. She was one of Denmark's most successful models.

"Can you give me a few more details? I'm not quite following. How did you end up with him?"

Dicta had perked up a bit.

"I'd seen his name in a few magazines and then yesterday I called him and he invited me in for a photo session."

Her speech was slurred.

"I took the train in this morning and we met at Café Ketchup and had brunch. His studio is right next door."

Louise was a little surprised at how uncomplicated and familiar she made it all sound.

"Do you usually go to Copenhagen like that?" she asked. "It sounds like you're familiar with the cafés."

Dicta shook her head and said that she'd never been there alone before. She and Liv had been to Copenhagen over summer vacation, but otherwise, she usually went there with her parents.

That reminded Louise that she had to contact them. "Do your parents know that you're back?"

"They think I'm at Liv's house," Dicta said, brushing aside Louise's objections.

"But they know you went to Copenhagen?"

This was starting to sound like an interrogation and Louise noticed Dicta receding into her own world again, so she restrained herself and let the girl go on with her story.

"His studio was really impressive compared with Michael's here," Dicta said, describing the walls, the different photographic backdrops, and all the lights and filters he used to tone down the light.

"What does Michael Mogensen have to say about your finding yourself another photographer?"

"He doesn't know I went there. Michael's totally not in the same league. Tue says that, too," she said, explaining that the Copenhagen photographer's name was Tue Sunds and that he had already explained to her over the phone that if she was really dreaming about making it big on an international level, she was going to have to stop wasting her time in a Podunk like Holbæk.

"Michael is really just small potatoes, a provincial photographer," Dicta said with newfound disdain—clearly the product of her visit to the big city.

"Why did Tue Sunds want to meet you on a Saturday?" Louise interrupted. "I hope you didn't take your clothes off for him."

Dicta turned to face her angrily. She flung out her hands, whacking the back of one of them against the edge of the table. "Are you crazy? I wouldn't do that!"

"Did you two go anywhere else?"

The girl sat for a bit before responding that they'd only been to the café and then he took a couple of pictures of her.

"Just a couple?"

That seemed strange, as the man had devoted his entire Saturday to this. In that case, he probably just wanted to make as much money as possible, Louise supposed.

"I mean, he is a professional," Dicta retorted quickly. "He's totally not like Michael, who spends several hours on a single pose. Tue works for the big magazines."

"But you didn't get home until now? Or had you already been back in Holbæk for a while when I met you?"

Dicta had to think about that one for a minute. Maybe she couldn't remember how or when she'd come back, Louise thought with concern.

"I took the train home and had just gotten back. And then standing there outside the station I suddenly had to throw up."

Louise shook her head at the girl. "What did you guys do for the rest of the day?"

"We went out and drank champagne to celebrate our new collaboration." Dicta sounded proud. "He said one of the heads of the big modeling agencies often came to the same place and that he would introduce us."

Louise sat there with her arms crossed.

"Did you go back to his place after that?" she asked.

Dicta nodded, her long blond hair falling down over her face in wisps. "We drank more wine and ate the sushi and caviar he ordered before I left for home."

"Did you sleep with him?"

Dicta gave Louise a shocked, offended look. "You have no right to ask me that. He thinks I have a lot of potential." She was still having trouble speaking clearly. "He says I could make it as far as Lykke May or Louise P."

"Did he do anything to you against your will?" Louise asked when Dicta didn't respond to her question.

"What do you mean?" Dicta seemed sincerely confused.

"Did he force you to do anything you didn't feel comfortable with?" Louise really couldn't put it any more clearly than that.

Dicta closed her eyes and hid her face in her hands as she shook her head. After a while, she moved her hands to give Louise a dark look. "You're like my mother. Why don't you believe that amazing things can really happen?"

Louise was about to protest, but she saw how tired and wretched Dicta looked. "Of course they can really happen. I just want to make sure that he didn't take advantage of you. You're a little off-balance these days after what happened to your friend. That can make it harder to make good decisions."

"He didn't. He just thought I was pretty, and he really wanted to help me. We kissed a little. Okay?" she added spitefully.

Louise couldn't tell if she was being honest about everything that had happened. But she wasn't actually all that concerned as long as the girl hadn't been molested on top of being marinated in champagne.

Louise stood up, supporting Dicta under her arm to help her up.

"I'll drive you home."

Dicta stood there unstable, looking as if she wanted to protest, but Louise started pulling her along right away.

It was dark in the big house when Louise parked outside, but by the time she reached the front door Charlie had already started barking loudly and several lights along the driveway snapped on. She rang the bell and supported Dicta while they waited for the door to open.

"No one's home," Dicta said after they'd waited awhile.

Louise looked at her in surprise. "Then why are we standing here waiting for someone to open the door?" She helped Dicta as the girl tried to extract her keys from the little chest pocket of her jean jacket.

Dicta shrugged and laughed a little foolishly. "I forgot it was the weekend," she said, getting the door open without letting the dog out. "My mom spends most of her weekends at dog shows or agility courses, and my dad goes along. Otherwise they'd never see each other."

She spoke like she had heard the explanation repeated so many times that it had become a kind of mantra. Louise had the sense that Dicta didn't care about her parents' priorities, not that they upset her. Louise stood in the front door watching the girl slip off her jacket and toss it on the floor. Once she had ascertained that Dicta was heading for her bedroom she yelled good night, shut the door, and drove back to the hotel.

19

What are we doing about those tires?" Storm asked, irritated, looking at Skipper and Dean.

It had now been almost two weeks since Samra had been found, and the whole group was sitting around the table in the command room. So far, they hadn't gotten anything out of the crime scene investigations, the dinghies out in the cove, the search of the al-Abds' home, or the string of witness statements that Louise and Mik had spent the intervening days working on along with Bengtsen and Velin. They'd trawled through everything—acquaintances, work relationships, family, neighbors. Storm had even considered whether he ought to have Interpol send one of them to Jordan to speak to family members there, but it would have a big financial impact on the investigation if that kind of questioning was to be permitted and he still hadn't found a way to justify it.

Skipper reached for a little stack of papers he had on the table in front of him.

"Well, there is a report here from the crime scene investigators that we've been working with for the last several days. They compared the tire tracks secured out at Hønsehalsen with the tires of Ibrahim's red Peugeot. In one of the treads in the crime scene track they found a milled groove, which was measured at 1.3 millimeters deep. In comparing that with the corresponding tread on the Peugeot's four tires, the corresponding depths were measured at 1.4 on the left front tire, 1.7 on the left rear tire, 1.6 on the right front tire, and 1.8 on the right rear tire," Skipper said, reading aloud from the pages and then setting them down again. "Therefore, there are no specific parameters that can serve as a basis for identification between the plaster cast from the scene and Ibrahim's car," he concluded. "But we also can't rule out that the impressions at the site were made by his car. The tire impressions are of the same dimension with an equivalent pattern and wear. We'll just never be able to prove it."

"All right, then let's drop that," Storm said gruffly. "There's no reason to throw more resources at it." He went on to explain that there hadn't been anything in the dinghies close to where the body was found, nothing besides remnants of fish blood, which had aroused interest until Dean reminded everyone that Samra hadn't bled.

Louise sighed and looked around at the rest of the team. She sensed that they had all been banking on the tire tracks being unique and matching the car Samra's father usually drove. There was no doubt that Samra's body had been dumped into the water from a boat, but the family could easily have driven her out to the site and then just rowed her out from there instead of crossing the entire sound with her in the boat.

Since they couldn't rule out the possibility that the tire track had been made by any random driver, Skipper and Dean had issued a press release asking people who owned cars with the same type of tires to contact them if they'd been out at Hønsehalsen in the days before the killing. There had also been a great deal of talk about tires and tire tracks in the media and on the police's website. But no one had come forward.

"We have to keep looking," Storm said, nodding at Bengtsen. "Should we expand our search for witnesses?"

Bengtsen stopped him by thrusting a hand up in the air. "We've talked to a lot of people. It isn't likely that we'll suddenly find one who saw the girl."

"Well then, we'll focus on the audio surveillance of the family, and we may have to consider starting to put some pressure on them to see if there's any reaction."

Søren seemed to support that decision. "We'll keep going with the digital room bug. There's a wiretap on their landline, too," he said.

Storm nodded and appeared satisfied. Louise didn't feel the same way. They'd been working hard, reviewing everything in the hope that they'd overlooked something, but nothing new had turned up. She thought about Dicta. Louise hadn't talked to her since that night at the hotel, but maybe it was most considerate to let that episode be, she thought, getting up as the meeting ended.

❧

"There are women strong enough to fight their way out of the iron grip of their damn families. They break free to escape forced marriages and violence and mentally ill husbands who feel so confident that they own these women that they rape them around the clock and dominate them and damn well believe that they have the absolute right to use them any way they will." Camilla realized she had begun to yell and took a deep breath, lowering her voice. "But that's a tiny fraction compared with all the women who stick around and put up with the whole thing because they don't have the same strength." She was sitting across from Terkel Høyer in his office and had just turned in two articles for the next day's paper. But after she'd seen the look on his face, she'd realized that she couldn't count on even a mention on the front page.

"It's been almost two weeks since the girl's body was discovered, but instead of going to the police and pressuring them to reveal whatever the hell they're doing, you turn in two articles about honor and shame and about women who never get a real chance to integrate into Danish society, because, according to you, they're bound by cultural traditions."

Camilla kept a straight face.

"What the hell are you thinking?" thundered her editor. "Our readers couldn't care less about cultural traditions if they cause a couple of parents to kill their daughter. No one is going to accept that kind of thing in Denmark, no matter what the girl did to get on her family's bad side. If they choose to live in Denmark, then it's up to them to fucking follow our cultural norms! You're not going to get anywhere with that angle, and you can't be cramming crap like that down my readers' throats. This paper does not condone that kind of thing."

Ah, so now they are his *readers*, Camilla thought. Her voice was icy as she got up to stand in front of his desk. "I don't agree with you," she said simply. "What I wrote has nothing to do with getting Danes to accept this. But it can't hurt to try to understand where it's coming from, to get to the bottom of why people are doing these things, which we very obviously don't understand and which of course we will not tolerate. Your readers may well be stupid, but I don't fucking think they're that stupid."

She spun around and, once she was out of the office, slammed the door shut behind her so hard the wall shook. She got to her office and slammed her own door, still enraged.

Camilla sat down at her desk and looked at her screen: LONE-
LINESS IS WORSE THAN FEAR. She had promised Sada some sort of
redress in the paper, and she was ready to go to some lengths to
make good on her promise. But right now that felt impossible.
Terkel was going to have to back down a little, or she was going to
have to come up with some news from Holbæk. There just wasn't
any news, though. Obviously she'd been keeping tabs on develop-
ments. What was he thinking?

Since Sada had come to see her at the hotel, Camilla had been
working on the two articles, along with everything else she'd written. She had spent a lot of time getting all her research in place,
talking to women who had managed to break free, and even with
a Pakistani woman whose husband kept her locked in their small
apartment and brutally raped her whenever he wanted to have sex,
which was at least once a day. If she begged him to leave her alone,
he beat her.

Camilla had striven to distinguish between religion and culture
in the articles, to explain that the two things didn't have anything
to do with each other when it came to concepts like honor and
shame.

*When you lose your honor, you lose your worth as a person and a
social being*, Camilla had written, linking that to the Arabic saying
"Honor is what distinguishes people from animals."

It had shaken her that honor killings in the Middle East were
increasing. And there was obviously a big difference between the
shamefulness of an act and the consequences for it. Women's sexu-
ality was considered worst of all, especially acts like being unfaith-
ful and having sex outside marriage. Only hardened criminality
came after that. She shook her head and felt deeply indignant on
behalf of her sex.

Camilla had determined that the consequences of such an act
depended a lot on where you lived. In traditional families in rural

areas, honor and shame meant much more than in modern families in urban environments, so obviously it was impossible to generalize. She had made a big deal of elaborating on that.

When she was almost done, she had stumbled across something that had made her reconsider whether she ought to write the story at all. She'd run into contradictions that hadn't made any sense; she wondered if she'd ever truly comprehend the whole thing.

In the Koran it said that you mustn't force someone to marry against their will. So how the fuck could parents still be forcing their wishes on their children? There was obviously also something cultural going on, Camilla had realized. She just didn't see how people could so blatantly be going against the Koran, especially when it was so clear. She had decided not to include that in the article, but the book was sitting there as a note on her desk and she had to admit that it was all quite complicated. So she had gone to see Terkel with her two articles, considering them very important in the debate that had been raging steadily in the press since Samra's murder.

Now in a fit she had crumpled them both up and tossed them into the corner of her office. She swung her legs onto her desk and sat there lost in thought, her eyes focused on the many drawings Markus had made for her, which she had dutifully hung up on the wall as a border all the way around her desk.

She had actually been planning to drive to Holbæk that evening to find out if there'd been any progress that hadn't left the police command room yet. Markus was with his dad, so that would have worked great. But after her run-in with Terkel she suddenly didn't care. It was one thing for him to have his opinions, but it surprised her that he had voiced them aloud. It was inappropriate for an editor to so blatantly take sides.

It made her jump when he flung open the door without knocking and fired off his torrent of words in one long sentence: "If you can find some kind of Danish angle in your articles, we'll run them. Otherwise, forget it. We're not publishing a manifesto here."

He was gone before she'd processed what he'd said and the door had already clicked shut by the time she yelled that it *was* a manifesto if he was going to be so freaking one-sided.

20

W e're going to release the body," Storm said from their office doorway, and then asked if Louise didn't need to take a spin back to Copenhagen to water her plants. If so, could she swing by the morgue and bring the certificate back? The family had requested permission to fly Samra back to Jordan so she could be buried in Rabba, where she'd grown up and where her grand-parents still lived.

"I'm sure my plants would love that. I suppose I might as well go do it now?" she said, looking from Storm to Mik, who both nodded.

"Of course you could also stay for a cup of tea before you go," her partner coaxed once Storm had left. "Bengtsen brought in some of Else's macaroons."

Louise smiled and held her hands up in refusal.

In the car she called Flemming Larsen's direct number and said she was on her way in to pick up Samra's death certificate. Did he have time to step out for breakfast or a cup of coffee?

"I'm going to have trouble getting out of here," he said and explained that he was about to start an autopsy. "But if you want, we could have a cup of coffee here when you arrive. I'd really like to see you before you leave town."

Louise laughed into her headset. The tall pathologist was a master at making her feel like she was special, which made her cherish their friendship.

"I'm in the basement," Flemming said. "Just come on down and we'll get the death certificate all sorted out, too."

When she arrived at the Teilum Building, she said hello to one of the pathology techs whose name she couldn't remember and found out that Flemming was in the first room on the right at the bottom of the stairs.

Her heels echoed. She'd been down to the cold-storage rooms several times, but had never attended a postmortem there. She wasn't usually there until they did the formal autopsy. She knocked and waited a bit before pushing the door open.

"Hi," Flemming said, walking over to her in his white lab coat. Louise stayed out in the hallway, but saw that the deceased on the table was an older man. She received a quick peck on the cheek from Flemming.

"Give me ten minutes and I'll be ready. I picked up some pastries across the street from the cafeteria at the Rigshospitalet," he said, indicating a chair a little farther down the hallway.

"I'll wait," she said, smiling at the thought that he'd gone out of his way to pick up pastries for her.

Down the hallway a heavy steel door opened and a man in a gas mask came out. She raised her eyebrows at Flemming, wondering what that was about.

"They just started embalming your Jordanian girl," he said. "That has to be done before she can be sent abroad. Have you ever seen how they do that?"

Louise shook her head and followed him to a glass window in the wall. It was a small room that was dominated by a steel table, which was screened by a thick plastic curtain on all four sides. Above that there was an enormous exhaust fan, under which Samra's naked body lay, on a table.

"They slowly fill her up with formalin," Flemming explained, pointing to a pump next to the body. Several tubes were attached with needles to the girl. "About four to five liters will be pumped in via the major arteries, also filling the lungs and the chest cavity. The formalin will cause her organs to shrink a little, and then they'll keep for quite a long time after that."

The pathology tech in the gas mask came back, rolling a zinc coffin in front of him.

Louise stood there for a bit looking at the girl. You couldn't tell that her earthly remains were being preserved. She still looked like she had when her teacher identified her in the presentation room.

"Once she's been through a few Muslim burial rituals, the coffin will be sealed, and then she'll be sent home to Jordan, where the actual burial will take place," Flemming said.

He went back to finish his postmortem exam, and Louise took a seat to wait for him. The sentimental side of her, which she still struggled with from time to time, really wanted to see them apprehend the culprit before Samra left Denmark. Not because her departure brought up any technical problems; all the evidence had been secured. Louise would simply feel more confident that justice had been done if she could say good-bye to the girl knowing that someone was going to be punished for having robbed her of her young life. Instead Samra was being sent away without their knowing anything at all.

"There. Time for a coffee," she heard Flemming say, pulling her out of her reverie.

His office wasn't particularly big, and there were stacks of papers and folders everywhere. He cleared off a chair for her and stepped out for a moment, returning shortly with two cups and plates bearing a chocolate croissant and a Danish with rum frosting, which he squeezed onto the last available spot on the desk.

"How's it going in Holbæk?"

She shrugged, not up to explaining that they really hadn't gotten anywhere. Instead she told him that she'd tried sea kayaking.

"Sea kayaking?" He sounded just as surprised as she had been when Mik invited her to try it.

She smiled and nodded, breaking off a piece of pastry. "It's amazingly fun," she admitted, one eyebrow shooting up when Flemming set down his cup of coffee and said it was something he'd been wanting to try for ages.

"I've just never gotten around to it, but now I have a good excuse. It would be fun if we went kayaking together next spring."

Louise brushed some crumbs off her blouse.

"Well, I can't promise that I'll be so hooked I'm still doing it then, but if I am, that sounds nice," she laughed.

When they finished the coffee, she stuck the death certificate into her purse and said good-bye with the agreement that they'd go out for a couple of beers once she was back in town.

⚇

"I can't understand how this happened. How could this happen?"

Ibrahim's voice was husky and unclear, but the interpreter translated without adding any emotion to the words.

"You stopped taking care of her."

"Sada is accusing him," the interpreter explained.

Louise had let her bag and jacket drop to the floor when she joined the others back at the police station.

"Of the murder?" Storm asked, interested, leaning over the oval table, where they were all sitting tensely, listening to the previous day's recordings. They hadn't gotten much out of the tapes, but now that the girl's body had been released, her parents were suddenly discussing something that might be related to what had happened.

"I never stopped."

The Mobile Task Force's own interpreter sat listening with concentration before he repeated the words in Danish.

"Why do you even talk to him? Why don't you shut the door on him?"

"He humiliates me. I won't find any peace until he's dead. He's ruined us."

"Who is Ibrahim talking about?" Louise asked.

The interpreter stopped the recording and thought for a moment before shaking his head and saying, "It could be a friend, an acquaintance, someone from the family. I don't know. But it could also be himself. If he killed his daughter and is convicted, I would interpret that as self-reproach."

When he turned the playback on again, they heard deep sobbing and a sentence so drowned out by the sobs they had to play it several times before Fahid was able to tell them what had been said.

"It would have been better if she weren't dead, but alive." Again, Fahid turned it off and looked at them.

"That is a very strong expression he used there," he explained. "He means they might have been able to find a different solution than taking her life."

"Well then, he's admitting it, isn't he?" Skipper exclaimed.

"No, I wouldn't interpret it that way. I would say he's acknowledging that someone is responsible for her death and that he might know who it is. I don't consider it an admission."

"You still don't think they should be questioned about what

they're saying here?" Mik asked, looking at Storm, who shook his head.

"They shouldn't find out we've been listening in on them until we arrest him, if we do. We can use this in court to get the court order extended if we need to, and we can also confront them with the most important sections of the recordings and ask them to explain themselves. We can even compare things they haven't disclosed and false statements up until that point if they don't know we're listening."

It was obvious that Louise's partner did not agree with that plan, but he gave in and continued paying attention as Storm signaled to the interpreter to continue.

Sada's clear voice filled the room. "I told you you shouldn't kill her. She could have gotten married."

He was still crying when he again said something. "I didn't do it. She was my daughter."

"Who did it then? It was your fault."

"There's a very unpleasant atmosphere between the two of them. It is completely obvious that his wife is accusing him, but he is denying it. I think he sounds extremely unhappy," Fahid said once the sequence had finished playing.

"Does he say anything we could charge him with?" Storm asked, not allowing himself to be swayed by the sympathy the interpreter seemed to be feeling for Ibrahim.

"No, quite the contrary. He seems agitated and unhappy."

"He's alluding to a third person, isn't he?" Louise asked, her eyes on the interpreter.

She couldn't tell if Fahid was feeling trapped, as if his loyalties were divided, or if he had really changed his opinion on the father partway through this session. At first, he had seemed like he believed Ibrahim was incriminating himself, but now he was leaning toward believing Ibrahim was profoundly unhappy.

"There's something about this family that isn't right," Skipper said in his calm, deliberate manner. "That story Camilla Lind wrote about the rabbit made that quite obvious."

Her friend had called her one evening after talking to Samra's friend Fatima, who had related an episode that had taken place a month before Samra was killed. One night Samra's parents served their daughter's pet rabbit for dinner, but told her it was chicken. It was only after she'd eaten it that her father asked her to go out to the yard and look in the empty rabbit cage. Camilla's story had taken up the whole front page.

"Yeah, but that doesn't mean they killed her," Fahid objected, eyeing them steadily. "Ibrahim explained that he'd done that to punish Samra, because she'd come home so late one night after visiting her aunt and uncle in Benløse. They'd had a clear agreement that she would be back at a specific time. And yet she didn't get home until several hours later."

"That's quite a severe punishment for a young girl," Mik said, staring at the wall.

According to Fatima, Samra ran straight into the bathroom and threw up until there wasn't anything left in her stomach, and after that she refused to eat, no matter what her mother served.

"Why don't we just charge the family?" Velin asked, looking at Storm in irritation, as if losing faith in his boss's ability to make decisions.

"Because we'll get more out of waiting until we're sure that we have enough to hold them," Storm replied sharply.

The interpreter finished his work, and Louise walked back to her office with Mik with an uncomfortable sense that the atmosphere at work was becoming rather tense. Good thing the weekend was almost here, so they wouldn't all have to spend every minute in such tight quarters for a couple of days.

21

Saturday morning, Louise was on Ahlgade trying to pick out a face cream when someone grabbed her arm and spun her around. Anne Møller said hello with a big smile, and Louise immediately got the sense that Dicta's mother had not heard about her daughter's overindulgences. She also decided that the mother didn't need to hear about it from her.

"Hi," Louise said, smiling back.

"You've practically moved out here to the boondocks for good," Anne joked. Then she asked Louise if she wasn't getting tired of eating at the Station Hotel every night.

"It is starting to get a little old," Louise admitted.

"If you want, you're very welcome to come over and eat with us. Dicta comes home for dinner, even if she goes back over to Liv's afterward. She's starting to do a little better, but of course the whole thing is still a terrible shock to her. As it was to all of us, of course," she hurried to add. She said that she'd seen Storm on TV the evening before and understood that some family matter was behind the killing, not that that made the crime any more understandable, but at least there was no reason to walk around feeling afraid there was some maniac on the loose.

Louise hadn't seen the report, but thought maybe her boss ought to have kept his statement to himself, since he didn't want to detain the suspects yet. She politely declined the dinner invitation.

"I'm afraid I'm getting together with one of my colleagues tonight," she said. "Perhaps we could do it another time?"

"Of course."

"I'm glad to hear that," Louise said, seizing the opportunity to get out of the conversation as an employee walked over to them. She quickly said good-bye to Dicta's mother.

Indian summer. *Wish I knew how long this weather was going to hold out*, Louise thought that afternoon as she biked out to the Rowing Club. It was a week into October and the sun still felt warm. She'd borrowed an old bike from Mik; she was pedaling hard and her pulse was up, her body covered in sweat. She was slightly out of breath as she rode down the gravel path to the club and the Turkish baths.

After the recent class, Mik had convinced her to keep going with Beginners 1 and 2, which were each four hours long. He had also emphasized that she didn't need to try to be the best. She should just be satisfied to learn enough techniques so she felt safe going out paddling on her own.

But it wasn't that easy. From the very beginning, all some of the men could talk about was when they would finally learn to do an Eskimo roll. When the first beginners' course ended, they'd practiced turning around and doing a half roll, and Mik had gotten them all worked up by promising that in the next class he would teach them how to go all the way around. Louise had felt sort of left out, but she had still said "Of course" when he'd asked her earlier in the week if she was ready for Beginners 2. No matter what, it was better than sitting around staring at the walls of her hotel room.

She zipped up her life jacket, tossed her bag, which contained a change of clothes, next to the shed, put on a hat with a visor so the sun wouldn't blind her, and she was ready. There were six of them, two women and four men, and she was intent on ignoring their boyish outbursts and putting the daunting task of learning to roll the kayak all the way around out of her mind.

"I'd rather get soused than learn how to roll a kayak," she'd said when Mik had leaned in over her desk the day before and asked if she was going to give it a try, too, when all the men rolled their boats.

Now she took a couple of deep strokes with the paddle and moved quickly away from the landing platform. The sun glimmered on the water, shrouding Cape Tuse on the other side of the sound in a lovely golden mist, and she felt blissfully calm when her kayak shot out. She lost all sense of time. When Mik got his kayak into the water a couple of minutes later and the lesson was under way, she had put all thoughts of work and murderers behind her and just wanted to follow the others farther out.

She left her bike at the Rowing Club afterward, climbing into the passenger seat of Mik's car and driving out to the farm with him. She was still laughing and he was still complimenting her.

Before the lesson was over—and while the four lumbering men in the class had fooled around with their paddles sticking up in the air and the water sloshing around them because they couldn't succeed in finding the right angle that would get their kayaks to flip all the way around without having to bail out partway—Louise slid up alongside Mik. She had spent the day's training session learning to fall into the water and then right the kayak again on her own, using her paddle and a bilge pump to empty the water out. She had tipped her kayak many times before she started feeling secure that she would be able to do it someday when she was out on her own. Now, without making a face, she tapped him on the shoulder with her paddle. Then she put her weight out to the side and put her paddle into the water and with all her might and the technique he'd just shown the guys, she disappeared underwater and came up again, becoming the first of the students to have successfully completed the eagerly discussed full roll.

At first Mik didn't realize what she'd done, even though she was sitting there in front of him, soaking wet, with a huge grin on her face. It wasn't until the men in the group started catcalling that he exclaimed, "What the hell are you doing? You can't just do a roll like that!" But then he started clapping, too, and smiling at her, impressed and not mentioning what he was probably thinking: that this was probably due more to astoundingly good luck than to her technique.

Louise's heart was still pounding, and she was a tad shaken that it had even occurred to her to do that. She couldn't comprehend how humiliating it would have been if she hadn't made it all the way around. At any rate, she couldn't help but be glad that she could still get it into her head to do things without overthinking them to death.

"So I guess that means you picked the Eskimo roll instead of getting drunk?" Mik said when they were standing around the clubhouse afterward having a soda.

Louise nodded, but still agreed when he suggested they celebrate her Eskimo roll with a beer back at his farm.

They drove out past Strandmølleengen and Holbæk Marina, which was full of pleasure boats. The road narrowed as they continued out toward the golf course and Dragerup, where Mik's red U-shaped farmhouse stood. The roof was thatched, the house freshly whitewashed, and the timber framing had been tarred over that summer. Everything looked like you would expect for a Copenhagen dweller who moves to the countryside and puts his all into realizing the dream of a pastoral idyll. But Mik wasn't from the city; he'd taken over the farm from his parents and fixed it up himself with the help of a couple of friends and the local roof thatcher.

"Do you want to see the puppies?" he asked once they'd gotten out of the car.

Louise followed him to the house, but took a step back when an exuberant wirehaired pointer came running out and started dancing around them until it lost interest and continued around behind the house into the yard. Mik waved for her to follow and then went into the kitchen, where the puppies were sleeping in a big basket.

"They're not always this calm," he said, leaning down and petting the mother, a black Lab, who stood up when they came in.

Louise knelt next to the basket and stuck her hand down to touch the soft puppies, who were beginning to move. A second later they were wriggling. They came tumbling over to curiously sniff her hand and then started nudging it. Mik came over and picked up a puppy for her. She put her cheek down next to it and felt its muzzle against her skin. When it started getting fidgety, she carefully put it back in with the others and stood up.

"Every time I get close to a puppy, I forget I don't want a dog," she said, shaking her head and smiling. Then Mik said that one of the puppies was still for sale.

She followed him as he grabbed two beers from the fridge and they strolled back out into the yard again.

"Shall we sit here?" He gestured to a wooden bench bearing the inscription DAD'S BEER-DRINKING BENCH.

Louise winced to think Mik didn't have enough taste to acquire a nicer bench, but at the same time had to concede that the view couldn't be better. She stood for a second, enjoying the sight of the fields and woods on the other side of the road.

"Don't you ever miss the countryside?" he asked once he'd sat down.

She shook her head and said she probably never would miss it enough to picture herself moving back.

"But every now and then I do need to get out of the city," she admitted, looking at the horses in the corral in the field opposite them.

"Do your folks still live out here?" he asked, watching her as she took a swig of beer.

She nodded and smiled at him. She'd misjudged him. She didn't have to pull every word out of him. In fact, he was the one who was grilling her.

She told him about her parents' place, which was between Roskilde and Holbæk, and said that her brother still lived out there, not in an old farmhouse, but in a house in a new development that didn't have even a smidge of the charm her folks' country home or his farm had.

"Actually, what is the difference between a country home and a farm?" she asked, then volunteered an answer to her own question: "Isn't it mostly that you tend a farm while a country home is mostly just for fun?"

Mik nodded. That pretty much summed up the definition. "How much land do you have here?" she asked him. "Are you growing anything?"

"Almost seventy acres, but I lease it to the farm over there." He nodded toward the large farm on the other side of the narrow road, the one with the horse corral. "They have the machinery and a barn."

Mik brought them another two beers and a blanket Louise could wrap around herself.

"My parents are dead, but I'm sure I told you that," he said after he sat down again.

Louise nodded.

"My mom died this spring, but it's been almost six years since my father died. His heart just stopped one morning while he was out checking on the cows. But if he had to go, I couldn't imagine a more fitting way for him to do it."

Louise watched him as he spoke. He sagged a little and was picking at the label on his beer bottle, but he didn't seem as if he felt any pressure telling her about himself.

"It didn't take more than a few months after my father died for my mom and me to move. She couldn't manage this whole place on her own and I had a small house on Fasanvej in town." He nodded in the direction of Holbæk. "And then I have a sister in Dubai. She moved out there with her husband almost ten years ago and I really doubt they're coming back. The kids go to a European school and she stays home and does her thing, so she wasn't interested in taking over this place."

Louise explained that her parents hadn't bought their country place until she was old enough to start school. Before that, they'd lived in a big apartment in Østerbro. "My mom's a ceramics artist," Louise explained. "She needed more room, a bigger kiln, and space for her potting wheel." She sounded out the words like they were alien to her, making it clear that she had not inherited her mother's creative abilities.

"What does your dad do?" Mik asked curiously.

"He's an ornithologist," she replied, and then quickly elaborated. "He works for the Danish Ornithological Society a couple days a week doing conservation and preservation work, and he edits their journal. He's one of those guys who lives his whole life with a spotting scope around his neck."

Mik laughed out loud, and something boyish came over his face that Louise hadn't seen before. She smiled and waited for him to explain what was so funny.

He shook his head a little before explaining that that was the last thing he would have imagined.

"I pictured him as maybe a detective or a lawyer. How the heck did you end up a cop?" he asked, looking at her with interest.

She gave him a look of mock affront. "Why? Is that so odd?"

"I don't know. With parents with skills and abilities like that, I would have figured some of it would have rubbed off on you." He said it as if she'd been cheated out of something marvelous.

An awkward silence settled between them as she contemplated this. Why had she chosen to join the police?

He interrupted her thoughts. "Would you like an Irish coffee?" he asked quietly. She had the sense he didn't want to interrupt her thoughts.

She nodded absentmindedly, her thoughts locked on her parents. It had never occurred to her that she could have followed in her mother's footsteps. She didn't think she had even a hint of creativity in her, but she had never really put herself to the test to see if that was true.

Mik came back with a tray of mugs, coffee, whipped cream, brown sugar, a bottle of Tullamore, and three large, square candles that were stacked up on the tray, threatening to tip over onto the coffee fixings.

"I grew up with birds," Louise said as he put brown sugar and whiskey into her cup, mixed them together, poured coffee over them, and topped it off with freshly whipped cream. "I got bird posters, bird books, and stuffed birds, while all my friends were getting Barbies and pop-music posters. And my mother walked around in her work clothes all the time, covered in splotches of clay with a towel around her hair. I didn't want to look like that when I grew up."

"Did you rebel?" he asked, handing her the cup.

"Maybe, but that's not how I saw it. I didn't go in a different direction to defy my parents. I just did it because what they did didn't interest me. I went to one of those forest kindergartens in Langelinie as a kid, one of those places where school is held outdoors all day regardless of the weather. I know they chose that because they wanted what was best for me. But I really would have rather gone to a kindergarten where you sat on little chairs and drew or played with puzzles and cleaned up nicely after yourself after each meal, instead of relying on the public restrooms out by the *Little Mermaid* statue and never eating a hot lunch, just sandwiches from our lunch boxes, even in the rain."

Mik listened without interrupting.

"I like there to be some kind of structure, something to grab on to."

They'd finished their drinks and when he offered her another, she was well aware it was time to say no thanks and force herself to be on her way. He'd said she could borrow his bike, since they hadn't brought her loaner bike along from the Rowing Club.

Instead she nodded and held out her cup. She thought about the next morning. How smart was it to show up to work with a hangover? Sure, tomorrow was Sunday, but they were going to meet anyway. On the other hand, hadn't they pretty much been working around the clock for the weeks since the case had been open? They needed to unwind a little.

He stood concentrating, letting the whipped cream slide down onto the warm coffee so carefully that it spread out like a white comforter.

She didn't think. Before she knew it, she was on her feet, still wrapped in the blanket, kissing him. Somewhere in the back of her mind she heard stern warnings that what she was doing was extremely unwise, but she ignored them, letting the blanket fall as he reached around her shoulders and pulled her toward him. She stood up on her toes, pressing her cheek against his, and noticed the short stubble against her skin in the few pauses between their kisses. Nibbling, yearning, hungry, and indulgent.

Where had that come from? she wondered. They still hadn't made eye contact, she didn't dare, couldn't deal with what she'd set in motion, but also didn't want to run away from it.

"Do you think this is wise?" he asked, his mouth against her throat as both of his hands slid up over the skin on her back.

She sought out his mouth again even as she shook her head. It wasn't wise at all, and wasn't she supposed to be the one saying that? It was anything but wise. They shared an office, and they were still going to be sharing it the next day and the day after that. No one knew how long she was going to be in Holbæk. But they had already crossed this line, so no matter what they did it was going to be awkward and totally wrong to see each other at work after this, she thought. And besides, he wasn't her type at all. Not the way he looked, not his interests, not his Dad's Beer-Drinking Bench. All he had going for him was that he hadn't turned his head away when she kissed him.

She released his lips and inhaled in short bursts to calm her breathing.

"Let's stop here," she said, releasing her firm hold on him. Still she allowed herself to be pushed along as he guided her backward, both hands on her hips, away from the Irish coffee toward the house. As they walked slowly so she wouldn't stumble, her eyes bore into his to determine how big a catastrophe this was. What did he think of her? Had she pressured him into this? Did he feel like he couldn't turn her down? How crushing a failure would it be when he said this was all a mistake? That they should have stopped before they even started. He didn't seem like the type to turn down a colleague, so maybe she'd already really overstepped his boundaries. And he had already suggested this wasn't particularly wise. She couldn't read anything from his eyes. They were just blue eyes smiling at her and they didn't seem to be suffering from any kind of crisis of conscience or harassment.

After he settled her onto the sofa and brushed her dark curls away from her face, he carefully pulled her sweater up over her head. After that he removed her blouse, then finally her jeans. He sat there caressing her stomach, letting his fingers glide gently over her body, until his hand settled softly around the back of her head. He leaned over and kissed her. Tenderly and intensely, slowly, the whole way down her body.

"Do you really want to stop?" he asked, once he'd pulled his own shirt over his head and loosened his belt.

Louise shook her head in silence without opening her eyes. No, she did not.

22

The melody was so insistent and the volume so loud, it couldn't be ignored. Louise did a rapid mental check before opening her eyes to be confronted with the mess she'd gotten herself into the night before. They had ended up in his bed after first making love on the sofa, then on the living room floor. She had no sense of when they had collapsed from exhaustion. *Actually, that's not so bad*, she thought.

Mik's cell phone was ringing off the hook and she shook him awake. The worst thing was that at one point he had whispered to her that this seemed like something she had really needed and she had hungrily agreed with him. After which she had really let go and abandoned herself to a level of enjoyment she could scarcely control.

To hell with the fact that she'd whispered a bunch of words she couldn't really recollect now, she thought. What did it matter that she had let him see her like that? Well, maybe that wasn't totally inconsequential. And she wasn't proud of it, either. She couldn't believe she'd sold herself out by admitting that she had needed a man.

That she was understimulated, and that she possessed a level of desire she herself couldn't control once it had been let loose. She had a hard time excusing herself for that.

Mik had the cell phone to his ear and was talking quietly, intensely. He was already out of bed and standing by the dresser, pulling out clothes. Louise could feel him looking at her, but she kept her eyes closed so there was no contact.

"You're going to have to wake up," he whispered, stroking her cheek.

"What time is it?" she mumbled, not wanting to face reality.

"Almost six."

He leaned over and kissed her until she opened her eyes and their eyes met. It wasn't as bad as she had feared. He smiled at her and she focused on his left front tooth, which was missing one small corner. Then he straightened back up and explained that that had been the duty officer down at the station on the phone.

"They just got a nine-one-one call from a woman who found a dead teenage girl in the parking lot behind Nygade," he told her. "That's the street that goes up to your hotel."

Louise was out of bed and on her way to the living room, where her clothes lay in a heap on the floor. He followed her and kept talking as she got dressed.

"They've already cordoned off the area."

He gave her a serious look before he went out to tend to his dogs before they left the house.

"It looks like one side of the girl's head was crushed and she was very badly beaten," he said, walking back into the living room with his car keys in his hand.

Louise cast a quick glance around the living room to see if she'd forgotten anything.

"I'll catch a ride over there and—" she started, but was interrupted when he reminded her that that would make it obvious to everyone else that the two of them had spent the night together.

That hadn't even occurred to her, but she quickly agreed that he was right.

The October morning was still dark and, while he drove around the small turn and back in past Holbæk Marina, she sat next to him speculating.

"How am I going to slip into the hotel if they've cordoned off the area?" she finally asked, suddenly unable to assess the situation.

"I can let you off a little ways away, if you'd like. But I don't mind in the least if the others see us together. I mean, it's not like we did anything illegal."

"We shouldn't arrive together," she said, a tad harshly. "I'll wait over at the station for half an hour before I head over."

He didn't remark on her stern pronouncement, but pulled over to the curb so she could grab her bag from the backseat.

Louise was standing there with her bag with the car door open when she realized this was all too ridiculous.

"I'll just walk in there," she said, blowing him a kiss.

He shook his head. Then he got out, walked around the car, and kissed her good-bye—not a long kiss, but with an intensity that reassured her.

"Talk to you soon," she said, once their lips had parted. "Definitely soon."

He got back in and drove the last four hundred yards past the police station over to Nygade.

23

Louise walked along Jernbanegade in the early morning with her kayaking bag over her shoulder and the feeling that she'd been in a dream for the last eight hours, a dream in which she couldn't completely take responsibility for her actions or vouch for her own conduct. She had pushed the thought of yet another body to the back of her mind and was too tired to think about it until she reached the hotel and the local police and the red-and-white-striped police tape with POLITI printed on it at regular intervals. Then she spotted Storm and Skipper, who were standing under a large streetlight outside the hotel's small outdoor seating area, well dressed, their hair nicely arranged, with their hands in their pockets, looking out over the empty early-morning pedestrian shopping street.

She looked down at herself. She was wearing the same clothes she'd had on the day before, her hair was more tousled than curly, and she had forgotten to bring a hairband that could hold back her dark mane. She quickly ran a hand through it and as she walked the last few yards tried to make herself a smidge presentable. She had one foot on the steps leading up to the hotel's front entrance when Skipper spotted her.

"Good morning, Rick."

She stopped midmotion, turned, and started walking over toward them.

"Good morning," she said, dropping her bag with a thump. Neither her temporary boss nor Skipper looked at it, nor did they comment on her arriving from outside the hotel.

They nodded over toward the police cars, most of them with their lights on, and asked if she'd heard all the commotion.

She shook her head, watching Mik's outline disappear into an alleyway next to the Gyro Hut.

"There's a teenage girl with a crushed skull back there," Skipper said, pointing in the direction in which Mik had disappeared.

"Do we know which teenage girl?" she asked, to get them talking and make it seem like she was on the ball. But she was completely unprepared when Storm turned to her and nodded.

"It's Dicta Møller."

Suddenly her stomach churned. She tasted bitterness as the bile from her stomach shot up into her mouth. But she held it back. She had vomited once before in front of a male colleague, and that was something she preferred never to repeat. She sank, supporting herself against a lamppost.

Fatigue suddenly overwhelmed her. While Louise had been reveling in her own pleasure, Dicta's skull was being smashed in. It seemed wrong.

"I'm going to run upstairs and take a quick shower," she said. "I'll be down in ten minutes."

She didn't wait for a response, already on her way up to her room.

What the hell is going on here? she thought, feeling for the first time in a long time like she didn't have a handle on squat.

Pretty, sweet young Dicta, who should have been a star, was now a victim. And the thought that this was how she was finally going to get her picture in the paper was unbearable, Louise thought sadly as she wrapped up her shower with an ice-cold rinse and hurriedly threw on her clothes.

The ambulance was still there. Storm and Skipper had moved over to the parking lot, where they were now standing with Søren Velin and the ambulance paramedic, who had established that Dicta was dead. Her old partner nodded at her somberly as she reached them.

"This is nasty," Velin said. He pulled her a little way away from where the body was located as he explained that a woman had found it when she was bringing some clothes over to the Salvation Army donation bin after getting off the night shift at the hospital. The area was still illuminated by a couple of big, portable spotlights.

Louise could just make out Dicta, lying at the edge of the parking lot. The lot was mostly empty. Quickly surveying the area, Louise counted eleven cars. At the far side, out by the ring road at the end of the lot where Dicta was lying, was a large building that housed Nordtank Shipping. And Lindevej ran between the ring road and the parking lot, but that was quite a small street. At the perimeter of the parking lot down by the main street there was a small service station. And out by Nygade was the back of the Gyro Hut. Louise spotted Dean, and noted that the only person she hadn't seen yet out here was Bengtsen.

Søren Velin said that one side of Dicta's cranium had been crushed. He spoke so softly that Louise had to strain to hear the words. Maybe he was trying to spare her or himself a little of the gruesomeness of what had happened.

"She obviously took a lot of blows to the face and definitely also to the body," he said, explaining that her clothes were covered in blood. The local police had locked down the scene when they arrived and now everyone was just waiting for the crime scene technicians and the coroner, who were on their way.

"But it looks ghastly."

She stared at him, astonished. He didn't usually react like that, and if he was putting it that way, she had no doubt he meant it. "What did you do with Bengtsen?" she asked after a brief pause.

"He went to the hospital with the woman who found the body. He was the first one here and since she didn't have anyone who could go and stay with her, he did it. He'll stay with her until she calms down."

Louise stood there for a bit before she started walking over to the body of the girl whose secrets she knew. She sank down into a squat when she reached her and sat there for a bit looking at the dead figure. Just as Søren Velin had said, the right side of her face was crushed, and her long blond hair was stuck in the thick bloodstain that radiated from her head like a dark shadow. A little farther away on the asphalt lay a yellow hairband tinged red with blood. Louise rested her elbows on her knees and supported her face in her hands. Under her jacket Dicta was wearing a small, yellow top. She had gotten dressed up before she'd left her house to visit Liv. Louise felt a jab of pain in her chest as she stood back up to return to the others.

Camilla had arrived in Holbæk late Saturday night. She had decided to drop the whole thing after her run-in with Terkel, but in the end her stubbornness had compelled her to head back out to see if she could make any progress on the story. Even if it robbed her of her Sunday, it would be a victory after their spat if she came home with something none of the other journalists had. She had called Louise from the road. Even before Camilla left Copenhagen she was looking forward to meeting Louise at Bryghuset and chatting for a while over a beer, but Louise's cell phone just kept going to voice mail. Camilla gave up around midnight.

Then early that morning the sirens from the first responders' vehicles sliced through the walls of her room at the Station Hotel with their high-pitched howl. She had strolled out toward the parking lot to check, but they'd cordoned off the area around the body; with all the police tape, she couldn't get close enough to see anything, so she called the desk officer at the station to find out what had happened. When he wouldn't tell her anything, she called Storm directly.

She hadn't gotten more than the name out of him, but that had been enough to start with. She had promised to keep it to herself until the girl's parents had been notified. Camilla had known whom he was talking about right away. In the days following Samra's death, she had interviewed Dicta along with a couple of other girls from Samra's class. When she finished talking to Storm, she went back to the hotel to dig out her notes from her conversation with the girl, and after that, she went down to the restaurant and got the cook to make her a little breakfast. She picked up a copy of *Ekstra Bladet* that the cook had sitting next to the stove along with a pot of coffee. She tried to reach Louise again, but her cell was still going straight to voice mail, so Camilla went back out to the restaurant with her breakfast to wait until there was some news from the police.

She saw the picture in the paper, read the brief text, and then leaped up, dropping everything. Her coffee sloshed onto the tablecloth and the bread basket tumbled onto the floor.

With the paper tucked under her arm, she ran out onto the street and over to the parking lot. Storm and Skipper were standing there talking, but she ran right past them, and continued to where Velin stood to ask about Louise. Just then she spotted her friend coming over from the other end of the parking lot, where the body was. Her face was blank and her eyes trained on the ground. Camilla ran over to her, holding out the paper.

"You have to see this," she called from a distance.

Louise looked up and was about to protest, but Camilla ignored her friend's rebuff and pulled her over to a walkway between the walls of two buildings, so they were away from the others. Camilla unfolded *Ekstra Bladet*, turned to page nine, and pointed to a large color photo of an almost naked Dicta Møller.

"This is today's paper," Camilla said, waiting for a reaction. Dicta's long blond hair was falling down over her breasts.

Her body was turned slightly with her head tilted a tad, and one hip pushed forward in a diminutive white crocheted bikini, which was tied together by a thin string, not leaving much to the imagination.

Louise slowly reached for the newspaper. "Well, she doesn't look like that anymore," she said in a subdued tone after having studied the picture.

"How does she look?" Camilla quickly seized the opening her friend had given her.

Louise stood there for a moment, appearing to consider whether she could tell Camilla anything.

"One whole side of her head is caved in after multiple, powerful blows," Louise finally said. "I would imagine that most of her cranium is crushed, and her face is one big, bloody pulp."

Camilla put her arm around Louise and held her. She knew Louise had spent a fair amount of time with the girl and that she must be working hard now to contain her emotions so they didn't overwhelm her. Camilla gave her shoulder a squeeze, and Louise folded up the paper and gave her a little smile.

"Thanks for showing me that," she said, preparing to go join Storm and Skipper.

"I know the photographer who took this picture," Camilla called after Louise. "He's a disagreeable chap. Sad that she fell into his clutches."

Louise stopped and came back over. "Disagreeable in what way?" she asked.

"Not in a way that I think would lead him to crush a girl's skull, but certainly a girl's heart. I always sort of got the sense he was ambitious, and there've been a few stories going around about him that haven't cast him in a favorable light." Camilla explained that some stories had been about violent behavior. "Although not against the girls, as far as I know," she hurried to add, before saying that, on the other hand, there had been rumblings about how he couldn't keep his hands off the young girls who came to his studio. "But that's not to say—well, I don't know how much is gossip and how much is truth. He's never been convicted of anything as far as I know and of course he's quite active professionally. So it could well be that he just has a bad reputation," Camilla concluded, so she couldn't be accused of having contributed to spreading the rumors.

"Interesting," Louise said. Then she said that she had just been asked to drive out and inform Dicta's parents.

Camilla stood and watched her as she walked away with the newspaper under her arm.

24

Louise stopped twenty yards from the Møller family's driveway. She had driven two wheels up onto the sidewalk and was sitting in the cruiser with her phone pressed to her ear. Before she'd left, she had told Storm about *Ekstra Bladet* and shown him the picture. Now he was calling her on her cell to have her tell Dicta's parents about it.

"Oh, no," she exclaimed. "I don't know if I can make myself do that."

"It's going to be hard to keep it hidden," Storm quickly retorted. He was right. "Maybe you can ask them how much they knew about her free time, while you're discussing it with them," he suggested.

"We'll see," Louise replied curtly, still not having the faintest desire to bring it up.

She turned her phone off and drove the last little bit to the driveway. It was only a few minutes before eight in the morning, but there were no cars in the garage and the house looked empty.

Louise was suddenly afraid that it might be hard to find them. They could have left early to go to a dog show.

The police usually sent two people to inform a family so that one officer wasn't alone if the parents had a violent response to the shock. In this case, Louise had opted to talk to them by herself because they already knew her; she had arranged with Storm that he would keep one officer ready to assist her, should that be necessary.

The dogs out back started howling as Louise walked up to the front door and held her finger on the bell for a long, sustained ring. She pushed the button again and heard the chime spreading through the house. She did not hear the gate in the wall to the yard opening, so she jumped when Dicta's mother was suddenly standing in front of her with a cheerful morning greeting and a large bowl in her hand.

"I was just out with the dogs. I usually run them early in the morning, and then we do our training later," she said, holding out the bowl as if that explained why she had it.

Louise nodded and said that she'd come to speak to the woman and her husband.

Anne Møller gave her a questioning look, but there was no trace of worry on her face.

"There's coffee made. Henrik just popped out to the bakery." She opened the door and held the dog. "But Dicta isn't here," she added, still leaning over Charlie with a grip on his collar. "She's spending the night at Liv's."

Anne set coffee cups out on the table, and it wasn't until they were sitting across from each other that a shadow came over her face.

"You didn't come over to talk to Dicta, did you?" she asked, to encourage Louise to begin.

The coffee in the cup was steaming and the milk had turned it a creamy, golden color.

"I would really like to speak to both you and your husband. How about if we just wait for him?"

Now that that was said, the worry was more palpable. Louise sat up when she heard the car door shut. A second later Henrik Møller was standing in the doorway, astonished to see her.

"You're here early," he said, walking over to shake her hand. Dicta's mother stayed in her chair, following her husband with her eyes, obviously apprehensive.

Henrik Møller tossed a bag of breakfast rolls and the newspaper onto the kitchen table, then walked over and took a seat next to his wife, as if he was expecting that this would all be wrapped up quickly so they could return to their quiet Sunday-morning routine.

Louise took a deep breath and jumped in.

"Early this morning Dicta was found in a parking lot behind Nygade," she said slowly. "I am very sorry to be the bearer of such terrible news. Your daughter is dead, and there is no doubt that she was murdered."

Both parents sat in shock, still looking at her with expectant expressions. It took a few more seconds for the news to hit them.

"Dead. Murdered?" Anne Møller stammered, not seeming to understand how this had anything to do with her.

"How can she be dead?" Henrik Møller asked, his voice extremely calm. "What happened?"

Louise started to explain. "She sustained a number of powerful blows to the head." She paused to allow the parents a chance to respond further.

Dicta's mother sat completely still, nodding automatically.

Louise doubted she could even hear what was being said. She turned to look at the father.

"Extremely powerful blows," Louise emphasized, hoping he wouldn't ask her to go into more detail.

"My darling little Dicta," Anne Møller croaked hoarsely. She collapsed into tears.

"Did she die quickly?" Henrik Møller asked, reaching out to hold his wife's hand.

They always wanted to know the same thing. All parents wanted to be reassured that their children had died without pain and without fear.

"Is that what the big emergency response in town was for this morning?" he continued. His voice was no longer in control and his eyes shone. "They were talking about it at the bakery."

Louise nodded and told them about the woman who had gone down early that morning to drop off some clothes in the Salvation Army bin.

"We don't know exactly what time the attack happened," Louise acknowledged, explaining that it could have been anytime between midnight and when she was found a little before six. "We have one witness who works at the Gyro Hut, who says that Dicta definitely wasn't there when he got into his car last night. We got hold of him early this morning and he's the only one we've talked to so far who was at the location so late. The owner of the gyro place lives upstairs from his business and contacted his employees when my colleagues were looking for witnesses."

"What was she doing out so late? She was supposed to be staying at Liv's," her mother cried.

Her husband lit a cigarette and inhaled deeply.

"So, Dicta was planning to spend the night at Liv's last night," Louise repeated. "What else did she do yesterday?"

"She was out most of the afternoon," Anne replied mechanically. "She left as soon as we were done with lunch. I went out to look at a new dog, and after that I took my car over to the shop. They're going to do a tune-up on it Monday morning. When Dicta came home, we ate dinner and then she went over to Liv's."

Anne's voice was monotone, as if she were simply reading from a report. As if she weren't talking about her daughter.

"I drove out to the golf course after lunch, along with Anne. Dicta walked," Henrik Møller explained, "and I didn't get home until evening."

Suddenly, with a heartrending cry, Anne leaped up from her chair so fiercely that it tipped over backward.

"No, no, no." Her shrieks seared into Louise's skin.

Henrik was at his wife's side in an instant, pulling her to him. He started rocking her soothingly back and forth, like a child. He seemed composed, directing all his attention at her. He tenderly stroked her hair, and Louise left them alone until Dicta's mother had calmed down a bit.

Henrik moved his chair next to his wife's so he could sit and hold her while they kept talking.

Quiet settled over the room. Anne looked at Louise, her face streaked with tears, her head resting limply against her husband's shoulder, as if all the energy had drained from her body. Only small, almost imperceptible tremors ran through her.

Louise felt the knot in her stomach and turned her attention to Henrik.

"Did you talk about anything before she went over to Liv's?" Louise continued, aware of how awkward it was to ignore the mother's agonizing pain.

"I think she was talking about the two of them going to the movies," Anne whispered with her eyes closed.

There were good reasons for and against telling them about the *Ekstra Bladet* photo, Louise thought. She almost couldn't bear to do it because she was pretty sure they weren't aware of their daughter's Copenhagen adventure. On the other hand, it would be worse if they didn't know about it and happened to hear from somewhere else that a photo of their daughter posing practically naked had appeared in the paper the same day she was found murdered.

Maybe they already know, Louise thought, allowing a third option.

Giving herself no more time to come up with excuses, she just asked flat-out if they knew Dicta was that day's page-nine girl, and if they knew anything about the Copenhagen photographer who had taken the picture of her.

The silence in the kitchen was deafening. Finally, Henrik spoke.

"Let's see it," he said, and it didn't sound as if it surprised him.

"You knew the pictures had been taken?" Louise asked, startled at having misjudged him.

"Well, there's knowing and then there's knowing...She didn't tell me, but I definitely figured she was up to something we weren't involved in," he said.

"What sort of nonsense is this?" Dicta's mother exclaimed. "She wasn't involved in anything we didn't know about. She wasn't like that."

She began to choke up, but Henrik's vehement response stopped her crying. "If you didn't know anything about this photo in *Ekstra Bladet*, then she must have been hiding something from us."

Louise cringed. Suddenly she found herself in the middle of a much-too-private conversation.

Henrik's wife didn't react, didn't even look at him, but sank deep into her own thoughts until she quietly spoke again, asking, "Why that newspaper? Why that kind of picture?"

"You knew that she wanted to be a model, right?" Louise asked.

"Don't all young girls?" Henrik responded. "I don't think she dreamed about it more than many other girls her age."

"But unlike many others, she managed to get in touch with a photographer here in town," Louise continued. "And she had been used as a model for a couple of local stores."

The girl's mother nodded and said that she was well aware of her daughter's dream, and that they had also talked about how that was all right as long as they were proper pictures, and it didn't get in the way of her schoolwork.

"I met Michael Mogensen and saw the pictures he's taken of her. She's a beautiful girl," Dicta's father said, sounding a tad proud. "Do you think this was the same person who killed Samra?" he continued, staring out the kitchen window and scratching Charlie behind the ear.

Louise shrugged and responded that she could easily understand where he was coming from, but the way things looked, that didn't seem to make sense.

"There's nothing similar about the two deaths, so it's hard to connect them. Samra's death was carefully planned, while your daughter's murder looks like an impulsive act. In terms of profiling the culprit, each of those things pulls the investigation in a different direction," she explained. "But of course, that's something we'll look into."

"Can I see her?" Anne suddenly asked. "I would like to see my daughter as soon as possible."

"I'm not sure that's a good idea," Louise said softly. "It might be better for you to remember Dicta the way she looked the last time you were with her."

"Will there be an autopsy?" Henrik interjected, and Anne squeezed her eyes shut tight.

Louise nodded. "I'm assuming that it will take place later today," she said.

It was as if picturing that happening triggered something in Henrik. He bent his head, supporting his forehead in one hand, and crumpled over the table.

25

Louise had just returned from Dicta's parents' house and was sitting in her office with a cup of tea when Mik came in and shut the door behind him. On his way over to his desk, he leaned over and kissed her on the forehead.

"What a morning," he said, sitting down behind his computer. Louise didn't know what to think about the intimacy that suddenly existed between them. It was unavoidable, but she didn't like it and it could easily get messy, she thought. Still, she smiled at him.

"We have to talk about what happened last night," she said after looking at him for a minute. Normally she did not do things that were rash and poorly thought out. The last twelve hours she'd done nothing but.

He looked at her and smiled. "Didn't you think it was nice?" he asked in a teasing tone, which made her wince. "We don't need to make a major deal out of it," he added, beating her to the punch.

"Obviously it wasn't particularly smart. But now it's happened, and I had a lovely night."

"We share an office!" Louise exclaimed, irritated at his relaxed attitude.

He nodded. "I still think it was lovely, and I promise I can control myself."

Louise couldn't help but smile. He had just kissed her, but apparently that didn't count, she thought, shaking her head. "Of course we can control ourselves, but it never should have happened, and I know it's my fault," she said emphatically. "But promise me anyway that we'll keep this just between the two of us."

He grinned and Louise hid her head behind her hands, suddenly overwhelmed by a wave of fatigue that she had suppressed while she was with Dicta's parents. Now it had come back in full force. The few hours of sleep had made her sensitive to the cold, and her body was weak and tender from the unfamiliar amount of lovemaking it had all of a sudden been subjected to.

She glanced over at him, not feeling very proud of the situation. And now of all times, when she had finally gained some autonomy, she thought. Something for which she had actually been longing for many years, but hadn't gotten around to doing anything about. She sat for a bit lost in her thoughts until she suddenly heard Camilla's voice in the back of her mind: *Now is the time to hook up with a few lovers. Lovers are so liberating; there's no pressure of having them around permanently.*

Louise smiled down at her clasped hands and thought, Well, *that* was what Mik was—a lover. She just wasn't used to that. What were you supposed to do with them after you'd made love? Where did you stash them after you were done with them, and how did you get them back out again? Or did you just scrap them all from time to time?

She pushed her hair back and looked over at him. "I'm tired, but it was nice," she said, meaning that sincerely. "Still, I wish we'd managed to sleep a little more. Especially to face a day like today."

Louise thought about Dicta and pictured the girl. "How did it go at her parents' place?" Mik asked.

She told him how Anne and Henrik Møller had reacted and that they really wanted to see their daughter if possible.

"The message from the pathology lab was that they were going to do the autopsy this afternoon, and we're supposed to be there."

Louise couldn't bear to think about the autopsy or the new investigation that was just starting up. She stood up to go get more coffee and asked if he wanted any.

"I'll come with you and find out if there's anything new. We've gotten in touch with a bunch of people who work close to the parking lot, but I think we'd better take a drive out and see that friend Dicta was supposed to spend the night with," Mik said.

Storm and Bengtsen were sitting with Ruth in the command room with steaming coffees in front of them when Louise and Mik walked in with their empty mugs.

"We just got her cell phone back from the tech guys," Storm said once they'd sat down. He pushed the phone across the table and asked Louise and Mik to read the last set of text messages in Dicta's inbox.

Louise pulled her chair close to Mik's and they both leaned over to read.

"They must have been sent while she was with Liv," Louise commented when she saw the time.

"We'll drive over there and talk to her before we head to Copenhagen," Mik added and received a nod before Storm continued.

"Velin is working on printing out all the phone info so we can see which towers it was routed through for the last few days," he said.

"This number doesn't have a name entered, but it belongs to Tue Sunds, the girl's photographer," Bengtsen said. Louise had already figured that out after having read the first of the messages, which said, "Unfortunately, I have to cancel for this evening."

Louise reached over and took the phone out of Mik's hand and scrolled down to the next message, the second that had come from Tue Sunds within a short time window.

"Yes, of course, you mean something, but not in that way. Please keep yourself away from me."

She moved to the next one.

"No, we can't meet tomorrow, either. I never promised anything. You're done; history. Quit bugging me."

As if she were a child he had brought to a candy store and not a young, naive woman.

"Don't threaten me and quit coming here, or things might get uncomfortable for you."

That was the last one, and it was received a little after ten thirty. Louise didn't even want to look when Mik switched over to the sent messages. She couldn't bear to see how Dicta had begged to try to avoid Tue's rejection.

What a pig, Louise thought, as she drained her cup and got up to accompany Mik on a visit to Liv, the last person Dicta was known to have seen.

Louise hardly recognized Liv without the thick, black eye makeup and the black clothes. Her hair was still black, but she was wearing totally normal clothes, and there was nothing provocative or rebellious about her as she stood there at the front door and let them in. She'd clearly heard what had happened and had been crying, and she certainly wasn't done yet. They promised her parents they would make it quick and followed the girl into the dining room, which was dominated by a large window with a panoramic view of the yard. They were looking for simple, straightforward answers. What time had Dicta left Liv's place Saturday night, and where had she been going?

Liv reported that Dicta hadn't left until a little after eleven, although she'd said earlier that she would be leaving around eight thirty because she was supposed to meet up with her photographer. Liv had assumed she meant Michael Mogensen, but she hadn't asked about it because she was mad that Dicta had used her as an excuse to go out without her parents' permission.

Liv said they'd watched a little TV, but that Dicta had seemed distracted and kept looking at her cell phone and sending text messages most of the night and when she finally left, she seemed more depressed than when she'd arrived.

They thanked Liv, and Louise said that they might need to come back and talk to her again.

Liv nodded and watched as Mik pulled away from the curb and turned the car onto the suburban street.

"It's hardly even worth discussing it with you," Camilla snapped into her phone so gruffly that people at the other tables in the café looked at her. "You're so goddamn judgmental, you've got me wondering if I can even keep working for your newspaper."

She would never have dared talk to her boss this way if he hadn't stepped on her toes by trashing her articles on Sada. He had exposed an unseemly side of himself, and she knew he would go to great lengths to cover it up.

"I completely agree that it's the same as admitting we were wrong," she continued, lowering her voice. "But we *were* wrong, and right now there is no indication that the al-Abd family killed their own daughter in some kind of honor killing. Quite the contrary; it would appear that there's a murderer on the loose in town."

She listened patiently while Terkel Høyer spoke.

"I can't keep smearing the family in the absence of any new information to point in their direction," she repeated into her phone. "There must be a reason the police haven't arrested the Jordanian girl's father yet."

Her editor kept insisting that they had to keep going with their angle so they didn't suddenly start working against their own stories.

"Well, now. You were the one who slanted the story so hard from the beginning," Camilla said again when he started blaming her for having stuck to such a hard line in the articles she'd written from Holbæk. She listened for a bit and then sighed tiredly. "If you print the two articles in the paper tomorrow and refrain from linking them to the killing of Dicta, then you will already have changed the tone, so the paper's stance isn't so severe."

Camilla could picture Terkel. It wouldn't be easy for him to do, but he could see she was right.

"I'm planning to stay in Holbæk for the rest of the day," she said, "but it might be a good idea to get someone to look into that photographer who took the pictures of Dicta for *Ekstra Bladet*. I know the police are interested in him."

Camilla didn't have to pick her son up from soccer until six, so she had plenty of time before she had to drive back to Copenhagen. Markus was playing in a tournament, so he wouldn't be done until five thirty. She had only tried once to be there, ready at the doorway when the flock returned home, sweaty and in high spirits in their oversize soccer jerseys with the team logo on the front and their own last names on the back, and her effort had not been well received. First, they'd had to eat a few pieces of crispbread slathered in Nutella and hold their postgame strategy meeting so they were ready for the next game. She either had to wait while they did that or come back half an hour later.

She called Louise in the hope of luring her out for a cup of coffee, although she figured Louise wouldn't take her up on it now that there had been another murder.

"A quick one," Louise said. "I have to go in and observe the autopsy in two hours and I could definitely use a pick-me-up before that."

Surprised that it hadn't taken more convincing, Camilla hung up and hurried to the café farther down the main street.

"You look like hell," she exclaimed when she spotted Louise. Louise yawned and nodded as Camilla suggested a latte and some water.

"Didn't you get any sleep last night?" Camilla asked, concerned. "What time was Dicta found?"

Before the coffee had even arrived at the table, Louise was filling Camilla in on her evening, the words pouring out in one long stream. Louise was just getting to her visit to Mik's farm when Camilla got up to order them some more drinks.

"With him? Really?" Camilla asked, incredulous. "He's pretty much as close to the opposite of Peter as you can get, if that's what you were going for. The man wears Wranglers, for Christ's sake!"

"How do you know that?"

"I notice that kind of thing," Camilla said with a grin. "He also wears police-issue Ecco shoes."

"Henning wore sandals," Louise reminded her.

Camilla's eyes sank down to the marble top of the café table.

Yes, he'd been wearing sandals—worse yet, with socks—the first time she met him, but she'd fallen for him anyway.

She looked up and smiled at Louise. "Well, are you going to see him again?"

"I don't see any way around it. We work together. There's no way I can avoid seeing him," Louise said.

"Oh, my God, that is by no means worse than someone screwing a colleague at a Christmas party. Life goes on," Camilla comforted her, knowing full well that Louise didn't belong in that category. "If it didn't mean anything other than a bit of fun, well then, it's already over. Was he good to you?"

Louise smiled and nodded. "He was very good, really sweet, and I can't remember it ever being like that before. But it felt so strange. That's the part I'm not crazy about."

"Then I suppose you'll just have to do it again, so it starts to feel more familiar." Camilla nudged her friend and laughed.

"No thanks. I think that was enough," Louise said. "I'm not sure he thought it was a particularly good idea, either, although he may be handling it a bit better."

"You mean that maybe you seduced him against his wishes?" Camilla teased.

"You could say that." Louise grinned sheepishly and Camilla smiled at her. In Camilla's mind it didn't really matter what Louise needed to do to shake off Peter's shadow. Which made her think of Henning, which made her heart hurt. If anyone was stuck on a relationship that was over, it was clearly her, and she just couldn't see any light at the end of that tunnel.

They paid and Camilla grew serious again. "What do you have on the new case?" she asked before they parted ways.

Louise considered her question, as if deciding whether it was okay to answer, finally sharing that they would bring the Copenhagen photographer in for questioning.

"We don't have anything, but now we have to see what the autopsy shows," Louise said, checking her watch. "It appears that there may be something to the rumors you told me about this morning." She stepped out onto the sidewalk and set off toward the police station.

Camilla stood there a minute watching her go before pulling out her phone and calling Terkel Høyer again.

"You should work the Tue angle, hard. He had something going with the girl," Camilla said succinctly. Then she headed back into the café and ordered a glass of organic Søbogaard fruit juice while she tried to get her thoughts in order. She wanted to write a story for the next day's paper with quotes from several of Dicta's classmates and a summary of the mood in the town. Then, once her censored articles ran, she would contact Sada again and ask about her reaction to the murder of her daughter's friend.

26

Louise felt like the day would never end. It was late afternoon, and she and Mik had just arrived at the morgue. She'd had her eyes closed most of the way there in the car, thinking how typical it was that on the one day she didn't show up to work perky and well rested, all hell broke loose. Her father had once told her something that had never been more true: If you're up to partying all night, then you darn well ought to be up to doing your job the next day!

Åse was already there, and Flemming Larsen was ready when they walked into the autopsy room. It was the same setup as before, aside from the fact that it was now Dicta's beaten, ill-treated body lying on the table waiting to be examined in minute detail by professional eyes and hands. Louise took a couple of deep breaths. Her hand brushed against Mik's as she walked past him to lean up against the wall while Flemming prepped. A strip of images from the CT scan of Dicta's skull was hanging in front of a large light box to the left of the door.

"Can you tell what happened?" she asked, looking at Flemming.

He walked over and stood next to the light box, pointing up at the first picture.

"It is evident that she sustained several severe blows to the left side of the head—there are many bone fragments. The advantage of a CT scan, in a case where the injuries are as severe as these, is that we can see the lesions inside the skull. When I open it up later, most of her cranium will just fall apart, which can make it hard to tell how the blows impacted," Flemming explained, turning to start securing Dicta's bloody clothes. After that, every inch of her naked body was meticulously examined for particles. Several times, Åse leaned over and dabbed a piece of tape against her bare skin in the hope of removing some evidence, and Flemming used Q-tips to search for anything that could be used for a DNA analysis. Meanwhile, Louise leaned against the wall, following along, prepared to work all night if that would bring them a step closer to whoever was responsible for this crime.

"There are fresh abrasions and subdermal hematomas on the chest." Flemming pointed to the large, dark splotches scattered above and below the girl's breasts. Then he leaned over and drew the big, round operating lamp farther down Dicta's body.

"That looks like maybe a footprint," he said, making room for Åse, who moved in with her camera. "I think she was kicked after she fell down."

Rage, Louise thought, everything she saw in front of her radiated unleashed rage.

Flemming carefully used his hands to examine Dicta's head injuries before walking over to the cabinet at the end of the room to retrieve a set of electric hair clippers, which he plugged in and used to start shaving the left side of the girl's head.

Louise closed her eyes for a second. It was almost unbearable to see those long blond locks, Dicta's pride and vanity, stripped away from her, leaving her bald and naked.

"Let's see how the skin looks," Flemming said as he switched off the clippers, long tufts of light-blond hair strewn in heaps on the floor. "She was severely beaten," he said, confirming that the whole left side of her cranium was caved in.

Åse took her pictures and said it looked like there were more contusions.

She made room for Flemming, who leaned over Dicta's head and studied it in detail. He straightened up and said, "I'd say we're dealing with a pattern injury here."

"What do you mean?" Louise asked.

Flemming pulled the lamp closer and beckoned Louise forward.

"Can you see those marks there? They appear to be identical. She was struck multiple times with a blunt object, which seems to have a distinctive appearance. It has two rounded protrusions spaced an inch and a quarter apart."

"Do you have any guess what it might be?" Louise asked.

Flemming shook his head. "Nothing other than the fact that it's heavy and if you found the object of interest, I could easily tell you if it was the one."

"Well then, that's what I'll try to do," she said, smiling at him. "What about the cause of death?"

He took a breath.

"Dicta Møller asphyxiated on the blood from the severe cranial lesions. It ran down into her throat as she lay unconscious in the parking lot."

Images from the crime scene swam before her eyes. She forced herself not to react, not to think about how long Dicta had lain dying in the parking lot, alone. Louise took a seat on a stool by the wall while Flemming completed the exam. She didn't get up until Mik put away his notes. Then she followed him down to the car in silence.

⚹

Louise didn't get back to the hotel until around 8 p.m. Before she went up to her room, she stopped in the restaurant to order a little food she could bring upstairs with her. When she and Mik had returned from Copenhagen an hour earlier, the others were already eating, but she had declined the invitation to join them. The image of Dicta was still too vivid.

Hunger had eventually won out and now she made her way up the stairs, balancing a brown wooden tray with a hamburger patty, boiled potatoes, and all the fixings.

It was ten past three when she woke up with the tray on her stomach and the TV on. It was a miracle that the gravy and potatoes hadn't tumbled onto the bed. She went and brushed her teeth before climbing into bed again to sleep for the few hours left before the alarm clock would ring at six thirty.

27

They'd set aside the next morning to question the photographer Tue Sunds at the Holbæk Police Station. The plan was for Louise and Mik to pick him up in Copenhagen at eight and bring him out to the provinces. When Louise opened her eyes that morning, she fantasized for a minute about calling first just to make sure Tue would be home, but she knew that idea was out of the question. It was better if they caught him unawares. So she swung her legs out of bed and set her feet on the rough hotel carpet.

She quickly made herself a cup of Nescafé, and then she was ready to meet her partner. They had agreed that he would pick her up in front of the hotel at seven.

As Louise stood outside in the cold October morning air, she realized she had a couple of butterflies fluttering in her stomach. The drive to Copenhagen was going to be long, and she and Mik would be alone together in the car the whole way. The day before, Louise had dozed on and off, but today the silence in the car would be so oppressive there would be no way to keep it from feeling a little awkward, she thought, pacing a little to stay warm. The train station across the street was already in full swing. The waiting taxis had nothing to do, but the town's commuters were busy trying to make their morning trains into the city.

She waved at him when he pulled over into the loading zone in front of the hotel, coming to a stop right next to the curb in front of her.

He had brought freshly buttered morning rolls with a Thermos of coffee. The milk was in a little Tupperware pitcher, and she smiled at him when he told her to help herself. She hoped that he had inherited the pitcher from his mother. There was just no way she was going to have a thing with a man who bought himself Tupperware products, she thought, ruefully acknowledging that she might already have done precisely that.

"How thoughtful. Did you get up early?" Louise asked. By the time she had poured coffee for both of them, Mik was already heading down Roskildevej toward the highway at a decent pace. "Yeah, you could say that," he said with a yawn, explaining that one of the puppies had been having stomach trouble all night and had made a mess of the kitchen.

"It's unbelievable what all can fit into such a small tummy," he said. "But the little guy was whimpering so much that in the end I had to call the vet."

Louise looked at him with concern and offered to drive. That made it two nights in a row he hadn't gotten more than a couple of hours of sleep. But he shook his head, saying he was fine.

"How's the puppy now? Is he doing any better?" It was hard not to be concerned about the little fur ball.

"He was sleeping when I left," Mik said and added that he'd enlisted his neighbor, who would look after things until he got home.

After all that, he'd still managed to bring coffee and rolls for them. Louise smiled at him, gradually starting to relax.

※

It was five minutes to eight when they rang the doorbell of Tue Sunds's large penthouse apartment, unsurprisingly located in the heart of an exclusive part of the inner city, right up under the roof of an old red building on Grønnegade. It was a combination apartment and photo studio, as far as Louise understood from Dicta's description the night she'd found her in front of Holbæk Station.

They had to ring the buzzer several times before the photographer came and opened the door, barefoot and wearing a bathrobe. They'd obviously caught him in bed, and Louise had the fleeting thought that now she would be meeting whatever new young model had taken Dicta's place.

"Tue Sunds?" Mik asked.

The photographer nodded.

"We're from the Unit One Mobile Task Force," Louise continued, trying hard to be polite. "We're working on a serious murder case. Would you mind coming back to the station with us for questioning?"

Sunds took a step back and ran his fingers through his hair. "Yes, I would mind. Now just isn't a good time," he responded, shaking his head a little. "Can't do it. I've got appointments all day."

"Would it be possible to move the appointments to another day?" Louise continued, in the same polite tone, avoiding looking at Mik.

"No, it's not something you can just rebook," he said with a touch of condescension and amazement that she could even imagine his being a man with appointments that could just be changed at a moment's notice.

Now Mik took over. "Yes, well, let me phrase it this way. If you don't accompany us of your own free will, we will be forced to place you under arrest."

Louise looked at her partner. There was quite a contrast between the cheerful, considerate side of him that she had begun to get to know—the way he treated the high school teacher, herself, and, for that matter, his dogs—and the way he dealt with people professionally in situations like this.

"Then you'll have to arrest me," the photographer responded provocatively.

"This pertains to Dicta Møller, who was found murdered in a parking lot in Holbæk yesterday morning," Louise said. She hoped that some transparency would make him realize how serious the situation was. "We know you knew her, and that you were supposed to get together Saturday night, but that you canceled your rendezvous."

He seemed puzzled about how she knew this, but didn't ask. He pulled his bathrobe tighter, like a coat.

"Dicta?" he said.

"You know the person we're talking about?" Mik asked.

The photographer responded with a nod and confirmed that he knew the girl, but said he did not know she'd been murdered. He also confirmed that he had canceled a meeting with her, but did not provide any more details.

"It can hardly have escaped your notice that she died," Louise interjected. "She is one of your models, her face was in all the news broadcasts last night, and she's front-page news today."

"I haven't seen them," he responded standoffishly, casting a glance down at the papers that were still lying on his doorstep. One of them displayed one of his own photographs of her. He walked over, picked up the papers, and started reading.

Mik took the newspaper out of his hand and said that he would accompany Tue inside his apartment while he put some clothes on.

Louise followed Tue Sunds's facial expressions with interest. There was very little going on in that taut, polished, sunburned face. He was older than you'd think by just looking at him, she thought, guessing that the photographer wanted to appear younger than he really was. That being the case, the Bordeaux-and-black-striped terry-cloth bathrobe didn't suit him at all.

He was more respectably attired when Mik came back down with him five minutes later. Once on the street, Louise climbed into the backseat with him. He didn't ask what had happened to Dicta until they'd crossed Kongens Nytorv and were on their way along Kalvebod Wharf.

"We'll talk about that once we get to Holbæk," Louise responded tersely.

At first the photographer sat with his teeth clenched, watching the heavy morning traffic coming toward them, but once they were out on the highway, he leaned his head back and closed his eyes and sat like that, off in his own world, the rest of the way to Holbæk.

⁂

Louise grabbed a mineral water, a pitcher of coffee, and two cups before walking in and turning on her laptop. She'd sent Mik home to check on his dogs and rest for a bit while she handled questioning the photographer. At first her partner had been reluctant to accept the offer, but ultimately he'd conceded.

Tue Sunds was pacing restlessly when she entered the office. She asked him to have a seat and offered him coffee. While she poured, she asked if she could get him anything to eat as they had taken him right out of bed; he likely hadn't had any breakfast yet.

He sat down and accepted her offer. Out in the hallway she ran into Velin and asked if he could bring some bread from the cafeteria. Five minutes later there were two slices of French bread on a white paper plate with butter and marmalade in small packets next to it, and they were ready to get started.

"I'm rather surprised to be here," Sunds started as he opened a butter. "I don't have a damn thing to do with this case."

Louise could see that he was starting to build up some resentment, which she hurried to quash by saying that she didn't think he did, either.

"Well then, why am I here?" he asked.

"Because I would really like to hear about your relationship with Dicta. You sent her some messages on Saturday rejecting her quite cruelly after you canceled your appointment, and you weren't particularly eager to come when we asked you to."

"Yeah, but do you suspect I killed her? Because that's totally absurd," he continued. "It's true that I wasn't able to see her on Saturday after all and maybe I was a little harsh when she didn't seem to be getting the message, but I didn't see her at all that day, so there's no way I could have murdered her."

Louise asked him to tell her why she should believe that he hadn't committed the murder.

He paused for a moment before speaking. "First and foremost, I wasn't in Holbæk. Besides that, I actually liked her."

Now, this was starting to get interesting, Louise thought.

"It would also be totally foolhardy to take the life of a model I thought I could make some money from," he continued in a milder tone.

Louise smiled at that last one; she hadn't missed the touch of irony in his voice.

"Obviously," she said. "And that's exactly the type of thing that would help convince us that you're not our murderer. So if you don't have any objections, I'd like to ask you a few questions that might help me shed a little light on Dicta's life and your relationship with her."

He nodded that that was fine. As if he could have responded in any other way and still have appeared innocent, Louise thought.

"How did you get in touch with Dicta Møller?" Louise asked after Tue Sunds had eaten both slices of bread. And when he didn't respond, she continued, "How does a young girl with no contacts in Copenhagen find her way to you specifically? You're not that famous, are you?" she asked and leaned back a little to take the sting out of her words.

He cleared his throat before answering. "No, of course she didn't know me." He smiled with exaggerated modesty. "But I understood from her that she subscribes to both *Sirene* and *Bazaar* magazines and I've had big fashion spreads in both magazines in the last few months. That's where she came across my name, and with that information it wasn't hard for her to find me online."

Louise was familiar with the two fashion magazines, which were both targeted at teenage girls.

"So she called you?" she asked, looking him in the eye as he slowly nodded.

"Yes, she called my studio."

"Is that normal, for young girls to call you that way? If that were the case, I'd imagine you'd probably spend all your time doing nothing other than taking calls from starry-eyed teenage girls, no?"

He smiled a bit and shook his head. "It's not normal at all. I thought it was quite impressive that she had the guts. They usually send their pictures to the modeling agencies. But Dicta wanted to hire me to shoot a few portfolio shots of her that she could use for submissions. She was very ambitious and I could tell that she was really willing to fight to make her dream a reality."

"What was she supposed to pay for them?" Louise asked.

"Normally, she'd have to pay six thousand Danish crowns. But I said I'd do them for her for three thousand crowns. She paid for them with her confirmation money."

"And did she then owe you the other half?"

Sunds fidgeted imperceptibly in the chair and let his hands rest on the desk. Then he shook his head. "No," he replied. "There was nothing about how I'd bill her for the rest if she made it big. Three thousand crowns was the agreed price."

Louise sat for a little while, watching him, but couldn't read him, sitting there staring back with his bright-blue eyes, completely composed. He leaned back and wove his fingers together behind his head.

"What you're really asking me is if I was expecting anything else from her because I offered to do her pictures for half price," he said, his gaze shrewd.

She nodded and waited.

He sat and thought for a moment before he again began to speak. "I have an eighteen-year-old daughter. I got divorced from her mother four years ago, and one of her friends was spending a lot of time at our house around that time. My own daughter never harbored any dreams of becoming a model. She wants to be a veterinarian and just started veterinary school, but her friend was very taken with the modeling world and used to hang out in the studio when I was working with professional models. I actually thought she was thinking about becoming a photographer, that's why I let her watch. But she wanted to be a model and kept pressuring me to give her a break, like under the table, even though I explained that I couldn't just start using a completely unknown girl when magazines booked me for an assignment. Besides, they choose their own models."

He paused for a moment before explaining that one day his daughter's friend had gone to the police and reported him for rape and at the same time leaked the story to the media. She couldn't be charged with making a false statement because of her age, but she was examined by a gynecologist and the exam showed that she was lying. Although it happens that the hymen can remain intact after a rape, it is rare, and after the events she described it certainly wouldn't have been possible.

"I didn't do anything more about it apart from talking to her parents, because the most important thing for me was that they understood that the story was a lie. I've always gone out of my way to treat young models considerately."

Louise had a copy of the police report in front of her. Ruth had had it waiting when they got back from Copenhagen, and Louise could see that a caseworker had been there during the questioning, which was standard procedure whenever someone underage was involved. Something had obviously gone wrong in terms of updating the case, because it didn't say anywhere in the paperwork that the preliminary charge had been found to be baseless.

"There's also a report of assault?" Louise said, pulling out another piece of paper.

"The same day the girl went to the police, she sent an email out to several of the magazines and papers I work for and to the biggest modeling agencies in the city, telling her story." He admitted this reluctantly, as if he didn't really want to accuse her of such poor behavior.

"She was a young girl, and my daughter's friend. At that point my daughter didn't have any room for more upheaval in her life."

Louise was starting to get irritated. He was almost being too selfless about what he'd been subjected to for Louise to take him seriously.

"You beat up a man so severely that he was in the hospital for a long time with facial fractures," she said impatiently, interrupting what she saw as a self-aggrandizing, defensive soliloquy.

He nodded.

"The story about the girl was making its way around the city. A few people knew how it all fit together. I got the girl's parents to write a letter to the people the girl had contacted, in which they explained that the report was made up. But not everyone who had heard the story received such a letter. The incident you mention happened one night after I'd had a little too much to drink and was maybe a little touchier than usual, so it all got out of hand when another photographer started egging me on."

Louise nodded and asked him to explain in more detail. "There's nothing more to say. I just couldn't stand to listen to any more whispering behind my back and didn't feel like I should have to keep defending myself for something I didn't do. So my temper got away from me."

Louise nodded. "Did Dicta have what it took to make it as a model?" she asked, picturing her. Louise had no doubt the girl had radiated charisma, and the boys certainly turned to look at her in the street, but a modeling career was a totally different matter.

He contemplated that for a bit before nodding.

"I think she had a reasonable shot. She was just too impatient. She expected the agencies to line up the instant they heard about her and it just isn't that easy," he said. "She apparently posed a little for a photographer up here and he really stroked her ego, but reality isn't like that."

"She was actually used as a model here in town," Louise said to vindicate Dicta a little.

"It's a hell of a long way from a picture in a free small-town newspaper to the big magazines," he said arrogantly.

"Well, actually, it was *Venstrebladet*," Louise pointed out, grabbing the chance for a new angle. "Give me an idea how many visits it takes to a celebrity photographer to get three thousand crowns' worth of portfolio pictures."

That shook him a little, but he didn't respond.

"And does it often happen that you drag it out all day and invite them out for sushi after the pictures are taken?"

He stayed silent.

"Two weeks ago, on a Saturday around eleven p.m., I ran into Dicta in front of the train station here in Holbæk," Louise continued. "She was so drunk, she was hunched over in the middle of the bike racks throwing up."

He looked like he wanted to say something but she kept going, her voice still calm and steady.

"A visit to a café and sushi up in your penthouse apartment. Why did you want to impress her when she was already in high spirits?"

He sat there with a wrinkle in his brow, clearly growing angrier by the minute. She discreetly followed his attempts to control it.

"I think you misunderstood that," he said finally. "Did she tell you that story? It's true that we ate brunch and that I invited her out for a glass of champagne after the pictures were taken. I usually do that when I wrap up a job."

"But she made up the part about your opening multiple bottles that night?" Louise asked, watching him.

He nodded.

"Did she also make up your eating sushi together?"

He said that Dicta had been hungry before she went home.

"She had the money to pay you three thousand crowns, but not to buy herself a hot dog at Nørreport Station?" Louise let the question hang in the air and then continued, "How many times have you seen her since that day?"

He looked like he was going to deny that he had seen her at all since then so she reformulated the question. "How many times did you have contact with her?"

He stared at her in silence before finally saying, "She came by a couple of times so we could choose which pictures would go in her portfolio. But otherwise I didn't see her."

"Did you agree to her sending that picture to *Ekstra Bladet*?"

Finally, some response was visible in his eyes. They squinted and darkened. "What fucking picture?"

Louise explained about his picture of Dicta appearing in the tabloid.

"I didn't fucking send in any picture. How do you think it makes me look if people see my name next to a page-nine girl?" he asked, outraged and angry.

Louise scowled. "I don't give a rat's ass how you look. How do you think Dicta looks? Now, you tell me what the fuck went on between the two of you. I don't want to hear any more bullshit."

He pulled back slightly in his chair and seemed more surprised than threatened.

"There's nothing else to tell."

Louise took a deep breath before she spoke again.

"I'm sorry I got all worked up. But I knew Dicta Møller in connection with another case we're working on and it was terrible to see her lying down there in the parking lot with her skull crushed."

He said that that was perfectly all right, but his eyes hardened when Louise repeated the question about how his photo of an undressed Dicta had ended up in *Ekstra Bladet*.

"She must have sent it in herself," he said, almost snorting the words.

Louise stood up to go check with Storm if it would be a good idea to hold off on pressing Tue Sunds any harder until they'd ransacked Dicta's room and had maybe found more that would help them get a picture of the relationship the two of them had had.

"Agreed," Storm said and then told her that Dean had been in touch with *Ekstra Bladet*'s photo editor, who had just gotten back to him with the information that the picture was sent in by the girl herself with a return envelope that was addressed to her own address. Dean had also checked that the account the money was supposed to be deposited into was Dicta's.

Louise leaned against the wall and stood there for a moment, feeling the energy that had been coursing through her during Tue Sunds's questioning drain from her body.

Storm left her in the hallway. He was going to see Søren Velin, who was studying Dicta's laptop with a technician.

Louise returned to her office and told Tue Sunds that an officer would be ready to take him back to the city within ten minutes. She held out her hand politely and thanked him for coming in.

"Did I really have any choice?" he asked. He gathered his white sweater up from where it had fallen on the floor and tied it around his waist.

"Yes, you could have refused. Then we would have been forced to arrest you, and then I wouldn't have thanked you so nicely afterward," she replied, following him out.

28

Louise was scurrying to the command room for a meeting with the others and didn't notice their presence until she heard a hoarse male voice behind her.

"Did that man have something to do with the murders?" Ibrahim al-Abd asked from the row of chairs along the wall. Sada was sitting next to him, well hidden behind her veil, which was wrapped tightly over her face.

Something had happened to his face since she'd seen him last. It had become dry and stiff, like bread that had been left out too long. He had expressed intense grief when they had last been together; now he expressed nothing, and his eyes watched her with a lackluster gleam. She walked over and sat down next to them.

"We came because we're afraid the new murder will make you forget about our daughter," Ibrahim began. "I presume now you're probably only interested in the Danish girl, whom Samra knew?" Louise reassured them by explaining that murder investigations didn't work that way. You didn't just drop one case because a new one came along.

"Yes, at the moment, we're trying to identify who murdered Dicta Møller. But you can rest assured, we're still doing everything we can to find out what happened to your daughter."

Sada gazed at her with a dark, unhappy look, which made Louise want to put her arm around the woman and comfort her. Instead she said that the police would really like to speak to them at some point in the near future, to find out what they knew about Dicta and the two girls' friendship.

"Please don't let our daughter end up on the back burner," Ibrahim pleaded. His voice cracked, and his wife looked down at the gray laminate floor.

Louise knew what he meant. So she tried to calm them down by explaining that a team of eight people was still working on their daughter's murder around the clock.

"We promise to let you know as soon as there's anything new," she said, holding out her hand as she stood up to join everyone else in the command room.

"Was it the same killer?" Storm asked as she opened the door.

The others were sitting around the table and the meeting was under way.

Bengtsen shook his head and was backed up by Skipper, who had extensive training in criminal profiling.

"The two girls' murders can't be compared." Skipper stood up and walked over to the dry-erase board, where he drew the two girls as stick figures and wrote ORGANIZED and DISORGANIZED over their heads.

Louise pulled out a chair and accepted the cup of coffee Søren handed her.

"One murder was committed by someone organized, one by someone disorganized," Skipper continued. "The organized one was thinking about his or her own safety and planned how to dispose of the body in advance, and we can certainly assume that the culprit doesn't live in the proximity of Hønsehalsen. The act suggests that there was a relationship between the killer and the victim."

Everyone seemed to agree.

"The murder of Dicta Møller, on the other hand, appears to have been committed by someone disorganized, and in terms of motives I think it's obvious that it was an emotional act stemming from a feeling like revenge or jealousy, for example. It was a spontaneous killing, and the murderer could easily have been seen from one of the surrounding apartments. Everything suggests that the location where the body was found was also the scene of the crime."

Louise had noticed that there were first- and second-floor apartments with windows looking out over the parking lot and had thought that the murderer was lucky no one had seen anything.

Storm stood up and moved to stand next to Skipper, from where he addressed the room.

"At present there are no commonalities between the murders of these two friends. Thus, we will continue to investigate the two cases individually," he said and added that still they should remain more attentive than usual to the coincidence that both girls were in the same class.

"A number of the parents have already called, expressing serious concern," Ruth interrupted. "They're afraid more students in the class may be in danger."

"I have a hard time believing that we're dealing with a murderer who has set out to systematically wipe out a whole school class," Storm said, running his hand through his hair, "but of course it's impossible to rule that out at this point."

He turned to Bengtsen and said, "Maybe you should drop in on the class and fill them in a little on our work. A small bit of information often goes a long way in calming people's fears."

Bengtsen nodded and said he'd do that right away.

"We should talk to the local photographer who worked with Dicta," Storm said and looked at Louise.

She sat there for a moment as Bengtsen left and the others stood to go. She was thinking about Dicta Møller and all her dreams. Yes, when Mik came back, they'd have to get hold of Michael Mogensen, but first they had to go out and take a look at Dicta's room. There had to be something there that could advance the case.

29

The pastor was sitting in the kitchen with Dicta's parents when Mik and Louise came to the front door. Both Anne and Henrik Møller came to greet them when they rang the bell. A bunch of bouquets of flowers, still wrapped in cellophane, along with small white cards that hadn't been opened or read yet sat on the counter. The pastor stood up and shook hands with Mik and Louise.

"It appears that sorrow has settled over our town for the time being," he said.

There was something forthright and inspiring about him, and the kitchen felt peaceful even though the grief was palpable and visible in both parents. The mother's eyes were red and puffy, her nose bright and shiny and rubbed almost raw from countless handkerchief dabs. The father's face was ashen and withdrawn, his eyes glassy, but there was no sign of tears. So he hadn't gotten that far yet, Louise thought, but it would come. In some people, the flood of tears came right away, while in others the grief had to take root in their cells before the reaction surfaced.

"We would really like permission to look around Dicta's room. Do you mind?" Louise asked, after they'd both said no thank you to coffee or joining the parents at the table.

"Of course we don't mind," Henrik said immediately. He stood up and led the way and opened the door, but remained frozen in the hallway, as if he didn't have the strength to go into the bedroom that still contained so much of his daughter's spirit in all of her things.

They could hear that Anne had started crying again and the pastor was comforting her. Louise turned her attention to the girl's room. She'd been there before, but with Dicta, and hadn't been so interested in the things in the room, but rather in what the girl had been telling her.

There was a big round disco ball hanging in one corner of the room above a small, circular table that was so covered in thick pink pillar candles, there was only space for an old-fashioned alarm clock with a bell on top. The bed was a futon, which was currently made up as a sofa adorned with two cream-colored pillows.

At the end of the bed, hidden behind the open door, hung a large vanity mirror with bare bulbs screwed into a wood frame all the way around it, like you might see in a theater dressing room or like a professional makeup artist might have. Under the mirror hung an open shelf with more body-care products, makeup, perfumes, and hair products—along with a curling iron and a flat iron—than Louise had seen gathered anywhere else, even at Camilla's place. Overwhelming and completely unnecessary for a young woman as beautiful as Dicta, Louise thought. Along the opposite wall there was a narrow desk and a tall bookshelf. To the left of the desk a little stereo system was mounted on the wall, and in the corner there was a tall, narrow CD holder.

A Fatboy bean bag chair filled up the space just to the left of the door. The trendy, oversize version of the classic 1970s bean bag chair was pink and matched the candles on the table. On the floor next to that there was a big pile of fashion magazines. A quick glance showed that they were *Costume*, *Eurowoman*, *Sirene*, and *Bazaar*. There was also a TV and a small black iPod on the table under the disco ball. The only thing missing was the computer Bengtsen and Velin had already picked up. On the wall over the desk there was a photo collage that Dicta had made herself with pictures of several of the biggest international models on catwalks from around the world.

"She was a beautiful girl," Mik said as Dicta's father stood in the doorway.

Henrik nodded and asked if they needed him to stay while they looked through her things.

"No, we can manage on our own," Louise hurried to say. It would be better if she and Mik could talk freely without worrying about offending the girl's parents.

"We'll see if she wrote anything about her meetings with Tue Sunds," Louise said once she'd taken a seat on the sofa to get an overview. Mik had gently put his arms around her waist as he slipped around her to enter the room, and she could still feel his hands on her body. It irritated her that she was receptive, but it still wasn't okay that he touched her that way. He would never have done that before their night together.

She followed him with her eyes as he opened Dicta's closet and started slowly flipping through her hangers. Not surprisingly, the closet was crammed full. The floor of it was littered with shoes and boots. The room seemed tidy on the surface, but as soon as you opened something, an awful mess was revealed. This young woman obviously had not yet developed any sense for order, or she just hadn't been interested in that.

Louise got up and started with the bottom shelf in the bookcase. It was mostly textbooks and three-ring binders; the two shelves above that were books, both children's and young adult; and then there were computer games, *The Sims* and *The Sims 2*. Louise guessed they hadn't been used in a while because there weren't many kidlike things left in the room.

Then there was the shelf with the photo album and a thin scrapbook. Louise took both of them over to the sofa.

A lot of pictures had been taken of Dicta. Louise could see that this must have been done over a long period of time, possibly over a year, because she had changed. Louise left the album sitting on her lap and flipped open the scrapbook. Several stores in town had used Dicta in their ads, and Michael Mogensen had used her often as a model in the photos accompanying stories in the local paper. There were also clippings showing her as a movie extra. He had apparently done what he could to make her dream of a modeling career come true, Louise ascertained, lingering for a bit over the clippings Dicta had pasted on the front page of the scrapbook and drawn a thick border around with a felt-tip marker. They were quotes from a couple of the biggest names in Danish modeling.

Remember your goals. A single picture can ruin your career.

That was surely true, Louise thought, letting her eyes move down to the next frame.

The first time you see your picture on the cover of Vogue, *the sky falls, and the world opens up. That's the best.*

Dicta had double-underlined *the best*. Louise read the first quote to Mik.

"Then why the hell did she send a picture to *Ekstra Bladet*?" he asked.

Louise shrugged. She started looking through the rest of the shelf to see if maybe there was a calendar or day planner that Dicta might have written something in. Something like that might also reveal how many times she'd been to Copenhagen, and Louise would take great satisfaction in slapping it down on the table in front of Tue Sunds and asking him to provide more details on his first statement.

"It was probably, like Sunds said, because she was impatient to be discovered," Louise said after a long pause.

Mik had picked up a little athletic bag from the bottom of the closet. He started spreading out the contents on the floor. Skimpy tops, short skirts of both denim and softer material. He picked up a narrow yellow belt and a small white bikini the size of the one Dicta had been photographed in.

"Could this be the one she took to Copenhagen?" he asked, checking the bag's exterior pockets. A small picture of a young, very blond-haired boy fell onto the floor as he pulled out a flowered, worn standard-size notebook with the word PRIVATE written neatly on the front.

Mik sat down with his back against the open closet door and opened the book. Louise watched him, curious.

"Read it out loud," she urged, annoyed at his silence.

He looked up at her after having skimmed a few more pages. "It isn't Dicta's."

Louise gave him a quizzical look.

"'My big brother got a job at Kvickly today,'" Mik read. "Dicta was an only child."

Louise nodded, and he turned the page in the book.

"'Saving up for a bigger cage for Snubby.' This was written last summer," Mik said, after glancing at the date in the top corner, but Louise was already up off the sofa. She snatched the flowered notebook out of his hands before he had a chance to react.

"It's Samra's," she said, sitting down with the book in her hands. Flipping through it, she could see that the girl had started the diary in May the previous year.

"There are big jumps in the dates every once in a while, and near the end, several pages are missing," Louise said after quickly skimming it.

Mik got up from the floor and sat next to her. They read in silence until they came across a poem Samra had written about her white rabbit.

You and me. Me and you. We'll never get out. You in a cage. Me behind a wall. We are the same. We'll never be free. But happiness can touch us now. Your soft fur and tiny nose undo the big knot within me and make me happy inside. Thank you. I love you, my little furry creature.

"That's the one they killed and served to her to punish her for coming home late," Louise said drily.

After searching through the pages, she found the episode in which her parents had made their daughter believe that they were eating chicken, and only after the fact had they told her it was actually Snubby.

I will never, never speak to Father again, and I will not eat Mother's food. I told them I was going to live with Dicta. Father went ballistic and started hitting me.

"How can parents treat their children like that?" Mik asked, and Louise shrugged. Even though neither she nor Mik had children, it seemed totally incomprehensible.

Louise flipped through to the last entries in the diary. Something in her resisted nosing around in another person's most confidential and private space, but, given the situation, the journal could be an important key to the investigation.

I got permission to go home to Grandma and Grandpa's for
Christmas. I'm flying to Amman on my own and then they'll
pick me up there. Maybe everything will work out. Father is
sweet.

The short sentences in her naive handwriting were written the
day before Samra died. She must have hidden the diary in the bag
when she was at Dicta's house that Tuesday, Louise thought.

"That doesn't make sense," Mik said, looking blankly at Louise,
who left the book sitting in her lap while she tried to figure it out.
They started reading backward through the diary and sat in silence after reading each page.

There was a soft knock on the door and Henrik Møller stuck
his head in to ask how it was going and whether they'd like coffee.

They declined. Louise showed him the book and pointed to the
bag. "Did you know that Samra had some things hidden in your
daughter's closet?" she asked.

He stared at her with a puzzled face and then looked down at
the contents of the bag, which were spread out on the floor in front
of the closet.

Then he shook his head and said that it was possible his wife
knew something about it. He stepped out, and a moment later
Anne came in.

She nodded when she saw it and kept saying sorry, that she actually had known but hadn't given it a thought.

"It was some of the clothes her parents wouldn't allow her to
wear. Maybe I shouldn't have turned a blind eye to it."

Louise showed her the diary and asked if she was aware of that
as well. But Anne shook her head. She had never pried into the
bag's contents.

"Did Dicta keep a diary as well?" Mik wanted to know before
Anne left.

The mother shook her head again. Not as far as she knew. "Did she have a calendar or day planner?" Louise asked.

"Yes, she had a nice one from Louis Vuitton that she got as a Christmas present. Maybe it's in the living room. I can go look for it," she offered as she walked out.

A moment later she was standing in the doorway with the large brown monogrammed planner, holding it out to them.

Mik took it and said they would like permission to take Samra's bag and its contents and Dicta's planner back to the station so they could go through them there instead of taking up the Møllers' time, but Louise wasn't paying attention. She felt the blood surging through her body. Her intuition told her that the diary was important, and at the moment she couldn't think of anything other than getting back to the station and being able to study it in peace.

"Dicta was in Copenhagen four times after she had those first pictures taken," Mik said once they were back at the station. "He obviously photographed her several times, or at least the planner has them listed as 'photo sessions,' but she went into the city twice in the evening and for those it says: 'Restaurant.'" Louise was absorbed in a drawing that covered two pages of the flowered diary. At the top of the corner of one page someone had drawn a picture of a girl's face, a girl with long, smooth hair like Samra's own. Tears were flowing from her eyes; both ruled pages were densely packed with the itty-bitty, round tears.

She flipped to the next page, where she read,

He did the worst to me and says it's my own fault.

There were very short, incoherent sentences filling the pages around the crying girl's face.

If I say anything, he'll give away my secret.

Mik was still talking on the other side of the desk, but Louise had blocked out his words; she was too preoccupied with the pages in front of her to listen. She flipped farther ahead in the journal.

They were laughing together as we ate. The whole family was there, and my mother was in the kitchen.

Louise interpreted the small scenes as a form of short prose, taken out of context, but the fragments were far more alarming and powerful the way they appeared here in brief snippets.

I will never, never trust anyone again. How could he do that to me when he says he loves me?

Louise stood up and walked out the door holding the diary. She didn't notice Mik's questioning look and didn't hear him get up and follow her.

Storm was sitting in the command room talking on the phone when she walked in. Louise stood in front of him and waited impatiently for him to finish.

"We need to bring Samra's parents in now," she said as soon as he hung up.

She showed Storm Samra's self-portrait, explained where they'd found the diary, and summarized briefly the rest she'd managed to read.

"A few pages were ripped out, but what's here says plenty," she said.

He read a little himself before standing up and handing back the diary. Then he went to find Skipper and Dean and ask them to drive out and bring in Samra's parents.

"They should bring the brother," Louise called after him. She was starting to see what Samra might have been subjected to.

Then she returned to her office and her close reading of Samra's tormented pages.

30

The more Louise read of Samra's diary, the more the knot in her gut tightened.

The pages drew a picture of a young girl who was torn between two worlds. On the one hand, she was trying to meet her parents' expectations and demands, while on the other she was trying to adapt to her new country and new friends. It was clear that she was having a hard time finding the balance. Was she Danish or was she still a Muslim girl from Jordan? Louise understood that what Samra was really trying to achieve, was putting all her effort into, was being a Muslim Danish girl. On the surface this sounded easy enough, but reading her diary made it clear that it was far from that.

Louise had been taking notes on the things that would be of particular interest when they questioned Samra's family again. It was clear in a couple of places that Samra had started having thoughts of love—at least, emotions had begun to occupy more significance in the words she wrote. Louise guessed that she might have fallen in love, but it was not clear that she had begun a relationship. She had written short poems about what she thought it would be like for two people to share a life. "The person I love and me," she wrote in her script. She also wrote a story about what it would be like when they went up to the old Crusaders' castle in Jordan together and sat looking out over the valley and then after that walked home to her grandmother's house and drank tea and ate sweet cakes.

Louise was a little surprised that Samra dreamed of walking home with her boyfriend in Rabba instead of along the sound in Holbæk.

"Did you know that your daughter kept a diary?" Louise asked once she'd brought Ibrahim in.

He did not appear to understand what she meant.

Louise held up the book, so he could see it. "Do you recognize this?" she asked instead.

He hesitated and shrugged. "Maybe."

"It's your daughter's diary. Where she wrote down her secrets." His face remained expressionless, so she continued.

"This book gives me reason to believe there's something you're not telling us. Something that made Samra very afraid. In several places she expressed outright fear that she might have to die."

Ibrahim looked away from her but didn't say a word.

"Did you kill your daughter?" Louise asked bluntly after several minutes of silence.

He shook his head.

"I could never hurt my little girl," he finally said just as Louise was giving up on hearing him say anything.

"I know that you hurt her. It says that clearly here in the book, but that happened long before she died. Something happened during the last few months of her life. What was it that made her so unhappy and afraid?"

He thought about it for a long time before he spoke. "Maybe something at school?" he suggested.

Louise shook her head. "I think your daughter had a secret she was trying to hide from her family. But she didn't succeed and then she became really, really scared."

Ibrahim went pale but remained silent.

"Did she have a boyfriend?" Louise asked, even though Dicta had already told her that Samra had never said anything that would suggest that.

Ibrahim didn't make eye contact, but he shook his head.

"It's strange," Louise said, "that I thought it was you she was afraid of, but this here confuses me."

She read the last page of the diary out loud, then stared intensely at him to gauge his reaction.

She read, "'I got permission to go home to Grandma and Grandpa's for Christmas. I'm flying to Amman on my own and then they'll pick me up there. Maybe everything will work out. Father is sweet.'"

Now Ibrahim hid his face in his hands and sat silently rocking back and forth.

Louise cleared her throat.

"I think you should tell me about this. The fact is, we know that something happened. And it won't just go away," she said, trying to sound kind.

While she waited patiently, she wrote on a piece of paper that she didn't think he knew about the diary. She got up and walked into the office next door, where Mik was questioning Hamid. Without saying anything, she set the piece of paper on the desk and waited while he wrote back to her: *Hamid does. And the bag.*

She returned to Ibrahim, who lifted his head as she entered. "I didn't hurt my daughter," he repeated after Louise was seated.

"You mean other than by killing her pet rabbit and forcing her to eat it." It slipped out before she could stop herself. She instantly regretted it, because now she was going to have to do some coaxing if she was to have any hope of getting him to talk. *Idiot*, she thought to herself, rubbing her face with both hands. She watched him as he sat there like a statue, then she sighed and said: "Maybe it wasn't you who physically killed her. But I think you know what happened to her and what she was afraid of. She writes that she had lost her faith in the people who loved her. And the people she was referring to were her family. In other words, you. My colleague is sitting next door talking to your son. He's not as reluctant to tell us what he knows. For example, he was well aware that his sister hid a bag of clothes at her friend's house. Clothes she didn't dare keep at home because you wouldn't allow her to wear the same things her classmates wore. Hamid also knew about the diary, and I think he was aware that his sister confided in Dicta Møller."

At that moment, something struck her, and she got up and left the office with a quick apology. Storm and Ruth were sitting in the command room, studying the big whiteboard where details about Samra's life and actions during the period leading to her death were recorded in blue ink. Next to that was a similar summary of Dicta's final days. Bengtsen and Velin had reconstructed the days up to the time when Dicta had been found in the parking lot.

Louise stopped in the doorway and started talking, rapidly. "Could Samra's family be behind both killings?"

She explained that Hamid had just admitted that he knew about the bag and the hidden clothes and the diary at Dicta's house.

"If Samra was really hiding a secret that would be so damaging to the family's honor that they felt they had to kill her, wouldn't it be possible that they went one step further if they realized that she had confided in her friend from school?"

A thoughtful silence settled over the room as they each tried to picture that scenario.

Ruth got up and walked over to the window, where she gazed out over the square in front of the old police station. Grass and big trees filled the space between the building and the sidewalk on Jernbanegade.

A couple of uniforms were called in to keep an eye on Samra's family members and make sure none of them left the police station while the team was quickly gathered.

"You're onto something," Storm said, nodding at Louise. "That would also explain why the one murder was so carefully thought out and the other seemed impulsive. If they felt threatened by what Dicta knew, they would have acted fast."

"Let's arrest the father and son for killing Samra," Velin said. "Then we can add charges later to cover Dicta's murder."

"Yeah, or we could charge them with both killings from the get-go," Skipper suggested.

Louise was sitting on the edge of the table.

"We don't know what she was hiding," Mik reminded them. "Let's be cautious now not to read too much into this."

"No, but we know there was a secret and we know she feared for her life. That's enough for me right now," Skipper interjected. "What we don't know is which of them killed her. That's why we charge them both."

"Often the person chosen to do the killing is the person the family can most easily do without," Dean explained and said that this could be either someone who didn't have anyone else to look after or someone who wasn't able to contribute by sending money back to the remaining family members in the old country. "Of course, it's also true that that person is sometimes a minor," he concluded.

"You're saying you think it was Hamid who killed his sister?" Bengtsen said.

"I don't know what I think; I need a little more to go on. I'm just telling you what kinds of factors I would expect families living according to strict cultural traditions to contemplate."

Storm had remained silent, but he now cleared his throat, interrupting their conversation. "I'm not sure we have enough right now to hold them on," he said, "but we'll do it, and gamble on more coming out during questioning. We may also get lucky and have something turn up in a new search, and then we have to hope it'll be enough."

"What about Sada?" Louise asked.

"She can go home to the two little ones, and then we'll follow the audio surveillance closely and have it interpreted as we go. We can assume there will be increased activity if we're holding her husband and oldest son." Storm asked Ruth to get hold of the interpreter they'd had listening to, transcribing, and translating the tapes from the last several weeks in installments of several days' worth at a time.

"It's Monday, October ninth. The time is four fifty-five p.m. You are under arrest for the murders of your daughter Samra al-Abd and her friend Dicta Møller," Louise said when she returned to the office.

Ibrahim jumped as if he'd received an electrical shock. He stared at her with his eyes agape, then collapsed in his chair with his head bowed and his chin resting on his chest.

Louise thought for a minute that he'd fainted and moved toward him. She could see Mik standing out in the hallway with Hamid, ready to walk him down to the uniforms downstairs so the arrest could be processed.

"I have to ask you to follow me," she said quietly, watching him as he slowly collected himself and stood up.

Neither the father nor the son said anything as their names were entered in the arrest log and they were searched, their possessions placed in clear plastic bags.

"We'll walk you over to the jail," Louise said, holding the door for them. Ibrahim had kept his eyes on the ground, but when he was even with Louise, he raised his head and directed his profoundly unhappy gaze right into her eyes, as he almost imperceptibly shook his head.

Two officers were waiting in the jail to accept the men. They said hello to Mik and nodded at her. Before they took Ibrahim and Hamid away, Louise stopped them and walked over to the two men.

"If there's anything you want to say, just ask to come talk to Mik Rasmussen or me," she said and then watched as they started walking down the hallway toward the jail cells.

Louise and Mik returned to their office and started reading through all the previous transcripts of questioning sessions with the family members before they started with the father and son again.

It was only just seven when the deputy chief of police walked into the office and said he wanted to request a preliminary hearing that evening so they could get it over with.

Louise was up out of her desk chair so fast that it shot backward and slammed into the wall.

"Out of the question," she said, giving him a stern look. "We need the full twenty-four hours for the questioning we need to get through."

Mik was also standing, but he said nothing.

The deputy chief paced back and forth a little bit before he leaned against the wall and looked from Mik to Louise.

"I read the whole thing and I'm not sure I have enough to keep them in custody," he finally said.

Louise pulled her chair back to her desk and sat down. "But this isn't a presentation of evidence. You just need to convince the judge that there is reason to suspect that if we let them out they could sync up their stories and sway other people," Louise said and referenced section 762 (1), paragraph 3. "Now just give us a little peace to do our work."

The deputy chief hesitated. "Fine. We'll hold off on the preliminary hearing until tomorrow afternoon," he said. "But by then I will also expect you to have something more for me."

31

At ten past eight the following morning, the squad was once again gathered in the command room. There was a carafe of coffee, and Velin had stopped by the bakery on his morning jog to make sure there were pastries, too.

"We're going to search the family's home again," Storm began once they had all helped themselves. It was obvious that there'd been a break in the case, and the mood was tense and focused. The deputy chief of police had stopped by again to make it clear that he expected more before he had to appear for the preliminary hearing, but Storm had explained that if the man just had faith that the case would hold, then he already had enough.

Now Storm looked at Skipper and Dean. "Go through everything, you two. And tear things apart. We need something more to connect the family to Dicta Møller's murder, and we have to find the murder weapon."

They received a brief description of the bludgeon with the two distinctive rounded protrusions that had been used to hit Dicta. According to Flemming Larsen, it had to have a certain heft.

"The crime scene technicians finished at the site yesterday, and two of them will join you out at Dysseparken," Storm continued.

"Do we know the murder scene is where the body was found?" Mik asked, looking at Skipper and Dean, who had helped process the parking lot.

"Yes, there's no doubt about that. She was bleeding so much we would have found traces of blood in other places in the parking lot if she'd been transported there," Skipper said.

"It's sheer coincidence that no one saw the attack," Dean said, shaking his head. "It was so violent."

"It may also be a coincidence that it happened right there," Storm said, repeating his supposition that there had been strong emotions involved.

"Rage," Louise suggested. Storm nodded.

Bengtsen briefly cleared his throat and then said, "Could that young girl have tried to use what she knew to pressure Samra's family? Just a thought. But maybe that could have been the provocation?"

Everyone around the table went silent, trying to picture that. "What the fuck did she want to get out of it?" Skipper asked. "I couldn't say. But if Dicta felt sure that Samra's family had murdered her friend, we can't rule out that she confronted them with her suspicion. Maybe the brother, whom she knew better than the parents."

Storm shrugged.

Louise's first impulse was that the theory was way out there, but she decided not to say anything because ultimately she just couldn't figure out what had been going on in Dicta's head. If she had sent her own pictures to *Ekstra Bladet*, she had already stepped well beyond what Louise would have imagined her capable of—and she had also snuck off to Copenhagen and gone traipsing around with a much older man without filling anyone in on her adventures.

In that light, it was hard to dismiss the idea that it might have occurred to Dicta to use what she knew against the family. If she had done that, it surely wouldn't have been to pressure them, Louise thought, but to let them know that she knew something. It wouldn't have been very well thought out. It just painted a picture of an immature, naive young girl. All in all, that fit quite well with the Dicta who had shown new sides of herself during the time Louise had known her. She was not quite who she seemed or who she tried to convince others she was.

"We can't rule out that she was seeking justice for her friend's death, if Samra had confided something to her, and she may well have confronted Hamid with it," Louise said, reminding them that even the first time she'd appeared at the police station, Dicta had expressed concern about the family in connection with Samra's disappearance. "Maybe she hoped she could get them to turn themselves in."

"That's not a bad theory. Let's bring them in from jail so we can proceed," Storm said, wrapping up the meeting.

❧

"What the hell are you doing?" Camilla shouted when she burst into Louise and Mik's office five minutes later. She flailed her arms, wearing gray sweatpants and a sweater, no makeup, and her bedhead hair gathered into a loose ponytail—clearly she'd come darting out of her hotel room the second she'd gotten off the phone. No doubt that was also the reason Mik didn't recognize her immediately, even though he'd met her before. The last time he'd seen her, she'd been dressed the way her vanity required: in a skirt, shoes with impressive heels, a little formfitting jacket, and perfect makeup. Louise had never understood how Camilla could stand to put all that on just to go to work, but that was one of the discussions they had that never got anywhere, just as Louise could never make her friend understand how she could leave her apartment without makeup.

"Are you people stupid or what?" Camilla railed on. "What are you trying to do?"

Her yelling had brought Storm to the doorway, where he stood listening.

"Good morning, Ms. Lind," he said with a smile when Camilla finally spun around and glared at him.

She stepped toward him. "Are you getting desperate? Or are higher-ups starting to breathe down your necks?"

The lead investigator seemed to be enjoying this, and on some level Louise was impressed at her friend's courage, because crime-beat reporters depended on being on good terms with guys like Storm. At the same time, Louise was also embarrassed for her. Camilla could act as if she owned the Danish media, and on many occasions that was far from flattering. But she did have a point.

"You must see how you'll look if you end up having to release them."

Storm was looking serious again and asked if it might not be a good idea for Camilla to join him for a quick cup of coffee. Louise didn't have trouble figuring out that it didn't particularly serve Storm's interests that news of the arrests had leaked out, since he wasn't sure yet that the judge would allow the two men to remain in custody.

Louise looked over at Mik.

"What just happened?" he asked.

If he had been a comic-book character, his jaw would be hanging down to the floor, Louise thought and smiled at him.

"Camilla's right," she finally said after sitting a moment in silence. "If the judge lets them go, we're in for it. Because it'll look
like the arrests were based solely on racial profiling."

Mik sat up straighter. "But we actually did arrest them based on
evidence," he reminded her. "And we can't be politically correct
just to protect our reputations," he continued, irritated.

Louise sat for a moment before saying she didn't agree with
the interpretation. She was just trying to provide her best guessti-
mate about how things would look if the judge let Ibrahim and
Hamid go.

"We have enough to keep them in custody," Mik said tersely
and asked if they should get started on the questioning so the
deputy chief would feel prepared when he presented the arrestees
to the judge.

Louise nodded and got up. She glanced at him over her desk as
she gathered up her papers and acknowledged that now was not
the time for them to lose their nerve.

Camilla was still worked up when she left the police station. She
went back to the hotel and had breakfast in the restaurant. She was
seated at a table by the window, looking over at the train station,
when she spotted Sada, who was trudging toward the hotel with
her eyes down, holding hands with Aida and Jamal. Camilla got
up and went out to greet her, and with her arm around the slender
woman's shoulder and Aida's little hand in hers, she brought them
into the restaurant.

"Have you had something to eat?" Camilla asked, looking at
the kids, pointing into the next room where the continental breakfast buffet was still set up. Camilla had ordered à la carte because
she hadn't felt up to sitting with all the other hotel guests, mostly

consisting of the German and Danish tradesmen who populated the hotel on weeknights. Camilla had only seen Samra's little sister once before, the time she had almost been thrown out of the family's apartment by an enraged Ibrahim, but apparently that hadn't had any negative impact, because now the little girl smiled and handed Camilla her doll.

"Oh, for me?" Camilla said, smiling back.

Aida nodded and followed Camilla's suggestion to go in to the buffet, even though her mother and little brother were seated at the window table and appeared satisfied with cups of tea.

Camilla wasn't used to little girls, but she just couldn't resist this one. Her heart went all soft when Aida looked at her with those delightful, kind dark eyes.

Sada's eyes widened at the sight of the two large pastries Aida had placed on her plate, but she didn't say anything, not even when Aida climbed up onto a chair next to Camilla instead of sitting by her mother and Jamal. Sada just sat there looking down and stirring her tea.

"They're going to end up in jail," she said finally, setting down her spoon.

Camilla tried to comfort her, saying that nothing was certain until they'd seen a judge, and that she'd been by the police station to find out what had made them decide to make the two arrests.

"They found your daughter's diary at Dicta Møller's house," Camilla said.

Storm hadn't told her much beyond the fact that the diary seemed to connect the two cases.

"Haven't they told you anything?" Camilla asked when Sada didn't react to the information.

"The police say that they're not coming home right now," Sada said, arms desperately wrapped around herself, as if she was trying to warm up her fingers. "I don't know what's going to happen."

Camilla wished she could reassure the woman, but she didn't want to raise false hopes.

"Can you tell me what you think the police might have read in Samra's diary? They wouldn't arrest two men if they didn't have a reason," she said.

Sada remained silent. Camilla had the sense that she was struggling with an internal battle of doubt and trust.

"I don't know anything," she finally said and took a little sip of her tea.

Aida had finished both pastries. Her mother then pulled a sketch pad and a box of puzzle pieces from her purse, spread out a small blanket on the floor, and asked Aida and Jamal to sit down and play.

Without objections, the girl went over to her mother and took the things she handed her, and a second later the two kids were both busy down on the blanket. That would never have worked with Markus, Camilla thought.

"Do you know what this might have to do with Dicta Møller?" Camilla persisted, even though she was afraid of putting too much pressure on Sada.

"They were friends," came the answer.

"You mean that your daughter might have confided in her friend?" Camilla fished. That was also her guess at the police's connection.

Again, there was a nod.

It was hard to tell if Sada was telling the truth or if she didn't dare divulge what her daughter had been hiding. But now at least she admitted that there had been something.

"Let's try and think about it from the police's perspective. Are they assuming it was an honor killing?" Camilla started, asking Sada to think through what might have triggered Ibrahim's anger. She had a strong hunch that deep down, Sada was afraid her husband's temper had gotten away from him and that in a fit of rage he had killed their daughter, but Sada categorically rejected that.

"That kind of thing never happens as long as no one outside the family knows about what took place," Sada slowly explained, as if she was trying to select each correct word individually. "My daughter didn't do anything that our family is aware of."

Camilla asked her to clarify.

"When girls are killed, it's because you can't defend the family's honor to the rest of the family—I mean, the extended family."

Sada reached out for Camilla's white paper napkin and asked to borrow a pen.

She drew a little circle.

"This is my immediate family, at home in Dysseparken." Then she made a larger circle around that.

"This is the rest of our extended family who live in Denmark," she explained.

Yet another ring around those.

"This is the entire extended family back home in Rabba."

She looked earnestly at Camilla and set the tip of the pen down on the outer circle.

"When the extended family knows there are problems with a daughter, they will want you to get her under control. If you can't do that, things can turn out badly."

She moved the pen to the innermost circle.

"We loved our daughter. If there are problems, then you help your child. Things don't turn out badly here."

Camilla tried to follow. "What you're saying is that the rumor that something is wrong has to make it farther than this small nuclear family before it would result in an honor killing?"

Sada nodded.

"And the problems that involved Samra weren't something that anyone outside your immediate family knew about?"

Sada shook her head, apparently not realizing that by doing so she was confirming that there had been problems. She stood up quickly and packed up her kids' playthings as she thanked Camilla for the tea.

"I can't make them understand," Sada said on her way out the door.

Camilla sat there lost in her thoughts for a long time. She didn't doubt that Sada felt trapped in the prejudices about her native culture, and somewhere deep down inside she also seemed to feel unsure of what she herself should think about Samra's fate.

As Camilla left the restaurant, a crowd of teenagers on the other side of the street caught her eye. They had surrounded Sada and her children, who hadn't made it to the bus stop yet, and instead were trapped in front of the large train station.

Camilla ran out the door and marched over to the group. Once she had pushed her way through, she positioned herself between the crowd and Sada, and shouted that if they did not leave this family alone, she would call the police faster than they could repeat the *T* in *towelhead*, just one of the insults she'd heard them using.

Instead of dissipating as Camilla had hoped, the teens started aggressively closing in. They were somewhere between sixteen and eighteen years old, she guessed, and their anger at Samra's mother hung like a thick cloud around them.

"Girl killer!" one of the boys hissed at Sada as she and her kids started backing away from the group. Word of the arrests had spread quickly and, in a small town like Holbæk, the response was quite evident.

Camilla heard Aida crying and, outraged, she stepped up to the group's apparent ringleader.

"What the hell are you doing, you little prick?" she snarled, sensing more than seeing how a couple of the boys jumped. She whipped her press pass out of her purse.

"If one of you has a beef you want to get off your chest, then I would love to hear it. Bring it to me, not to a woman walking down the street with her children. That's just pathetic."

Camilla overheard some of them mumbling that she ought to "shut her mouth" and quit butting in where she didn't belong. She ignored a shove to her left shoulder. She maintained eye contact with the boy she had spoken to.

"Until someone is found guilty of murder, you need to shut up and quit bullying people. But actually, I'd really like to write about your anger. Maybe I can even get your pictures in the paper," she said, her words heavy with sarcasm.

Then she turned and followed Sada, who was headed over to the buses. She stayed until Sada and the kids were safely seated.

By the time the bus pulled away, the boys were gone.

32

The preliminary hearing started at three, and it was fair. The whole investigative team attended and listened along as the judge found that there was sufficient reason to hold the father and son and that they could remain in custody for fourteen days.

"He wasn't sure there was enough to hold them for four weeks," Storm said once they had returned to the command room and were seated around the table drinking sodas, which Ruth had retrieved from the fridge. Still, his relief was obvious. "Well, now we'll have a little space to work."

Skipper and Dean had finished searching the al-Abd family's home in Dysseparken right before the preliminary hearing began, so no one had heard if they'd turned up anything new yet. "Nothing," Skipper said, shaking his head. "No murder weapon, no diary pages or anything else that in any way revealed new details about Samra's private life, and now I think I can say that there won't be anything, either. There's no place that hasn't been searched, so we need to change tacks."

"Louise and I are on our way to have a chat with the photographer Michael Mogensen," Mik said, draining his Fanta. "And early tomorrow we'll bring Ibrahim's brother in. He was with the parents around the time of Samra's death. We need to ascertain where he was when Dicta was killed."

Louise caught his eye. She left her Coke on the table and stood up to signal that she was ready to go. She was having a hard time coming down from the adrenaline rush she'd felt during the preliminary hearing, so heading out right away suited her just fine.

Michael Mogensen answered the door quickly when they rang the bell on the front of the large yellow-brick home he lived in. He rented the upper floor from his grandmother and also had a large room in the basement, which he used for his studio and computer equipment.

"We would like to speak to you about the two murders that occurred here in town," Mik began.

A shadow immediately fell over the photographer's eyes, and he lowered his head and nodded.

"May we come in?" Louise asked.

He quickly stepped aside to make room. "Of course. Should we go down to my workspace or up to where I live?" He sounded uncertain and uneasy with the situation.

"Your call," Mik said, but when it didn't seem as if anything was happening, Mik suggested that they go down to the basement. "You knew Dicta as a result of your work, so that seems fitting." Portraits of babies, couples, brides, grooms, and businesspeople from town lined the walls, and there were advertising photos and an enlarged reporting series from the School of Arts and Crafts on the outskirts of Holbæk.

The photographer offered them coffee once they were seated by a small coffee table; he rolled his own desk chair over, so he was sitting across from them, looking at them expectantly.

"I just can't understand it," he began, seeming more exhausted than Louise had first noticed.

"Tell us how you and Dicta became acquainted," Louise requested.

He sat silent for a moment, pensive.

"There'd been a game down at the stadium, and I was on my way home to submit my pictures to my editor. On the way home, I stopped to get a bite to eat and that's where I saw her. I was standing up at the corner by the Kebab House and she came walking toward me."

"How long ago was that?"

"That was last fall. She wasn't that old, but we did a few catalog photos for one of the sporting equipment companies in town and then the rest came later."

"The rest?"

"The jewelry and clothes." He pointed over at some pictures showing a hand with various rings and a neck with an elegant gold chain.

"Did you use other models besides her?" Mik wanted to know.

Mogensen nodded and looked over at a filing cabinet. "But little by little it was mostly her I used. She was good and my customers were happy with her. But there were some things she was too young for, of course. Women's clothes, for example. I do some work for an optician's shop and they really wanted their models to be a little older."

"How was she as a model?" Louise asked.

"She was great—natural talent and a pleasure to work with," he said without hesitation.

"Had she ever tried modeling before you originally stopped her on the street?"

He shook his head. "No, never. But like I said, I could see that she could become something. Which is why I devoted the time to helping her feel comfortable in front of the camera. Those pictures would just remain in the cabinet. It was an investment for both of us, which ultimately brought in more gigs."

"What do you know about the photographer she went to see in Copenhagen? Did she tell you about her plans?"

Michael Mogensen shook his head and said a little defensively that she wasn't obligated to stick with him, that they'd never drawn up a contract that she would work exclusively for him. There was no way he could have afforded to honor that.

"But if you were volunteering your time and energy to mentoring her, wasn't it a little frustrating that she disappeared just as she was getting good enough to make more money in the jobs you were getting?" Louise asked, eyeing him with curiosity.

He sat for a moment before he shrugged and said, "That's life, isn't it?"

"Didn't you ever dream about working for some of the big magazines?" Mik asked.

The photographer looked at him and smiled for the first time. "It's better to be a big fish in a small pond than a small fish in a big pond," he said, becoming solemn again.

"Were you close, you and Dicta?" Louise wanted to know.

He nodded and said that he thought they had grown close over the time they'd known each other.

"You have to trust each other, otherwise it shows in the pictures."

Louise smiled to herself. There was something touching about his self-importance, but she had no doubt that he took his work seriously even if he was unlikely to ever achieve the sort of recognition that a photographer like Tue Sunds had.

Mik had gotten up and was walking around a little. He stopped in front of the filing cabinet and asked if he could look in it.

Michael Mogensen said of course and explained that the pictures were divided into categories, but the top two drawers were portraits.

He and Louise talked a bit more about his friendship with Dicta over the year they had known each other.

"It got so I could tell if she was in a good or a bad mood, if there were problems at school, or if she was tired. It's hard to hide that kind of thing when you're standing in front of a camera lens."

Louise nodded and listened the same way people skim books. She picked up on what sounded interesting and let the rest slip right by.

Mik cleared his throat and pulled a picture out of the filing cabinet drawer.

A girl with long, straight dark hair and large dark eyes was smiling warmly from the picture. "You knew her?" he asked, walking over to Michael with the portrait of Samra.

The photographer nodded and reached for the picture. He sat with it for a bit, as if lost in thought, before he explained that Dicta had sometimes brought her friend along when she came straight from school.

"She was also a pretty girl," Michael said, setting aside the picture.

"Did she ever pose for you?" Louise asked.

"I asked her to, but she didn't dare because of her parents."

"But you still photographed her?"

He nodded, but said it was just a personal photo.

Louise smiled and tried to picture Samra. Although she'd never known the young Jordanian girl, Louise knew she would have liked her. She had given herself permission to be photographed and feel the freedom of following a dream, knowing the whole time that the pictures must never be shown. She wanted the full experience. She'd had it, but definitely knew that her parents mustn't find out.

"Did you get the impression that the two girls confided in each other?" Louise asked.

The photographer thought for a moment before answering. "I'm not sure what you mean by that, but they were best friends."

"If one of them had a secret, do you think the other would have known about it?"

He mulled that over. "I'm not sure."

"When did you last see Dicta?" asked Mik, who had once again taken a seat next to Louise.

"I was with her last Saturday, the day before she was found dead. We had an appointment to take a few pictures down behind Hotel Strandparken that afternoon."

"Did she seem like she felt threatened or scared of anything to you?"

Michael Mogensen considered her question.

"I hadn't considered that, but I also hadn't seen much of her lately."

Once Louise and Mik were back in the car, she said that it seemed Dicta had withdrawn from Michael a little while she tried her luck with Tue Sunds.

"Yeah, you almost wish she hadn't been so ambitious, but had stuck with Michael. She probably would have gained more good experience that way," Mik said as he pulled up in front of the hotel and gave Louise a quick kiss on the cheek before she got out.

33

DICTA MØLLER WAS ONE OF THE MOST TALENTED AND PROMIS-
ING MODELS I'VE WORKED WITH. SHE HAD A NATURAL LUMINOS-
ITY THAT GLOWED THROUGH THE CAMERA'S LENS AND STUCK. I
DON'T DOUBT FOR A SECOND THAT SHE HAD A BIG INTERNATIONAL
CAREER AHEAD OF HER, ON PAR WITH OTHER GREAT DANISH
FASHION MODELS LIKE LOUISE P OR LYKKE MAY. IT'S A GREAT
LOSS FOR THE DANISH MODELING WORLD THAT SOMETHING SO
DREADFUL COULD HAPPEN TO HER.

Oh, just shut up, Louise thought, shaking her head once she was
done reading. She folded up the newspaper and dropped it on
Mik's desk. She'd spotted it when she was eating breakfast and had
brought the paper back with her. Tue Sunds occupied the whole
front page and two pages inside the paper.

"He damn well isn't upset about it," she said, nodding at the front page.

"No, it looks like he knows how to promote himself," her partner agreed, pulling the paper over to skim through the article.

"When are we going out to Benløse?" Louise asked and added that they really ought to pick up Ibrahim's brother before he drove in to open his shop at ten o'clock.

"We're leaving as soon as you're ready," Mik said, tearing himself away from the paper.

There was a relaxed intimacy between them. She had spent a second night out at his farm and the situation had transformed from being a painful mistake to a controlled attraction, which filled her with warmth. They agreed that what they had together was nice, but that it shouldn't interfere with their work. She watched him as he put on his jacket. He had a calming effect on her, and although his slightly edgy manner and lanky frame weren't things she immediately associated with security, he held her in a way that made her feel like she'd come home.

"I'm eager to hear what he has to say about their arrest," Louise said as she led the way to the car.

"I'm never going home to my parents again. Their wrath is so great and they're so ashamed of me it has clouded their minds and warped their hearts. How can people who are tied together by blood be so cold to each other? How can anyone who used to love me suddenly want me dead? I ran into my aunt on the street and when she saw me she crossed to walk on the other side. I don't know how much longer I can take this."

Camilla was far away, lost in her own thoughts, when the door to her office opened and Terkel Høyer came in.

"What did you want?" he asked, standing in the doorway.

Camilla picked up the clipping and read aloud.

"Will it never end?" he sighed when she was done. Then he continued. "That was good spotting. We'll bring it up again to show that strict rulings and long sentences aren't enough to stop this kind of thing. Find the girl and write her story. If she doesn't want her picture in the paper, she can be anonymous, but get hold of her."

Since the arrests of Samra's father and older brother, letters to the editor had been pouring in. People were sick to death of hearing about cultural differences and "honor," and anger was building such that the vast majority felt the sentencing guidelines ought to be made even stricter, a policy the minister of justice had just come out in favor of. A large percentage of the letters basically said that in cases involving crimes based on religious beliefs, cultural traditions, or issues involving honor, the judge should order deportation once the sentence was completed.

In Holbæk, anger and frustration at the two killings was so palpable that one night the living room window and a large, frosted pane in the front door were smashed at Dysseparken 16B, where Sada al-Abd was now living alone with her two youngest children.

"Find her," the editor repeated. "Or find someone else with the same story. There are enough of them out there that it shouldn't be that hard."

"Nah, it won't be that hard," Camilla agreed, her eyes trained on him. She sensed the rage starting to build within her, but wisely held it in check and continued calmly: "The girl who wrote it is ethnically Danish. Her name is Pernille and she's from Præstø." Camilla took a deep breath. "But I won't be talking to her because she took her own life ten days ago. She was born into a family of Jehovah's Witnesses and had just turned sixteen when she broke with the church."

Terkel Høyer was on his way out the door but stopped and took a step closer to her.

"And now you just listen here," Camilla continued, and before he had a chance to say anything, she started reading another account from fifty years ago: "'If I have to bear this child, I would rather end it all.'

"That was written by a very young woman who came from a fishing family in West Jutland—an evangelical family. She got pregnant at a very young age by one of the local farmers and turned to Mødrehjælpen, the National Council for Unmarried Mothers, in the hope of getting permission for an abortion. She was denied. That same day she took her own life by walking out into the waves to avoid having to go home to her family, who wanted her dead anyway."

"What are you getting at?" Terkel asked, walking over to her desk.

Camilla was geared up for another confrontation, entirely prepared for Terkel to reject the angle she'd found for the current case.

"As a small parenthetical comment on the debate," Camilla said, "I want to draw people's attention to the fact that Danish families also expel relatives if they cast shame over the family. Of course, we don't kill them. They handle that on their own. But we shouldn't go around pretending that this could never happen in a Danish family," she said, her voice getting louder despite her efforts.

Terkel sat down on the edge of her desk. "Those aren't ordinary Danish families," he objected.

"I definitely think you could meet Jehovah's Witnesses who would be downright insulted to hear you say that," Camilla said. "Sure, they're part of a religious community, but otherwise they're completely ordinary, even if the rest of us might think they have bats in their belfries."

"They don't kill their daughters!" Terkel exclaimed.

"No, but that's the only difference. If Samra's family members were expelled by the rest of their Jordanian relatives, they would be treated the same way as Jehovah's Witnesses who were expelled by their community. The difference is that Samra's father had the option of restoring his honor by taking his daughter's life."

"We can't make that comparison. You're talking about a tiny group of religious fanatics."

"Well, it's not that small," Camilla retorted. "The current population of Denmark is five and a half million. That's about the same as the number of Jehovah's Witnesses in the world, so they're not exactly an insignificant group."

Her boss seemed to consider this.

"Motorcycle gangs," she said. "That's not news. If you get on bad terms with them, they'll fucking kill you. Their concept of honor is perhaps more developed than everyone else's, and that has certainly happened in Denmark. During the years when the Great Nordic Biker War was going on, we hardly read about anything else."

Høyer gave up on saying anything and just looked at her.

"This is about the fact that there are also Danes who feel like their honor has been violated and would expel someone as a result. I think that would be extremely interesting right now, with the debate at its peak, and everyone so busy distancing themselves from what's going on with Samra's family," Camilla blurted out. It was so irritating, if unsurprising, that they even had to discuss this.

"A very small percentage," he repeated.

Camilla tucked her hair behind her ears, looked at him seriously, and said, "It is also a very small percentage of Muslims who would commit an honor killing. Quit making it sound like you believe it's the whole lot of them who would do that kind of thing. The families who react that way usually come from rural areas, and they act the way we did fifty to a hundred years ago. My grandmother was from tiny Hvide Sande, and I can damn well remember her telling some terrible stories about the girls—and boys, for that matter—who had sex out of wedlock. It just irritates me that now we've totally forgotten how it used to be here, too."

Terkel opened his mouth to say something, but Camilla cut him off.

"I'm still not saying that we accept it. Not that we accept what happened fifty years ago in that West Jutland fishing family, either. It's just good common sense to look at the similarities."

She was totally winded, but could tell by looking at him that he had heard her. It would be lunacy not to slap this in as an aside before Holbæk descended into a character assassination of all Muslims.

"Did you also know that the Jehovah's Witnesses' Danish headquarters are in Holbæk?" she asked. "*The Watchtower*'s office is out by Stenhus, the old boarding school. Not that they have any connection with this case, but since the folks who live out there now are all working themselves into a frenzy about Samra's family and the other immigrants in town, it's a great local hook for this story."

"I wasn't aware that this specific topic meant so much to you," her boss said.

"I don't know if it does," Camilla replied after having contemplated it for a moment. "But I've been curious to find out what's going on ever since a family killed their daughter just to maintain their honor."

"Well, get to it," Terkel said, wanting to know when he could expect her article.

"You can have it this afternoon. There's just one part I need to read up on," she said, thinking she wanted to contact the National

Council for Unmarried Mothers to see what they had to say about these types of stories.

⚘

Camilla had her hand on the phone, about to dial. She was lost in her thoughts about girls who had either knowingly or inadvertently offended their families and what had happened to them as a result. She and Louise had gone to school with a girl who came from a well-respected Roskilde family. She was seventeen when she got pregnant. The family had shut down anything having to do with her. The baby was given up for adoption and the girl was sent to France to be an au pair for one of the father's business associates. At the time, Camilla had found the whole thing exotic and exciting, but she was sure the girl probably hadn't seen it that way. Rumor had it she had married a rich car dealer in Provence, and that she had shocked people by not attending her own mother's funeral a couple of years ago.

Camilla was torn from her recollections when the phone rang.

"He's dead."

At first, she didn't recognize the voice, but then she felt her stomach tense up and her heart begin to pound faster.

"What happened?" she whispered, clenching the phone.

"He managed to hang himself in his cell," her ex-boyfriend Henning said, referring to his brother.

It felt like a tower of blocks had collapsed in her chest. A loud, piercing voice inside her said she ought to hang up, that this didn't concern her. She had struggled so hard to deal with the breakup and had only now finally started to accept that he no longer wanted to be with her. He couldn't just call her up and drag her back into his life again.

"I'd really like you to come to the funeral," Henning said.

"Why?" she blurted out, even though her mind was screaming for her to say no.

"He left a farewell note. He asked that you participate in his final journey."

How pathetic, Camilla thought. Henning continued: "And I think you owe it to him to come."

Camilla felt the tears coming, her throat tightening. "Do you want me there, too?" she asked quietly.

"It's not about me, and it doesn't have anything to do with us," Henning responded tersely. "He's going to be buried in Sorø on Saturday at two o'clock."

Then he hung up.

34

Ahmad al-Abd was thin and immaculately groomed, with his dark hair combed neatly back. He was sitting in the living room with his wife and their three young children when Louise and Mik arrived at the apartment in Benløse, and he agreed right away to accompany them back to Holbæk. Apparently he didn't have anything against talking to the police anymore, nor did he seem to still be upset about the arrests. Although once they were seated in the cruiser, he did say, "It's a great tragedy for us all that they're in jail."

Louise didn't ask him what he meant by that, preferring to wait until they were sitting across from each other and could see each other properly, so she just nodded and looked out the windshield as they drove through the countryside back to Holbæk.

"How well did you know your brother's daughter?" Mik asked once they were seated in the office with black coffee in the station's standard-issue white plastic cups.

Louise had asked Mik to take charge of the questioning while she wrote up the witness statement on the computer. There had been something in Ahmad's manner, even when they were standing in his doorway in Benløse, that told her he respected Mik more than he did her, and they couldn't afford not to use that to their advantage.

"I knew her very well," he replied. "Our family is quite close."

"Tell me about Samra as you knew her," Mik said.

Already in the car Mik had made it clear to Ibrahim's brother that the police expected him to cooperate even though arrests had already been made in the case.

"Of course," the man had said and added that it was his duty to help the police and that he was very sad about what had happened.

"Samra was a delightful child, a happy, easy little girl," he began.

"How did things go as she got older, became a teenager?" Mik wanted to know.

Ahmad drew out his response a little, looking down at his hands, as if he was considering the weight of his words.

"That, of course, is a difficult age," he finally said. He rubbed his hands together.

Ahmad was thirty-six, seven years younger than Ibrahim, Louise calculated as she sat watching him.

"In what way was it difficult?" Mik asked, to get Ahmad to continue.

"Yes, well, she did as she pleased. There were friends and boys, who suddenly became more important than her family."

Louise quickly glanced over at Mik, and their eyes met. This was an account of Samra's life they hadn't heard before.

It was as though Ahmad had picked up on their sudden uptick in interest. He paused for a moment and then started to explain that of course it was fine for young women to live their own lives,

SARA BLAEDEL

but his niece was only fifteen, so it was expected that she would respect the rules her father set for her.

"Could you expand on that?" Mik asked.

Ahmad hesitated a little before he continued. "There are guidelines for how young girls should behave," he began. "They mustn't run around with boys and they must obey their fathers."

Mik interrupted. "What do you mean when you say that she ran around with boys?"

"Just that young girls should behave in such a way that the family can continue to be familiar with them," Ahmad explained.

"And Samra didn't do that?" Louise asked.

Samra's uncle looked irritated that Louise was getting involved in the conversation, then he shrugged and fell silent.

Mik took over again.

"It sounds to me like you're saying that Samra was a little more interested in boys than was acceptable. Whom did she see?"

Ahmad al-Abd didn't even look up when Mik asked the question, so Louise didn't expect him to answer.

But Mik kept staring at him expectantly. A long, awkward silence filled the office.

"Did she have a boyfriend?" Mik finally asked directly.

Ahmad raised his shoulders a bit and kept his eyes focused on the desk. After another pause, he nodded a couple of times.

"Was this a relationship other people knew about?"

Again, it took a while before Ahmad answered, and when he did, his answer was hard to interpret: He shrugged while at the same time shaking his head and mumbling a weak "Perhaps."

"Did her parents know about it?" Mik asked.

Louise was on the edge of her seat. "Someone did," Ahmad finally responded.

It was obvious that he was not inclined to provide any more details.

"What boyfriend are we talking about?" Mik asked. "Was he Danish?"

Louise had leaned back and watched Ahmad, wondering why he was telling them this, something that frankly would not help Ibrahim's or Hamid's case, and why Ahmad was the one who was providing them with this information, considering how many people they'd talked to who had all denied that Samra had a boyfriend. Maybe the girl had confided in her uncle. Even though he was obviously male and a chauvinist to boot, he was younger than her parents and she had spent a fair amount of time at his house.

Samra's uncle nodded.

"Can you tell us who he is?"

Now Ahmad shook his head and apologized.

Louise caught Mik's eye and held it a second before standing up and excusing herself from the room.

Out in the hallway she quickly headed for Skipper and Dean's office and found them each sitting with a big piece of chocolate cake in front of them. She stopped abruptly in the door, pissed off for a second that they were just sitting there chilling out and having fun while she and Mik were slaving away on the investigation.

"It's Else," Skipper said, pointing at the cake, as if that explained how it had ended up on his plate.

"There's more," Dean said, smiling at her, although he seemed to sober up when he saw her serious expression.

She quickly filled them in, telling them she and Mik had brought Samra's uncle in and that he had just told them his niece had had a Danish boyfriend.

"Or, at any rate, a friend," she corrected herself, looking at

Dean. "Why do you think he's telling us that? He could just as easily have left that out. He's just reinforcing our suspicions of Ibrahim and Hamid. Now we have a concrete reason for them to have killed her."

Dean took another bite of his cake, considering her question.

"So there will be no doubt that the act occurred to restore the family's honor," he finally responded after he'd finished chewing. "He's not saying it to help us. It's a signal to the rest of the family and their social circle that the matter has been dealt with."

Louise pulled on a heavy sweater and strolled down toward Nygade to eat lunch at the small local brewery, where the beer was every bit as good as the Czech draft beer at Svejk back home in Frederiksberg. Mik was driving Ahmad back to Benløse, and after lunch she would pay the Møller family a visit.

She ordered a large beer and the herring plate, on which the head brewer had included a beer-marinated pickled herring. Perhaps it wasn't the best idea to have a meal like this in the middle of the day, but honestly she didn't care. She needed it.

It irked her that Samra's uncle was only now starting to share what he knew. He hadn't said a word about this the first time Mik had talked to him. Although, true, she didn't know if he'd been asked, but it certainly would have been nice if they'd known this before they started questioning people.

Now they had to ascertain that Samra's friends either hadn't known about any relationship or were holding back and didn't want to get mixed up in anything.

She drank half of her large beer in one go. Then she glanced quickly around the restaurant to see if anyone had noticed, but no one seemed interested in the beer-guzzling woman seated on her own in the corner. Her herring had just arrived when her cell phone started ringing.

"Hello," she said when she saw it was Camilla. It took a little while before she could understand what her friend was saying. The sobbing made her voice unclear and her words came out in hiccups.

"He killed himself?" Louise asked once she'd finally pieced together a bit of sense from the stream of words in her ear. "Of course I'll go with you, but are you sure it's a good idea?"

She sat there holding her phone with one hand and drinking her beer with the other while Camilla explained that she couldn't decide what to do. Finally, Louise repeated that she would go if Camilla decided to attend the funeral. That calmed her friend down and then, to distract her, Louise said they'd just brought Samra's uncle in and that he'd told them his niece had had a Danish boyfriend before she died.

"I think you're wasting your time by focusing so much on the family," Camilla said. "We're so full of prejudices about the way they behave and in reality, we Danes aren't a damn bit better ourselves."

It surprised Louise that she hadn't piqued Camilla's curiosity more. It wasn't like her not to ask for more information about a detail like the one Louise had just given her.

"What do you mean?" Louise asked, signaling to the waiter that she'd like a small draft beer.

"You can read all about it in *Morgenavisen*," Camilla continued.

The beer arrived on her table and Louise asked for the check. "Maybe you're the one who should hold back a little until you find out what our investigation turns up, so you don't waste your time on some dead end," Louise retorted, smiling at her phone. They had eventually found balance in their relationship, the police detective and the journalist, but that didn't stop them from giving each other a hard time when it was justified.

"Yes, well, let's just see which of us is on the right track," Camilla said, sounding a little less overwhelmed. "Are you going out to sit on that farmer's beer bench tonight?" she asked before they wrapped up the conversation.

Louise felt a little flutter in her stomach at the thought. "It's not out of the question," she said, happy that her friend couldn't see the sudden red glow in her cheeks.

35

Only after Louise had rung the doorbell for the second time did she notice the silence. There was no barking from the yard or from inside the house, but the big four-wheel-drive was parked in the driveway, which confused her.

She rang again, then walked over and peered in the kitchen window. The house seemed empty. She walked around it once. The curtains were drawn in several of the windows. She stopped for a moment, leaning against the wall, to think. She could call them when she got back to the station. This could wait. She just wanted to see how they were doing, given the two arrests, and talk to them about the funeral, which was scheduled for Monday.

An unpleasant mood had taken hold of the town as the rumors had spread that Samra's father and brother had been taken into custody, and the news that they were also being charged with Dicta's murder had ratcheted things up to a fever pitch. The police were prepared for a big turnout at Dicta's funeral and, along with the local detective inspector, Storm had agreed to send a handful of officers to keep the peace among the many teenagers who needed an outlet for their sorrow and anger. Anne and Henrik were informed of the situation, but had announced that everyone was welcome and said that afterward there would be beer and soft drinks at the youth hostel for anyone who wished to come.

Louise called them one last time. When they still didn't pick up, she climbed back into her car and drove downtown, but instead of heading for the police station, she turned onto Ahlgade and parked outside Henrik's chiropractic clinic.

She trotted quickly up the stairs and, after she introduced herself, asked the receptionist if she knew where Henrik Møller was.

"Yeah, of course. He's here," she said with a smile.

Louise looked at her in confusion. "I had understood that he wasn't coming in until after the funeral," she said, speaking quietly because of the patients in the waiting room.

"That was the plan, but he came in this morning and has been taking patients all day. I didn't have the heart to talk him out of it."

The receptionist's hair hung around her face in loose curls. She had warm, cheerful eyes, and when she spoke about her boss her voice contained equal parts concern and care.

"There is a break in his schedule when he's done with this current patient. Because I'm assuming you would like to speak to him," she said, eyeing Louise inquisitively.

"Yes, please. I'll make it quick."

Louise sat down and grabbed a magazine, but had only just flipped to the first page when the receptionist called her name.

❦

"I'm sorry to bother you. I hadn't realized you were back at work," Louise began once she was in Møller's office. She explained that she had just come to ask his receptionist whether she had any idea where he was.

"I hadn't planned on coming back so soon," he said, tipping his desk chair back. He rubbed his eyes, stretched his arms up in the air, and folded them behind his head.

He looked tired.

"I just stopped by your place, but there wasn't anyone home," Louise continued.

He gazed at her in surprise. "Anne wasn't there?"

Louise shook her head. "She didn't answer the door anyway." Louise felt bad for a second. Maybe she shouldn't have gotten involved.

Henrik closed his eyes.

"I didn't go home last night," he admitted. He brought his arms down from behind his head and leaned forward, supporting himself on his elbows on his desk. "I actually haven't been home since we found out you arrested the father and brother. She talks and talks and talks and blames me. I didn't tell her I suspected that Dicta might have been up to something she hadn't told us about."

He rubbed his temples and let his eyes rest on the top of his desk.

"I can't stand talking about it all the time. It's not going to hurt any less just because you keep putting words to it. At least not for me anyway," he said.

Louise watched him in silence, and when he looked up at her, their eyes met.

"Suddenly I can't stand her," he said, still looking Louise in the eye. "She ignores the fact that our daughter had a life that she wasn't involved in. Which is ridiculous and naive. The girl was fifteen."

Louise didn't know what to say, so she didn't say anything.

"Since that morning you came and told us what had happened, she's been walking around pretending this doesn't concern her. Sure, of course the pain and grief affect her. But she won't hear a word about *Ekstra Bladet*, Samra's diary, or the trips to Copenhagen. She doesn't think that has anything to do with our daughter and I just want to shake her."

Louise was stunned. Not so much because he was so incredibly irritated at his wife; she'd seen that before. It also wasn't new to her that two parents could respond so differently to grief and that the response one of them had could really set the other one on edge. She just hadn't thought it would be a problem for Anne and Henrik.

"The day after you came to our place we had a visit from a journalist from *Morgenavisen*, who wanted to write an article about Dicta. We spent several hours talking to her, and that triggered something. Suddenly it became clear how differently we perceived our family life and especially our daughter."

Louise listened to these private reflections a bit uneasily; she was no psychologist.

"Nor do I personally view it as the end of the world to see my daughter's picture in *Ekstra Bladet*. She was a pretty girl, and we have no reason to be embarrassed. But Anne thinks she must have been forced into that, drugged or something," he said with an awkward chuckle, and Louise smiled politely at his attempt to be funny.

"What about the funeral?" she asked.

He took a deep breath and said that he'd brought his dark suit with him when he left the house and wasn't planning to go home before the funeral. He explained that he had a small room and a kitchenette here at the clinic, and that was where he was living for the time being.

Instead of talking to him about the police turnout at the funeral,

Louse asked if his wife might have been out walking her dogs, since she probably hadn't gone anywhere without her car.

He looked at her with his zoned-out but friendly gaze and then shook his head.

"She put all the dogs into a kennel run by someone from the dog club. Even Charlie," he added. "That's how it is. She's putting life on hold while I'm trying to get it to keep moving. That's why we can't be together right now."

There still wasn't any answer when Louise went back to the Møllers' large home, but the bathroom window had been opened. After taking a turn around the house, Louise returned to the front door and left her finger on the bell for a while as she waited.

After ten minutes something finally happened.

Louise took a step back when Anne opened the door. Dicta's mother was in a thick red bathrobe, and her pageboy hairdo hung wetly down over her ears; her eyes looked small without makeup and she'd obviously been crying. The change was so pronounced, and had happened in such a short period of time, Louise wasn't sure she would have recognized her on the street.

"Hi, Anne," she said, stepping forward again. Dicta's mother looked at her but didn't respond.

"Could I come in?" Louise asked, stepping forward, gripping Anne gently around the shoulders and leading her into the laundry room. The flowers were still in their cellophane wrappers, the cards still unopened. There were cups, plates, and several empty wine bottles in the kitchen.

"I just went over to see Henrik. He thought you were probably still home even if you didn't answer the door when I was here earlier."

Louise was talking to bring some life to the room. She made

herself at home, started a pot of coffee, and followed Anne into the living room, where she sat down next to her on the sofa.

"How are you doing?" Louise asked. She tried to establish eye contact but didn't succeed.

Anne made a face. "What do you think?"

"Yes, well, good point," Louise conceded.

"My husband obviously thinks life goes on," Anne said tersely, and Louise realized she shouldn't have mentioned that she'd spoken to Henrik first. "I don't think it does."

"He's not doing that well himself, either," Louise said.

Finally, something that got a response out of Anne. "Well then, he's doing a fucking crappy job at showing it. It's like he has no reaction at all," she said in a more neutral tone.

Louise decided not to explain that that was also a type of reaction, and in the subsequent silence it seemed as if Anne Møller had slipped back into her own world. Her voice sounded frail when she spoke again.

"I only had one child, and she only had one life. I can't accept that it has all ended this way. And I don't want to hear any talk about moving on. I have no desire to move on. Not ever. It isn't fair. She's not even buried yet. No one can tell me to pull myself together. Why should I?"

"I noticed that your dogs aren't here," Louise said, trying to distract her.

Anne nodded. "I'm boarding them. They don't understand that I feel violated every time they wag their tails or jump up happily to get me to play. They don't understand that we don't do those things anymore, so it was better to send them away."

"Maybe it would've been good for you to have some kind of distraction," Louise suggested.

"I don't want to be distracted. I'm doing everything I can to hold myself together."

Her voice was starting to sound shrill.

Louise stood up. "Isn't there anyone you'd like to have here with you?" she asked as she went to get the coffee. She poured it into a thermos before setting it with a clean cup in front of Anne in the living room.

Anne Møller absentmindedly shook her head.

"Or someone you could stay with for a few days?" Louise tried again, but Anne just shook her head.

After Louise said good-bye, she stood out on the street for a second looking around at all the surrounding homes. It made her sad that Anne was so alone with her grief.

When she got back to the police station, Storm came rushing in and pulled her out into the hall.

"You have to hear this," he said and led her into the room where the National Police interpreter was listening to the wiretap recording from the al-Abd family's landline.

"Let's go back. Rick needs to hear this sequence from the beginning."

The interpreter nodded briefly at Louise and turned to read from a piece of paper; Storm explained that this was a conversation that had just taken place over dinner.

"Ahmad called Sada," the interpreter explained. He adjusted his glasses and started translating the conversation.

"'I've told the police now.'" The interpreter looked up at her and made it clear that Ahmad had said that to Samra's mother.

"Then she asks, 'What did you tell them?'

"'How it's connected.'

"Here, there's a long pause on the tape," the interpreter noted before he read more.

"Sada says that he's a sick man, and that he shouldn't ruin her whole family with his wickedness."

Louise had taken a seat; the interpreter's description of Ahmad's reaction made her jump forward.

"He says: 'You already ruined the girl with all that freedom and you're ruining the rest of our family. Samra's was only one life. We have a whole family to think about. I will not walk around feeling ashamed for the rest of my life because you couldn't control your daughter.' Sada sobs intensely and says that he has every possible reason to be ashamed, and that she's going to talk to the police, too," the interpreter continued, addressing Louise, before he read yet another of Ahmad's outbursts and explained that the voices were very heated there.

The interpreter lowered the piece of paper and said, "At this point, Sada hangs up, and there hasn't been any activity at the number since then."

Louise let the words sink in for a moment.

"We need to bring the mother in now and get her to tell us what she knows," Storm said.

36

The front door was open when Louise and Mik arrived at Dysseparken 16B. Mik walked in first and waved for Louise to join him. They stood in the doorway to the kitchen, looking at the three people.

Sada was sitting there, ready, with her coat on. She was still crying, and her face was swollen and wet. The two little ones were sitting on the floor with a roll of crackers, which they'd spread out, so they were surrounded by crumbs.

"Hi," Mik said, walking over to the table where Sada was sitting. "We would really like to talk to you. Is there someone who could look after the kids while you come down to the police station with us?"

Sada nodded and said that she had already called her sister. Samra's mother had her purse in her lap and was holding it with both hands.

"Were you on your way out?" Louise asked, stepping into the kitchen as well, so Sada could see her.

The slender woman glanced up at her and nodded. She opened her purse and pulled out a few pieces of white paper. Louise saw with surprise that they must be the pages that had been ripped out of Samra's diary.

Just then, there was a soft knock on the front door and a woman walked in. Aida leaped up from the floor and flung herself at her aunt with a squeal. The woman held the child pressed up against her, but nothing was said. The two women just exchanged a glance.

"Will you stay with them? Or could they go with you?" Mik asked the sister.

"I'll take them home with me," she replied simply.

Sada stood up and closed her purse. Then she stepped over and picked Jamal up off the floor and kissed him affectionately before she placed him in her sister's arms. After that, she stroked Aida's hair, kissed her forehead, and said something Louise couldn't understand. On the way out the door, the girl blew her mother a quick kiss and blinked her long dark eyelashes vigorously so no tears fell.

At the police station several minutes passed before Sada al-Abd's sobs subdued enough for her to start talking. As she set down her coat, Louise took a seat across from her to read the pages that had been missing from Samra's diary and Mik stepped out to inform Storm. Louise knew reading the pages would be painful, but she couldn't have prepared for how deeply they would hurt her. Something inside her broke.

My life isn't worth anything anymore. I'm dirty and contaminated and can never be washed clean. He says that if I tell Mother and Father, he will tell what I've done and the family won't be able to live with that. I don't dare sleep. I can hear him coming and feel his arms. If I scream, he'll tell Father.

Louise could picture the young woman. She felt like she could almost hear the words on the page in her voice, but the only sound in the small, dark office was Sada's quiet sobs.

He says that he just happened to see us, but I know that's not true. He must have been following me. I hate him and wish I'd never been born. If I ever have to go to Benløse again, I'll drown myself in the sound.

I can't take any more. He should kill me rather than letting this continue. I miss Grandma and home. Dear God, I pray that Mother and Father understand.

Louise glanced over at Sada to see if she was following along with Louise as she read, but the woman was sitting frozen in place with her head bowed, staring at her clasped hands. Only an occasional twitch of her shoulders and the faint sound of deep despair revealed any signs of life. Louise had a hard time understanding how Samra's mother could have kept the enormous pain that had filled her daughter at the end of her life to herself.

"I found the pages in her jewelry box after she died," Sada said quietly, without raising her eyes. "Where she kept her jewelry and private things."

Mik Rasmussen came and stood in the doorway, obviously struck by the mood in the small room. Without a sound he walked over and sat down.

Louise continued watching Sada.

"Tell me what happened," Louise pleaded. "What was your daughter subjected to and why did you cover up something that hurt her so much?"

She spoke calmly. It was as if all the tension had left the room, leaving a heavy calm. In a way, something had been put behind them, even though they hadn't really started yet, Louise thought, looking expectantly at Samra's mother. "Who is your daughter writing about?"

The woman was silent. Louise thought about Storm and Ruth, who were sitting in the command room, knowing that she was working on something that could resolve the case. She was afraid of being too aggressive with her questioning, or pushing too hard. Piecing together the rest of what happened could very easily depend on how Louise handled the mother, and what she said would have to be able to stand up in court later. Right now it was not about getting Sada to confess and sign a statement, because she could recant that once she was facing a jury. That kind of thing happened. Louise knew she had to get Sada to take responsibility for the pain she was feeling right now— to make her feel that, instead of protecting the men in her family, she needed to stick up for her daughter, who had had a right to live.

"Something had happened around the beginning of summer vacation that had turned Samra's life upside down. Something that caused her to be quiet and withdrawn," Sada said. "When Samra was home, she mostly stayed in her room with the door closed. She went to school, did her homework, and did her chores at home.

"But she avoided her father and wouldn't join us when the family was together," Sada continued, her breathing ragged.

The weekend before Samra died, Sada had found her lying on the bathroom floor. She was half unconscious; the acetaminophen pills hadn't totally knocked her out yet.

"I knew what she'd tried to do and got her to throw up all the pills," Sada said, trying to dry her eyes. "I gave her tea and a blanket and had my sister come take the kids."

Sada took a deep breath and Louise fidgeted a little in her chair, aware of how difficult it must be for the woman to tell this story. Mik sat completely motionless, listening along.

"Since spring, Samra had had a Danish friend, whom she saw in secret," Sada began, taking a deep breath before she could continue. "She didn't tell anyone about it, not even her girlfriends. But Ahmad found out, and he did something to her that she didn't dare tell us about."

Finally, Sada looked up, and there was something in the darkness of her gaze that tugged at Louise, asking for understanding and patience.

Louise nodded weakly in return.

"He raped her," Sada finally said. "Several times." Sada struggled to keep her voice under control.

"She couldn't tell anyone that, because then he would reveal her secret, that she'd been seeing someone."

Louise closed her eyes for a second. "But seeing a Danish boy could never be as bad as being raped by her uncle and having him threaten her?" Louise said quietly.

Sada nodded.

"Samra knew that he would spread the rumor that she was unchaste, and how bad we were at keeping her in line. So it was better to say nothing."

Total silence descended in the office. Sada's words still lingered in the air as Louise and Mik tried to understand what had held Samra back.

"It is a much more serious crime for an adult man to rape a girl than for her to be seeing a boy her own age," Louise tried again.

Sada made a strange motion with her head, which could have been interpreted as both a yes and a no.

"That's not the case where we come from," she finally said. "It's worse for a girl to be disobedient, because then she herself is to blame for what happens to her."

Louise was going to object, but held back.

"When a woman is raped, it's her own fault. She brings it on herself," Sada attempted to explain. "Ahmad says that if she can have sex with a Danish boy, then she can have sex with him, too."

Here was a cultural difference that was so impossible to understand, Louise decided not to even try. They had to just let the mother tell her story; they could go back in later and respond to what she'd said. The autopsy report had not said anything about whether Samra's hymen had been intact, because that wasn't part of the routine exam unless there was a suspicion of rape. As there hadn't been anything to suggest a sex crime, Louise hadn't requested the examination.

"What did you do when your daughter told you what had happened?" Louise asked.

"At first she refused to let me tell her father. But I explained to her that my husband would understand. I would no longer consider my husband's brother as family and if Ibrahim didn't understand, I would leave him and take the kids with me."

She paused for a moment.

"We told him Monday afternoon when he came home from the boat early. At first, he wouldn't believe it and got very angry. He hit Samra and said she was trying to break up his family and ruin things for him. He's a very proud man, and he wouldn't have anyone believing that he couldn't look after his family. She showed him the big marks that she still had on her body, and he blamed her for them, said her Danish boyfriend had made them. But she told him exactly what had happened in her uncle's bathroom in Benløse and in the end, he had to believe her. Several times, my husband's brother had brought our daughter in there and raped her on the changing table by their bathtub, and each time she took it without screaming even though her aunt and small cousins were just outside the door in the living room."

Louise understood from Sada's explanation that what had convinced Ibrahim his daughter was telling the truth was her description of a scar his brother had in his groin area. It was from an accident that had taken place when the two brothers were little and had been playing in the river. Ibrahim had accidentally stabbed Ahmad with a sharp knife that their father used to clean fish. Ahmad had been practically unconscious before they managed to stop the bleeding. The scar could only be seen when his penis was exposed.

Louise could picture the scene in the bathroom. Samra had been a slight, delicate girl. It would have been almost effortless for him to have his way with her. She hadn't stood a chance of resisting, although she hadn't tried.

"Then my husband got angry," Sada continued. "He grabbed our daughter and held her tight and promised that it would never happen again. He also promised that she would be at peace."

"What did he have to say about her seeing a Danish boy?" Louise asked when Sada once again fell silent, with her head bent and her hands folded.

"He said that she was free to live her life and that she was more important to him than his extended family or anyone else."

Her discomfort filled the room, made it cold and heavy with sorrow. Louise crossed her legs tightly and folded her arms across her chest.

"Then what happened?"

"He asked Ahmad to come over Tuesday evening, the night she disappeared," Sada began. When she looked up, her gaze was distant, as if she'd forgotten anyone else was in the room. "They argued. My husband said we refused to be threatened. He had made plans to send our daughter home to Jordan for Christmas. No one in Rabba would turn their back on him. And if she were ever touched again, he would report it to the police."

Louise looked at her in surprise.

"Ahmad got angry, too, and said that my husband wouldn't dare because he wouldn't be able to show his face in Jordan once the rumors got there about how his daughter had behaved here in Denmark. My husband said he didn't care, he was going to protect Samra, and finally kicked his brother out."

"The next day you went to Benløse. What did you talk about on that visit?" Louise wanted to know.

"Samra was missing. We wanted to ask if he'd taken her or seen her," came the response.

"Had he?" Louise asked.

Sada shook her head and started crying again.

"But you think he was the one who killed your daughter?"

It took a moment before Samra's mother gathered her wits and raised her head. "I don't know what to think, but I didn't think she was dead. I thought maybe she'd run away to get away from him or so she wouldn't have to be home when her father talked to him."

Louise had a hard time understanding how the mother could have had suspicions like this about her brother-in-law and not said anything to anyone. Worse, it seemed Ibrahim had had the same suspicions and had likewise said nothing.

She could tell that Mik was already preparing to bring Ibrahim's brother in for another round of questioning, but she remained seated when he stood up and let him leave on his own. Samra's story had been more gruesome than she'd imagined, and both she and Sada needed a moment to sit and let everything settle.

37

The scent of flowers was pungent. Camilla chose a discreet bouquet of bright-yellow blossoms and contemplated whether to include a little card. Maybe she should just leave it anonymous, because she didn't know what to write. Should she apologize because maybe she bore some of the blame for his arrest, and because his life was over now? She didn't hear the saleslady when she repeated her question about a card. Just held out her debit card and finally shook her head. The arrest wasn't her fault, she decided, and she wasn't going to carry that as a burden.

"Just send it," she said, handing the woman the address of the church in Sorø.

She walked out of the shop and stood on the sidewalk for a moment, thinking about the funeral. She didn't feel like she could share in grief that didn't concern her—and suddenly it was like something inside her had finally given in and relaxed. As if the love she'd felt for her ex-boyfriend had finally left her, allowing her to see clearly again. She didn't have room for him anymore and didn't want anything else to do with him. That chapter was over now.

Camilla strolled down the main street. She'd spoken with Louise and knew that Ahmad had been brought in for another round of questioning, and that he had opted not to have a defense attorney present because he stubbornly insisted that he hadn't done anything he could be charged with. That was all she'd found out, but that was enough to make her think she might have misjudged the situation and jumped the gun a little with her defense of the family. She was pretty much the only one who hadn't railed against the family and hung them out to dry long before they were ever convicted of anything. If that turned out to have been the wrong call, she was going to have to eat crow.

If it really was someone in the al-Abd family who had killed those two girls, of course the act was completely indefensible, she thought, crossing the wide thoroughfare, whose sidewalks were lined with planters full of flowers. She had never intended her articles to imply that it was acceptable for recent immigrants to kill their daughters just because ethnic Danes had done something similar at some point in the past. Of course, it had ticked her off that people were so quick to judge the immigrants even though the same phenomenon could be found in other subsets of Danish society, but she mostly just felt that she owed it to Sada for people to hear her side of the story.

Camilla had visited Sada after she'd been questioned at the police station. Sada had called and invited her over. Still deeply shaken by the experience, Sada had obviously felt that Camilla was the only person she could talk to if she was to have any chance of making someone understand what it was like to be trapped between two cultures. Sada had served her sweet tea and Camilla had quietly listened with Aida on her lap. While the little girl wisted Camilla's long blond hair into loose ringlet curls, it slowly dawned on Camilla that the familial schism Sada was talking about was so deep that it wasn't just about being good or evil. This woman's life had been ripped apart, both when Samra died and when Sada's conduct had been called into question, without her having any chance to set the record straight.

Sada might actually have suffered more than Samra had, Camilla thought sadly as she strolled down the narrow walkway that led to the harbor to get a little fresh air.

"Ahmad still denies that he killed Samra, and so do both Ibrahim and Hamid," Storm said once the team had gathered in the command room after spending the whole day questioning the three family members. "But we have to stick with it until one of them loosens up a little."

"That's going to take a while with this family. They're not going to say shit," Skipper said, adding that he had the impression Ahmad didn't believe he had anything to hide. "He actually acknowledged that he'd had sex with his niece, but he doesn't think it was rape because girls who go out with Danish boys are sex-crazed hussies." He stopped and glanced around at the others as he pulled his hand through his wavy gray hair. "I was really working on him, but he didn't give up a thing. Suddenly he can't even remember what the boyfriend looks like. Nothing besides the fact that he's blond and way too old for her. Ahmad stubbornly insists that he didn't see his niece after he left his brother's house Tuesday night. His wife confirmed that he came right home after the visit and that he didn't leave the house again until the next morning when he went to open his shop."

"She's not a credible alibi," Velin interjected critically.

"Of course not," Skipper said. "And at this point he doesn't really have anything else to say, although it doesn't seem like he understands how serious this crime is. He's said several times that Samra represents only one life."

Dean had pulled his chair back a little and was stretching out his legs. "This all suggests your basic honor/shame scenario," he said, looking at Skipper. "Only one life doesn't matter that much when you look at their entire extended family—the ones living here in Denmark and the ones back home in Jordan. This kind of thing generally has ripple effects on these people that they would prefer not to deal with."

Louise could tell that Mik was going to contradict him, but he stopped himself.

"What about Hamid?" she asked.

Louise hadn't talked to Hamid herself. She had concentrated on Ibrahim and felt that eventually the two of them had built up a decent rapport. Mik had continued with Hamid even though they still hadn't clicked.

"He's sick of it," Mik said. "And I also get the sense that he's afraid of what's going to happen. Whether they end up in jail or get kicked out of the country. He talks a lot about school and his friends, but he says he didn't know anything about his sister having a boyfriend. I had hoped, and still hope, that he could tell us who the boyfriend is. But apparently there isn't anyone who can."

"What did the techs find? There must be something that can tie them to the two killings," Louise said.

"What about the wiretap?" Dean asked.

"Nothing noteworthy," Storm admitted, "which is to say, no increased activity, but all three family members consented to let Bengtsen and Velin do a cheek swab on them, so we can check their DNA profiles. No DNA material was found on Samra and we have to assume that any that might have been there was washed away in the water, but we did secure several samples from Dicta. We just haven't heard back yet from the Forensic Genetics Lab about whether there was enough to construct a profile."

Storm moved on to the witness statements. "Several people saw Dicta down on the big lawn behind Hotel Strandparken on Saturday afternoon when she was doing the photo shoot Michael Mogensen told us about. She went home to eat a little past six and left her house again at seven thirty to bike over to Liv's place, where she was going to spend the night. She arrived there fifteen minutes later and stayed with Liv until a bit after eleven, when she left. Dicta said she was going to meet the photographer and promised to come back before the next morning, so Liv wouldn't have to explain to her parents where Dicta had gone."

"And she was exchanging text messages with Tue Sunds all evening," Louise interjected.

Storm nodded and continued. "After that, the father of one of her classmates saw her on Ahlgade entering a shop, and a couple of witnesses also saw her downtown at that late hour, but no one can tell us with a hundred percent certainty exactly where they saw her. But the route fits nicely if she went from Liv's place toward Nygade and then on up to the train station. After that there's no trace of her. Where was she going?"

"To Copenhagen," the detectives said, all speaking at once, and Storm nodded again.

"Yes, we're assuming that she went to the station to take the last train into the city at eleven forty-five p.m."

"But she never boarded," Bengtsen concluded, lost in contemplation for a moment. "Should we try to re-create the route she took from Liv's place to the scene of the crime?" he asked, looking slowly around the table.

"We have a good working relationship with *Venstrebladet*," Dean added, and said the paper had been known to include photos before, if the police requested it, to jog people's memories.

"That's not a bad idea," Bengtsen agreed, looking at his younger colleague. "Let's get one of their photographers to walk the route with us and take pictures of the locations where we know Dicta was seen and of the crime scene."

Storm nodded and thought for a moment. "Let's do it. But we can't do the same thing for Samra, because she wasn't killed out at Hønsehalsen. She was brought out there after she was killed."

"The duty officer just received a call from the harbormaster that someone vandalized Ibrahim's boat yesterday or last night," Ruth interrupted, having just walked in the door. She said that someone had painted vulgar messages all over it.

"Maybe that means we should start paying attention to the threats against the family. At least as long as the mother is still living in the apartment with those two little ones," Ruth said, taking a seat.

The group went silent. The newspapers had described the mood in town as a lynch mob out to get the al-Abd family and other Muslim families as well. People were lumping all the Muslims together, blaming them for the girls' deaths. But until now the anger that had arisen had not been manifested in any kind of physical assault.

They discussed assigning officers to protect Sada and her children or maybe moving them out of town.

"Let's contact *Venstrebladet*," Storm said, concluding the meeting. "We need to get those photos taken tomorrow."

They all stood up and trickled out into the hall, heading off to shut their office doors before going to eat, when Louise's cell phone started vibrating in her pocket. She saw that it was Camilla and answered it with a perky "What's up?"

She stopped abruptly, listening to her friend's frantic words. When she hung up, she called her colleagues together before they had a chance to disappear into their offices.

"Aida is missing," she said loud enough for everyone to hear her.

"What do you mean 'missing'?" Skipper asked, stopping in the doorway to his and Dean's office.

Louise explained that Camilla had just received a call from Sada, who had reported that the two children had had permission to go down and play in the sandbox before dinner. Dysseparken's minimal playground facility was off the end of the parking lot in front of the al-Abds' building.

Storm called them back into the command room and asked Louise to finish explaining.

"When Sada went down to get them, Jamal was sitting there alone playing, and when she asked him where his sister was, he just said she'd left. Sada spent the last hour running around looking for her daughter until she called Camilla a second ago and asked her what she should do."

"The little girl could have gone to visit someone," Velin suggested. "But we have to react given the threats people have been making against them the last few days. We have to go find that girl."

Louise agreed. They needed to act immediately. It really didn't matter what kind of mischief Aida might have gotten into. It was embarrassing that the police hadn't responded to the threats already. They had talked about providing some kind of protection for Sada and the little ones, but it just hadn't been done.

"Why the hell didn't she call us?" the MTF captain asked, irritated.

"Because—" Louise began, and Storm finished her sentence: "So far, we haven't done anything besides split up her family. So we're not her first choice to turn to when she needs help. We're going out there."

38

A small group of people "of ethnic background"—as Skipper put it—were gathered in the parking lot. Storm pulled Louise aside with a tug on her arm.

"Go find out what the mother says," he told her and then returned to the others to start a search.

Louise spotted Sada right away. She was sitting on a bench with Jamal on her lap surrounded by a crowd of people. Louise made it to the middle of the crowd and all the way in front of Sada before the woman noticed her and pointed over to the sandbox through her sobs. Just then Camilla came running up to them, and Sada made room for her on the bench.

Everyone standing around moved back a little, uneasy about the level of intimacy they perceived between the blond journalist and the Jordanian woman. Louise understood their reaction. This was an unfamiliar situation: An outsider was unreservedly offering the same degree of concern and caring they had been providing.

"Maybe she went over to someone's house?" Camilla asked when Sada looked up at her. Louise could tell from the way Camilla looked at the mother that Camilla was there as a private person and not as a journalist.

Sada shook her head. In the background Louise noticed that Mik and Skipper had started organizing the people who had turned out to help into a search party.

"Maybe somebody was bothering her, so she hid?" Camilla suggested, stroking Sada's arm as she spoke.

Louise looked at her. That wasn't unlikely based on what Camilla had told her the crowd of teenagers had done to Sada and the kids outside the train station.

Sada shook her head again. "Then Jamal would have been scared, too," she said, "but he was sitting here quite calmly, playing, when I came to get them."

"When did you last see her?" Louise asked, leaning over to hear Sada's quiet voice.

"Four o'clock. They came down to play when I started making dinner."

That was over two hours ago. That was a long time for a four-year-old girl to be away, but it normally wasn't long enough to report a person missing. But this wasn't a normal situation.

Louise walked over to inform the rest of the police officers what had happened, and over the next half hour the local police got a search going that would focus initially on the area around Dysseparken. There was still a small hope that she had gotten wrapped up playing with a friend and lost track of the time or had wandered off. It was well past dinnertime, and if she'd forgotten the hour, her hunger would soon remind her that it was time to go home.

Louise was picturing worst-case scenarios. How had the little girl been lured away from her younger brother? Had she struggled or had she gone along trustingly? Louise wished again that they'd managed to do something to provide more protection for Sada and the two children.

Word of the girl's disappearance had started to draw a crowd. Some people were standing off to the side in small groups, while others came over to ask if they could help with the search. People were ranting or chatting. While there were those who expressed fear for what might have happened to the four-year-old girl, there was also the suspicion that the family had brought the girl's disappearance on themselves, that they deserved it after what they'd done.

Storm had handed over command of the search to Bengtsen, who knew the town and all the local officers who'd been brought in to help. Two canine units were also on their way. His voice was stern and his words succinct and precise. There wasn't any room for mistakes. At the same time there was a push to appeal to the public so any potential witnesses would step up sooner rather than later. The faster they closed this case, the faster they could calm the anti-immigrant sentiment slowly taking over the town, which had already had too much of an impact.

"Dean will stay with Sada in case the girl turns up on her own. The rest of us will join the search. We'll split up the town into zones and each take charge of one area," Storm commanded.

"Should Ibrahim be informed?" Mik asked, but then shook his head at his own question.

Louise agreed. There wasn't anything he could do to help. Camilla came over to them. The autumn twilight was upon them, and that would only make the search more difficult.

"I'm going to help search," Camilla said once she reached Bengtsen, ignoring the protests of the local officers. She mentioned the unpleasant episode in front of the train station again. "Maybe I could recognize those guys if I saw them again. We have to find her tonight."

39

They called off the search for the night at 2 a.m., but Louise had trouble falling asleep once she was finally lying in her bed. At eight the next morning there were once again search teams throughout the entire town, and canine patrols fanning out so they were combing the area from all sides. About twenty to thirty volunteers had shown up to help, and Bengtsen had broken them up into groups and was in firm control of who was in charge of each individual search team and where they would be searching.

"All basements and attic spaces, stairwells and bike sheds must be checked," he instructed his people.

The missing person report ran every hour on the radio news update, but by midday there still wasn't any sign of the girl.

Louise was sitting in her office with a Coke and a slice of pizza before the meeting she and Mik had scheduled with a photographer from *Venstrebladet* to retrace the route Dicta had followed late Saturday night after she left Liv's house. Louise pushed the pizza container to the side and pulled a padded envelope from the pathology lab closer to her. Flemming had sent her the photos from Samra's autopsy and she slowly flipped through them. When she came to the page with the pictures of the back of Samra's head, she was puzzled by the vellum-colored marks on the back of the girl's neck. Suddenly she realized they bore a certain similarity to the rounded marks they had found on Dicta.

Flemming hadn't measured the distance between the marks on Samra's head, because he hadn't considered them relevant—they had been incurred after the girl's death. Now Louise borrowed the ruler from Mik's soccer mug and determined that the distance here was also an inch and a quarter. In other words, both girls had been in contact with the same object. Not that that brought them any closer to what might have made the distinctive rounded marks. Skipper and Dean hadn't found anything in the family's home during their search, nor anything in Ahmad's apartment or his shop. But for the first time they had something concrete that linked the two killings. Louise got up and went to the command room where Ruth was working alone. The rest of the group were still out with the search teams.

Louise set down the stack of photos and pointed out the marks.

"The spacing is the same as the ones Flemming found on Dicta," Louise pointed out. Right then she was interrupted by Mik, who had just walked in to let her know the photographer had arrived.

"Are you ready to go?" he asked.

Louise left the stack of photos on the administrative assistant's desk and they hurried down the hall to meet Michael Mogensen, who was on his way to their office.

"I'm a little late," he apologized. He had been on assignment with one of the search teams because they were doing a story on the girl's disappearance for the paper and had just returned.

They took the stairs down to the cars, discussing the missing girl as they walked.

＊

The suburban street where Liv lived with her parents was quiet. Only one lone car passed by while Michael Mogensen set up his tripod and got his large digital Canon camera ready.

"How wide should the shot be?" Louise heard him ask. "Is it going to be the whole road or just the driveway?"

"The driveway and a bit of the street so people can recognize the location," Mik responded, stepping over to hold some of the photographer's equipment as he unpacked things.

Louise followed them at a distance. Mik was the one who'd put together the list of locations they wanted to show in the paper: Liv's house; the kiosk up on the main road, which Dicta had been seen entering; then Nygade; and finally the parking lot behind that where she'd been found.

The photographer got ready and did a layout. He suggested that they put a small photo of Dicta in every picture so readers associated her face with the four locations.

When they were done on the street in front of Liv's house, he led the way in his car down to the kiosk on the main street and they parked right behind him. He jumped quickly from the car, fishing his equipment out of the trunk. He set the camera up on the tripod and adjusted the height so he could get the kiosk and a little of the main street with it.

"I'll take a couple of shots," he said, moving the tripod a little farther out into the street. "Then we can look at them and decide if we're done."

Mik had gone into the kiosk to buy something to drink and a couple of bags of candy, so Louise nodded to the photographer that

that was okay. She smiled at his thoroughness. To her it was just a couple of pictures of a kiosk on a main road, but he made it seem like a bigger assignment in which the angle, lighting, and width of the shot were crucial to the success of the project.

He changed lenses and said that he wanted to take a couple more shots with a wide-angle lens and asked her to hold the tripod while he squatted down to organize all his various lenses. Every time a car drove by, Louise followed it with her eyes to see if there was a little dark-haired girl in the backseat. The whole time her eyes were checking front steps, gates, and stairs leading down to basement doors. She watched the pedestrians walking toward her and thought: *Could they have done it?*

"It may make the most sense to leave the cars here," Michael said when he was done. "Once we've got it all, I think you should come back to the studio and select the specific photos you want to run with. Then I can send them to the editor right away."

He swung his weighty camera bag up onto his shoulder; Louise quickly reached out and grabbed the tripod so he wouldn't have to carry everything. It *was* pretty heavy.

As they headed toward Nygade, a young couple emerged from the brewery, and she heard them talking about the dead girl's little sister who had disappeared. Louise turned around to get a closer look at them and tripped over the edge of a sidewalk slab that was slightly uneven. She was losing her balance and the tripod toppled from under her arm, but her reflexes were faster than her brain, and she stretched her right leg out in an attempt to prevent the plate at the top that the camera screwed onto from smacking against the ground at full force. It hammered into her shin instead.

"Fuck!" she muttered, struggling to rescue the tripod.

"Let me take that," Michael said, quickly coming over to help her out.

Louise moaned and shot an angry look at Mik when he briskly asked if she had everything under control.

As they proceeded, her leg throbbed, and she felt a drop of blood trickling down toward her sock. Up by the alley she found a place to sit down and watch the photographer work. Just as conscientiously as before, he got his camera ready, set up the tripod, and took pictures of Nygade and the alley leading into the parking lot. Once those were done, they gathered up all the stuff and continued down the alley toward the parking lot to wrap things up at the location where the body had been found.

Mik gave Michael his instructions. There were still flowers there, both recent additions and the bouquets that had been left there since Dicta's savaged body had been found. The photographer was moved to find himself at the scene of the crime and pointed out a large bouquet of white roses that he himself had brought. Still he remained meticulous and focused as he got started photographing the site, so the readers could see that Dicta had been lying in the rear corner of the parking lot, down by Lindevej.

Louise reached out to take the tripod when Michael started packing up, but gladly left it to Mik when he offered to carry it back to the cars.

40

They both said yes to Michael Mogensen's offer of coffee, and he hooked his digital camera up to his computer to download the photos before disappearing up into his apartment to put the coffee on. Louise noticed that the gash on her shin was still bleeding and walked over to pull a paper towel off the roll that stood on a small table under the window.

She sat down on the sofa and rolled up her pant leg. The blood had spread into a smudged stain. She carefully dabbed it clean and held a fresh paper towel against her leg to stop the trickle. Michael came back down with the coffee, mugs, and a carton of milk under his arm.

"Well, are you ready to look at them?" he asked as he sat down in front of his monitor.

Louise walked over to the trash with the paper towel. As she was about to toss it in, she was struck by the familiar and distinctive rounded marks her blood had left. This time she didn't need a ruler to know there was exactly an inch and a quarter between them.

For a moment she forgot to breathe. Then she turned around slowly and studied Michael Mogensen, as every piece of the puzzle fell into place.

Mik had not noticed Louise's silence as he poured their coffee. Louise stood and gathered her thoughts for a moment, then calmly walked over and sat down next to the photographer. For a few minutes she watched as he brought photos up on the screen.

Then she asked her question.

Her partner only reacted the second time she asked. Michael Mogensen had his eyes glued to the screen, but his fingers had stopped moving on the keyboard. He looked at her for a moment, and the look in his eyes convinced her that she was right in her suspicion.

"Why did you kill them?" she repeated, waiting for his response.

Mik came over and stood next to her, but Louise didn't take her eyes off Michael Mogensen, leaving her partner to follow along as best he could. She could see him putting the pieces together as she passed him the paper towel with the two red marks that the screws on the plate to which the camera housing attached had left on her leg. His face was serious and his voice calm as he closed in on the photographer.

"Did you take Aida as well?" he asked.

Finally, Michael Mogensen turned his body toward them, allowing his eyes to remain locked on the screen and the picture of the suburban street where Liv's home was.

He hesitantly shook his head, speaking in such a low voice that they had to lean in to hear him.

"That wasn't me," he said.

Louise reached out and grabbed him. She forced him to look at her.

"I don't know where she is," he continued in the same quiet tone. "I could never do anything to her."

He looked down, avoiding her angry face.

"Why should I believe that when you've been so hypocritical—leaving flowers for both Samra and Dicta even though you were the one who killed them?"

He mumbled something she didn't understand, and she glanced up at Mik, who shrugged.

"I'm going to ask you again. Were you behind her disappearance?" Mik said in a harsh voice Louise had never heard before.

"I haven't touched her," the photographer repeated, this time with more strength in his voice.

The answer came so quickly and clearly that they believed him. Louise got up and went out into the hallway to call Storm and tell him they'd found their murderer but that he denied having anything to do with Aida's disappearance. She told him that they needed no assistance. They would handle the arrest themselves and he would hear from her again soon.

She returned to the studio, hot with rage, but determined to keep it under wraps. She exerted a great deal of effort to make her voice sound relaxed. There was no reason to fight him now when gaining his trust was key to getting him to talk.

"Tell us what happened between you and the two girls," she encouraged.

The photographer sat, his back hunched, nearly collapsed in on himself, but before he had a chance to say anything, she continued.

"When it comes to Dicta, I'm guessing it was anger that made you kill her. Anger that she'd turned her back on you in favor of a Copenhagen fashion photographer. She hurt your feelings."

Louise avoided pointing out how small-minded this reaction was, because it wasn't her place to define these things. A forensic psychologist would have the opportunity to do that later.

"She humiliated me," Mogensen corrected her immediately.

Louise could tell that it wouldn't be hard to get him to talk; sure enough, the words started flooding out of him.

"She mocked me and became cruel. She said that I was a second-class, provincial photographer who would never make a name for myself any farther away than the village of Vipperød." Louise nodded. That was what she'd figured. She would get the details of his explanation later during the official interrogation at the police station. But the answer to the next question wasn't so obvious.

"Why Samra? You hardly knew her, right?" She tried to establish eye contact with him.

Something changed in his face. He turned to look her in the eye, and what Louise saw in front of her was a big boy who was slowly falling apart.

"I loved her," he said, his eyes moist.

There was no trace of guilt there, just a deep despair that confused Louise.

"You were her Danish boyfriend?" Mik asked. Now Louise was the one left out in the cold.

"If that was the case," she said hesitantly, "then why did you kill her?"

Again, there was a long pause during which Louise tried to put the last pieces of the puzzle together herself.

"She didn't want me," he finally whispered. "She said she wanted to go home to Jordan and marry someone from there. Someone Muslim like herself."

He spoke softly, but there was nothing tentative about his words. He really wanted to make them understand.

"Why did she want that?" Louise asked, bewildered.

His response took her completely by surprise and didn't fit with the image she had formed of Samra.

"Because she wanted someone who was like her and fit in with everything she knew," he said, as if he didn't quite understand it himself. "And then she said that Danish families didn't have the same kind of solidarity that families had where she came from. She didn't want to be part of a family where people never really spent any time together even though they lived in the same house. She thought it seemed empty and wrong that I didn't have more to do with my grandmother, since we lived so close together, and that I'm not really in touch with my other family members. In Jordan the whole family sticks together, they all take care of each other. If one person is sick, the others bring food. It's never lonely, and she missed and longed for that kind of familiar togetherness. That's why she wanted to go home to Jordan and marry a man from there."

"But she was happy enough to risk a lot to see you in secret, even though she didn't want people to know about your relationship," Mik prompted.

"Was it because she knew that her parents would object to her picking you instead of a man from her own background?" Louise asked and noticed the adrenaline rushing through her body again.

Michael started crying and hid his face in his hands as his shoulders shook.

They let him be until he dried his face with both hands and looked up.

"It wasn't like that. She knew that they wouldn't object. She was the one who didn't want it, even though she was free to follow her heart. That's what I couldn't understand. I've never loved another person the way I loved her. She also claimed she loved me. But she still wouldn't consent to being a couple."

"She was much younger than you. Far too young to know whom she wanted to share her life with," Louise interjected.

Michael shook his head.

"Her father had given her permission to go home and visit her grandparents for Christmas. She said maybe she could find someone to settle down with."

When he saw Louise's dumbfounded face, he continued, "She said that on Tuesday night, when she came over after her parents were asleep. I'd given her a necklace and asked her if she would marry me."

"You killed her because she said no?" Mik asked.

"Samra tried to convince me that I would always be in her heart even though we weren't together. I couldn't understand that and for me it wasn't enough, either. She was the one I wanted," he said.

The photographer let his chin fall down against his chest and closed his eyes.

"And when she went home she said she wasn't following her heart but that it would be easier for her. But it was all just lies. Because if she really wanted to, she could have just moved in here with me."

Louise cleared her throat. "Unfortunately, I don't think it was that easy for her," she began, picturing the pages from Samra's diary.

The room was silent. Only the sounds of their breathing made the air vibrate.

Louise thought of Ibrahim and Hamid. It surprised her that neither one of them had distanced himself more vociferously from the crime. That alone had cast suspicion over them. Sure, they had denied it and hadn't wavered on their statements, but they hadn't seriously defended their innocence. Now that it was clear they weren't behind the killings, she realized that each of them must have suspected the other after the crime Ahmad had subjected his niece to.

Ibrahim must have thought his brother was behind the murder, but hadn't wanted to turn him in until he was sure of what had happened.

That was what he'd been trying to figure out when he went to see Ahmad the day after Samra disappeared. Maybe he had also been afraid that Hamid had acted on his own initiative to make his father and uncle happy, if he knew about his sister's secret.

Meanwhile, Ahmad had probably suspected Ibrahim of killing his own daughter so she wouldn't cast shame over the family once the relationship with the Danish man was revealed. That would have made sense to Ahmad. Louise also knew from Camilla that for a while Sada had suspected her husband was behind the murder, although later her suspicion had passed to Ahmad. No one in the al-Abd family had ever really suspected anyone from outside the family.

"I must now officially inform you that the time is six twenty-one p.m. and you are under arrest, charged with the murders of Samra al-Abd and Dicta Møller," Mik said to Michael Mogensen.

Then he asked the photographer to stand up in order to frisk him, before putting a hand on his elbow and leading him out to the patrol car.

41

Let's issue a press release right away," Storm said when Louise and Mik returned to the police station with Michael Mogensen. The photographer was received by two officers who were ready to process him so Louise and Mik could join the others in the command room.

"It's important that we let the media know that this case did not involve an honor killing. Maybe that will make whoever's behind Aida's disappearance come to their senses," Dean said.

"We'll release Ibrahim and his son immediately and tell them what's happened," Storm said, looking over at Ruth. "I wonder if we'll be fined for their arrests. We're sure to receive a fucking claim for compensation for wrongful imprisonment that's going to hurt more than just our public image."

The administrative assistant raised an eyebrow and agreed.

"But there was no other choice with the situation the way it was," Skipper said.

"All the family members seemed to suspect each other and no one was telling us what they knew, so it's really not that surprising that we suspected them as well," Louise said, reaching for a bottle of Coke before she started telling everyone about Michael's arrest. "Late Tuesday evening, after Ahmad had gone home and once her parents were asleep, Samra snuck out to see her boyfriend. Out of fear that her parents and brother would discover their relationship, Samra hadn't allowed any phone calls between them. Instead they arranged their future meetings in person when they were together. Michael Mogensen thinks it was about eleven when she came over. He had lit candles and bought her flowers, because he had been planning to ask her to marry him that night, so it took him completely by surprise when she said she had come to tell him that she had arranged with her parents that they were to send her back home to Jordan."

"Ouch," mumbled Bengtsen, passing cookies around as Louise continued.

"He gave her the thin gold chain she was wearing when she was found. But he didn't understand why she didn't want him, or why she would rather find a husband in Jordan when the time came."

"Who says that's what she wanted?" Skipper asked.

"That's what Michael Mogensen said," Mik responded and then let Louise continue.

"Michael thinks it's because Samra wanted the kind of close extended family life she would have had with someone from her own traditional background. After having read her diary, I don't think the family relationship was the main reason. I mean, just think about what her uncle did to her. It might have been part of the reason, but I think mostly she was looking for an excuse to call it off."

"To escape from the double life she'd been leading, which was making it hard for her to be a 'normal' Danish teenager," Dean added, and Louise nodded.

"I know that a lot of Muslim girls who suddenly choose to go back to their family's traditional values do it to achieve some peace of mind," Louise continued. "The struggle that the young immigrant girls have to fight is twice as hard because by becoming 'normal Danes' they know they can expect to end up lonely and isolated, cut off from their families and their closest friends. And that network doesn't just get replaced by a new one. In that sense it's a totally different kind of women's liberation than what Danish women have been through," Louise concluded, letting her elbows sit on top of the table as she pensively rested her chin in her hands.

"Poor girl," Ruth said, staring straight ahead.

Mik cleared his throat. "Michael Mogensen has a boat that he keeps out in Hørby Marina by Cape Tuse," he said. "Michael says he suffocated Samra with a sofa cushion, then carried her out and put her in the trunk of his car and drove out to his boat."

"His tripod was in the trunk, too, and that's where the marks on the back of her head came from," Louise added. She was annoyed that she hadn't realized the photographer had access to a boat back when she'd seen the pictures of Dicta that had been taken on the deck. She honestly just hadn't given it a thought, because their suspicions had been focused elsewhere.

"We'll get it checked out," Storm said. "And obviously the same goes for his car and his studio. And you'd better remove the wiretap in Dysseparken now that they're being released," he added with a look at Velin.

"That also means that those tire impressions we found out at Hønsehalsen are completely irrelevant, right?" Skipper asked, and Dean nodded.

"But how does Dicta's murder fit into this story?" Ruth asked, looking over at Louise.

"It really doesn't. It doesn't sound like Dicta knew anything about the relationship between her best friend and the photographer. Apparently Samra hadn't told anyone. Dicta was presumably not in the best mood when she left Liv's place after her humiliating rejection by Tue Sunds, and was pretty much primed to take it out on someone. Michael Mogensen thinks it was a little past midnight when he happened to see her crossing the street in front of the train station. He pulled up alongside her and she said that she had missed her train and he offered to drive her home. After she got in, she started mocking him, and he pulled into the parking lot to let her out. But after she got out she kept belittling him and eventually he lost it."

"You can pin down all the details when you talk to him," Storm said, then asked Louise and Mik to start preparing to question the photographer, so they would be ready for the preliminary hearing.

An hour later news of his confession was everywhere. The local TV news crew was getting ready to do a live interview with Storm when they went on the air around nine o'clock, and the *Dagbladet* journalists had already started gathering in the lobby of the police station, waiting for the press conference Storm had called for immediately after his television appearance. Louise was trying to block out all the commotion so she could concentrate on Michael Mogensen's questioning, which she and Mik were going to begin as soon as the uniforms were done processing the arrest.

The crime scene specialists had just arrived in town and had started turning the photographer's apartment upside down. The car and the sailboat at Cape Tuse would be brought in for thorough examinations, but even after just a cursory look at the tripod they had agreed that that was what had been used to crush Dicta's skull. The weight, the size, and the location of the rounded screw heads fit the lesions with the inch-and-a-quarter spacing.

Louise was sitting in her office behind a closed door, reviewing the notes from the first questioning session they'd had when they visited the photographer. When her phone rang, she didn't answer till the fourth ring, and even then she was dismissive and snappish with her greeting.

"I just heard," Henrik Møller said, without paying any attention to her standoffish tone. "I'm heading home to tell my wife. I wasn't sure if she'd heard the news. I'd really like you to come over right away." He hung up, giving her no time to object.

Louise felt like she'd been stuffed into a deep, black hole. The last thing she wanted to spend her remaining energy on now was Dicta's unhappy, unbalanced mother.

She stood and Mik looked up. "What was that?"

"Henrik Møller. He just told his wife that Samra's parents are innocent and that the actual murderer has been caught. He wanted me to come over right away."

"Do you want me to come, too?"

She shook her head. "You don't need to do that. I think he just wants me there to confirm that the case is really closed. It won't take long."

Both of the family's cars were in the driveway when Louise arrived, but there still weren't any dogs barking as she walked up to the front door. The dogs' absence left her with an empty feeling. The doorbell echoed through the house, and a second later the door opened.

Henrik Møller was pale and nodded briefly when she said hello. She reluctantly followed him into the house and down the hallway toward Dicta's room. There was an open moving box in front of the door, and a few toys were spread out on the carpet.

Henrik stood in the hallway and pushed open the door to the room. Big piles of little girls' toys filled the floor. The bed was unmade, but by the headboard Louise spotted a head of dark hair.

42

Anne Møller didn't even look up when Louise walked into the room. She was sitting like a statue, watching the little girl sleep in her daughter's bed. Dicta's mother was holding a grayish-white teddy bear in her hands, one that looked like it had seen many years of affection and play.

Louise took a deep breath of relief, and watched as Dicta's father nodded at his wife, turned on his heel, and returned to the kitchen without a word. Anne appeared to be unresponsive. She hadn't noticed that anyone had entered the room.

Louise walked back out to the hall and found Mik's cell phone number.

"I need two ambulances," she said. "I think Aida is alive, but Anne Møller is in shock or some sort of trance, or whatever the hell you'd call it. I suggest that we call Jakobsen, the crisis psychologist at National Hospital whom Department A uses. I don't know of anyone out here who can handle this kind of thing. If he can't come here, we'll have to bring her in to him because she needs help ASAP, and her family-practice doctor doesn't seem to have seen fit to follow up on her condition."

Louise went back into the bedroom and said Anne's name. Silently and without startling Anne, she walked over, sat down next to her on the edge of the bed, and tugged slightly on the comforter that was covering Aida's little body. The girl was breathing peacefully, and as far as Louise could tell there were no signs of violence or assault. She was sleeping with her hair spread out over the pillow.

Louise briefly considered whether she ought to pick up the girl and take her somewhere safe. But there was nothing in the room that gave her a reason to believe she was in danger.

On the other hand, she had no doubt that Anne Møller was beyond reach. Her grief had firmly taken root and was controlling her actions. But there was no sign of evil intent in her face. Anne had taken the child because she'd thought they'd taken hers.

The sirens sliced through the peaceful, upscale neighborhood. Two ambulances arrived at the same time, immediately followed by police cars. Henrik came in without saying anything, and Louise took Anne's hand and said that now Aida had to go home to her mother again.

"My little girl came back," Anne said, looking at Louise through unfocused eyes.

They heard footsteps in the hallway and an EMT stepped into the room, followed by a colleague. Suddenly the room seemed very small. Anne stood up and bent down over Aida, who had started to stir. The little girl sleepily rubbed her eyes and stretched her small body.

Louise was still sitting on the bed looking at the girl, relieved that she was in good condition, when Anne suddenly moved. Her hands locked around the girl's throat in a choke hold that squeezed a deep gurgle out of her mouth and made her eyes shoot open in fear.

The two men were on Dicta's mother in a heartbeat, but she had a firm grip and put all her weight into her efforts. The girl twitched a couple of times and a moment later she stopped moving.

At that instant, Louise swung Dicta's heavy photo album against Anne's head with all her might. The blow flung the mother off the bed, and Louise scooped up the unconscious girl and was quickly out of the room with her in her arms. She laid Aida on the kitchen floor and stayed by her side while the EMTs started CPR. She kept calling the little girl's name until Aida finally opened her eyes and looked around in confusion. Her eyes were bloodshot and radiated terror, but her cries were soundless. The pain in her throat held them back.

Louise heard Camilla at the door and made room as Henrik led her in. Louise knew Camilla had been at the police station along with the rest of the journalists, waiting for Storm's press conference. Maybe Storm had thought she could help; with Camilla, the girl would feel safe and protected through the shock of waking without her family.

Anne Møller was carried out. Henrik turned away when they walked by with his wife, but the pain in his eyes was so obvious that it sliced through Louise.

"Don't you want to ride with her?" Louise asked, stepping over to him.

He shook his head almost imperceptibly, but walked slowly out to the ambulance anyway. Louise stood there in the doorway watching as he climbed in to sit down next to the gurney.

Camilla was sitting with Aida in her lap. She was stroking the little girl's hair and kept saying that there was nothing else to be afraid of.

Louise walked over and tapped her shoulder.

"Let's go," she said, holding the front door open for them.

There were seven or eight cars outside. Several of them contained folks from the press. They must have seen the massive police response in town and followed the sirens to the Møller family's house. Louise ignored them and left it to Camilla to decide how she wanted to tackle the intrusive photographers, one of them from her own paper.

Louise held open the door to the backseat of the police cruiser for Camilla, who was cradling Aida in her arms. Once the door slammed shut, Louise got behind the wheel and headed toward Dysseparken 16B.

The couple had seen them from the window, and Ibrahim and Sada were standing in the doorway when they came up the stairs. With tears in their eyes, they reached for their youngest daughter. In the living room, Hamid sat glued to the large TV screen, as if he still wasn't ready to accept input from the world around him.

Aida clung to Camilla's neck before she let herself flop down into her mother's arms.

"We need to take her to the hospital," Louise said from where she stood in the background.

"But we think she should have a few minutes with you before she undergoes the medical tests," Camilla added, smiling at Sada. Then she gave Aida a kiss on the forehead and started back down the stairs.

Louise followed her, but promised before she left that the family would receive a detailed description of what had happened. One of the ambulances had followed them to Dysseparken and was now standing by to transport the family to Holbæk Hospital.

When Louise got back to the station, she went straight into her office and shut the door firmly behind her. She needed to gather her thoughts and pack away all her personal and private feelings before questioning Michael Mogensen. It wouldn't do her any good to sit there face-to-face with the charged man and his appointed defense lawyer with her emotions still raw.

Annoyed, she grabbed the envelope that had been placed on top of the case file on her desk. Then she got curious, because it was anonymous, with no police logo, nor any name. Mik was absorbed in something on his computer, taking notes from whatever he was reading.

Louise tore open the envelope and pulled out a photocopy of a map. Confused, she tried to find Cape Tuse or Hønsehalsen on it. She assumed it was a map of the crime scenes that she was supposed to use during the questioning, but she couldn't make any sense of it.

"It's Växjö, in Sweden," Mik told her from the other side of the desk, tossing her another anonymous envelope. "Here's a little about the route we'll paddle."

She stared at him, completely thrown off-guard.

"I'm not paddling any route," she finally said.

"Yes, you are. In eight days you and I are going to Sweden to do a little paddling on a lovely system of lakes. It's right in the middle of mushroom-picking season and we'll camp and cook our food over an open fire."

She stared at him with her mouth open and was about to protest vehemently, but he beat her to it.

"That's the kind of stuff people do with their good friends," he explained. "If you and I were dating, I'd have invited you to Paris. But we're not, are we?"

Her eyes fell, and she closed her mouth as she considered this. She shook her head. No, they weren't. Then she pulled out the contents of the second envelope and started studying them.

"Well, then. I can't wait," she finally said with a smile, as she stood up with the case folder under her arm, ready to accompany him down to the interrogation room.

ACKNOWLEDGMENTS

From my very first publication and onward, I've been a stickler for thorough research, which is essential if the goal is storytelling that is believable, authentic, and realistic. I've had enormous help along the way. Special thanks go to Ove Dahl, former head of the Homicide Department, and to my now old friends at Copenhagen's Police Headquarters, without whose help the framework around Louise Rick wouldn't hold.

A big, fat, massive thank-you to Kurt Kragh and Tom Christensen, Flying Squad, who have been with me all along the way, and who have generously contributed with talk and details as the book was in process. Deep gratitude for your time and compassion.

Heartfelt thanks go, as always, to my brilliant friend, forensic expert Steen Holger Hansen, who is there to help out when a plot needs to be spun together. Without you there would be no books.

Great thanks to my talented Danish editor, Lisbeth Møller Madsen, and to my publisher, People's Press. It's a pleasure to work with you.

A billion thanks to my wonderful, super-smart American editor, Lindsey Rose, and to the spectacular, endlessly committed team at Grand Central. It is a thrill, an honor, and an enormous joy to work with you all. I appreciate every single effort you've made on my behalf. So happy to be here.

Thank you so very much to my fabulous and savvy American agent, the unparalleled Victoria Sanders, who works magic for me, and to your incredibly wonderful associates, the lovely and talented Bernadette Baker-Baughman and Jessica Spivey, whose great work, all around the world, leaves me filled with gratitude and aware of just how fortunate I am.

Thank you to clever and tireless Benee Knauer, who knows what I am thinking and what I mean, and how to capture it perfectly. It means so much to know you are there, to have you behind and beside me.

I want to express my heartfelt appreciation to the American crime-writing community, and to my dear American readers. I cannot sufficiently convey how much your warm welcome has meant to me; you have made my dream come true. I love this country so much and am delighted to call it my second home.

My warmest thanks must go to my son, Adam, whom I love with all my heart, and who has traveled every step with me along the way on this indescribable journey.

If you enjoy Sara Blaedel's Louise Rick suspense novels, you'll love her Family Secrets series.

An unexpected inheritance from a father she hasn't seen since childhood pulls a portrait photographer from her quiet life into a web of dark secrets and murder in a small Midwestern town…

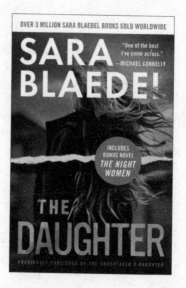

Please see the next page for an excerpt from *THE DAUGHTER*.

Available Now.

1

"What do you mean you shouldn't have told me? You should have told me thirty-three years ago."

"What difference would it have made anyway?" Ilka's mother demanded. "You were seven years old. You wouldn't have understood about a liar and a cheat running away with all his winnings; running out on his responsibilities, on his wife and little daughter. He hit the jackpot, Ilka, and then he hit the road. And left me— no, he left *us* with a funeral home too deep in the red to get rid of. And an enormous amount of debt. That he betrayed me is one thing, but abandoning his child?"

Ilka stood at the window, her back to the comfy living room, which was overflowing with books and baskets of yarn. She looked out over the trees in the park across the way. For a moment, the treetops seemed like dizzying black storm waves.

Her mother sat in the glossy Børge Mogensen easy chair in the corner, though now she was worked up from her rant, and her knitting needles clattered twice as fast. Ilka turned to her. "Okay," she said, trying not to sound shrill. "Maybe you're right. Maybe I wouldn't have understood about all that. But you didn't think I was too young to understand that my father was a coward, the way he suddenly left us, and that he didn't love us anymore. That he was an incredible asshole you'd never take back if he ever showed up on our doorstep, begging for forgiveness. As I recall, you had no trouble talking about that, over and over and over."

"Stop it." Her mother had been a grade school teacher for twenty-six years, and now she sounded like one. "But does it make any difference? Think of all the letters you've written him over the years. How often have you reached out to him, asked to see him? Or at least have some form of contact." She sat up and laid her knitting on the small table beside the chair. "He never answered you; he never tried to see you. How long did you save your confirmation money so you could fly over and visit him?"

Ilka knew better than her mother how many letters she had written over the years. What her mother wasn't aware of was that she had kept writing to him, even as an adult. Not as often, but at least a Christmas card and a note on his birthday. Every single year. Which had felt like sending letters into outer space. Yet she'd never stopped.

"You should have told me about the money," Ilka said, unwilling to let it go, even though her mother had a point. Would it really have made a difference? "Why are you telling me now? After all these years. And right when I'm about to leave."

Her mother had called just before eight. Ilka had still been in bed, reading the morning paper on her iPad. "Come over, right now," she'd said. There was something they had to talk about.

Now her mother leaned forward and folded her hands in her lap, her face showing the betrayal and desperation she'd endured. She'd kept her wounds under wraps for half her life, but it was obvious they had never fully healed. "It scares me, you going over there. Your father was a gambler. He bet more money than he had, and the racetrack was a part of our lives for the entire time he lived here. For better and worse. I knew about his habit when we fell in love, but then it got out of control. And almost ruined us several times. In the end, it did ruin us."

"And then he won almost a million kroner and just disappeared." Ilka lifted an eyebrow.

"Well, we do know he went to America." Her mother nodded. "Presumably, he continued gambling over there. And we never heard from him again. That is, until now, of course."

Ilka shook her head. "Right, now that he's dead."

"What I'm trying to say is that we don't know what he's left behind. He could be up to his neck in debt. You're a school photographer, not a millionaire. If you go over there, they might hold you responsible for his debts. And who knows? Maybe they wouldn't allow you to come home. Your father had a dark side he couldn't control. I'll rip his dead body limb from limb if he pulls you down with him, all these years after turning his back on us."

With that, her mother stood and walked down the long hall into the kitchen. Ilka heard muffled voices, and then Hanne appeared in the doorway. "Would you like us to drive you to the airport?" Hanne leaned against the doorframe as Ilka's mother reappeared with a tray of bakery rolls, which she set down on the coffee table.

"No, that's okay," Ilka said.

"How long do you plan on staying?" Hanne asked, moving to the sofa. Ilka's mother curled up in the corner of the sofa, covered herself with a blanket, and put her stockinged feet up on Hanne's lap.

When her mother began living with Hanne fourteen years ago, the last trace of her bitterness finally seemed to evaporate. Now, though, Ilka realized it had only gone into hibernation.

For the first four years after Ilka's father left, her mother had been stuck with Paul Jensen's Funeral Home and its two employees, who cheated her whenever they could get away with it. Throughout Ilka's childhood, her mother had complained constantly about the burden he had dumped on her. Ilka hadn't known until now that her father had also left a sizable gambling debt behind. Apparently, her mother had wanted to spare her, at least to some degree. And, of course, her mother was right. Her father *was* a coward and a selfish jerk. Yet Ilka had never completely accepted his abandonment of her. He had left behind a short letter saying he would come back for them as soon as everything was taken care of, and that an opportunity had come up. In Chicago.

Several years later, after complete silence on his part, he wanted a divorce. And that was the last they'd heard from him. When Ilka was a teenager, she found his address—or at least, an address where he had once lived. She'd kept it all these years in a small red treasure chest in her room.

"Surely it won't take more than a few days," Ilka said. "I'm planning to be back by the weekend. I'm booked up at work, but I found someone to fill in for me the first two days. It would be a great help if you two could keep trying to get hold of Niels from North Sealand Photography. He's in Stockholm, but he's supposed to be back tomorrow. I'm hoping he can cover for me the rest of the week. All the shoots are in and around Copenhagen."

"What exactly are you hoping to accomplish over there?" Hanne asked.

"Well, they say I'm in his will and that I have to be there in person to prove I'm Paul Jensen's daughter."

"I just don't understand why this can't be done by e-mail or fax," her mother said. "You can send them your birth certificate and your passport, or whatever it is they need."

"It seems that copies aren't good enough. If I don't go over there, I'd have to go to an American tax office in Europe, and I think the nearest one is in London. But this way, they'll let me go through his personal things and take what I want. Artie Sorvino from Jensen Funeral Home in Racine has offered to cover my travel expenses if I go now, so they can get started with closing his estate."

Ilka stood in the middle of the living room, too anxious and restless to sit down.

"Racine?" Hanne asked. "Where's that?" She picked up her steaming cup and blew on it.

"A bit north of Chicago. In Wisconsin. I'll be picked up at the airport, and it doesn't look like it'll take long to drive there. Racine is supposedly the city in the United States with the largest community of Danish descendants. A lot of Danes immigrated to the region, so it makes sense that's where he settled."

"He has a hell of a lot of nerve." Her mother's lips barely moved. "He doesn't write so much as a birthday card to you all these years, and now suddenly you have to fly over there and clean up another one of his messes."

"Karin," Hanne said, her voice gentle. "Of course Ilka should go over and sort through her father's things. If you get the opportunity for closure on such an important part of your life's story, you should grab it."

Her mother shook her head. Without looking at Ilka, she said, "I have a bad feeling about this. Isn't it odd that he stayed in the undertaker business even though he managed to ruin his first shot at it?"

Ilka walked out into the hall and let the two women bicker about the unfairness of it all. How Paul's daughter had tried to reach out to her father all her life, and it was only now that he was gone that he was finally reaching out to her.

2

The first thing Ilka noticed was his Hawaiian shirt and longish brown hair, which was combed back and held in place by sunglasses that would look at home on a surfer. He stood out among the other drivers at Arrivals in O'Hare International Airport who were holding name cards and facing the scattered clumps of exhausted people pulling suitcases out of Customs.

Written on his card was "Ilka Nichols Jensen." Somehow, she managed to walk all the way up to him and stop before he realized she'd found him.

They looked each other over for a moment. He was in his early forties, maybe, she thought. So, her father, who had turned seventy-two in early January, had a younger partner.

She couldn't read his face, but it might have surprised him that the undertaker's daughter was a beanpole: six feet tall without a hint of a feminine form. He scanned her up and down, gaze settling on her hair, which had never been an attention-getter. Straight, flat, and mousy.

He smiled warmly and held out his hand. "Nice to meet you. Welcome to Chicago."

It's going to be a hell of a long trip, Ilka thought, before shaking his hand and saying hello. "Thank you. Nice to meet you, too."

He offered to carry her suitcase. It was small, a carry-on, but she gladly handed it over to him. Then he offered her a bottle of water. The car was close by, he said, only a short walk.

Although she was used to being taller than most people, she always felt a bit shy when male strangers had to look up to make eye contact. She was nearly a head taller than Artie Sorvino, but he seemed almost impressed as he grinned up at her while they walked.

Her body ached; she hadn't slept much during the long flight. Since she'd left her apartment in Copenhagen, her nerves had been tingling with excitement. And worry, too. Things had almost gone wrong right off the bat at the Copenhagen airport, because she hadn't taken into account the long line at Passport Control. There had still been two people in front of her when she'd been called to her waiting flight. Then the arrival in the US, a hell that the chatty man next to her on the plane had prepared her for. He had missed God knew how many connecting flights at O'Hare because the immigration line had taken several hours to go through. It turned out to be not quite as bad as all that. She had been guided to a machine that requested her fingerprints, passport, and picture. All this information was scanned and saved. Then Ilka had been sent on to the next line, where a surly passport official wanted to know what her business was in the country. She began to sweat but then pulled herself together and explained that she was simply visiting family, which in a way was true. He stamped her passport, and moments later she was standing beside the man wearing the colorful, festive shirt.

"Is this your first trip to the US?" Artie asked now, as they approached the enormous parking lot.

She smiled. "No, I've traveled here a few times. To Miami and New York."

Why had she said that? She'd never been in this part of the world before, but what the hell. It didn't matter. Unless he kept up the conversation. And Miami. Where had that come from?

"Really?" Artie told her he had lived in Key West for many years. Then his father got sick, and Artie, the only other surviving member of the family, moved back to Racine to take care of him. "I hope you made it down to the Keys while you were in Florida."

Ilka shook her head and explained that she unfortunately hadn't had time.

"I had a gallery down there," Artie said. He'd gone to the California School of the Arts in San Francisco and had made his living as an artist.

Ilka listened politely and nodded. In the parking lot, she caught sight of a gigantic black Cadillac with closed white curtains in back, which stood first in the row of parked cars. He'd driven there in the hearse.

"Hope you don't mind." He nodded at the hearse as he opened the rear door and placed her suitcase on the casket table used for rolling coffins in and out of the vehicle.

"No, it's fine." She walked around to the front passenger door. Fine, as long as she wasn't the one being rolled into the back. She felt slightly dizzy, as if she were still up in the air, but was buoyed by the nervous excitement of traveling and the anticipation of what awaited her.

The thought that her father was at the end of her journey bothered her, yet it was something she'd fantasized about nearly her entire life. But would she be able to piece together the life he'd lived without her? And was she even interested in knowing about it? What if she didn't like what she learned?

She shook her head for a moment. These thoughts had been swirling in her head since Artie's first phone call. Her mother thought she shouldn't get involved. At all. But Ilka disagreed. If her father had left anything behind, she wanted to see it. She wanted to uncover whatever she could find, to see if any of it made sense.

"How did he die?" she asked as Artie maneuvered the long hearse out of the parking lot and in between two orange signs warning about roadwork and a detour.

"Just a sec," he muttered, and he swore at the sign before deciding to skirt the roadwork and get back to the road heading north.

For a while they drove in silence; then he explained that one morning her father had simply not woken up. "He was supposed to drive a corpse to Iowa, one of our neighboring states, but he didn't show up. He just died in his sleep. Totally peacefully. He might not even have known it was over."

Ilka watched the Chicago suburbs drifting by along the long, straight bypass, the rows of anonymous stores and cheap restaurants. It seemed so overwhelming, so strange, so different. Most buildings were painted in shades of beige and brown, and enormous billboards stood everywhere, screaming messages about everything from missing children to ultracheap fast food and vanilla coffee for less than a dollar at Dunkin' Donuts.

She turned to Artie. "Was he sick?" The bump on Artie's nose—had it been broken?—made it appear too big for the rest of his face: high cheekbones, slightly squinty eyes, beard stubble definitely due to a relaxed attitude toward shaving, rather than wanting to be in style.

"Not that I know of, no. But there could have been things Paul didn't tell me about, for sure."

His tone told her it wouldn't have been the first secret Paul had kept from him.

"The doctor said his heart just stopped," he continued. "Nothing dramatic happened."

"Did he have a family?" She looked out the side window. The old hearse rode well. Heavy, huge, swaying lightly. A tall pickup drove up beside them; a man with a full beard looked down and nodded at her. She looked away quickly. She didn't care for any sympathetic looks, though he, of course, couldn't know the curtained-off back of the hearse was empty.

"He was married, you know," Artie said. Immediately Ilka sensed he didn't like being the one to fill her in on her father's private affairs. She nodded to herself; of course he didn't. What did she expect?

"And he had two daughters. That was it, apart from Mary Ann's family, but I don't know them. How much do you know about them?"

He knew very well that Ilka hadn't had any contact with her father since he'd left Denmark. Or at least she assumed he knew. "Why has the family not signed what should be signed, so you can finish with his…estate?" She set the empty water bottle on the floor.

"They did sign their part of it. But that's not enough, because you're in the will, too. First the IRS—that's our tax agency—must determine if he owes the government, and you must give them permission to investigate. If you don't sign, they'll freeze all the assets in the estate until everything is cleared up."

Ilka's shoulders slumped at the word "assets." One thing that had kept her awake during the flight was her mother's concern about her being stuck with a debt she could never pay. Maybe she would be detained; maybe she would even be thrown in jail.

"What are his daughters like?" she asked after they had driven for a while in silence.

For a few moments, he kept his eyes on the road; then he glanced at her and shrugged. "They're nice enough, but I don't really know them. It's been a long time since I've seen them. Truth is, I don't think either of them was thrilled about your father's business."

After another silence, Ilka said, "You should have called me when he died. I wish I had been at his funeral."

Was that really true? Did she truly wish that? The last funeral she'd been to was her husband's. He had collapsed from heart failure three years ago, at the age of fifty-two. She didn't like death, didn't like loss. But she'd already lost her father many years ago, so what difference would it have made watching him being lowered into the ground?

"At that time, I didn't know about you," Artie said. "Your name first came up when your father's lawyer mentioned you."

"Where is he buried?"

He stared straight ahead. Again, it was obvious he didn't enjoy talking about her father's private life. Finally, he said, "Mary Ann decided to keep the urn with his ashes at home. A private ceremony was held in the living room when the crematorium delivered the urn, and now it's on the shelf above the fireplace."

After a pause, he said, "You speak English well. Funny accent."

Ilka explained distractedly that she had traveled in Australia for a year after high school.

The billboards along the freeway here advertised hotels, motels, and drive-ins for the most part. She wondered how there could be enough people to keep all these businesses going, given the countless offers from the clusters of signs on both sides of the road. "What about his new family? Surely they knew he had a daughter in Denmark?" She turned back to him.

"Nope!" He shook his head as he flipped the turn signal.

"He never told them he left his wife and seven-year-old daughter?" She wasn't all that surprised.

Artie didn't answer. *Okay*, Ilka thought. *That takes care of that*.

"I wonder what they think about me coming here."

He shrugged. "I don't really know, but they're not going to lose anything. His wife has an inheritance from her wealthy parents, so she's taken care of. The same goes for the daughters. And none of them had ever shown any interest in the funeral home."

And what about their father? Ilka thought. *Were they uninterested in him, too?* But that was none of her business. She didn't know them, knew nothing about their relationships with one another. And for that matter, she knew nothing about her father. Maybe his new family had asked about his life in Denmark, and maybe he'd given them a line of bullshit. But what the hell, he was thirty-nine when he left. Anyone could figure out he'd had a life before packing his weekend bag and emigrating.

Both sides of the freeway were green now. The landscape was starting to remind her of late summer in Denmark, with its green fields, patches of forest, flat land, large barns with the characteristic bowed roofs, and livestock. With a few exceptions, she felt like she could have been driving down the E45, the road between Copenhagen and Ålborg.

"Do you mind if I turn on the radio?" Artie asked.

She shook her head; it was a relief to have the awkward silence between them broken. And yet, before his hand reached the radio, she blurted out, "What was he like?"

He dropped his hand and smiled at her. "Your father was a decent guy, a really decent guy. In a lot of ways," he added, disarmingly, "he was someone you could count on, and in other ways he was very much his own man. I always enjoyed working with him, but he was also my friend. People liked him; he was interested in their lives. That's also why he was so good at talking to those who had just lost someone. He was empathetic. It feels empty, him not being around any longer."

Ilka had to concentrate to follow along. Despite her year in Australia, it was difficult when people spoke English rapidly. "Was he also a good father?"

Artie turned thoughtfully and looked out his side window. "I really can't say. I didn't know him when the girls were small." He kept glancing at the four lanes to their left. "But if you're asking me if your father was a family man, my answer is, yes and no. He was very much in touch with his family, but he probably put more of himself into Jensen Funeral Home."

"How long did you know him?"

She watched him calculate. "I moved back in 1998. We ran into each other at a local saloon, this place called Oh Dennis!, and we started talking. The victim of a traffic accident had just come in to the funeral home. The family wanted to put the young woman in an open coffin, but nobody would have wanted to see her face. So I offered to help. It's the kind of stuff I'm good at. Creating, shaping. Your father did the embalming, but I reconstructed her face. Her mother supplied us with a photo, and I did a sculpture. And I managed to make the woman look like herself, even though there wasn't much to work with. Later your father offered me a job, and I grabbed the chance. There's not much work for an artist in Racine, so reconstructions of the deceased was as good as anything."

He turned off the freeway. "Later I got a degree, because you have to have a license to work in the undertaker business."

They reached Racine Street and waited to make a left turn. They had driven the last several miles in silence. The streets were deserted, the shops closed. It was getting dark, and Ilka realized she was at the point where exhaustion and jet lag trumped the hunger gnawing inside her. They drove by an empty square and a nearly deserted saloon. Oh Dennis!, the place where Artie had met her father. She spotted the lake at the end of the broad streets to the right, and that was it. The town was dead. Abandoned, closed. She was surprised there were no people or life.

"We've booked a room for you at the Harbourwalk Hotel. Tomorrow we can sit down and go through your father's papers. Then you can start looking through his things."

Ilka nodded. All she wanted right now was a warm bath and a bed.

"Sorry, we have no reservations for Miss Jensen. And none for the Jensen Funeral Home, either. We don't have a single room available."

The receptionist drawled apology after apology. It sounded to Ilka as if she had too much saliva in her mouth.

Ilka sat in a plush armchair in the lobby as Artie asked if the room was reserved in his name. "Or try Sister Eileen O'Connor," he suggested.

The receptionist apologized again as her long fingernails danced over the computer keyboard. The sound was unnaturally loud, a bit like Ilka's mother's knitting needles tapping against each other.

Ilka shut down. She could sit there and sleep; it made absolutely no difference to her. Back in Denmark, it was five in the morning, and she hadn't slept in twenty-two hours.

"I'm sorry," Artie said. "You're more than welcome to stay at my place. I can sleep on the sofa. Or we can fix up a place for you to sleep at the office, and we'll find another hotel in the morning."

Ilka sat up in the armchair. "What's that sound?"

Artie looked bewildered. "What do you mean?"

"It's like a phone ringing in the next room."

He listened for a moment before shrugging. "I can't hear anything."

The sound came every ten seconds. It was as if something were hidden behind the reception desk or farther down the hotel foyer. Ilka shook her head and looked at him. "You don't need to sleep on the sofa. I can sleep somewhere at the office."

She needed to be alone, and the thought of a strange man's bedroom didn't appeal to her.

"That's fine." He grabbed her small suitcase. "It's only five minutes away, and I know we can find some food for you, too."

The black hearse was parked just outside the main entrance of the hotel, but that clearly wasn't bothering anyone. Though the hotel was apparently fully booked, Ilka hadn't seen a single person since they'd arrived.

Night had fallen, and her eyelids closed as soon as she settled into the car. She jumped when Artie opened the door and poked her with his finger. She hadn't even realized they had arrived. They were parked in a large, empty lot. The white building was an enormous box with several attic windows reflecting the moonlight back into the thick darkness. Tall trees with enormous crowns hovered over Ilka when she got out of the car.

They reached the door, beside which was a sign: JENSEN FUNERAL HOME. WELCOME. Pillars stood all the way across the broad porch, with well-tended flower beds in front of it, but the darkness covered everything else.

Artie led her inside the high-ceilinged hallway and turned the light on. He pointed to a stairway at the other end. Ilka's feet sank deep in the carpet; it smelled dusty, with a hint of plastic and instant coffee.

"Would you like something to drink? Are you hungry? I can make a sandwich."

"No, thank you." She just wanted him to leave.

He led her up the stairs, and when they reached a small landing, he pointed at a door. "Your father had a room in there, and I think we can find some sheets. We have a cot we can fold out and make up for you."

Ilka held her hand up. "If there is a bed in my father's room, I can just sleep in it." She nodded when he asked if she was sure. "What time do you want to meet tomorrow?"

"How about eight thirty? We can have breakfast together."

She had no idea what time it was, but as long as she got some sleep, she guessed she'd be fine. She nodded.

Ilka stayed outside on the landing while Artie opened the door to her father's room and turned on the light. She watched him walk over to a dresser and pull out the bottom drawer. He grabbed some sheets and a towel and tossed them on the bed; then he waved her in.

The room's walls were slanted. An old white bureau stood at the end of the room, and under the window, which must have been one of those she'd noticed from the parking lot, was a desk with drawers on both sides. The bed was just inside the room and to the left. There was also a small coffee table and, at the end of the bed, a narrow built-in closet.

A dark jacket and a tie lay draped over the back of the desk chair. The desk was covered with piles of paper; a briefcase leaned against the closet. But there was nothing but sheets on the bed.

"I'll find a comforter and a pillow," Artie said, accidentally grazing her as he walked by.

Ilka stepped into the room. A room lived in, yet abandoned. A feeling suddenly stirred inside her, and she froze. He was here. The smell. A heavy yet pleasant odor she recognized from somewhere deep inside. She'd had no idea this memory existed. She closed her eyes and let her mind drift back to when she was very young, the feeling of being held. Tobacco. Sundays in the car, driving out to Bellevue. Feeling secure, knowing someone close was taking care of her. Lifting her up on a lap. Making her laugh. The sound of hooves pounding the ground, horses at a racetrack. Her father's concentration as he chain-smoked, captivated by the race. His laughter.

She sat down on the bed, not hearing what Artie said when he laid the comforter and pillow beside her, then walked out and closed the door.

Her father had been tall; at least that's how she remembered him. She could see to the end of the world when she sat on his shoulders. They did fun things together. He took her to an amusement park and bought her ice cream while he tried out the slot machines, to see if they were any good. Her mother didn't always know when they went there. He also took her out to a centuries-old amusement park in the forest north of Copenhagen. They stopped at Peter Liep's, and she drank soda while he drank beer. They sat outside and watched the riders pass by, smelling horseshit and sweat when the thirsty riders dismounted and draped the reins over the hitching post. He had loved horses. On the other hand, she couldn't remember the times—the many times, according to her mother—when he didn't come home early enough to stick his head in her room and say good night. Not having enough money for food because he had gambled his wages away at the track was something else she didn't recall—but her mother did.

Ilka opened her eyes. Her exhaustion was gone, but she still felt dizzy. She walked over to the desk and reached for a photo in a wide mahogany frame. A trotter, its mane flying out to both sides at the finishing line. In another photo, a trotter covered by a red victory blanket stood beside a sulky driver holding a trophy high above his head, smiling for the camera. There were several more horse photos, and a ticket to Lunden hung from a window hasp. She grabbed it. Paul Jensen. Charlottenlund Derby 1982. The year he left them.

Ilka didn't realize at the time that he had left. All she knew was that one morning he wasn't there, and her mother was crying but wouldn't tell her why. When she arrived home from school that afternoon, her mother was still crying. And as she remembered it, her mother didn't stop crying for a long time.

She had been with her father at that derby in 1982. She picked up a photo leaning against the windowsill, then sat down on the bed. "Ilka and Peter Kjærsgaard" was written on the back of the photo. Ilka had been five years old when her father took her to the derby for the first time. Back then, her mother had gone along. She vaguely remembered going to the track and meeting the famous jockey, but suddenly the odors and sounds were crystal clear. She closed her eyes.

"You can give them one if you want," the man had said as he handed her a bucket filled with carrots, many more than her mother had in bags back in their kitchen. The bucket was heavy, but Ilka wanted to show them how big she was, so she hooked the handle with her arm and walked over to one of the stalls.

She smiled proudly at a red-shirted sulky driver passing by as he was fastening his helmet. The track was crowded, but during the races, few people were allowed in the barn. They were, though. She and her father.

She pulled her hand back, frightened, when the horse in the

stall whinnied and pulled against the chain. It snorted and pounded its hoof on the floor. The horse was so tall. Carefully she held the carrot out in the palm of her hand, as her father had taught her to do. The horse snatched the sweet treat, gently tickling her.

Her father stood with a group of men at the end of the row of stalls. They laughed loudly, slapping one another's shoulders. A few of them drank beer from bottles. Ilka sat down on a bale of hay. Her father had promised her a horse when she was a bit older. One of the grooms came over and asked if she would like a ride behind the barn; he was going to walk one of the horses to warm it up. She wanted to, if her father would let her. He did.

"Look at me, Daddy!" Ilka cried. "Look at me." The horse had stopped, clearly preferring to eat grass rather than walk. She kicked gently to get it going, but her legs were too short to do any good.

Her father pulled himself away from the other men and stood at the barn entrance. He waved, and Ilka sat up proudly. The groom asked if he should let go of the reins so she could ride by herself, and though she didn't really love the idea, she nodded. But when he dropped the reins and she turned around to show her father how brave she was, he was back inside with the others.

Ilka stood up and put the photo back. She could almost smell the tar used by the racetrack farrier on horse hooves. She used to sit behind a pane of glass with her mother and follow the races, while her father stood over at the finish line. But then her mother stopped going along.

She picked up another photo from the windowsill. She was standing on a bale of hay, toasting with a sulky driver. Fragments of memories flooded back as she studied herself in the photo. Her father speaking excitedly with the driver, his expression as the horses were hitched to the sulkies. And the way he said, "We-e-e-ell, shall we…?" right before a race. Then he would hold his hand out, and they would walk down to the track.

She wondered why she could remember these things, when she had forgotten most of what had happened back then.

There was also a photo of two small girls on the desk. She knew these were her younger half sisters, who were smiling broadly at the photographer. Suddenly, deep inside her chest, she felt a sharp twinge—but why? After setting the photo back down, she realized it wasn't from never having met her half sisters. No. It was pure jealousy. They had grown up with her father, while she had been abandoned.

Ilka threw herself down on the bed and pulled the comforter over her, without even bothering to put the sheets on. She lay curled up, staring into space.

3

At some point, Ilka must have fallen asleep, because she gave a start when someone knocked on the door. She recognized Artie's voice.

"Morning in there. Are you awake?"

She sat up, confused. She had been up once in the night to look for a bathroom. The building seemed strangely hushed, as if it were packed in cotton. She'd opened a few doors and finally found a bathroom with shiny tiles and a low bathtub. The toilet had a soft cover on its seat, like the one in her grandmother's flat in Bagsværd. On her way back, she had grabbed her father's jacket, carried it to the bed, and buried her nose in it. Now it lay halfway on the floor.

"Give me half an hour," she said. She hugged the jacket, savoring the odor that had brought her childhood memories to the surface from the moment she'd walked into the room.

Now that it was light outside, the room seemed bigger. Last

night she hadn't noticed the storage boxes lining the wall behind both sides of the desk. Clean shirts in clear plastic sacks hung from the hook behind the door.

"Okay, but have a look at these IRS forms," he said, sliding a folder under the door. "And sign on the last page when you've read them. We'll take off whenever you're ready."

Ilka didn't answer. She pulled her knees up to her chest and lay curled up. Without moving. Being shut up inside a room with her father's belongings was enough to make her feel she'd reunited with a part of herself. The big black hole inside her, the one that had appeared every time she sent a letter despite knowing she'd get no answer, was slowly filling up with something she'd failed to find herself.

She had lived about a sixth of her life with her father. *When do we become truly conscious of the people around us?* she wondered. She had just turned forty, and he had deserted them when she was seven. This room here was filled with everything he had left behind, all her memories of him. All the odors and sensations that had made her miss him.

Artie knocked on the door again. She had no idea how long she'd been lying on the bed.

"Ready?" he called out.

"No," she yelled back. She couldn't. She needed to just stay and take in everything here, so it wouldn't disappear again.

"Have you read it?"

"I signed it!"

"Would you rather stay here? Do you want me to go alone?"

"Yes, please."

Silence. She couldn't tell if he was still outside.

"Okay," he finally said. "I'll come back after breakfast." He sounded annoyed. "I'll leave the phone here with you."

Ilka listened to him walk down the stairs. After she'd walked over to the door and signed her name, she hadn't moved a muscle. She hadn't opened any drawers or closets.

She'd brought along a bag of chips, but they were all gone. And she didn't feel like going downstairs for something to drink. Instead, she gave way to exhaustion. The stream of thoughts, the fragments of memories in her head, had slowly settled into a tempo she could follow.

Her father had written her into his will. He had declared her to be his biological daughter. But evidently, he'd never mentioned her to his new family, or to the people closest to him in his new life. Of course, he hadn't been obligated to mention her, she thought. But if her name hadn't come up in his will, they could have liquidated his business without anyone knowing about an adult daughter in Denmark.

The telephone outside the door rang, but she ignored it. What had this Artie guy imagined she should do if the telephone rang? Did he think she would answer it? And say what?

At first, she'd wondered why her father had named her in his will. But after having spent the last twelve hours enveloped in memories of him, she had realized that no matter what had happened in his life, a part of him had still been her father.

She cried, then felt herself dozing off.

Someone knocked on the door. "Not today," she yelled, before Artie could even speak a word. She turned her back to the room, her face to the wall. She closed her eyes until the footsteps disappeared down the stairs.

The telephone rang again, but she didn't react.

Slowly it had all come back. After her father had disappeared, her mother had two jobs: the funeral home business and her teaching. It wasn't long after summer vacation, and school had just begun. Ilka thought he had left in September. A month before she turned eight. Her mother taught Danish and arts and crafts to students in several grades. When she wasn't at school, she was at the funeral home on Brønshøj Square. Also on weekends, picking up flowers and ordering coffins. Working in the office, keeping the books when she wasn't filling out forms.

Ilka had gone along with her to various embassies whenever a mortuary passport was needed to bring a corpse home from outside the country, or when a person died in Denmark and was to be buried elsewhere. It had been fascinating, though frightening. But she had never fully understood how hard her mother worked. Finally, when Ilka was twelve, her mother managed to sell the business and get back her life.

After her father left, they were unable to afford the single-story house Ilka had been born in. They moved into a small apartment on Frederikssundsvej in Copenhagen. Her mother had never been shy about blaming her father for their economic woes, but she'd always said they would be okay. After she sold the funeral home, their situation had improved; Ilka saw it mostly from the color in her mother's cheeks, a more relaxed expression on her face. Also, she was more likely to let Ilka invite friends home for dinner. When she started eighth grade, they moved to Østerbro, a better district in the city, but she stayed in her school in Brønshøj and took the bus.

"You *were* an asshole," she muttered, her face still to the wall. "What you did was just completely inexcusable."

The telephone outside the door finally gave up. She heard soft steps out on the stairs. She sighed. They had paid her airfare; there were limits to what she could get away with. But today was out of the question. And that telephone was their business.

Someone knocked again at the door. This time it sounded different. They knocked again. "Hello." A female voice. The woman called her name and knocked one more time, gently but insistently.

Ilka rose from the bed. She shook her hair and slipped it behind her ears and smoothed her T-shirt. She walked over and opened the door. She couldn't hide her startled expression at the sight of a woman dressed in gray, her hair covered by a veil of the same color. Her broad, demure skirt reached below the knees. Her eyes seemed far too big for her small face and delicate features.

"Who are you?"

"My name is Sister Eileen O'Connor, and you have a meeting in ten minutes."

The woman was already about to turn and walk back down the steps, when Ilka finally got hold of herself. "I have a meeting?"

"Yes, the business is yours now." Ilka heard patience as well as suppressed annoyance in the nun's voice. "Artie has left for the day and has informed me that you have taken over."

"*My* business?" Ilka ran her hand through her hair. A bad habit of hers, when she didn't know what to do with her hands.

"You did read the papers Artie left for you? It's my understanding that you signed them, so you're surely aware of what you have inherited."

"I signed to say I'm his daughter," Ilka said. More than anything, she just wanted to close the door and make everything go away.

"If you had read what was written," the sister said, a bit sharply, "you would know that your father has left the business to you. And by your signature, you have acknowledged your identity and therefore your inheritance."

Ilka was speechless. While she gawked, the sister added, "The Norton family lost their grandmother last night. It wasn't unexpected, but several of them are taking it hard. I've made coffee for four." She stared at Ilka's T-shirt and bare legs. "And it's our custom to receive relatives in attire that is a bit more respectful."

A tiny smile played on her narrow lips, so fleeting that Ilka was in doubt as to whether it had actually appeared. "I can't talk to a family that just lost someone," she protested. "I don't know what to say. I've never—I'm sorry, you have to talk to them."

Sister Eileen stood for a moment before speaking. "Unfortunately, I can't. I don't have the authority to perform such duties. I do the office work, open mail, and laminate the photos of the deceased onto death notices for relatives to use as bookmarks. But you will do fine. Your father was always good at such conversations. All you have to do is allow the family to talk. Listen and find out what's important to them; that's the most vital thing for people who come to us. And these people have a contract for a prepaid ceremony. The contract explains everything they have paid for. Mrs. Norton has been making funeral payments her whole life, so everything should be smooth sailing."

The nun walked soundlessly down the stairs. Ilka stood in the doorway, staring at where she had vanished. Had she seriously inherited a funeral home? In the US? How had her life taken such an unexpected turn? What the hell had her father been thinking?

She pulled herself together. She had seven minutes before the Nortons arrived. "Respectful" attire, the sister had said. Did she even have something like that in her suitcase? She hadn't opened it yet.

But she couldn't do this. They couldn't make her talk to total strangers who had just lost a relative. Then she remembered she hadn't known the undertaker who helped her when Erik died either. But he had been a salvation to her. A person who had taken care of everything in a professional manner and arranged things precisely as she believed her husband would have wanted. The funeral home, the flowers—yellow tulips. The hymns. It was also the undertaker who had said she would regret it if she didn't hire an organist to play during the funeral. Because even though it might seem odd, the mere sound of it helped relieve the somber atmosphere. She had chosen the cheapest coffin, as the undertaker had suggested, seeing that Erik had wanted to be cremated. Many minor decisions had been made for her; that had been an enormous relief. And the funeral had gone exactly the way she'd wanted. Plus, the undertaker had helped reserve a room at the restaurant where they gathered after the ceremony. But those types of details were apparently already taken care of here. It seemed all she had to do was meet with them. She walked over to her suitcase.

Ilka dumped everything out onto the bed and pulled a light blouse and dark pants out of the pile. Along with her toiletry bag and underwear. Halfway down the stairs, she remembered she needed shoes. She went back up again. All she had was sneakers.

The family was three adult children—a daughter and two sons—and a grandchild. The two men seemed essentially composed, while the woman and the boy were crying. The woman's face was stiff and pale, as if every ounce of blood had drained out of her. Her young son stared down at his hands, looking withdrawn and gloomy.

"Our mother paid for everything in advance," one son said when Ilka walked in. They sat in the arrangement room's comfortable armchairs, around a heavy mahogany table. Dusty paintings in elegant gilded frames hung from the dark green walls. Ilka guessed the paintings were inspired by Lake Michigan. She had no idea what to do with the grieving family, nor what was expected of her.

The son farthest from the door asked, "How does the condolences and tributes page on your website work? Is it like anyone can go in and write on it, or can it only be seen if you have the password? We want everybody to be able to put up a picture of our mother and write about their good times with her."

Ilka nodded to him and walked over to shake his hand. "We will make the page so it's exactly how you want it." Then she repeated their names: Steve—the one farthest from the door—Joe, Helen, and the grandson, Pete. At least she thought that was right, though she wasn't sure because he had mumbled his name.

"And we talked it over and decided we want charms," Helen said. "We'd all like one. But I can't see in the papers whether they're paid for or not, because if not we need to know how much they cost."

Ilka had no idea what charms were, but she'd noticed the green form that had been laid on the table for her, and a folder entitled "Norton," written by hand. The thought struck her that the handwriting must be her father's.

"Service Details" was written on the front of the form. Ilka sat down and reached for the notebook on the table. It had a big red heart on the cover, along with "Helping Hands for Healing Hearts."

She surmised the notebook was probably meant for the relatives. Quickly, she slid it over the table to them; then she opened a drawer and found a sheet of paper. "I'm very sorry," she said. It was difficult for her not to look at the grandson, who appeared crushed. "About your loss. As I understand, everything is already decided. But I wasn't here when things were planned. Maybe we can go through everything together and figure out exactly how you want it done."

What in the world is going on? she thought as she sat there blabbering away at this grieving family, as if she'd been doing it all her life!

"Our mother liked Mr. Jensen a lot," Steve said. "He took charge of the funeral arrangements when our father died, and we'd like things done the same way."

Ilka nodded.

"But not the coffin," Joe said. "We want one that's more upscale, more feminine."

"Is it possible to see the charms?" Helen asked, still tearful. "And we also need to print a death notice, right?"

"Can you arrange it so her dogs can sit up by the coffin during the services?" Steve asked. He looked at Ilka as if this were the most important of all the issues. "That won't be a problem, will it?"

"No, not a problem," she answered quickly, as the questions rained down on her.

"How many people can fit in there? And can we all sit together?"

"The room can hold a lot of people," she said, feeling now as if she'd been fed to the lions. "We can squeeze the chairs together; we can get a lot of people in there. And of course you can sit together."

Ilka had absolutely no idea what room they were talking about. But there had been about twenty people attending her husband's services, and they hadn't even filled a corner of the chapel in Bispebjerg.

"How many do you think are coming?" she asked, just to be on the safe side.

"Probably somewhere between a hundred and a hundred and fifty," Joe guessed. "That's how many showed up at Dad's services. But it could be more this time, so it's good to be prepared. She was very active after her retirement. And the choir would like to sing."

Ilka nodded mechanically and forced a smile. She had heard that it's impossible to vomit while you're smiling, something about reflexes. Not that she was about to vomit; there was nothing inside her to come out. But her insides contracted as if something in there was getting out of control. "How did Mrs. Norton die?" She leaned back in her chair.

She felt their eyes on her, and for a moment everyone was quiet. The adults looked at her as if the question weren't her business. And maybe it was irrelevant for the planning, she thought. But after Erik died, in a way it had been a big relief to talk about him, how she had come home and found him on the kitchen floor. Putting it into words made it all seem more real, like it actually had happened. And it had helped her through the days after his death, which otherwise were foggy.

Helen sat up and looked over at her son, who was still staring at his hands. "Pete's the one who found her. We bought groceries for his grandma three times a week and drove them over to her after school. And there she was, out in the yard. Just lying there."

Now Ilka regretted having asked.

From underneath the hair hanging over his forehead, with his head bowed, the boy scowled at his mother. "Grandma was out cutting flowers to put in vases, and she fell," he muttered.

"There was a lot of blood," his mother said, nodding.

"But the guy who picked her up promised we wouldn't be able to see it when she's in her coffin," Steve said. He looked at Ilka, as if he wanted this confirmed.

Quickly she answered, "No, you won't. She'll look fine. Did she like flowers?"

Helen smiled and nodded. "She lived and breathed for her garden. She loved her flower beds."

"Then maybe it's a good idea to use flowers from her garden to decorate the coffin," Ilka suggested.

Steve sat up. "Decorate the coffin? It's going to be open."

"But it's a good idea," Helen said. "We'll decorate the chapel with flowers from the garden. We can go over and pick them together. It's a beautiful way to say good-bye to the garden she loved, too."

"But if we use hers, will we get the money back we already paid for flowers?" Joe asked.

Ilka nodded. "Yes, of course." Surely it wasn't a question of all that much money.

"Oh God!" Helen said. "I almost forgot to give you this." Out of her bag she pulled a large folder that said "Family Record Guide" and handed it over to Ilka. "It's already filled out."

In many ways, it reminded Ilka of the diaries she'd kept in school. First a page with personal information. The full name of the deceased, the parents' names. Whether she was married, divorced, single, or a widow. Education and job positions. Then a page with familial relations, and on the opposite page there was room to write about the deceased's life and memories. There were sections for writing about a first home, about becoming a parent, about becoming a grandparent. And then a section that caught Ilka's attention, because it had to be of some use. Favorites: colors, flowers, season, songs, poems, books. And on and on it went. Family traditions. Funny memories, role models, hobbies, special talents. Mrs. Norton had filled it all out very thoroughly.

Ilka closed the folder and asked how they would describe their mother and grandmother.

"She was very sociable," Joe said. "Also after Dad died. She was involved in all sorts of things; she was very active in the seniors' club in West Racine."

"And family meant a lot to her," Helen said. She'd stopped crying without Ilka noticing. "She was always the one who made sure we all got together, at least twice a year."

Ilka let them speak, as long as they stayed away from talking about charms and choosing coffins. She had no idea how to wind up the conversation, but she kept listening as they nearly all talked at once, to make sure that everything about the deceased came out. Even gloomy Pete added that his grandmother made the world's best pecan pie.

"And she had the best Southern recipe for macaroni and cheese," he added. The others laughed.

Ilka thought again about Erik. After his funeral, their apartment had felt empty and abandoned. A silence hung that had nothing to do with being alone. It took a few weeks for her to realize the silence was in herself. There was no one to talk to, so everything was spoken inside her head. And at the same time, she felt as if she were in a bubble no sound could penetrate. That had been one of the most difficult things to get used to. Slowly things got better, and at last—she couldn't say precisely when—the silence connected with her loss disappeared.

Meanwhile, she'd had the business to run. What a circus. They'd started working together almost from the time they'd first met. He was the photographer, though occasionally she went out with him to help set up the equipment and direct the students. Otherwise, she was mostly responsible for the office work. But she had done a job or two by herself when they were especially busy; she'd seen how he worked. There was nothing mysterious about it. Classes were lined up with the tallest students in back, and the most attractive were placed in the middle so the focus would be on them. The individual portraits were mostly about adjusting the height of the seat and taking enough pictures to ensure that one of them was good enough. But when Erik suddenly wasn't there, with a full schedule of jobs still booked, she had taken over. Without giving it much thought. She did know the school secretaries, and they knew her, so that eased the transition.

"Do we really have to buy a coffin, when Mom is just going to be burned?" Steve said, interrupting her thoughts. "Can't we just borrow one? She won't be lying in there very long."

Shit. Ilka had blanked out for a moment. Where the hell was Artie? Did they have coffins they loaned out? She had to say something. "It would have to be one that's been used."

"We're not putting Mom in a coffin where other dead people have been!" Helen was indignant, while a hint of a smile appeared on her son's face.

Ilka jumped in. "Unfortunately, we can only loan out used coffins." She hoped that would put a lid on this idea.

"We can't do that. Can we?" Helen said to her two brothers. "On the other hand, if we borrow a coffin, we might be able to afford charms instead."

Ilka didn't have the foggiest idea if her suggestion was even possible. But if this really was her business, she could decide, now, couldn't she?

"We *would* save forty-five hundred dollars," Joe said.

Forty-five hundred dollars for a coffin! This could turn out to be disastrous if it ended with them losing money from her ignorant promise.

"Oh, at least. Dad's coffin cost seven thousand dollars."

What is this? Ilka thought. *Are coffins here decorated in gold leaf?*

"But Grandma already paid for her funeral," the grandson said. "You can't save on something she's already paid for. You're not going to get her money back, right?" Finally, he looked up.

"We'll figure this out," Ilka said.

The boy looked over at his mother and began crying.

"Oh, honey!" Helen said.

"You're all talking about this like it isn't even Grandma; like it's someone else who's dead," he said, angry now.

He turned to Ilka. "Like it's all about money, and just getting it over with." He jumped up so fast he knocked his chair over; then he ran out the door.

His mother sent her brothers an apologetic look; they both shook their heads. She turned to Ilka and asked if it were possible for them to return tomorrow. "By then we'll have this business about the coffin sorted out. We also have to order a life board. I brought along some photos of Mom."

Standing now, Ilka told them it was of course fine to come back tomorrow. She knew one thing for certain: Artie was going to meet with them, whether he liked it or not. She grabbed the photos Helen was holding out.

"They're from when she was born, when she graduated from school, when she married Dad, and from their anniversary the year before he died."

"Super," Ilka said. She had no idea what these photos would be used for.

The three siblings stood up and headed for the door. "When would you like to meet?" Ilka asked. They agreed on noon.

Joe stopped and looked up at her. "But can the memorial service be held on Friday?"

"We can talk about that later," Ilka replied at once. She needed time to find out what to do with 150 people and a place for the dogs close to the coffin.

After they left, Ilka walked back to the desk and sank down in the chair. She hadn't even offered them coffee, she realized.

She buried her face in her hands and sat for a moment. She had inherited a funeral home in Racine. And if she were to believe the nun in the reception area laminating death notices, she had accepted the inheritance.

She heard a knock on the doorframe. Sister Eileen stuck her head in the room. Ilka nodded, and the nun walked over and laid a slip of paper on the table. On it was an address.

"We have a pickup."

Ilka stared at the paper. How was this possible? It wasn't just charms, life boards, and a forty-five-hundred-dollar coffin. Now they wanted her to pick up a body, too. She exhaled and stood up.

ABOUT THE AUTHOR

Sara Blaedel's suspense novels have enjoyed incredible success around the world: fantastic acclaim, multiple awards, and runaway number one bestselling success internationally. In her native Denmark, Sara was voted most popular novelist for the fourth time in 2014. She is also a recipient of the Golden Laurel, Denmark's most prestigious literary award. Her books are published in thirty-seven countries. Her series featuring police detective Louise Rick is adored the world over, and Sara has just launched her new Family Secrets suspense series to fantastic acclaim.

Sara Blaedel's interest in story writing, and especially crime fiction, was nurtured from a young age. The daughter of a renowned Danish journalist and an actress whose career included roles in theater, radio, TV, and movies, Sara grew up surrounded by a constant flow of professional writers and performers visiting the Blaedel home. Despite a struggle with dyslexia, books gave Sara a world in which to escape when her introverted nature demanded an exit from the hustle and bustle of life. Sara tried a number of careers, from a restaurant apprenticeship to graphic design, before she started a publishing company called Sara B, where she published Danish translations of American crime fiction.

Publishing ultimately led Sara to journalism, and she covered a wide range of stories, from criminal trials to the premiere of *Star Wars: Episode I—The Phantom Menace*. It was during this time—and while skiing in Norway—that Sara started brewing the ideas for her first novel. In 2004 Louise and Camilla were introduced in *Grønt Støv* (*Green Dust*), and Sara won the Danish Academy for Crime Fiction's debut prize.

Originally from Denmark, Sara has lived in New York but now spends most of her time in Copenhagen. When she isn't busy committing brutal murders on the page, she is an ambassador with Save the Children and serves on the jury of a documentary film competition.